The Road to Avalon

The Road to Avalon

JOAN WOLF

CHICAGO
REVIEW
PRESS

Cover design: Sarah Olson
Cover image: Detail from *La Belle Dame Sans Merci*, exh. 1902,
by Sir Frank Dicksee (1853–1928). Oil on canvas. © Bristol
City Museum and Art Gallery, UK/The Bridgeman Art Library
International.

Copyright © 1988 by Joan Wolf
Reprinted by arrangement with the author
Foreword © 2007 by Mary Jo Putney
This edition published in 2007 by
Chicago Review Press, Incorporated
814 North Franklin Street
Chicago, Illinois 60610
ISBN-13: 978-1-55652-658-9
ISBN-10: 1-55652-658-X
Printed in the United States of America
5 4 3 2 1

For Aunt Betty

Foreword

MYTHS and legends reflect a nation's soul, and for Britain, the greatest repository of such tales is the Arthurian material known as the Matter of Britain. From the sixth century to the present, these stories have inspired countless writers and dreamers. My first Arthurian book was a child's version that had all the difficult bits edited out, and I was still enchanted.

There are so many possible interpretations of the Arthurian legends, and they can be constantly reimagined to offer new insights and reflect new realities. Sir Thomas Malory's *Le Morte d'Arthur*, one of the early books printed by William Caxton, England's first printer, harkened back to the noble days of chivalry. Edmund Spenser's *The Faerie Queen* was a long allegorical poem that was clearly intended to flatter Queen Elizabeth I. Alfred Lord Tennyson's *Idylls of the King* is much concerned with how the adultery of Lancelot and Guinevere introduced evil into the shining purity of Camelot. T. H. White moved from the playfulness of a badger tutor to looming war to a final spark of hope in *The Once and Future King*. Marion Zimmer Bradley's *The Mists of Avalon* brings a feminist and pagan slant to the story. Mary Stewart's wonderful Merlin cycle concentrates on the powerful sorcerer who is the catalyst to creating Britain's greatest hero. I could go on and on, but you get the idea.

Mary Stewart was the writer who first introduced me to an Arthurian saga set in a historically believable fifth-century Britain, which has been strongly shaped by centuries of Roman occupation. Though Joan Wolf's general story line follows Sir Thomas Malory, she places her marvelous *The Road to Avalon* in this Romanized Britain. Wolf's richly realized world has Roman roads and cities and memories of glory, but the legions have withdrawn and now the land is threatened by encroaching barbarian tribes. It is a time of transition, when the remnants of civilization are in danger of being destroyed forever. A land in need of a great leader.

I've read any number of Arthurian stories, and I even wrote a novella in which, in true romance writer fashion, I gave Arthur the happy ending I thought he deserved. But I've never read a version that had greater psychological resonance than Joan Wolf's treatment.

I first read her book when it was published in 1988, and I remembering blinking a bit when I saw Merlin as Arthur's grandfather and Morgan as Merlin's young daughter. But why not? There is no definitive version of the legends, so one of the lures of writing an Arthurian story is the chance to reimagine the relationships. Joan Wolf writes relationships brilliantly, and does so in effortlessly accessible prose. I was immediately drawn into the story of the young Arthur, a wounded, wary, and brilliant boy.

For me, Wolf's greatest achievement is that she returns Arthur to the center of his own story. Too often Arthurian tales concentrate on the Knights of the Round Table or the tragic love of Lancelot and Guinevere. King Arthur is treated like George Washington often is—as a hero who is so noble and so far above the common man that he seems more like a stuffed owl than a real person.

Just as Washington was a real man who surmounted his human weaknesses with wisdom and vision, Wolf's Arthur is a charismatic, utterly compelling king who earns the love and loyalty of his people. It is Arthur's understanding of horses and cavalry that enables him to build an effective army—and Joan Wolf really knows her horses. It's Arthur's wisdom and fairness that make him a king for the ages. As Guinevere learns, "When Arthur was present, you did not look at anyone else."

Perhaps the one irreducible element of the Arthurian legends is the tragic love triangle of Arthur, Guinevere, and Lancelot (the last of whom *The Road to Avalon* calls by the earlier British name of Bedwyr). There is tremendous power in this story of forbidden love, yet depicting Arthur as a cuckold undermines him as a hero.

Joan Wolf solves this problem by giving Arthur a powerful, passionate love that is also forbidden. This love claims his heart and soul, leaving no room for the beauteous Guinevere except as a friend and advisor. I believed in the bond between Arthur and grave, intuitive Morgan, who understands him better than anyone, just as I believed that Guinevere could love two men. It's refreshing to read an Arthurian story in which characters aren't drawn in black and white. Most are sympathetic, flawed people. Even Mordred is a stormy petrel of a young man, weak rather than evil.

Because of the human power of the Arthurian legends, there will always be new versions, all of them with their own insights and interpretations. But *The Road to Avalon* will remain on my keeper shelf. I'm very glad that it is available again for new readers to discover.

MARY JO PUTNEY

I

MORGAN
(446–452)

Chapter 1

*I*T had been raining earlier in the day, a chill spring rain, but with the twilight the skies began to clear. There were lanterns burning on the colonnade of the forum as Merlin rode into the main street of Venta. The Romans had been gone from Britain for many years, but Venta was still very much a Roman city. The praetorium, toward which Merlin was riding, however, was no longer the headquarters of a Roman governor but of a British high king.

The courtyard in front of the praetorium was paved and there were guards posted in the sentry boxes. One came forward immediately to challenge the stranger who had just ridden in. The sentry's voice stopped in mid-sentence, however, as he recognized the face illuminated by his lantern.

"My lord Merlin!"

Merlin nodded. "Yes. I have come to see the king."

"Let me take your horse, my lord."

Merlin dismounted, gave his reins to the sentry, and mounted the steps of the praetorium. Five minutes later he was being shown to the middle-size, comfortably furnished room that was the reception room of the king's private chambers. The man inside was alone, sitting beside a charcoal brazier that was burning against the cool of the spring night. He was a handsome man, his dark hair not yet touched by gray. The lines around his eyes and his mouth, however, gave away his forty-one years. He was dressed in the British style, with a purple-colored tunic worn over tan wool breeches. He did not speak as the older man came into the room.

"Good evening, Uther," said Merlin in Latin.

The king's eyes, a startling light gray under black brows and lashes, regarded him without expression. "Merlin," he said at last. "This is a surprise." He gestured to a high-backed red-cushioned chair. "Sit." Then, as his father-in-law obeyed, "Igraine is not here. She is still at

3

Durovarium. She was quite ill this time. The doctors feared for her life."

"So I heard." Merlin's voice was quiet. "That is why I was surprised to learn you had come to Venta. Is there trouble?"

The king shrugged wearily. "There is always trouble this time of year. The spring wind is a Saxon wind. You should know that by now."

"Yes." Both men spoke Latin with perfect purity and no trace of a British accent. "Uther," Merlin said carefully, "I came to see you because it is time to talk about the succession."

The king's face settled into harsher lines. There was a pause that seemed much longer than it actually was. Then, "Yes. I suppose it is time."

"Britain cannot afford a civil war over who is to inherit the high kingship after you." Merlin leaned a little forward in his urgency. "God knows, I hope you last another twenty years. But we must make provisions, Uther. The Saxons will pour through every crack in our unity."

At that the king rose to his feet. He was not a tall man, but his shoulders and arms were heavily muscled. He was the son of a Roman, and a Roman he remained, both in looks and in heart. "I know," he said, now bitterly. "But what is to be done, Merlin? God knows, the Celts will never unite under one of their own. Their jealousy would tear the country apart. And how the wolves would love that!"

Merlin was nodding agreement. "That is why it is so important to have a son of yours inherit. Your son would be both Roman, through you, and Celtic, through Igraine. A natural leader for Britain."

"For God's love, Merlin, I have no son! You know that well enough!" Uther rubbed his forehead as if it hurt. "Another stillborn child," he said heavily. "It is as if God has cursed us. Maybe he has, for the way we came together."

"You do have a son," contradicted Merlin. "You forget. There is still Arthur."

Uther went very still. Merlin watched the smoke curling above the brazier and waited. "We sent Arthur away and gave it out that he was dead. You know that. It is too late to think of Arthur now."

Merlin let his eyes return to Uther's face. "We sent Arthur away so he could not stand in the path of your true-born sons. But you have no true-born sons. No *other* true-born sons. Arthur is not a bastard. Technically, he was born in wedlock."

The king sat down abruptly. "Yes. He was born three months after we married. And until that time Igraine was wedded to another man. The child's paternity was very questionable, Merlin." He made a gesture in response to the flash of expression in Merlin's eyes. "Oh, not to me. Igraine swore he was mine, and I believe her. But the fact remains that when he was conceived, she was married to Gorlois."

"You killed Gorlois in single combat and then you married Igraine, even though she was noticeably with child. You would not have done that, Uther, if you had not been sure the child was yours."

Uther ran a hand through his black hair. "But there would always be a question. You yourself said so." A note of bitterness crept into the king's voice. "When Ambrosius died and I became king, it was you who suggested that Arthur be sent away."

"I know. I know. But Igraine was pregnant again . . ." Merlin drew a long breath. "Who could have foreseen all these stillbirths?"

Uther looked up from under his level black brows. "What do you propose I do?" he asked, and the bitterness had not quite gone.

"You need do nothing. I will go to Cornwall, fetch the boy, and bring him home with me to Avalon. He will be nine years old now; time enough for him to learn to be a Roman and a king."

"You remember where he is?"

"I remember where I took him. To Malwyn's village. I presume he is still there?"

"Yes. I send something to Malwyn every year. She will have taken good care of him. She was always more his mother than Igraine." He paused as they both remembered Igraine's refusal to have anything to do with her firstborn child.

"Igraine saw him as a visible sign of her adultery," Merlin said matter-of-factly. "His existence was a constant scourge to her pride."

"Well, there is no use now in going over past sins." Uther's voice was hard. "At the time, it seemed the prudent thing to send the boy away. We knew he would be cared for, and Malwyn could be trusted to keep the secret of his birth. But you are right, Father-in-law. Things have changed." Uther straightened his broad shoulders and his voice took on an unmistakable note of authority. "Go into Cornwall and get the boy, but do not tell him, or anyone else, who he is. Let us see first if he has the makings of a king."

Merlin had straightened too. "I will," he replied.

"And"—Uther's pale eyes held Merlin's—"we will say nothing of this to Igraine."

After a moment Merlin nodded.

"Good." The word from Uther was both an approval and a dismissal.

The following morning Merlin left Venta and rode west to Cornwall, the same journey he had made over eight years before when he had been escorting a woman and a baby into exile.

Malwyn's village was some miles east of Tintagel, a long weary ride from Venta. Merlin took Roman roads until he reached Isca Dumnoniorum, and from there he went along local tracks. He stopped at an inn once but otherwise made camp by himself. He was fifty-six years of age, but he had been a soldier under Uther's father, Constantine, and he had not forgotten his skills.

Malwyn's village, like most of the villages scattered throughout the Cornish peninsula, was purely Celtic. The Roman legions who had occupied Britain for so many hundreds of years had scarcely left a mark beyond the Tamar. It was early afternoon when Merlin rode into the circle of stone huts that composed the village. The sun was warm and he saw a number of small children and pigs, but no adults. Then an elderly woman came out of one of the huts and blinked in the sunshine. Merlin called to her and she waited while he dismounted. The mud squished under his feet as he approached her. "Which of these houses belongs to Malwyn?" he asked in British.

A blank look was his only answer. He tried again, speaking more slowly. "Malwyn," the old woman repeated. She squinted up at him, her eyes almost hidden in a mass of wrinkles. "She be the one with the bastard boy?"

It had been thought best to have Malwyn say that Arthur was her own child. Merlin's mouth folded at the corners. "Yes," he said.

"She be dead."

"Dead?"

"Aye. She died long years ago." The old woman looked dimly satisfied. "She were one of them Christians," she added, as if that should explain matters.

"If she is dead, then where is the boy?" Merlin asked sharply.

"He bides with Esus. Her brother."

"And which dwelling belongs to Esus?"

The old woman pointed and Merlin turned and walked through the mud toward the indicated hut. He bent his head at the door and called, but there was no reply. He ducked inside for a moment, long enough to see the bareness and smell the odor of animals and ascertain the single room was empty. Once outside, he took a deep breath of air. He had not remembered that the place looked like that.

Evidently some of the children had gone running for their mothers, for as he stood there, uncertain where to look next, two young women with children in their arms and at their skirts appeared from behind a clump of trees. Merlin led his horse toward them. "I am looking for Esus," he said slowly. "Do you know where he is?"

The women exchanged glances; then the smaller one spoke. "In the fields, with the other men."

"And Esus' wife?"

A surprised look. "Esus has no wife."

Merlin took a deep breath. "And the boy?"

The women looked at each other again, and this time the taller of the two answered him. "The boy is with the sheep, as usual."

"Where are the sheep?" Merlin asked, and the two of them pointed to a grassy hill about a mile in the distance.

Merlin rode slowly toward the sloping green hill where the village sheep were pastured, and his thoughts were not pleasant. They had not done well, he and Uther, by this boy. Someone, during all these years, should have come to see how things were with him. Uther's son. His own grandson. Living in that stinking hovel. For how long had Malwyn been dead?

The sheep were grazing on the hill and, seated under a hawthorn bush carving a piece of wood with a knife, was a boy. Merlin walked his horse slowly toward the seated figure and then, when he was almost in front of him, dismounted.

"Arthur?" he asked, his voice not as steady as he would have liked.

The boy had been watching him come. At the name he nodded warily, put down his carving, and stood up. Something about him reminded Merlin forcibly of an animal at bay.

"There is no need to be frightened," he said gently. "I won't hurt you."

The boy's face was blank and shuttered. He said nothing. Merlin softly stroked his horse's nose and looked at his grandson.

The boy was Uther's, there could be no mistake about that: the ink-black hair, the dark brows and lashes, the light gray eyes. But the bone structure was Igraine's. He was dressed like a peasant and his hair was greasy and there was a dirt smudge on one high cheekbone, but he wore his heritage in every lineament of his face.

Merlin searched for what to say. That blank, shuttered look rejected him before he had even begun. "Arthur," he began determinedly, "I am here as an emissary from your father."

The boy said nothing. The look on his face did not change.

"He . . . he did not know that your . . . that Malwyn was dead."

Still nothing.

"How old were you when she died?"

There was a long pause. Merlin was beginning to wonder if the boy had been able to understand him, when Arthur finally spoke. "I don't know." His British was the local dialect; his voice was sullen.

Merlin stared at his grandson in frustration. Finally he said baldly, "I have come to take you away."

Something flashed briefly behind those gray eyes before the shutters came down again. But it was a reaction. Encouraged, Merlin went on with the story he had prepared during his journey to Cornwall. It had to do with Arthur's fictitious father being an old army friend of his. Flavius, he named him. Flavius had been married, he told the boy, and so unable to marry Malwyn. But he had always intended to send for Arthur. When Flavius had died a few months ago, Merlin had promised to look out for the boy. And so here he was, come to take Arthur home.

The story had not sounded very plausible even when he thought it up. It sounded even less plausible now as he confronted the still, closed face of his grandson. No, Merlin thought heavily, they had not done well by Arthur at all.

For the first time the boy volunteered speech. "Will he let me go?" he asked.

"Do you mean Esus?"

"Yes."

"I have not yet spoken to him. But he has no claim on you, boy. He will let you go."

A breeze came rustling up the hill, making Merlin's cloak swirl around him, lifting the tangled black hair off Arthur's forehead. It should be a beautiful face, Merlin thought, but it was marred by that sullen, withdrawn expression. "Come," he said decisively, "we will go and find Esus."

It was not, in fact, quite as simple as Merlin had anticipated, the business of removing Arthur from his guardian. Esus, large, grim-faced, argumentative, was not inclined to give the boy up easily. It was a matter, Merlin finally gathered, of the yearly payments from Uther.

He got Arthur, finally, because of who he was. Even in Cornwall they knew of Merlin, the Romano-Celtic prince who had been one of Constantine's captains, who was the father of the queen. He got Arthur, although Esus had not liked it. All through the long discussion the boy had sat to the side and said nothing. When bidden, he had made a packet of his belongings and followed Merlin. He had said nothing to Esus at the parting.

It was late afternoon when they left the village, but Merlin had no disposition to linger within its inhospitable environs. He would be more comfortable sleeping under the stars than in that circular hut with the smoke and the pigs and Esus' hostility.

They made camp beside a small stream and Merlin shot a rabbit with his bow. The boy ate the meat hungrily and lay down obediently at Merlin's command. He was asleep almost instantly.

Merlin looked at the tousled black hair of his sleeping grandson, illuminated by the dying light of the fire. The boy was no dirtier than most village-dwellers, but he was a long way from Merlin's fastidious Roman standards of cleanliness. Tomorrow, he thought, he would bathe Arthur in the stream. He had brought fresh clothes for the boy in his own saddlebag. With a bath and clean clothes, the boy would look presentable enough to bring to Avalon.

Arthur made no objection when Merlin announced his intentions the following morning. The sun was bright and warm and Merlin even went so far as to strip himself and step into the cold, running water. Arthur followed suit a little gingerly. Clearly, bathing was not a familiar occupation for him. The sun slanted through the trees, casting dapples of light and shade on the water and on their naked bodies. Merlin watched Arthur's tentative splashes, and reached out toward the boy to wet his hair. Arthur, moving like lightning, leapt back out of his reach. Merlin was so startled he almost lost his balance.

The boy's fists were raised in front of him, his whole thin, child's body tensed. "Don't touch me," he snarled.

Merlin stared, stunned by the expression on the boy's face. After a moment, when he had recovered his breath, "I was just going to wash your hair," he said quietly.

"I'll do it," Arthur said. Then, "I don't like to be touched."

"All right," Merlin replied with as much composure as he could muster. "You do it, then."

When they were finished bathing, and Arthur was dry, Merlin brought out the clothes from his saddlebag. "For you," he said. He did not attempt to hand them to the boy, but laid them down and backed away so that Arthur could pick them up himself.

The mark on the boy's cheek had not been dirt but a fading bruise. And as Arthur had washed in the stream, Merlin had clearly seen the thin white scars that crisscrossed the boy's back and buttocks and thighs.

No wonder Arthur had made no complaint about leaving Esus.

Merlin's thoughts were bleak as he broke camp and prepared to start north and east. Whether Arthur would make a king or no, he was thankful he had come to Cornwall to find this grandson. He only hoped, for both their sakes, that he had not come too late.

Chapter 2

MERLIN got him a pony. There were only two horses in the village and Arthur had never ridden them, but he did not tell that to Merlin. Instead he watched carefully as Merlin mounted, and then he did the same.

The pony was splendid. Arthur let his legs hang down and relaxed into the horse's back. He could feel the stretch of muscles right through the saddle.

The man, Merlin, was talking. "We are going to my villa of Avalon. Avalon will be your new home. I think you will like it. It's called Avalon because of its apple orchards. It's famous for its apple orchards."

The man spoke softly, gently, clearly. As if he were speaking to an idiot, Arthur thought. He shot Merlin a look from under lowered lashes. He didn't know what the man's motives were, but he didn't trust him. It wasn't likely that he had ridden all the way into Cornwall just to collect the son of an "old friend."

"It used to be one of the most famous villas in the country," the man was going on. "My family were princes of the Durotriges tribe and they built the villa as their palace." The old man gave him a deprecating look. "It's not a palace any longer, Arthur. It is a working farm. But in these troubled days, it is luxury to have all you need at your fingertips, I suppose."

Princes of the Durotriges. Arthur was even more suspicious. What could this man want with him? A sudden thought crossed his mind. He had heard of what some men did with boys. His nostrils flared a little as he looked at the man riding so calmly beside him.

Iron-gray hair, still very thick. Finely drawn features. Blue eyes. His red woolen cloak was clasped at his shoulder by a brooch of obvious value. Arthur relaxed a little. Such a man would not need to seek out an obscure Cornish boy to satisfy his deviant tastes.

Merlin was still talking about this Avalon. "There are several other people living in the house besides myself. First there is Ector, my steward and my friend. He was a soldier under Ambrosius before he was wounded. He has a son who also lives at Avalon. Caius, or Cai as he is always called. You and he can have lessons together. He is about your age."

Arthur was not sure of his own age. He said, looking straight ahead, "How old is this Cai?"

"Ten. A year older than you."

Nine. The old man sounded very positive about that. "He's big for his age," Merlin was going on, "but very nice. You won't have to worry about Cai."

Arthur was not worried about any boy. He had learned long ago to take care of himself with other boys. He said, a little gruffly, "I don't know how to read. Or write."

"Of course you don't. How should you?" Merlin responded easily. "That will come first, naturally. I think I shall start by giving you lessons with Morgan. Morgan is my daughter. She's eight and it's time she learned to read and write too."

Lessons with a girl. Well, he would take lessons with a dog if he had to. He would do anything to learn to read.

And no matter what happened, or what the old man's motives were, at least Merlin had taken him away from *him*.

It was late in the afternoon of a golden spring day that Arthur first saw Avalon, of the apple trees. The orchards were in bloom and they rode in through a magnificent canopy of blossoms, pink and white against the green grass and the cobalt sky. For a brief moment Arthur found himself wondering if the old man might be one of the fairy folk taking him to an enchanted world beyond the earth.

Merlin was watching his face. "Arthur," he asked gently. "Do you never smile?"

Arthur stiffened and just then the house came into view.

It had been built as a palace, Merlin had told him, and it looked like a palace to Arthur. The single-story house was built of gray stone and stretched out on three sides of a great cobbled courtyard. "The main part of the house is the wing in front of us," Merlin was saying as they rode into the courtyard. "That wing," and he gestured to their right, "is mainly bedrooms, and this opposite wing contains the baths." He halted his horse and shouted. In a minute a man came running.

"Welcome home, my lord."

"Thank you, Marcus. Take the horses to the stable, please."

The stocky brown-haired man nodded and picked up both sets of reins. He glanced once at Arthur before he led the animals away.

"Come," said Merlin, and strode toward the great front door. Arthur followed.

The large double door opened into an imposing vestibule. Beyond the vestibule was a great mosaic-tiled room, with a marble dais at one end. The throne room of the princes of the Durotriges, Arthur thought with a mixture of derision and awe. He followed Merlin across the room and into another room that opened off it. This room was much smaller and distinctly more cozy. It was furnished with wicker chairs and leather stools, and an old couch leaned against the far wall. This floor too was of varicolored mosaic tile.

"Sit down," Merlin said, and gestured to one of the wicker chairs. "I'll find Ector and be right back."

Arthur sat warily on the edge of the indicated chair.

A long time seemed to pass. Then a voice spoke to him in Latin from the doorway and he looked up to find a small girl regarding him solemnly.

"I don't speak Latin," he said shortly.

The child came into the room. "I'm Morgan," she said in British. "Who are you?"

"Arthur," he replied, and looked at Merlin's daughter.

Her gown had grass stains on the skirt and her hair was hanging untidily down her back. It was light brown and it badly needed a comb. He looked at her face and met the biggest, most luminous brown eyes he had ever seen. The child crossed the room and pulled up a stool next to his chair. "Was that your pony Marcus brought to the stable?" she inquired, seating herself.

"Yes."

"He's nice. We can give him an apple later, if you like."

He didn't know that ponies liked apples. "You must have a lot of extra apples," he commented, and she laughed.

There was a heavy step outside the door, and then Merlin was back, bringing with him a tall broad-shouldered man with graying brown hair and a noticeable limp. "Oh, here you are, Morgan," her father said. "Have you met Arthur?"

"Yes." Morgan kissed her father on the cheek and Merlin said, "Ector, this is Flavius' son. His name is Arthur."

The man bestowed a smile upon him and said kindly, "Welcome to Avalon, Arthur."

Arthur watched the two men with a steady, unblinking stare, and nodded.

"It's almost time for dinner," Merlin said briskly. "I want a bath first, though. The roads are still full of mud. I'll show you to your bedroom, Arthur, and you can change your clothes."

The boy's face never altered, but he took a step forward. Then he felt a small hand slip into his own. "I'll show him, Father," Morgan offered. "He can have the bedroom next to mine."

There was a pause; then Merlin answered, "Very well. Show Arthur the bedroom, and then you can direct him to the baths if he wants, Morgan."

"I will." Arthur felt a strong tug on his arm. "Come along, Arthur," Morgan said. Then, when they were in the next room, "I want to show you my dog."

Morgan's dog was a mongrel, with one ear half chewed off. "Isn't he wonderful?" she asked as the dog came to thrust its muzzle lovingly into her hand. Her brown eyes were looking at Arthur with perfect naturalness and trust. She might have known him all her life.

Arthur had expected the daughter of a house like this to have a purebred. He caressed the dog's head gently and asked, "What's his name?"

"Horatius."

"Hello there, Horatius," the boy said, and squatted easily on his heels. The dog nuzzled him.

"I found him wandering in the woods one day," Morgan explained. "He was hungry and he'd obviously been in a couple of fights. Do you have a dog?"

He shook his head. He would not have brought a dog home to live with Esus.

"Horatius likes you. You can share him if you like."

He raised his head sharply and looked at her. "Why should you share your dog with me?"

The big brown eyes looked serenely back. No eyes had ever looked at him like that before, as if they were looking just at *him*, and liking what they saw. "Because he likes you," she answered simply. "He's afraid of most people. I think he must have been cruelly mistreated once. But he likes you."

Her words made him feel strange. "Your bedroom is next door," she said. "I'll show you."

His own room. There was actually a bed, a wooden platform with a mattress and blankets and pillows. The floor was red tile. There was a brazier for warmth.

"It's very nice," he managed.

She looked at him solemnly. "Are you going to live here now, Arthur?"

He answered cautiously, trying it out. "Yes. I am."

She smiled. He had never seen such a smile. "Oh, good," she said. "Then you can be my friend."

It was impossible not to respond to that radiant look. "Yes," he said. And felt something hard and tight and hurtful in his chest begin to relax.

He met Cai at dinner, a tall, big-boned boy with very steady hazel eyes. In deference to Arthur they all spoke British. They were dressed in British garb as well, and sat at the table on benches in the British fashion, but Arthur sensed that this was not really a Celtic household.

Their usual speech was obviously Latin. And the villa itself was nothing a Celt would have built. There was a whole wing devoted just to baths! The princes of the Durotriges had evidently embraced Rome with a whole heart.

Morgan sat on the bench beside him, dressed now in a clean blue gown and white wool tunic. Her hair was neatly combed and hung down her back to her waist. Her small hand with its fragile wrist dipped into the meat platter. Arthur followed suit.

Merlin was talking. "Tomorrow Cai can take you around the estate, Arthur. Show you the farms, the stables and orchards, all that sort of thing."

Cai nodded. "Be happy to," he said pleasantly to Arthur. Merlin looked at his grandson as well. The boy's face was perfectly expressionless.

"May I come too?" asked Morgan.

Cai sighed. "Morgan, whenever you come somewhere with me you are sure to find a bird with a broken wing or a cat with a cut paw, and then we have to come home so you can take care of it."

"Well, you wouldn't want to leave a wounded animal, Cai," Morgan said reasonably.

"No. But why is it *you* who always find them?"

"I don't know." Morgan was clearly puzzled by this herself. "I just do." She asked again, "Please, Cai, may I come?"

Cai was saying, "Oh, I suppose so," when Merlin chanced to look once again at Arthur.

The boy was watching Morgan, and on his mouth there was a very faint smile.

Chapter 3

Merlin looked at the three children who were seated around the large library table of polished wood. The spring sun slanted in through the window and pooled on the darker inlay in front of Arthur. Dust motes danced in the air, watched by Morgan with concentrated interest. The two boys watched Merlin. As Merlin's eyes touched Arthur's face, he realized, with a small shock of surprise, that it was almost two years ago to the day that he had brought the boy to Avalon.

In two years that sullen young savage had made great strides. He had learned to speak and read and write in fluent Latin and today was embarking on the course of study for which he had been brought to Avalon. Merlin was going to teach his grandson to be a leader of men.

Cai was to be included in the lessons as well. Merlin was fond of Ector's son; also, it would look distinctly odd if he singled Arthur out for special attention. The rumor already was that Arthur was Merlin's son. Not that it was necessarily a bad thing for the boy to think; nor was it far from the actual truth.

Merlin's eyes went from Arthur's face to Morgan. His daughter, of course, had no business at all being in this class. She should be with the women, learning how to weave and sew. But she wanted to do everything that Arthur did, and Merlin had given in to her without much protest. There was no doubt that Arthur was easier to handle when Morgan was present. Alone, he was reserved, impenetrable almost. With Morgan he was a different boy: relaxed and approachable. And so here she sat, his ten-year-old daughter, about to learn how to be a leader of men.

The boys were still watching him. "Today," he said pleasantly, "we are about to begin a series of lessons that will teach you both," he could not seriously include Morgan in this discussion, "how best to be of service to your country." He paused. "The high king has been

17

fighting the Saxons for over eleven years now, and still they come, pushing always from the east, trying to overwhelm us, to take Britain for themselves. In a few years you boys will be of an age to fight. Well and good. But the high king does not need just fighters. He needs leaders. Men who know how to command other men.

"This is what I wish to teach you, the art of competent leadership." He looked into Cai's serious hazel eyes and then into the cool gray gaze of his grandson. "I learned leadership myself from a master," he continued. "I learned from Constantine, the Comes Britanniarum, the Count of Britain, one of the greatest of Roman soldiers."

The children had heard often enough of Merlin's old commander, the Count of Britain.

"May we ask questions, sir?" It was Arthur's voice, still a boy's voice but with a cool and detached note that made it sound as if it belonged to someone much older.

"Yes."

"I have wondered how, if Constantine were such a great soldier, the empire spared him to Britain."

Merlin leaned back in his chair and stretched his shoulders. "A fair enough question," he agreed. "Britain was hardly one of the empire's first priorities, after all. Why, then, you wonder, should Rome send us one of her finest soldiers?"

At Arthur's almost imperceptible nod, he went on. "Very well. Constantine is as good a place as any to start." He frowned a little, fixed his eyes on the little splash of sunlight on the table, and began.

"Constantine came from a great Roman military family. When he was about your age," and his eyes briefly scanned the politely attentive face of his grandson, "he was sent to Constantinople to attend the Emperor Theodosius' Imperial School. This was a school for future Roman generals, and it included all the finest highborn barbarian princes, as well as Romans like Constantine. Alaric the Goth was one of the pupils."

"Alaric!" It was Cai's quick exclamation. "Do you mean the Alaric who sacked Rome?"

"Yes," said Merlin dryly. "I do."

"He learned his lessons too well," said Morgan. She was gazing now at her father, her small chin propped on her hand. She had begun to pay attention once Merlin started to talk about Constantine.

"So it would seem," Arthur murmured, and cast her a look of affectionate amusement.

Merlin went back to gazing at the splash of sunlight. "The Imperial School flourished until the year 394," he continued. "That was the year of the Battle of Aquileia against the traitor Arbogast. Constantine, along with most of the other boys from the school, fought in that terrible battle." He looked from the sun spot to Cai and then to Arthur. "We will study that battle someday," he promised.

Arthur's black eyebrows rose fractionally and he nodded.

Merlin continued. "Constantine's brave leadership at Aquileia caught the eye of the great Roman general Stilicho. He became a prodigy of Stilicho's and rose high in the ranks of the army. Then, in 408, Stilicho was treacherously executed by the Emperor Honorius, and Constantine was banished from Rome. In 410, as you know"—he cocked an eyebrow at Morgan—"Alaric sacked Rome. The last of our own legions were recalled from Britain, and we were left to defend ourselves as best we could against the Saxons and the painted people from the north. Britain continued to beg the empire for help, however, and in 415 Honorius created the position of the Count of Britain. The count's job was to assist the native British tribes defend what was left of Rome in Britain. In order to do this, Honorius detached a mobile field army from his legions in Gaul and sent it to Britain under the command of the count."

Merlin raised one elegantly groomed eyebrow. "The job of Count of Britain was not, as you correctly surmised, Arthur, a desirable one and so it was given to a man who had fallen from imperial favor: Constantine."

"Was Constantine successful in pushing back the barbarians?" asked Morgan.

"He was successful against the Saxons, but then the painted people began to raid across the wall. We went north, to try to push them back . . ."

Merlin broke off. Even after all these years, it hurt him to speak of that terrible time. He had been eighteen years old when he first joined Constantine and he had loved the Roman more than any other man in the world. "Constantine was betrayed," he said in a hard, cold voice. "It was said he was killed in a Pictish raid, but that was not true. It was the Celts. He was killed by one of Vortigern's men. I could never prove it, but I know it is so. The Celts were afraid Constantine would restore the empire in Britain, and so they killed him and set up one of their own, Vortigern, as high king. If I had not gotten Constantine's sons,

Ambrosius and Uther, away to Armorica, they would have been killed too."

The rest of the lesson was spent in recounting the history of Vortigern's rule and Ambrosius' triumphant return. The children were satisfactorily attentive and Merlin dismissed them two hours before dinner.

Morgan and Arthur went to their usual place by the river. They had constructed a platform in a beech tree the previous year, and they loved to sit there, high above the ground, screened from view by the beech's branches, and watch the river, read, or talk. Morgan had changed into breeches and she and Arthur sat now, crossed-legged and identically dressed, throwing dice and talking.

"Poor Father," Morgan said as she idly rolled the dice in her palm. "I think he finds it very frustrating not to be on better terms with Uther."

"I think so too," Arthur returned. They spoke in British, as they invariably did when they were alone. Arthur's thick black hair slid down across his forehead and he pushed it back with a quick, characteristic gesture. "Why isn't he, Morgan?"

She lifted her head, and the sun, shining through the leaves of the tree, dappled her hair and face with light. Her hair had just been trimmed and it hung like soft brown silk halfway down her back. Almost absently, Arthur reached out and touched the shining, evenly trimmed ends. Morgan said seriously, "He used to be, I think, until he married my mother."

Arthur rubbed his thumb gently back and forth across the lock of hair he held. "What do you mean?"

"I heard this from Justina, you understand," Morgan cautioned with amusement. Justina was her nurse and an inveterate gossip.

Arthur's eyes mirrored the expression in hers. "Go on," he prompted. He dropped her hair and she leaned back against the tree trunk and rested her arms around her drawn-up knees.

"According to Justina," she began, "my father and Uther used to be fast friends. As my father was friends with Ambrosius. When Ambrosius died and Uther became king and married Igraine, my father was his closest adviser. Then Merlin married my mother, and Uther and Igraine turned against him."

Arthur's black brows drew together. "But why?"

"Well, Nimue, my mother, was a granddaughter of Maximus, the Maximus the British legions raised to be emperor. Uther was afraid that Merlin was setting up a royal house to rival his own." Morgan waved an insect away from her face. "Actually, Justina blames Igraine for the quarrel more than Uther." She shrugged. "At any rate, both Uther and Igraine insisted that Nimue was an enchantress, to have seduced my poor old father into marriage. Father was furious, as you can well imagine. He does not think of himself as old."

Arthur grinned. "He does not," he agreed.

Morgan continued, matter-of-factly, "Then I was born and my mother died. Father and Uther made it up after a bit, but I don't think Father ever quite forgave Igraine."

"She never comes here." Arthur produced two pears and handed one to Morgan, who took a healthy bite.

"I met her once," she said around the pear in her mouth, "when I was little and my sister Morgause was married. She came to the wedding and left again almost immediately." Morgan finished chewing and said penitently, "I shouldn't be unkind. She has had a very sad life, Igraine. All those dead babies!"

"You have never been unkind in your life," Arthur said. His strong young teeth crunched into his own pear.

"But isn't it sad, Arthur?"

"It's sad for Igraine, I suppose." Arthur took another bite. "But it's even sadder for Britain. Uther has no son to follow him in the high kingship."

"Justina says it's a judgment on Igraine for betraying her first husband, Gorlois."

Arthur's fine nostrils quivered with derision. "Justina would." He finished his pear, picked up the three dice, and began to roll them in his palm.

Morgan watched his thin brown hand, a frown puckering her brow. "I think Father has started his own imperial school," she said after a short pause. Her eyes were still on his hand. "And it's not for Cai."

The hand stilled. "I know," said Arthur, and she looked at his face. His hair had fallen forward again, almost to the level black line of his brows. Their eyes met. "He has some plan for me. I wish I knew what it was."

"Everyone thinks it is because you are his son."

"Well, I'm not." They had talked of this before. "My mother told me too many times that I looked just like my father. I don't look at all like Merlin." There were two sharp lines between his brows. "My mother didn't lie."

Morgan nodded solemnly and took a last bite out of her pear. "We'll find out who you are one day." She tossed the core out of the tree and gave him a humorous look. "I liked it better when we were reading Virgil."

The frown lifted from Arthur's face. *"Pius Aeneas,"* he said. "So noble. And so tedious."

"Don't let Merlin catch you saying that," she warned, and he laughed.

"Never!" he said in Latin. Then, rising to his feet, "It's getting late. We'll miss dinner if we don't hurry."

The two children climbed out of the tree, Morgan as nimbly as Arthur, and began to walk hand in hand back to the house.

As time went on, Morgan continued to attend Merlin's lectures, but left the boys to themselves when they went into the field to learn the physical arts of war. Ector was their chief instructor at first; then, as the boys improved, Merlin began to import a series of "experts" for the various disciplines of war and leadership. Over the years, Avalon became accustomed to a procession of strange men who would spend a few months instructing Arthur and Cai before they departed as mysteriously as they had come.

The boys learned the correct use of the lance, pike halberd-ax, long-sweep sword from horseback, short sword for afoot, and the long sword. They learned about siege engines and circumvallation and entrenchment. They learned how to use their voices so they could reach every corner of a battlefield and still be understood. And every day Ector had them out on the grass wrestling. The sport that Arthur and Cai had once played merely as a release for excess boyish energy now became a daily occupation of forced excellence.

"Excellence" was Merlin's favorite word. "Your Christian religion teaches you why you are in this world: to serve God," he told them. "But the thing you must teach yourselves is that the highest service is to excel. It was to excel in everything that you were born into this world. If you do not excel, then you were born in vain."

Merlin's lectures were always addressed impartially to both boys, but Arthur knew the old man was talking to him. Why this should be so, he did not know. But that it was so, he was certain.

And it was in his nature to excel. He could feel it in himself as he answered the challenges constantly posed by his teachers. Even the wrestling with Cai became a challenge, and it was not long before Arthur had learned to use leverage to compensate for his slighter weight.

He could ride better than Cai, too. He could ride better than the cavalryman Merlin brought to Avalon to teach them. It was the use of horse in battle that most interested Arthur. He read all of Xenophon's comments on cavalry, and he questioned Merlin relentlessly on Constantine's use of horse.

"The Battle of Adrianople established definitively the value of heavy cavalry," Merlin told his pupil. "It was one of the most nearly total defeats ever suffered by a Roman army. The cavalry of the Goths cut the legions to pieces. From Adrianople on, cavalry formed an important part of the Roman army. Stilicho used it at Aquileia when he defeated Arbogast."

Arthur, however, drew his own conclusions from Merlin's talk. "It seems to me that the Romans never learned the proper use of heavy cavalry," he said to Cai one chill winter day when the boys were in the baths after some strenuous work with lances. "Constantine had light cavalry, but he never used it in direct attack."

"Don't say that to Merlin," Cai replied humorously. "You know how he feels about everything Roman."

"I know." Arthur ducked under the water and came up, his dark head sleek as a seal's. He gave Cai an ironic look. "The empire is more his religion than Christ."

Cai sat on the side of the bath. At fourteen he was very tall, with shoulders that would one day be massive as his father's. At present, however, he had an unfinished look. He had grown so quickly that the rest of his body had never quite caught up to his height. He was intelligent, kind, steady as a rock. He was a year older than Arthur, but had resigned himself without resentment to the fact that he would never quite be the younger boy's equal.

Arthur got out of the bath and began to towel his hair. Cai took the opportunity to study the scars on the other boy's back. If Arthur knew he was looking at them, he would be angry. He hated anyone to notice his scars, and he had a collection of them. There was one above his right eyebrow, one on the side of his chin, and a particularly wicked-looking one on his left knee. Cai had asked only once about them. It was then that he had discovered that Arthur had the nastiest tongue of anyone he had ever met.

He had learned the origin of those scars from Ector, and had immediately forgiven Arthur his bad temper. Over the years his feelings for the younger boy had coalesced into a mixture of pride, admiration, and protectiveness—the feelings of a generous-hearted older brother toward a particularly brilliant younger sibling.

Arthur tossed his hair back and began to dry his shoulders with another towel. At thirteen he had the body of a dancer, light-framed, graceful, quick.

"In some ways Merlin is right," he said to Cai as he began to dress. "*Romanitas* still stands for civilization. It stands for regulated government and the freedom to live in peace. But the empire itself is crumbling. We in Britain are only a small part of the fight against the darkness."

Cai too began to dress. "My father says that the Saxons are massing for a strike in the spring. The high king is trying to gather the Celtic princes to his standard to oppose them."

Arthur stared at him, a line like a sword between his straight black brows. "If only I were not so young!"

Cai reached out to put a hand on the other boy's shoulder. "Don't worry," he said comfortably. "The Saxons will wait for you, Arthur." And he reached for his own tunic.

Chapter 4

"LEADERSHIP is always the management of men," said Merlin. "Failure in the management of men cannot be compensated for by success in other things. A leader must always be aware of his public function. He cannot consider his affairs as private, even to himself."

The window was open and the soft air of July came blowing in. Merlin's pupil appeared to be listening attentively, but Merlin was certain his thoughts were elsewhere. The sound of laughter floated in the window with the breeze and Merlin looked out into the courtyard and saw his daughter. She was carrying a basket of berries and her pony was following her, trying to eat them.

Arthur was now Merlin's sole pupil. It had been a very long time since Morgan had come to class. And this year Cai, now sixteen, had gone off to join the high king's army. The Saxons grew ever more aggressive, and Uther was hard-put to contain them.

"The Celtic princes are sorry now for the error they made when they invited Hengist and his kind to settle in Britain," Merlin said, following this line of thought. He looked at Arthur, inviting a reply.

The boy's long lashes lowered, half-screening his eyes. "Vortigern may have been a Celt, but he was following good Roman precedent," he answered. "The painted people of the north were pouring across the wall and Vortigern could not contain them. So he invited one set of barbarians in to harry the other." He raised his lashes and looked at Merlin. "It worked often enough for Rome."

Merlin stared back at his grandson's light eyes and deeply suntanned face. Even now, after six years, it was difficult for him to know what Arthur was thinking. "It worked for Rome, but it didn't work for Vortigern. Why, Arthur?"

The boy had evidently worked that one out long ago; he didn't even have to think about his reply. "Vortigern did not have Rome's resources," he said. "Nor did he have any understanding of what was happening in the world around him. The barbarian tribes had been on the move for a hundred years before his time: the Huns, the Goths, the Alanni, pushing westward, always westward." Arthur's thin brown fingers played with the stylus he was holding. "Vortigern unwittingly opened the door of Britain to a part of this mass migration of people, the Saxons." He put the stylus down. "He let the wolf into the fold," he concluded soberly, "and now they come by the thousands, pushing ever further in from the coast, sacking our towns and laying waste the country, harrying our people as wolves harry the sheep in a time of famine."

"A very good analysis," Merlin said after a moment. "The Celtic princes saw their mistake only when it was too late. Then they killed Vortigern and welcomed Ambrosius back from Armorica and installed him as high king. They learned at last that it is Roman leadership and Roman ability that are Britain's only hope against the Saxons."

It was the gospel he had preached to Arthur for six long years. This time Arthur answered him quietly, almost casually, "The only hope for us lies in our forgetting that we are Celts or Romans and remembering only that we are Britons."

Merlin was staring at his grandson's profile when there came the sound of a dog's joyous bark from the courtyard. A smile touched Arthur's mouth. "Horatius has been reunited with Morgan," he said.

"Run along," Merlin said abruptly. "It's too lovely a day to be indoors."

In less than two minutes he saw Arthur join Morgan in the courtyard.

They took their ponies and went out to the open country, away from the vale of Avalon and into the hills. There was a particular place they often visited, a wild valleyside where the flowers were riotous and there were tufts of heather, and it was there that they stopped and unbridled their ponies to let them graze. Horatius stretched out in the shade near Morgan, and Arthur did the same, resting his head in her lap as she leaned back against a fir tree. It was cool here, out of the sun, and he closed his eyes in pleasure, confiding the weight of his head to her with long-accustomed ease. She put her hand on his black hair, tousled by the ride and now on a level with her knees.

"Father was unusually brief this morning," she said.

"There's nothing more he can teach me." His voice was matter-of-fact. Sleepy. He was clearly enjoying the touch of her hand. "He has his instrument, all tuned and ready. Now we must see what he plans to do with it."

"You're only fifteen," she said.

He looked up into her brown eyes. "I'll go next year," he said. "I must. Cai went at sixteen."

"I know."

He drew her hand down to his mouth for a minute, and then he sat up. "I'm too young!" he said fiercely. His eyebrows were tense with frustration. "Too young to go to war, too young to marry you. But I don't *feel* young, Morgan. I feel . . ." He ran a hand through his tangled hair. His peaceful mood had quite vanished. His nostrils were pinched-looking, his eyes narrowed.

Morgan bent her head. "I know," she said again.

He looked over at her. Her round head, with its long, evenly cut silken hair, was bowed. He could see the nape of her neck where her hair parted. It was milk-white, unlike the tanned skin of her cheeks and forehead. He could almost feel the softness of her nape under his hand.

Morgan belonged to him and he belonged to Morgan. If only they were not so young!

As always, her thoughts marched with his. "Promise me," she said, "promise me that you will marry me before you go away."

They looked at each other, and as they gazed, the mask of youth fell away from them. No one who knew them would have recognized the grave and adult expression that came across both young faces.

"Will he let us?" Arthur asked. "You are his daughter, and God alone knows who I am."

"I don't know. I don't care. We'll do it anyway."

He moved to sit beside her, putting an arm around her shoulder and holding her to him. He was always amazed at the strength and the resilience of her slight young body. "Yes," he said. "We'll do it anyway."

"Here the young people come now," Ector said heartily as Arthur and Morgan came into the dining room. He smiled at the two of them as they took their seats.

Ector was by far the least complicated member of the Avalon household. He was almost as fond of Arthur and Morgan as he was of his own boy, and he still thought of them all as children. Arthur and Morgan in particular he saw as children; they still roamed the woods on their ponies, spent afternoons nested high in their tree house, and roughhoused with Morgan's collection of animals.

The old steward looked now at Morgan, who was seated at his right hand. She was dexterously using her knife, and when he spoke to her she lifted her head to reply, her teeth flashing white in her small suntanned face. He watched her as she stuffed food into herself like the hungry child she was, and thought, not for the first time, that someday she was going to be a lovely woman. She was lovely already, with her long brown hair tucked behind her small ears and spreading in a smooth fan to her waist. Her remarkable brown eyes were fixed now on her plate, but he knew all too well how they dominated the small, pure oval of her face.

Little Morgan, he thought affectionately. So solemn, so gentle, mothering her collection of wounded, orphaned animals, binding up all the boys' cuts and scrapes from the practice field. Beside him her hand reached out for more meat. The fragile wrist was scored where a thorn bush had caught it, one finger wore a scab, and two others were stained yellow from the dye she had been making that morning.

She was fourteen. In a year or two, when it was time for her to marry, perhaps Merlin would think of Cai. Cai would like it, his father knew. Apart from its being a very good match, Cai had always been very fond of Morgan.

From across the table came Merlin's voice, asking him a question. Ector pulled his thoughts back to the present and made a reply.

Two days later Merlin left for Venta. He had seen Uther at least once a year since Arthur had come to Avalon, but now he was going to meet the high king for one specific reason. Arthur's education was finished; the time had come for Uther to acknowledge his heir.

How he has aged. It was Merlin's first thought when he was shown into Uther's presence. The sun was shining and the day was warm, but the high king had a brazier going and he sat next to it, huddled like an old man against the chill.

"Are you well, Uther?" Merlin asked sharply.

Uther's dark skin had a decidedly sallow cast. There was gray at his temples. "I've had a cough," he said. "It's getting better. Sit down, Merlin." He gestured impatiently to a chair. Then, when the older man was seated, "Well?"

Merlin permitted himself a smile. "He is ready."

"Ah." Uther's aquiline nose looked more prominent than once it had. He leaned back in his chair. "Tell me about him," he said.

Merlin had spoken of Arthur before, of course: of his progress, his intelligence. Now he said what he really thought. "This is a boy like a drawn sword, Uther. I have thought for several years now that the reason you and Igraine had no more children was that God had ordained Arthur to be our king. I think he was born for Britain, Uther. Born to lead us out from under the darkness of the barbarian nightmare. I think he will be a king such as we have never yet seen in this land."

Uther was staring at him; Merlin did not often indulge in hyperbole. "Are you serious?" the king said at last.

"Yes."

In the heat of the room Uther was wearing a cloak, and now he pulled it more closely around him. "He is fifteen," he said grimly. "Too young yet." His face became even sharper. "I hope to God I can give him a few more years, Merlin."

"Are you that ill?"

"I feel wretched," the king replied frankly. "The doctors tell me I will recover, however, so there is hope."

"Shall I bring the boy to Venta?"

"No. Not yet." Uther's hands clenched on the arm of his chair. "He is safe at Avalon; let's keep him there for now. I have another campaign in the north this fall, and I don't trust my allies. There are too many small kings who would like to become the next high king and would not be pleased to discover the existence of a son of mine. I might not be able to keep him safe in Venta."

Merlin frowned and nodded, remembering Constantine.

"I would like to see him myself, though," said Uther, and for the first time emotion showed on his face. "I will come to Avalon."

Merlin looked away from the longing in the king's eyes and slowly shook his head. "Not unless you are prepared to acknowledge him."

Uther's pale eyes blazed. "If I wish to see him, I will. This is not your decision."

Merlin turned his head and met that burning gaze. "Uther, the boy looks too much like you. At present he thinks I am his father, but once he looks at you . . ."

The expression on Uther's face was painful to watch. "He looks like me?"

"Yes. Your hair. Your eyes. His eyebrows even grow like yours. He has your complexion. The resemblance is too marked to go unnoticed. We have kept this secret for too long to have it come out prematurely now."

Uther was looking intently at his hands. "And no one has ever guessed whose son he might really be?"

"There is no one at Avalon who knows you. Except Ector, of course. I think Ector has had his suspicions, but he will never say anything. And the boy himself has no idea. As I said, the belief at Avalon is that he is my son. Let us leave it that way for now."

"Yes." The word was spoken with obvious reluctance. "Yes, you are right, Father-in-law. The most pressing need is that he be kept safe until I need him."

Merlin remained talking with the high king for a few more minutes and then he left Uther to seek out the apartment of his daughter, Igraine, the queen.

Igraine's rooms in the praetorium were richly appointed, furnished with lamps and rugs that had at one time come from Rome. She was sewing with her women when Merlin was announced, and she held out her hand to her father and offered him her cheek to kiss.

He performed the desired office and took the seat she indicated. She folded her work in her lap and asked pleasantly, "What brings you to Venta, Father?"

Merlin looked appraisingly at his daughter before he answered. She was several years younger than her husband, and when she had married Uther, Igraine had been the most beautiful woman in Britain. There was still no gray in her black hair, but there were distinct lines beside her dark blue eyes and at the corners of her mouth. Her skin may have lost its youthful resilience, Merlin thought, but no matter how old she got, the beauty of her bone structure would never fail her. She had given those bones to her son.

Merlin ignored her polite question and said bluntly, "Uther looks ill."

A shadow crossed Igraine's face. His daughter had never been an emotional woman. She had married Gorlois, a man three times her age, with cold calculation; she had wanted to be Duchess of Cornwall. She had scarcely looked at her son, and had never once asked after him in all the years since he had been sent away. All the passion in her nature was concentrated on Uther. For him she had betrayed her husband and publicly shamed herself and her family. For him, and his kingship, she had ruthlessly broken with her father and her father's second wife. When it came to Uther, Merlin thought his daughter was probably capable of murder.

And Uther felt the same for her. She could not bear him a living child; he had every reason to put her away and marry again. But he had not.

"He has been ill," she replied now shortly. "But he is getting better." Her beautiful winged brows drew together. "His life would be so much easier if he was not always worrying about his allies as much as he worries about the Saxons."

"There has always been unrest and ambition among the Celts," Merlin said. "Is there some particular problem?"

"Yes." Igraine's voice was hard and very cold. "My sister Morgause's husband, Lot. Rumors have reached us that he fancies himself as the next high king."

"Lot!" Merlin was clearly astonished. "Lot has no claim to the high kingship. At least Vortigern could claim marriage to one of Maximus' daughters. Lot is just the king of a particularly poor northern kingdom."

"What Lot is, is ambitious," Igraine said bitterly. After a moment she added, her voice low, "He also has three healthy sons."

Merlin did not answer. He had never been able to talk to Igraine about her childlessness. There was, unfortunately, nothing one could say.

There was a little pause. Igraine fingered the jewel she wore at her throat. "I imagine Morgause would like to be queen." The lines on her face were harsh now. She looked suddenly as old as Uther.

"Morgause has no ambition," Merlin returned. He lifted a humorous eyebrow. "Morgause doesn't think that far ahead, Igraine. You know that."

There was no returning humor in Igraine's face. Humor had never been one of her outstanding characteristics. Morgause had humor, Merlin thought. Humor and warmth. Igraine had neither. What Igraine had, however, was a marvelously astute brain. She knew her sister too well to suspect her of plotting. Morgause was one to float along and do whatever it was that was easiest to do. If Lot engineered a revolt, she most probably would follow where he led. But the guiding brain would never be Morgause's.

"You and Uther are perfectly capable of dealing with Lot," Merlin said. "The northerners may go along with him, but Cador and Maelgwyn and the kings of the south will never agree to accept Lot as high king."

Igraine was looking at the sewing in her lap. "I know. But it is

one more worry for Uther, and at a time when he is not feeling himself
. . ." She stroked the material on her lap. He could almost see her
gathering her forces. When she looked up, her face was calm. "And
how is my youngest sister?" she asked. "We must begin to think of a
marriage for her."

Merlin thought about his daughters as he rode home from Venta the
following day. Igraine and Morgause were the children of his first
marriage. They had been born eight years apart and had never been
friends. They were too much opposites.

It had been Igraine who arranged Morgause's marriage to Lot. The
King of Lothian would never have crossed Merlin's mind as a possible
candidate for his daughter's hand. Lothian was far in the north, out of
the Roman sphere and, to Merlin's mind, scarcely civilized. Lot was a
Celtic king. He wore patterned, multicolored cloaks and hung himself
with gaudy jewelry. He was big and fair and arrogant, and Morgause
had been hot to have him the moment she first laid eyes on him.

Merlin had consented. He had understood Morgause's eagerness
well enough. In spite of his barbarous trappings, perhaps even because
of them, Lot was a splendid specimen of a male. He would keep
Morgause happy in bed and give her babies, and that was all Morgause
needed out of life.

Igraine's motives for introducing Lot to Morgause were far more
subtle. Merlin had still not fathomed them—unless it was simply that
she wanted her sister out of her way. It seemed now that Igraine was
regretting her choice.

The apple orchards of Avalon came into view and Merlin's thoughts
turned at last to his third daughter and youngest child. He smiled. The
best of the lot, he thought fondly. Never would he marry Morgan so
far away from him. Nor would he let Igraine pick this sister's husband.

There was no hurry, he thought. Morgan was but fourteen. Plenty of
time to worry about marriage.

It was rather a shame, he thought idly as his pony came into the
courtyard of the villa, that she could never marry Arthur.

Chapter 5

SEPTEMBER was a perfect month that year and the apples hung heavy in the Avalon orchards. Ector had wagonloads of produce to take to the Glevum harvest fair, and for the first time Merlin allowed Arthur and Morgan to accompany his steward on this annual journey. Merlin himself could not go, but he sent Justina to look after Morgan and gave Ector strict orders to keep a close watch on Arthur. He had hesitated about the wisdom of allowing Arthur to leave the confines of Avalon, but both children had begged so hard that he had eventually given in. The Glevum fair was so close to Wales, he thought, that there was little likelihood of anyone being present who would notice the boy's likeness to the high king.

The morning of their second day at the fair, Arthur left Morgan alone at a stall selling herbs and medicines and went off to explore on his own, promising to be back in an hour. Morgan was deep in conversation with the old woman who ran the stall and paused only long enough to give him a half-smile and say, "Go along. I'll be fine by myself."

"The young lady is very knowledgeable," the old crone who was selling the herbs said with unmistakable astonishment.

"Thank you," Morgan replied modestly. "Now, what do you recommend for boils?" Arthur grinned and began to walk toward the livestock area.

He went directly to the area where the horses were stabled. Most of the horses for sale were hill ponies, small and sturdy, no different from the horses they had at Avalon. Arthur walked up and down the roped-off area, looking, and shaking his head when asked if he wanted to buy. When he got to the end of the line he stopped and looked back, a faint line between his black brows. Was there a horse in all Britain that would make a cavalry mount?

"You don't look as if you care for our ponies." The voice spoke

British colored by the soft lilt of Wales, and Arthur's head swung around. A young giant was standing next to him. Arthur looked up and encountered the very blue eyes and fair gilt-colored hair of the pure Celt. The expression in those blue eyes was not friendly.

Arthur's reply was noncommittal. "They're nice ponies."

"But, from the look on your face, not good enough for you." The boy's voice was soft but its expression was as unfriendly as the look in his eyes.

"I was looking for something bigger," Arthur said.

"You?" The blue eyes measured him derisively.

"Yes."

The blond threw back his head. "I have a horse you might like." He smiled maliciously. "He's big. Very big. And a stallion. Want to try him?"

"Yes," said Arthur without hesitation. "I do."

He followed the big Celt out behind the pony area, beyond the tents and stalls, to a place which was obviously a camp. "Over here," the boy said across his shoulder, and led the way to where a single horse was picketed. "Sodak," he said softly, and a black head looked up from its grazing.

Arthur stood like a statue and stared. The black was the most magnificent animal he had ever seen: huge, muscled, his coat glowing like polished silk in the brilliant sunshine.

"Want to ride him?" the blond boy asked.

Arthur nodded mutely.

The other boy misunderstood his silence and smiled. "I'll saddle him for you," he said.

The stallion's ears went back as soon as he was approached with a bridle, and it took the two of them to get it and the saddle on. "Ready?" the blond said, grasped Arthur's knee in his hands, and tossed him into the saddle.

The black's head came up and Arthur could feel all its muscles tense. The stallion felt like a coiled spring beneath him. Before he could get his head down to buck, however, Arthur smacked him behind the saddle with his hand. Hard. The stallion changed his mind and sprang forward, at a dead run.

There was a field behind the encampment and Arthur headed there, leaning forward on the stallion's back, almost lost in the streaming black mane.

Never had he felt such power. After a few turns around the field the black's pace slackened and Arthur was able to take a feel of his mouth. He pressed with his leg and steered to the left and the black obediently followed his aids. Arthur laughed out loud. This was heaven.

It was with great reluctance that he finally brought the stallion back to its owner walking quietly. The blond boy took the bridle and grinned up at him, blue eyes full of undisguised admiration. "I'm sorry," he said. "Gods, but you can ride!" Then, as Arthur slid to the ground, "My name is Bedwyr. What's yours?"

"Arthur," Arthur replied, and returned the grin. "What a horse! Is he for sale?"

A shadow flickered across Bedwyr's smile. "No, he's not. And he's not my horse, he's my father's." He looked at the sweating animal. "I'm going to be in trouble if my father sees him like this. I should never have let you ride him."

"You thought he would just buck me off and go back to grazing," Arthur said excusingly.

Bedwyr nodded. "You didn't *look* as if you could ride him," he replied.

"I'll help you walk him out," Arthur offered, and the two boys stripped the stallion's saddle off, ducking the lashing hooves dexterously, and began to walk him slowly around the field, Bedwyr holding the reins and Arthur walking on the horse's other side.

"Where did your father find such a horse?" Arthur asked.

"He comes from Gaul. My father bought him from a Goth a few years ago to improve our own stock."

"He breeds those ponies to him?" Arthur asked in astonishment.

"No." Bedwyr gave Arthur a disgusted look. "We have some good mares at home. These," and he waved toward the ponies, "are the stock we are trying to unload."

"And you were insulted when I didn't want to buy them," Arthur said dryly.

Bedwyr's white teeth flashed. "Well," he said. And shrugged.

"Where do your people live?"

"In Dyfed. My father is King Ban."

So. This big blond boy with the magnificent horse was a prince. That accounted, Arthur supposed, for the obviously valuable arm rings that Bedwyr wore. Arthur reached up to pat the muscled neck of the stallion, and the horse turned on him with bared teeth. Arthur removed his arm from the path of the snapping teeth and said to Bedwyr, "Is he always this nasty?"

"He killed a man on the boat from Gaul," Bedwyr replied with what sounded suspiciously like pride. "He's a vicious brute, but his foals are magnificent. My father gave me one of his colts this spring."

When the horse was breathing quietly they brushed off the saddle marks and picketed him to graze. As they moved off together in the direction of the fair, Arthur said, "I have to meet my friend."

"I'll come with you," Bedwyr offered, and Arthur nodded. The two boys had reached the fairgrounds and were making their way up a narrow alley behind a row of stalls when there was the patter of feet behind them and suddenly Bedwyr was surrounded by four men. Arthur had been a little in front, and when he heard Bedwyr's yell he turned. The men were grabbing for Bedwyr's arm rings, but the blond boy fought them off with startling ferocity. Without a moment's hesitation, Arthur plunged in to help.

Bedwyr was enormously strong, and two of the men, recoiling from his blows, turned to the smaller, slighter boy who had come back to assist his friend. One man found himself thrown across Arthur's shoulder. Another, coming at him with upraised fists, got a chop on the side of the neck that stopped him dead. Bedwyr's fist sent a third flying through the air. Abruptly the boys were alone.

They regarded each other with mutual satisfaction. "You shouldn't wear all that fancy jewelry around a fair," Arthur said reprovingly.

Bedwyr's eyes were brilliantly blue. "Gods," he said. "Where did you learn to fight like that?"

"At home," Arthur replied laconically. He looked up at the sky. "Come on. I'm late meeting Morgan."

Morgan was sitting on an old saddle in front of the herbwoman's stall when she saw him coming toward her, accompanied by a big boy with long silver-blond hair. "Sorry," Arthur called as soon as he was within earshot. "I got delayed."

"That's all right," Morgan replied equably, and got to her feet.

Bedwyr stared at the small, fragile-looking girl. "Is *this* your friend?" he asked Arthur.

Before Arthur could reply, however, Morgan spoke. "Whom were you fighting?" she asked Arthur, and looked with resignation at the blood on his lip.

"Some men jumped us," he answered cheerfully. "They wanted Bedwyr's arm rings. Morgan, this is Bedwyr. He has the most magnificent horse. You must come to see him."

Morgan's brown eyes moved to Bedwyr. "Hello, Bedwyr," she said. "Do you mind if I come to see your horse?"

Bedwyr found himself smiling at her. "You'll have to be careful," he cautioned. "He isn't safe."

Morgan's brown head nodded in acknowledgment. "Before we leave, though, perhaps you ought to take off those arm rings."

Bedwyr grinned and complied, slipping them inside his tunic as the three of them walked off. He would never have taken them off at anyone else's suggestion, Arthur thought with amusement as they weaved in and out among the stalls. Wait until he saw Morgan with his vicious stallion!

They were moving through the area of food stalls and the crowd was getting thicker. Arthur took Morgan's hand. "You go first, Bedwyr," he said as he slipped Morgan deftly between the Celt and himself. "You're the biggest."

The black was still grazing when they arrived back at the Dyfed camp. He raised his head and looked at them suspiciously as they approached.

"Oh, Arthur," Morgan breathed.

Arthur nodded tensely. "Bedwyr says he came from Gaul."

"Hello, my beauty," said Morgan, and began to walk toward the horse.

"Watch out!" Bedwyr reached to stop her but his own arm was caught and held immobile by steel-hard fingers.

"Wait," said Arthur. "Watch."

Bedwyr stood still, astonished by the strength of those thin fingers, and did as he was commanded. The stallion watched Morgan approaching him, his ears flicking back and forth. Bedwyr was amazed to see that he was trembling. The girl was talking to him in a series of chirps and soft sounds that the Celt had never heard before. She reached the stallion and stood quietly before him, still talking. He snorted, but his eyes never left her. Then she raised a hand and patted the side of his neck. For a moment the two stayed thus, as if carved in marble, and then the stallion lowered his head and she was rubbing his forehead. He began to nuzzle her clothes.

"I don't believe it. Is it magic?" Bedwyr turned to Arthur and surprised a very revealing expression on the other boy's face. Oh, thought Bedwyr, so that's how it is.

Then the expression was gone, and Arthur said to him, "Not magic, just Morgan. She can do anything with an animal."

"It is amazing," Bedwyr replied slowly, and looked thoughtfully back at the girl who was gentling his father's vicious horse. "Where do you two come from?" he asked.

"From Dumnonia," Arthur replied. "From the villa of Avalon."

Avalon was a name that Bedwyr knew. His head jerked around. "Merlin's villa?"

"Yes." Arthur's face was composed, unreadable.

"But who are you?" Bedwyr asked in confusion.

"Morgan is Merlin's daughter." There was an almost imperceptible pause. "And he is my guardian," Arthur added.

"I see," said Bedwyr, although he didn't.

Arthur absently flexed one lean brown wrist. "We came to sell our produce at the fair." Morgan was coming toward them now. She reached the boys and looked up. The top of her head reached to Arthur's eyes; Bedwyr towered over her. The sun shone on her peach-colored cheeks.

"Your dream horse," she said to Arthur. Then, looking at Bedwyr, "Are there more like him?"

"His oldest get are now three-year-olds," Bedwyr replied.

"But there are more in Gaul?" It was Arthur speaking now.

"I suppose so. Among the Goths, at any rate." He looked at the two of them in some bewilderment. "Why is it so important?"

Arthur's eyes, so arrestingly light in his deeply tanned face, looked Bedwyr up and down. Bedwyr found himself holding his breath. It was suddenly of vital importance to him to be found worthy of this black-haired boy's confidence.

Arthur had made up his mind. He smiled at Bedwyr and said casually, "One day I want to form a cavalry unit to fight against the Saxons."

The blue eyes blazed. "A cavalry unit? Like the Goths?"

"Yes," said Arthur. "Heavy cavalry. Like the Goths."

Bedwyr's splendid face was perfectly serious. "When you are ready to form your cavalry unit," he said, "send for me."

"Yes," replied Arthur with equal seriousness, "I will." And it did not seem strange to either boy that Bedwyr, the prince, had put himself at the other's command.

Over that winter Horatius began to fail. Moving was an obvious effort for him and he would lie for hours near the charcoal brazier in Morgan's room, watching her out of dreamy, half-closed eyes. Several times a day Arthur would carry him out to the grass at the back of the house and then carry him back to Morgan's room.

In March he began to refuse food. Merlin wanted to end it for him, but Morgan refused, saying he was not in pain. "Let him die in his own way," she said to Arthur.

On an early spring day of diffused sunshine, Arthur carried Horatius out to the grass for the last time. Morgan sat with him as he lay with his head on his front paws, his eyes clouded, his sides trembling with each breath.

He was still alive when Arthur came down after his morning practice session with weapons, and so both youngsters were with him when he died.

They told no one at first. Arthur dug a grave for him in the woods behind the house and carried him out to it, a long walk burdened with Horatius' deadweight. Morgan put some hay in the bottom of the grave to soften it; then they put the dog in and covered him over.

"How is Horatius?" Merlin asked his daughter at dinner.

Arthur answered for her. "He died this afternoon, sir. We buried him in the woods."

"I see," said Merlin quietly. He looked at his daughter's averted face and said nothing more.

After dinner Morgan slipped away to look at Horatius' grave. Then she took her pony out to the tree house, where she sat huddled against the trunk, staring at the willows on the other side of the river that were just starting to turn green.

After ten minutes she heard Arthur's voice calling her name.

"Here!" she called back.

She heard his pony coming through the woods, but did not look over the edge of the platform. He swung himself up onto the planking and stopped, looking at her gravely. A lock of black hair fell across his forehead and he brushed it back.

"It's foolish to grieve for his death, I know," she said. "He was ready. But, oh, Arthur, I shall miss him so!"

"It's not foolish to grieve for the loss of a loved one," he replied and, coming to sit beside her, he gathered her into his arms. She nestled against him, her head falling against his arm, her face turning into his shoulder. She began to cry and he held her closer, his heart aching. He put his cheek against the silky round top of her head.

Her tears stopped, but still they stayed as they were. Arthur felt her against him, so soft and warm, the very heart of his own being. He turned his cheek so that his mouth was against her hair.

She let out a long, uneven sigh and sat up, looking at him, her face very close to his. There were still tears on her cheeks and he touched one with a careful, delicate finger.

"Morgan," he breathed. Her eyes were so dark and yet so luminous. He leaned his face closer and, very gently, his mouth touched hers.

It was a very soft kiss, very tentative. Close as they had been for all these years, they had never before done this. Their lips parted and two pairs of eyes, one dark and one light, searched each other. Then, with one accord, they moved again into each other's arms. He kissed her mouth this time with trembling fierceness, and she reached her arms up around his neck, and her hair streamed like a silken mantle down over his wrists and spilled on the wooden planks of the tree-house floor.

Chapter 6

ON the far side of the river Camm, at the very northern border of Avalon, lay the forest. Morgan often went berrying there, bringing back to the villa baskets of blue and red and purple berries for the cook to bake into breads. She also gathered herbs for the medicines she was becoming so adept at making. The only stipulation Merlin made was that if she went to the forest, Arthur was to go with her; and he was to bring a knife.

The berries were particularly good that spring, and Arthur and Morgan were coming back through the forest with laden baskets one especially warm afternoon, but the harmony that usually prevailed between them was absent this day. Arthur kept glancing at Morgan worriedly as they made their way in silence to the river. The small boat they used to cross the river was tied to a beech tree, and both young-sters jumped into it with the ease of long practice. Arthur picked up the oars and in less than two minutes they were on the opposite shore. Arthur tied the boat to a wooden stake and lifted out the baskets of berries.

"We don't have to go back right away," he said over his shoulder to Morgan as he performed this task. "We have time."

She nodded and sank to the grass. "I think I have a stone in my shoe," she said, and proceeded to remove her rawhide moccasin. She turned the shoe upside down, and then, instead of putting it back on, removed the other one as well and wiggled her bare toes with plea-sure. Her feet were small and narrow, with high-arched insteps. They were dirty from the trek through the woods. Her short-sleeved saffron-colored tunic was dirty as well. Arthur came to sit beside her.

"How many scratches did you get?" he asked, and held out his forearm for her to see the long red lines that marred its deep tan. Morgan lifted her own arm in reply and showed him two deep crimson marks that scored the silken white flesh above her wrist. He circled her wrist with his fingers and looked into her eyes. "What's the matter?" he asked softly. "You've been unhappy all day."

Her eyes slid away from his. Her expression was somber, astonishingly mature, very different from the face she showed to the adults at home. "In another month," she said, "you will be sixteen."

He let out his breath. "We can't stay children forever." He tried to keep his voice light.

"I wish we could."

"I don't." The lightness was gone. His voice now was intense, almost fierce. "Don't you understand?" he said. "Don't you feel how hard it is to be young?" His hand on her wrist tightened. "There's everything I want, everything I'm ready for, and I'm too *young*."

She looked at him, her brown eyes grave. "Yes," she said at last. "I do understand. But I haven't your courage. I'm afraid . . ." She shivered and the hand on her wrist pulled her closer, and then she was in his arms. She closed her eyes and rested her cheek against his shoulder, feeling his hard young body pressed against hers. She wanted to keep him here beside her like this forever, and she was afraid because she knew she could not. After a minute he released her and said in a rough voice, "We'd better be starting back."

The following day it rained, a soft drizzling rain that held off at times. Arthur read history in the library with Merlin in the morning and then went to look for Morgan. She wasn't in the house or in the herb garden and so he took a pony and went out to search all their usual haunts. She wasn't at the tree house. She wasn't watching the carpenter or the blacksmith. She wasn't in the valley. The air was heavy and gray with mist as Arthur turned back toward the villa. He was halfway home when the drizzle turned into a heavy rain. The storehouse where they kept the grain was near, so he took shelter there, bringing his pony in and tying it up. He had been in the barn for five minutes when the door opened again and Morgan came in.

She recognized his pony immediately. "Arthur?" she called.

His head appeared over the side of the loft. "Here," he answered. "I was looking for you. Where were you?"

"Oh, here and there," she answered vaguely, and began to climb up to the loft to join him. Arthur had made himself comfortable on a nest of old sacks. It was dim up under the roof and it was not until she sat down beside him that he realized how wet she was.

"Morgan!" He was half-laughing, half-concerned. "You're soaked!"

"It's raining," she replied. "Hand me one of those sacks and I'll wrap it around myself."

He did as she requested and she draped the sack, shawlwise, around her shoulders. She shivered and he reached an arm around her and drew her against him. Her head fell onto his shoulder.

The rain beat on the roof of the barn. Below them they heard the pony snort. The smell of grain filled their nostrils. When he bent his head to find her mouth, she was waiting for him.

Their kissing had become expert over the last month, but there was something between them now that had not been there before. There's everything I want, everything I'm ready for, he had said to her yesterday, and she had understood what he meant. She ran her hands up and down his back, feeling the hard young muscles. The heat of his body warmed her own chilled flesh.

"Do you want to take off your wet gown?" His voice was scarcely recognizable to her. She said yes and with her own hands pulled the wet material over her head.

He touched her with wonder. Her skin was like silk under his rough, callused fingers. Passion came up in him, stroke after stroke, undeniable, like the clanging of a great bronze bell within. She was so soft . . . the force within him so irresistible. He leaned over her and looked into her face. She put her arms around his neck and his heart blazed up in a flame of joy. She was so lovely, she was such a bliss of release . . . she was his love.

He hurt her, but she didn't mind. She nestled against him, listening to the slowing beat of his heart, the quieting of his breathing, and was fiercely glad that she had been able to do this for him.

The rain beat steadily on the roof of the storehouse, and they lay in one another's arms and were at peace.

At dinner Merlin and Ector talked about the new Saxon offensive, and Arthur, who would ordinarily have listened closely, scarcely heard a word they said. His whole being was concentrated instead on the girl who sat across the table from him. Ector and Merlin might have been ghosts, so unreal and insubstantial did they seem to him now.

Ector broke off to say something to Morgan, and she smiled, showing him the mask of a happy and unconcerned child. As she turned away from Ector, her eyes met Arthur's. The look they exchanged was not childlike at all.

Merlin said something. Then, with a touch of exasperation: "Arthur. I am speaking to you."

Both Arthur and Morgan turned toward his voice with identical startled looks. Then Arthur said calmly, "I'm sorry, sir. I didn't hear. What was it?" Across the table, Morgan's eyes dropped and she began to eat her venison.

It was not difficult to cover their tracks. They had been constant companions since childhood and it simply had never occurred to Merlin that the relationship between his daughter and his grandson could be other than that of sister and brother. They had many long afternoons alone, and the weather was beautiful.

"Wake up, Arthur! Look at the bird!" Morgan was tugging at the lock of black hair that always seemed to slip down over his forehead, and he raised his lashes drowsily.

"What?"

"Look. Over there." He followed her pointing finger and saw a beautiful yellow-and-black bird rising from the hawthorn bush near them.

"I see." He narrowed his eyes against the glare of the sun and said with faint reproach, "I was asleep."

"I know you were." She leaned over him so her long hair tickled his bare chest. "You were snoring."

His gray eyes smiled. "Was I?"

"No." She sat up straight again. "But it's getting late. They'll be looking for us."

They. The unreal ghosts of Merlin and Ector and Justina and the others; everyone, in fact, who was not Arthur or Morgan. He sighed and raised himself effortlessly to a sitting position. He was wearing only brown wool breeches and he looked around now for his tunic. He rubbed his head.

Morgan's eyes watching him were filled with tenderness. He swiveled around to reach for his clothing and the tenderness darkened and sobered. Very gently she put out a hand and traced the thin line of a scar on his shoulder. She felt the muscles tense under her finger.

"You'll carry them on your flesh all your life," she said. "I wish I could do something to erase them from your mind."

He turned to look at her. The skin under his eyes looked suddenly bruised. She was the only one he had ever spoken to about Esus. "It wasn't the pain," he said. "I could live with that. It was that I *let* him do that to me. That I *allowed* it."

"Arthur"—her voice was matter-of-fact, revealing none of the terrible pity that possessed her—"you were a child. You were helpless. There was nothing you could have done."

The darkness around his eyes did not fade. "I don't think about it," he said.

"You dream about it sometimes."

He stared at her, his face naked.

She made herself go on. "Blame Esus. He was a wicked, evil man. But don't blame yourself. *You* are not the one at fault." Her calm broke and she said fiercely, "I would like to plunge a dagger into his black heart."

A little of the darkness lifted from the skin beneath his eyes. "You," he said. "You would probably feel sorry for him."

"Never." She made a thrusting movement with her hand. "Never would I feel sorry for that man."

A glimmer of a smile touched his mouth. "Oh Morgan," he said. "How I love you. Come here."

His tunic was forgotten as they lay back together on the saddle rug Arthur had spread. He ran his hands over the skin with which he had become so familiar; he knew all its soft silkiness, knew where the scratches and cuts were, where she liked most to be touched. Over the last month their bodies had learned each other very well.

Afterward, on their way back to the villa, they carefully arranged their faces to meet the ghosts who were awaiting them.

On his sixteenth birthday Arthur planned to speak to Merlin about marrying Morgan. But on his sixteenth birthday Merlin was not at Avalon; he had gone to Venta to see the king.

Uther did not look well. "The time has come," he said to Merlin almost as soon as he had dismissed his servants. "I do not think I have much longer to live."

Merlin looked at him for a long moment in silence. Then he said only, "When? And how?"

"I have called a council for three weeks' time. The message has gone out to all the kings and princes of Britain. I have said the purpose of the council is to name my heir." The ghost of a sardonic smile crossed Uther's thin face. "That will bring them all running." He leaned back in his chair. "We will do it then."

Merlin nodded. Then, offering the only reassurance he could find: "He is ready, Uther."

The pale eyes commanded with something of their old fire. "I want to see him before the council, Merlin. Bring him to Venta."

"Yes," said Merlin. "I will do that."

"Does . . . does he know yet?"

"Arthur knows nothing." There was a pause and then the older man asked, "Shall I tell him first? Or do you want to?"

Uther raised a hand to his brow. The bones of his temples were too prominent in his wasted face. "You tell him," he said. "You know him. You will know how it should be done."

"I know him as well as anyone, I suppose," Merlin said a little enigmatically. "All right. I shall tell him."

"Bring him immediately." Uther dropped his hand. "He needn't stay here. In fact, it would be best if he didn't, if he went back to Avalon until the council. Surprise is a factor that will work on our side. But I want to see him first."

Merlin stared at the king. "Does Igraine know?" he asked.

"No." Uther's wasted look was now very pronounced. "I will tell Igraine."

Merlin rose to his feet. "I can have him here tomorrow."

"Good. I will be waiting," said Uther, and Merlin looked away from the hungry light in the high king's eyes.

It was late when Merlin returned to Avalon, although the sky was still light with the dying sun. He was tired and thought he would go to sleep the minute his body felt the comfort of his own bed, but he found his mind was too busy.

How ought he to handle Arthur?

They would leave for Venta tomorrow. Should he tell the boy first, or wait until they were on the road?

After much tossing and turning, Merlin decided to wait. Tell Arthur here at Avalon, and Ector would know. And Morgan. And everyone in the household. Better give the boy a chance to see Uther first.

Once that was decided, Merlin was able to fall asleep.

He overslept the following morning and was irritated when no one could tell him where Arthur was. He finally found the boy down at the stables with Morgan. The two youngsters were getting ready to go for a ride, and when Merlin called Arthur's name, they turned to him with looks of bemused astonishment.

THE ROAD TO AVALON • 47

Then, "Hello, Father," Morgan said. "I hope you had a pleasant journey."

"You were asleep, sir," said Arthur, "so we thought we'd go for a ride."

"You are going for a ride, but it is with me," said Merlin. "We are going to Venta, Arthur. Come back to the villa and change your clothes. You cannot meet the high king looking like that."

"Meet the high king?" Arthur said. His gray eyes searched Merlin's face. "Today?"

"Today. I would like to arrive in time to get a decent night's sleep, so you will please come along." There was something disturbing about the expression in the boy's eyes, and Merlin spoke more sharply than he had intended.

Arthur glanced at Morgan. "There is something I have been wanting to speak to you about, sir," he began, but Merlin cut him off.

"Not now. There isn't time." The youngsters looked at each other again. Morgan had probably found a baby wolf she wanted to raise, Merlin thought impatiently. "He will be back tomorrow, Morgan," he said to his daughter. "Whatever it is will keep until then."

The relief in her brown eyes was unmistakable. "Of course, Father." She touched Arthur's hand. "Go along," she said. "And remember to take your new white tunic."

Their eyes met and held and then Arthur nodded almost imperceptibly before he turned to follow Merlin.

They were on the road to Venta by noon. "Uther is just back from the north," Merlin had told Ector, "and this is a good opportunity for Arthur to meet him."

"Has the army returned to Venta as well?" Ector asked, and Merlin had smiled and answered, "Yes. And I promise to bring Cai home for a visit if I can."

This conversation was in his mind now as he remarked to Arthur, "It will be good to see Cai again."

"Yes," said Arthur.

The boy was not making it easy. He had responded politely to all of Merlin's comments, but his face had an abstracted expression that said he was not listening very closely to his grandfather's conversation. There was nothing about him to offer a clue as to how he was going to react to the news Merlin had to impart. You know him, Uther had said. Merlin thought he knew his brain. He knew the trained skill of that young body. But he did not know Arthur. He doubted anyone did. Except, of course, Morgan.

Merlin cleared his throat. "Arthur," he began determinedly, "the time has come to speak about your parentage." Merlin stared at the road ahead, not at the boy beside him. Arthur did not answer. "I know you think you are my son," Merlin went on, "and, indeed, you have cause to think so . . ." There was a movement from Arthur, and Merlin turned.

The boy's gray eyes were perfectly steady. "But I have never thought I was your son."

For some reason, this revelation sounded a note of warning. Merlin tried to shake it off. "You are probably the only person at Avalon, then, to feel that way," he said with an attempt at dry humor. Arthur's face did not change. "Why didn't you think so?" Merlin asked curiously.

"I remember well my mother telling me that I looked like my father," the boy replied. "I don't look like you."

Dear Christ, thought Merlin with unaccustomed blasphemy. "Whose son did you think you were?" he asked at last.

"I have no idea." Arthur looked at him. "Are you going to tell me?"

"Yes. Well . . ." Merlin took a steadying breath. "Malwyn told you true when she said you looked like your father. You will see for yourself shortly, although the resemblance is not so clear since he became ill. Arthur . . ." Here he stopped his horse. Arthur's pony stopped as well. "Your father is Uther Pendragon, High King of Britain."

There was not a flicker of expression on the boy's face.

"Did you hear me?"

"Yes. I heard you." Dark shadows suddenly appeared under Arthur's eyes. "So *he* is the one who sent my mother to Cornwall."

"No." Merlin leaned a little forward in his eagerness to explain, and his horse, feeling the shift in weight, walked forward again. Merlin halted him. "You don't understand, Arthur. Malwyn was not your mother. She was Igraine's serving woman, and when it was deemed necessary to send you away, she assumed the role of your mother. But the woman who bore you is Igraine. You are the son of Uther and Igraine, Arthur. The *legitimate* son, born three months after they were wed. And you are heir to the high kingship of Britain."

Chapter 7

*I*T was still light when they rode into Venta, but even though this was Arthur's first visit to a city of this size, he scarcely noticed his surroundings. There were columns on the front of the high king's house, and soldiers guarding the door. Then he was shown to a bedchamber that did not look unlike his bedchamber at home, and was told to wait until he was sent for. Arthur merely nodded and stood, tense and watchful, until the door closed behind his grandfather.

As the door closed shut, a tremor of relief ran all through him. Alone. He began to pace back and forth across the mosaic floor, free to think now that he was no longer expending all his energy to guard his face.

He was the son of Uther and Igraine. One day he would be king. He could not take it in.

He wished desperately for Morgan. Her calm good sense would help buttress the turbulence of his own emotions. She would help him deal with this.

The son of Uther and Igraine. Arthur suddenly stopped dead, his chin lifting as a throught struck him. Morgan was Igraine's sister.

It can't be, he thought. Then: Don't panic. Think it out. He stared straight ahead with unfocused eyes, and under his tan he was very pale. *Not* her sister, her half-sister. They had had different mothers. That meant . . . the only relative he and Morgan had in common was Merlin. Merlin: his grandfather, Morgan's father.

The blood bond was not that close; no closer, certainly, than first cousins. Arthur's legs carried him forward again and he sat limply on the side of the bed. He and Morgan would be all right. Within the various tribes of Britain, first cousins married all the time.

He and Morgan would be all right. After all, how could Merlin refuse her hand to the High King of Britain?

The High King of Britain. He was back to that again. Could it actually be true?

The window was open to let the warm air into the room and Arthur got up and went to look out at the scene before him. The summer sun was setting, and the sky was filled with brilliant color. Against the dramatic oranges and pinks, the colonnade of the forum stood out with a pure beauty it did not normally possess. As Arthur stood there looking out at the sky, the colors slowly began to change and fade. And with the fading sunset came belief.

It had to be true. This was what Merlin had been preparing him for all these years. This was why he had been brought out of Cornwall and into the security of Avalon. Merlin had only been waiting for this day.

This day. The day he was to meet his father.

I can't. His breath came hard through constricted nostrils. The scene before his eyes was a blur. *He has had a chance to prepare himself for this. I haven't.*

Uther. His father. The man who had left him to Esus.

"Arthur." The voice at the door was Merlin's. Arthur stood at the window, rigid, his fists clenched so tightly at his sides that the bone showed yellow through the skin. "Come with me," Merlin said from the door, and Arthur forced himself to walk forward.

As they passed through the corridor on their way to Uther's chambers, Merlin kept glancing at the boy out of the side of his eyes. Arthur's face wore the look that Merlin most dreaded: reserved, withdrawn, faintly hostile. When Arthur looked like this, his grandfather thought despairingly, he was impossible to deal with. It was not going to be easy for Uther.

They were at the king's door. "Go in," said Merlin. "He is waiting for you." He rarely touched the boy, nothing about Arthur ever invited contact, but he found himself putting a comforting hand on his grandson's shoulder. The muscles under his fingers were rocklike with tension. Arthur did not pull away, but turned to give him a quick questioning look. Merlin smiled reassuringly. "It will be all right," he said. "Go on."

Arthur opened the door and went in.

Uther was alone, sitting in a chair on the far side of the room. Outside, the sun had almost set, but the room was bright with lamplight. Arthur stopped just inside the door, his eyes on the man who was watching him so intently.

Uther had always looked like a king. His dark head, now so liberally sprinkled with silver, was held with all the arrogance of power. He wore a white tunic trimmed with imperial purple and about his dark brows the slender gold circle of his office. "Come here," he said in a deep, level voice. Arthur crossed the room slowly.

When he reached the king he stopped. Then, remembering Merlin's instructions, he went down on his knees, bowed his head, and said, "My lord king."

"Rise, Arthur," the king replied. To Arthur's ears his voice sounded distant. Only Uther knew that inside the fine wool of his beautiful tunic, he was trembling. "Let me look at you," he said, and let his eyes roam hungrily over the figure who was standing before him.

The boy's thick straight hair was his own, as were the eyes and the brows. But the face . . . It was as if a blade turned in Uther's heart. The fine-boned, beautiful face that was looking back at him with such disciplined immobility was Igraine's.

"You will be king before the year is out," he said to that still face. "Are you ready?"

The boy's discipline was equal to the challenge. His gray eyes met his father's and did not look away. "I don't know," Arthur said. "I have not quite adjusted yet to my new . . . identity."

His voice was cool and clear and edged with faint irony. He made no pretense of concern for his father. Fair enough, Uther thought heavily. Aloud he said only, "Merlin says you are ready. He told me you were ready last year, but I did not want to move prematurely. I wanted to keep you safe for as long as possible."

There was the faintest glimmer of derision in Arthur's gray eyes before he lowered his lashes to conceal them. "I see," he said politely.

Uther closed his hands over the chair arms to conceal their trembling. "You do not need to tell me that you should have been reared as a prince, not hidden away at Avalon for all these years," he said harshly. "But it was for your own safety, Arthur."

"Oh, I understand, my lord." The gray eyes were once again on Uther's face. "And I was quite content . . . at Avalon."

The boy could use his voice like a weapon, Uther thought. Its cool, clear tone was so respectful on the surface, so full of contempt in its undernotes.

Uther answered the unspoken challenge. "This is not an apology," he said. "There is no apology that can be made for what happened when you were a child." The expression that flickered like lightning across the boy's face caused Uther to tighten his hands to fists on the chair. He forced himself to continue evenly. "But I will explain why I did as I did."

He drew a long, steadying breath. "Did Merlin tell you how you were born? That Igraine and I had been married but three months?"

Arthur nodded. He was looking white about the lips and nostrils. Uther continued. "Then you know there was always the possibility of questions being raised about your paternity. Igraine had been married to Gorlois. The kings of Britain would never have accepted Gorlois' son as their high king. Too many of them considered themselves of greater importance than a mere Duke of Cornwall.

"At the time, you understand, there was no reason to suppose Igraine and I would not have more sons."

The boy's head was bent, the thick black hair had fallen forward to screen his face, but Uther could see that he was listening intently. "I knew you were my son," he continued soberly. "I cannot pretend that I did not. But it was the politic thing to remove you from the position of heir and put in your place a child whose birth was unblemished. You must understand, Arthur, that Britain could not survive a civil war. In order to fight the Saxons, we *must* be united.

"I did not act as a father, I acted as a king.

"Nor do I think I was wrong in what I did. What *was* wrong was to leave you without adequate knowledge of how you were faring. I knew Malwyn would take good care of you. She loved you as if you were truly her own. But I did not check. I did not know that she had died and that her brother had the keeping of you. In this I was grievously at fault. I wish I had it all to do again. But I do not."

The effort this speech had taken was almost beyond Uther's strength. He leaned back in his chair now, exhausted. Very briefly he closed his eyes. When he opened them again it was to find his son regarding him with a faint frown.

"Are you all right, my lord? May I pour you some wine?"

"Yes," said Uther. "Thank you, Arthur." He willed his hand not to shake as he took the goblet from the boy. He drank off half the cup, then leaned back again. "When it became clear that Igraine and I were to have no more children, Merlin brought you to Avalon. He and I are the only two who know who you are.

"We kept the secret, Arthur, because there are those who would not be overjoyed to learn that the high king has a son."

The boy pounced immediately on the one fact that Uther was anxious to disguise. "The queen did not know I had been brought to Avalon?"

Uther could not meet his son's eyes. "No," he said. "She did not know."

There was only a glimmering of light now from the window. In the pause that followed, Uther took another drink of wine.

"Who is it, my lord, who would not like to find you have a son?" Arthur asked pleasantly. "Lot of Lothian?"

Uther stared at the contained young face before him. "Lot, yes. Lot principally. He wants to be high king. He is only waiting for my death to make his move."

"He has support?"

"Yes. In the north, at least." Uther put the goblet down. "You must understand, Arthur, that the high kingship is essential. Even the most independent of the Celtic princes realizes that. There will be a new high king elected because there must be a leader in the battle against the Saxons. But Britain will tear itself apart if one Celtic king tries to take precedence over the others. That is why it must be you.

"You are the last Roman, Arthur. Constantine's grandson. Yet you are British too, through your mother. It must be you."

Arthur nodded calmly, coolly, practically. To his amazement, Uther realized that the boy had completely pushed aside the painful personal aspect of their relationship. He was analyzing the facts that Uther had just put before him.

Abruptly Uther realized that Arthur was still standing. "Bring over that stool," he said.

Arthur obeyed and then sat, quite naturally, in front of Uther's chair. The boy's brow was furrowed in concentration. "How large is your army?" he asked his father. "I mean the army apart from the levies contributed by the kings and princes. Who are your generals? Can you count on their loyalty? Which of the kings support you? Which ones support Lot? Which ones have to be won over—"

"Wait a minute." Uther's voice was breathless. "One question at a time."

It was another hour before Arthur finally quitted the king's chamber. He went to his bedroom, his brain teeming with information, and lay awake half of the night analyzing it. When finally he slept, his rest was deep and dreamless.

Uther was not alone for five minutes before Merlin was announced. "Well?" the older man asked as soon as he had crossed the threshold. "What did you think?"

Uther laughed. In the wasted sallowness of his face, his eyes were bright. "He will be a king," he said. "I don't believe I've ever had my brain scoured more ruthlessly."

Merlin's own face relaxed. "I was afraid when I left him with you," he confessed. "Arthur is not always the most . . . approachable of boys."

A little of the glow died out of the king's eyes. "I think we understand each other," he said. "We both have a job to do, and we will work together very well."

"Arthur is a joy to work with," Merlin said. "Impossibly demanding because he is so intelligent, but a joy."

"When the time comes, he will be ready." Uther looked suddenly exhausted.

Merlin was blunt. "Does he know that you are dying?"

Uther lifted a dark, ironic eyebrow. "Oh, yes. He wanted to know how much time he had."

There was a pause. Then Merlin said slowly, "He finds it hard to forgive what we did to him."

Uther shook his head. "Oddly enough, I don't think that is it at all. I think he has just decided to accept me, not as a father but as a man whose job he must learn. He needed to know how much learning time he had, and so he asked." The eyebrow was raised again. "I can scarcely expect him to love me, Merlin."

"No." Merlin looked away from Uther's face. "No, one could scarcely expect that." He looked back. "What shall we do next, then?" he asked, his voice brisk. "Return to Avalon?"

"Yes. Take him to Avalon until the council. I will send Claudius with you. He has been my second-in-command for years. He knows our dispositions and fortifications better than anyone else. Arthur will find him helpful."

Merlin nodded. "Good idea."

"Leave early," Uther continued. "The fewer people who see him, the better. He wears his heritage too clearly on his face."

"I told you he looked like you."

"No," Uther replied. "He looks like Igraine."

The name fell into the room with the rasp of a high-pitched sound along raw nerves. "You said we should leave early," Merlin said carefully. "Surely Igraine wishes to see him before we go."

Lamplight flickered along the hollows of Uther's face. "I don't think so," he said after a minute. Then: "She was not pleased to learn that I had been keeping a secret from her all these years."

Merlin took two steps forward. "She must see him, Uther!" His voice was sharp. "What will Arthur think if she does not?"

"Does he know she is in Venta?"

"Yes."

"How?"

"He asked me and I told him." There was another pause and then Merlin said, "There is no reason, Uther, for her to refuse to see him. Certainly none that I can decently explain to Arthur. In my opinion, we have had to make far too many explanations to Arthur as it is."

There was surprise on Uther's face. "You love him," he said, an odd note in his voice.

"Is that so strange?"

"You have always spoken of him so . . . dispassionately. I did not realize. That is all."

Merlin was refusing to meet Uther's eyes. "He's a difficult, prickly, self-contained young devil, but yes, I love him." He looked up at the king. "He fascinates me," he admitted. "There is something about him that is so compelling . . ."

"Like my father."

"Even more so. And Arthur is only sixteen. What will he be like, I wonder, when he is thirty?"

Silence fell between them. From outside they heard the sound of the sentries' voices as the guard was changed. Then Uther said, "I will ask Igraine to see him before you leave tomorrow morning."

"I think he deserves that."

"Yes." Uther's hooded gaze was troubled. "I hope he is not expecting a tender reunion scene."

"Do not worry. He would be horrified should Igraine attempt such a thing. Arthur is as good as she is at keeping himself to himself."

"Yes," said Uther dryly. "I noticed."

Chapter 8

IT was very early the following morning when the summons for Arthur came from the queen. Merlin, ushering his grandson toward Igraine's apartments, felt a moment of panic. This meeting was his doing. Perhaps he should have left well enough alone.

A serving woman opened the door at his knock, then slipped out as they entered, closing the door behind her. The well-furnished chamber was empty save for the woman seated in a carved chair in front of the window, with the merciless morning light falling directly on her face. Whatever her faults, Merlin thought as he put a hand on Arthur's elbow to guide him across the room, vanity wasn't one of them.

"Good morning, Father." Igraine's voice was chill. She addressed Merlin, but her dark blue eyes were on Arthur.

"Good morning, Igraine," Merlin replied. Then: "I have brought you your son."

"Arthur." Igraine's eyes were as cold as her voice. They had reached her chair and Merlin put pressure on his grandson's elbow.

The boy knelt. "My lady," he said, and raised his face to his mother's.

Merlin was watching Arthur, not Igraine, and was relieved to see that the boy's face was not wearing the look he most dreaded. Instead he was gazing at Igraine steadily, his straight black brows drawn slightly together, his profile intent and concentrated. He seemed to be searching for something in his mother's face.

"You may rise," the queen said, and Arthur stood. His face was composed now, his eyes quiet.

All the lines in Igraine's skin were brutally visible in the light from the window. Lines or no, Merlin thought, she was still the most beautiful woman he knew. Each time he beheld her he wondered anew that she was a child of his. The queen looked from her son to her father. "You did not think to tell me that he was at Avalon for all these years?"

"Uther did not want you to know."

They were talking about Arthur as if he were not present, but he stood easily and did not seem to mind. Igraine's long fingers drummed nervously on the arms of her chair. Her golden gown spilled dramatically against the dark purple of its covering. "Uther has called a council to present him as the heir," she said, and the look she gave her son was not friendly. She rose to her feet, brushed by Arthur as if he were a servant, and began to pace the floor. "It is not necessary," she said over her shoulder to Merlin. "Not yet. It may well precipitate a civil war. Lot will never accept this boy as Uther's heir. You know that, Father!"

Merlin was appalled. This was worse than he had ever imagined it could be. He glanced apprehensively at Arthur, fully expecting to find him wearing his most shuttered look. Instead he was looking at his mother with an expression of polite curiosity. Merlin said harshly, "There is no one who can deny Arthur's birth, Igraine. By the blood of Christ, you have only to look at his face!"

Then Arthur spoke. "I fear, my lady, that you are saddled with me. In the absence of a better candidate."

His voice was absolutely pleasant. Igraine stopped pacing and stared at him. He gave her a brief businesslike smile.

Merlin let out his breath. It suddenly occurred to him that, of the two of them, it was Igraine who was the more vulnerable. "You don't understand anything about it," she was saying to her son.

"On the contrary, I understand very well. The king needs me. Britain needs me. Not because I am Arthur, but because I am the son of Uther and Igraine." She was standing almost the width of the room away, but he could pitch that flexible voice of his with effortless ease. "Uther has held Britain together for years. He was the only one who could do it, could consolidate the Celts and the Romans in a fight against the Saxons. He is called high king but he is really the war leader, the Comes Britanniarum that his father was. He needs a son because Britain's only hope of unity lies in the continuation of the high kingship."

"You tell me nothing I don't already know." She stared at him with passive antagonism, like a hawk in a cage. "My point is that in acknowledging you now, he will precipitate the very division he is trying so desperately to avoid."

"Lot must be faced sooner or later. The king knows that." The boy's voice was patient and, Merlin realized with astonishment, kind. "He is tired, Igraine. He has carried this burden for many years. The time has come for him to share some of it." And then he answered her real fear. "If Lot objects to me, I will deal with him."

Igraine began to come toward him. "You?" she said. "You are just a boy." But her voice had changed.

"I am a boy," he agreed. "But I have nothing better to do."

She had reached his side. She was a tall woman, almost as tall as her son. "Promise me, Arthur," she said fiercely, "promise me that you will not let him ride to war against Lot."

"I promise," he replied, and Merlin saw that Igraine was satisfied.

The meeting had not followed any of the lines Merlin had imagined. He did not have a chance to speak to Arthur alone until they were once more on the road to Avalon. They were traveling with Claudius Virgilius, Uther's first general, and Cai, but the two soldiers obligingly dropped back when Merlin indicated that he wished to speak to his grandson.

The road was dusty and their horses' hooves raised little brown pools of haze as they rode forward at a brisk walk. When the others were out of earshot, Arthur asked, "What precisely is wrong with the king?"

"His heart."

"I see."

"Yes. So does everyone else. Except, it seems, Igraine."

"She perceives me as an acknowledgment of his death." Arthur's eyes were narrowed slightly against the sun.

"I fear that is so." Merlin spoke slowly, testing his words. "Now that you have met her, perhaps she will be easier for you to understand. It is true that Igraine had no care for you when you were a child. But she has never cared for anyone, my boy, except Uther. For him, she is a veritable flame of emotion." Merlin sighed. "I fear for her when Uther dies. Nothing will comfort her."

"Perhaps not. But keeping Lot and Morgause off the throne will at least keep her busy." There was the faintest irony in the lift of Arthur's brows.

Merlin stared at him and could find nothing to say in reply.

The breeze stirred Arthur's black hair and his expression suddenly changed. He turned to Merlin with a rare boyish smile and asked lightly, "What do you think Morgan will say when she hears the news?"

Arthur's voice changed when he said Morgan's name. It always had.

There was no reason, Merlin thought, for that sound to send a shiver of apprehension through his heart.

As they drew nearer to Avalon the country around them grew flatter, more gently rolling. Cai pushed his horse up to Arthur's side and Merlin tactfully dropped back to give the boys a chance to talk.

Arthur looked his friend up and down. "You've grown even bigger than Ector," he announced. "What do they feed you in the army, Cai?"

Cai laughed. "Nothing to boast about. I'm looking forward to the cooking at Avalon."

Arthur became serious. "How did this last campaign in the north fare?" he asked, and listened intently as Cai talked.

When Arthur was finished asking questions, Cai turned to personal matters. "When are *you* going to join the army, Arthur? I thought I might see you in Venta sometime this summer."

The corners of Arthur's mouth quirked. "I suppose you might say I have joined the army. Claudius Virgilius is coming along to Avalon in order to instruct me." Cai said nothing, just looked at him. Arthur stared straight ahead. "You see, Cai," he explained almost apologetically, "I have turned out to be Uther's son."

"You look like him." Cai did not sound surprised. "The first time I saw Uther I thought: By God, he looks like Arthur. And then I began to fit some pieces together. I always knew you were important. You had to be for Merlin to have taken the kind of trouble he did. Like everyone else, I always assumed you were his son. But when I saw the high king, I began to think otherwise."

Arthur was staring at him. "You might have let me know," he said in exasperation.

"It was just a suspicion. I had no proof of anything."

"Well, it's been one hell of a twenty-four hours," Arthur said. It was good to have Cai there. "First Merlin tells me I'm the high king's son, then he throws me into the loving arms of my father and mother. I feel as if I've been at the wrong end of a siege engine."

Cai grinned. "One thing about the army Claudius won't tell you," he said. "We could use heavy cavalry."

The gray eyes lit and Cai's grin spread. He knew his Arthur. For the rest of the ride the two boys talked horses.

Avalon of the apple trees. Arthur felt as if he'd been away for years instead of overnight, so much had happened to him. He had ridden away a nameless bastard and returned the heir to Britain. His gray eyes were brilliant as they rode into the villa courtyard. Wait until Morgan heard!

Ector came out to greet them and Merlin brought them all into the great reception room that had never, in Arthur's memory, been used before. Merlin sent for wine.

"Where is Morgan?" her father asked, sparing Arthur the necessity.

"I don't know," Ector replied, and Merlin frowned and sent a slave out to look for her.

The old soldier Claudius, whose father had come from Rome with Constantine, was looking around the room with frank admiration. It had always been one of the most classically Roman rooms in Britain: the floor was mosaic, with the tiles depicting a muscular Aeneas carrying his aged father safely away from a burning Troy; the marble in the columns came from Carrara in Italy, as did a large marble-topped table with beautifully carved legs. The company had chosen to sit in the high straight-backed chairs that circled the dais even though the gilded Roman-style couches that were against the wall looked to be more comfortable.

A slave came in with wine, and as it was being served, Morgan appeared. "I knew you had come back," she said to Arthur, not to her father. She was wearing a yellow gown that hung softly from her young throat and delicate wrists. She had evidently been in the garden, for the skirt of her gown was stained from kneeling in the dirt and there was a smudge on her small straight nose.

Cai made a movement and her eyes went to him. "Cai!" she said, and went to kiss him on the cheek. Cai's serious hazel eyes watched her with love.

"Sit down, my daughter," Merlin said, and Morgan took a gilded stool and went to sit beside Arthur. They exchanged a quick look before she turned to her father, who was obviously getting ready to speak.

"I have a story to tell you," Merlin began. "Some of you may know its ending already, but I am going to start from the beginning and tell it all. I will start with my daughter Igraine, who, when she was the wife of Gorlois of Cornwall, fell in love with Uther Pendragon. . . ."

"And so," he was saying some minutes later, "I went to Cornwall to fetch the boy and bring him home to Avalon. The rest of the story you all know. Arthur is that boy, the son of Uther and Igraine. He will be proclaimed Uther's heir in three weeks' time, before a council of the kings and princes of Britain." Merlin paused, sipped his wine, and watched his daughter.

Morgan sat rigid on her stool, staring straight ahead of her at the bust of the Emperor Hadrian that adorned the big marble table on the far side of the room. Arthur was looking at her as well, Merlin saw.

"I always thought the boy looked like Uther," Ector was saying. "But I had no idea of the truth. The story was that the queen's son had died."

"Well," said Merlin, "we did not need Uther's enemies searching for Arthur and perhaps trying to use him against his father. It was best for everyone to think him dead."

Morgan finally spoke. "You are saying that you deliberately left him alone with that man for all those years?"

Every eye in the room swung to her in astonishment. No one had ever heard that tone of voice from Morgan. Arthur could sound like that, but not Morgan.

"It was inexcusable," Merlin said at last, very soberly.

Her face was taut with emotion. "Inexcusable!" she began.

Only Merlin saw Arthur's hand close on a strand of her hair and give one quick tug. Morgan did not look around at him, but she stopped whatever else it was she had been about to say.

It was Arthur's voice that filled the sudden awkward silence. He spoke to Ector. "The king has sent Claudius Virgilius to help school me on the present state of the army and our fortifications, sir."

"Well, you will find you have an apt pupil, Claudius Virgilius," Ector said heartily. "Nor do I think you will find Arthur's knowledge of military matters lacking."

"Certainly not, if you have been his instructor," the grizzled veteran of thirty years of war against the Saxons returned courteously. He had known Ector in the days before Ector's injury had forced him to retire from the army.

They had another goblet of wine and then Merlin and Claudius and Cai went to the baths to wash off the dust of the road. Arthur said he would join them, but instead he and Morgan went to the river.

"You're very quiet," he said after they had picketed their ponies to graze and were sitting side by side on a thick carpet of grass and wildflowers.

"They just left you there!" Her profile was tense with anger. "How could they have done such a thing?"

"Morgan," he said. "Don't." She turned to look at him. "There is nothing to be gained from harboring old grudges."

"There is something more at stake here than grudges," she answered, but her brown eyes were searching his face. "I knew something had happened," she said. "I could feel it. You were upset. What happened? Did you meet Uther and Igraine?"

"Yes." They could hear a small animal scurrying in the high grass. He looked at her ruefully. "Merlin waited until we were halfway to Venta before he told me who I was. Then, almost as soon as we had arrived, I had to meet him." He plucked a piece of grass, put it between his teeth, and squinted at the river. "You might say I was upset. In fact," and he shot her a look, "I wanted to bolt right back here and put my head in your lap. I didn't know how I would feel, you see. I hadn't had time to think about it at all."

"I think Father must be mad," Morgan said fiercely.

Arthur shook his head. "No. Not mad, just too clever." A little breeze had blown up from the river and it ruffled the hair at his brow. "Then, there I was," he said. "And there he was. And it was not as bad as I had feared." He frowned, trying to explain. "It wasn't personal. I could see him as a man, not as a father. A man and a king." His mouth closed in a grim line around the stalk of grass. "He has not had an easy life, Morgan. He has been in arms against the Saxons since he was a boy. He is worn out. In fact," and now his gray eyes were as grim as his mouth, "he is dying. He says I will be king before the year is out."

Morgan's brown eyes seemed to take up all of her small face. Arthur laughed, although the sound held no amusement. "Yes," he said. "King."

"King," she repeated. "I hadn't quite thought about that."

His eyes softened. "You were too busy being indignant for my sake."

"What did you think of Igraine?" she asked abruptly.

"Oh, meeting her was easy enough. I could never think of her as my mother. Malwyn was my mother." He lay on his back and looked up at the sky. Clouds were moving in rapidly to cover the sun. "She doesn't look at all like you."

Morgan suddenly felt as if something were squeezing all the air out of her lungs. "Arthur," she said, "Igraine is my sister!"

"I know. I thought of that." She continued to look stricken and he sat up. "Don't look like that, Morgan. It will be all right. I thought it all out. She is only your half-sister. You and I are no closer in blood than first cousins. And first cousins marry all the time."

Her brown eyes were thinking. "That is true."

"Our relationship poses no difficulty," he said with perfect confidence.

"Our relationship." She stared at him in outrage. "But Arthur . . . I am your aunt!"

He grinned. "Half-aunt." His tone changed, became overly solicitous. "And how are you feeling today, old dear?"

"You're so funny . . ." She reached out to pull his hair and then they were both down on the grass engaged in a mock wrestling match. He let her manhandle him a little, laughing and cowering away in pretended fear, loving the feel of her elastic young body against his. Then he rolled so that she was under him. Their laughing faces were very close.

"Kiss me," he whispered, and she reached up her arms and drew him down to her.

Chapter 9

*I*T began to rain before Arthur and Morgan reached the villa. They met Claudius and Merlin in the corridor as they were going to their bedrooms to change.

Claudius looked at the two youngsters and smiled with pleasure. Morgan's face was flushed with rain, fresh and dewy as a newly opened flower. Arthur's black hair was sleek against his head and his wet clothing only served to bring out the fine lines of bone and muscle. He would never be a big man, Claudius thought, his eyes going over the young male body appraisingly, but he moved with the grace and coordination of a cat.

"When you said you would take a bath, I didn't realize you meant in the rain," said Merlin.

Arthur grinned. He looked lit-up with happiness, Claudius thought. It was difficult to look away from him.

"I wanted to talk to him," Morgan answered her father.

"I hope you got all your talking done," Merlin returned austerely. "Arthur is going to be too busy these next weeks to go larking about Avalon with you, Morgan."

Merlin's words proved to be true ones. Arthur was closeted for most of each day with Claudius Virgilius, going over lists and maps and troop dispositions. Claudius was impressed by his pupil. "He has a grasp of tactics that is astonishing in so young a boy," he told Merlin and Ector. The two old men were delighted. They considered Arthur their own personal creation and had him out on the practice field every day to demonstrate his prowess to Uther's general.

Arthur performed without complaint. As he said to Morgan one night, "I need Claudius Virgilius. I need all of Uther's officers. I cannot command an army if I don't have the loyalty of its leaders. If Merlin thinks I should dance for Claudius, I'll dance."

They were in Morgan's room, in Morgan's bed. For the first time they had begun to take advantage of the fact that their bedrooms were next to each other. Arthur's days were not free any longer.

Arthur had not yet spoken to his grandfather about marrying Morgan. She wanted him to wait until after the council. In her deepest heart, Morgan was not as confident as Arthur that there would be no obstacle in the way of their marriage. She wanted to keep things the way they were . . . for a little while longer, at any rate.

What would she do . . . what would Arthur do . . . should Merlin object to their marrying? Before, there had been no doubt. When they were just Arthur and Morgan, nothing and no one could have kept them apart. Before. Before Arthur was Britain's next king.

Amazingly, Arthur himself seemed to have no doubts. His major fear had always been that his birth was not good enough for her, and now that that concern had been put to rest, he was confident that their future was secure. He wanted to speak to Merlin, wanted everything out in the open. She had to beg him before he would agree to wait.

On the day before they left for Venta for the council, Merlin presented Arthur with a sword.

"One day you will have your father's sword," he said to the boy. "Constantine's sword. But this was forged for you alone." The whole household was gathered in the reception room of the villa and in the quiet one could clearly hear the general intake of breath as Merlin handed the sword to his grandson.

It fitted into Arthur's hand as naturally as if it had grown there. Arthur flexed his wrist and light glinted, quicksilver bright, off the blade. The pommel was set with a magnificent ruby. "The Emperor Hadrian presented that ruby to my ancestor," Merlin told Arthur. "It is fitting that an emperor's gift should grace the sword of the High King of Britain."

Arthur's dark face was very still. Then he raised glowing eyes. "Thank you, sir," was all he said, but Merlin was satisfied.

"I have a gift for you too," said Morgan, and ran out of the room. She was back in a minute carrying a white hound puppy. "Here, Arthur"—she put the puppy into his arms—"for you." The puppy promptly began to lick his face.

"Have you named him?" Arthur asked Morgan around the licks.

She shook her head. "No. That is for you to do."

"I'll call him Cabal," said Arthur, and scratched the puppy's nose.

"How typical this is," he managed to say a little breathlessly to Cai's grinning face. "Merlin gives me a sword, and Morgan gives me a dog!"

Cai and Ector began to laugh, and after a minute Claudius Virgilius joined in too.

The kings and princes of Britain were gathered in Venta when Merlin's party rode in the evening before the council. Venta had been a district capital during the days of Roman rule, and the council was to be held in the building where the Civitates, or local legislature, had once met.

The first thing Merlin's party noticed as they approached the city was the number of men quartered in tents on the outskirts. "They are northerners," Claudius said grimly. And indeed it was easy to place the strangers from the checked pattern of their tunics and breeches. "Lot's men," Claudius added, and looked quickly at Arthur.

The boy's dark face was unperturbed. "He comes rather heavily escorted for a council."

"It's a show of strength," said Ector, and Arthur nodded.

"I wonder if Lot brought Morgause," said Morgan.

The men stared at her. It was Merlin who chose to explain. "If Lot has fighting on his mind, he would hardly risk his wife as a hostage."

Morgan's brown eyes were wide. "Oh," she said. "Does he want to fight? I thought he wanted the high kingship handed to him."

Arthur was the one whose eyes registered comprehension. "In which case, a fruitful wife and three healthy sons would be a distinct asset. Particularly if the wife is the sister of the present queen."

"Oh," said Cai, as understanding dawned for him too. "I see what you mean. And Lot, of course, knows nothing of Arthur."

Arthur laughed. "What odds will you give, Cai, that we meet a whole clutch of Lothians at Venta?"

"This is not a laughing matter," Merlin snapped.

"No indeed," echoed Claudius with a worried frown.

Arthur winked at Morgan and she had to look away to maintain her gravity.

Almost the first words Uther uttered as he greeted his son and his father-in-law an hour later were, "Lot's brought Morgause and his sons."

"We must make Morgan a member of the council," Arthur murmured to Merlin under his breath.

Merlin glared. He thought Arthur was taking this new development far too lightly.

"I have had to give house room to all of them." Igraine was furious.

The king and queen, Arthur, and Merlin were alone in Uther's chamber. A cozy family party, Arthur thought, and stared at the floor so no one could see the hilarity in his eyes.

"Of course," said Merlin, "Lot knows nothing yet about Arthur."

Uther's face wore its most sardonic look. "It might have been a clever move," he conceded. "With Morgause already quartered in the praetorium, it would not seem so odd for Lot to move in also as the next high king."

Igraine's beautiful face was stamped with satisfaction. "Well, he has overreached himself at last," she said. "Uther already has an heir."

Arthur, who had not yet spoken, threw his mother a look that was the duplicate of his father's.

Merlin spoke quickly. "You might say that Lot has actually played into our hands. He will not risk a fight until he has his family safely home in Lothian."

Igraine's voice was cold and sharp as an icicle. "They will not be going home to Lothian. Have your wits gone wandering, Father? They will stay right here, hostages for Lot's good behavior."

Merlin stared at his daughter. "Are you serious, Igraine? Morgause is your sister."

Arthur spoke for the first time. "The queen is always practical."

Igraine gave her son a long, hard look. Arthur's gray eyes were guileless. Merlin thought, with irritation, that he was enjoying himself.

"Lot was a fool to bring them here," Igraine said to Arthur, "and we would be fools not to take advantage of his mistake."

They all looked to Arthur. It was not until later that Merlin thought how strange it was that the three of them should turn to the boy so naturally. Nor did Arthur seem to find it unusual that he should be the one to take charge. "Now that they are here," he said pleasantly, "it would be a shame to lose Morgause's company too quickly. Do you think she would like to spend some time at Avalon?"

For the first time Igraine regarded her son with approval. "Very good. We can give it out that Morgause has a desire to visit her old home."

Uther was frowning. "It is a good idea." He shifted his weight in his chair as if he were uncomfortable, and Igraine's eyes sharpened. He gave her a faint reassuring smile before he went on, "We'll send

Morgause and the boys off tomorrow, as soon as the council gets under way. We don't want to give Lot time to act."

"Are we to carry them off kicking and screaming?" Merlin asked sourly.

"Of course not, Father. We have more finesse than that. I will think up some story to convince Morgause that it is Lot's wish that she go. She is easy to satisfy." Igraine raised a finely groomed black eyebrow. "In fact, I wager she'll be delighted to go. A few weeks' respite from the rigors of the north will look very attractive to my dear sister. She spent two hours at the baths this afternoon. In Lothian they must make do with a miserable tin tub before a fire."

"It is only for a little while, sir," Arthur said to his grandfather. "Just until Lot and his men are safely back in Lothian. Then Morgause and her sons can go home."

Merlin sighed. "Oh, very well. But I do not want Morgause or the children frightened."

"Neither do we," said Uther. He let a little pause fall before he changed the subject. "Now, about tomorrow . . ."

The chamber of the Civitates was filled the following morning when Merlin entered to take his place on one of the benches by the dais. He had brought Cai and Ector with him even though they could not vote. He thought Arthur would appreciate seeing a few familiar faces in the crowd. The one person Merlin knew his grandson would most like to be present was barred from the all-male assembly. In fact, Morgan would not even be in Venta by the time this meeting was concluded. They had decided last night that she should accompany Morgause and her sons to Avalon.

The chamber of the Civitates was a smaller and poorer version of the Senate building in Rome. The chamber was a single rectangular room, heated in winter by a hypocaust and cooled in summer by a series of small windows placed high along the walls of the long sides of the building. There was a dais on one short wall, with a chair set for the presiding officer. In the days of Rome the officer had been the provincial governor, the *vicarius*. Today it was the high king.

The main door of the building was on the wall facing the dais and it was through this door that Merlin and his companions entered. There was one other small door behind the dais, placed in order to allow the provincial governor to escape without having to encounter the Civitates' members on his way to the door. At one time a purple wall hanging had concealed the door, but the wall hanging had gone long before the last of the legions pulled out of Britain.

The two long walls of the room were flanked with benches, and on these benches sat the kings and princes and chiefs of the various kingdoms and tribes of Britain. As Merlin took his seat his eyes went along the benches, mentally noting who was present and who was likely to prove friend or foe.

The three Welsh kings were there, Maelgwyn of Gwynedd, Magach of Powys, and Ban of Dyfed. All three of them had brought their sons, the princes of their line. Merlin's eye was particularly caught by one of Ban's sons. He was a magnificent-looking boy: big, golden-haired, blue-eyed, a pure Celt. They held very much to the old ways in Dyfed. It was one of the few areas of Britain that was still not Christian.

Further down the bench, past a few tribal chiefs whom Merlin did not recognize, was Gwyl of Elmet. Merlin stared at the King of Elmet's shrewd, weather-beaten old face. Gwyl had always supported Uther, but of late he had seemed very thick with Lot. Then there was Urien of Rheged, who was new to his throne and a definite question mark; and Edun of Manau Guotodin, who was securely under Lot's thumb.

On Merlin's side of the room sat Cador of Dumnonia, who, along with the Welsh, could probably be counted on to support Arthur. Cador was frowning and looking impatiently toward the door. The only missing king, Merlin realized, was Lot.

"Where is—?" Cai was beginning to whisper into his ear, when there was a stir at the door and Lot came striding in.

"A good entrance," Ector said to Merlin out of the side of his mouth.

They watched as Lot paused, looking around the room to see who was there. When he saw Merlin, he came over to greet him.

"I saw Morgause last night, and my grandsons," Merlin said in response to the King of Lothian's opening remark. "But you are not availing yourself of Uther's hospitality, Lot?"

Lot smiled genially. Like the young Prince of Dyfed, he was obviously a Celt. His big wide-shouldered body was dressed in the brightly checked material they wove in the north. He wore a magnificent gold torque about his neck, and his muscular arms were circled with bronze and gold arm rings. Unlike the clean-shaven, Romanized south, the men of the north wore beards. Lot's beard was the same dark blond color as his hair. His blue eyes did not reflect the geniality of his smile. "I stayed with my men," he said. "To make certain they behaved themselves."

"You appear to have quartered half of Lothian outside Venta."

Lot flashed a set of excellent teeth. "Not half, Father-in law. I have plenty more men at home. But the roads are dangerous these days. A man can't be too careful."

"True," said Merlin. He did not return Lot's smile. "A man can't be too careful."

A boy dressed in a white tunic with a scarlet dragon embroidered on the shoulder appeared in the main doorway. "My lords," he announced in a shrill, clear voice, "the High King of Britain, Uther Pendragon." Lot moved quickly to his seat and the rest of the assembly rose as Uther came into the room and advanced with dignity to the dais. He walked slowly, but his posture was perfectly erect. He looked every inch a Roman, Merlin thought with pride as the king sat and gestured for the rest of them to resume their places.

"I must thank you all, my lords," Uther said when they were seated and looking at him with unconcealed expectancy, "for coming so promptly to my call. We have weighty matters to discuss at this council, and I appreciate the effort you made to reach Venta by this day."

The room was perfectly silent. Uther's voice was weak but clear as he addressed his audience from the dais. "I have been high king for sixteen years," he said as his eyes circled the room, "and during that time we have managed to keep the Sea Wolves from our doors. But the fight is not yet over. Indeed, it is only begun." He paused and Merlin could see that he was fighting for breath. They waited.

Uther set his face. Never had Merlin seen the force of his will exerted more clearly. When he spoke again the breathlessness had gone. "We defeated the Saxon offensive under Cerdic in the north this spring, but they are wounded, not beaten. Cynewulf will not be held by the borders of Kent, nor Offa by the boundaries of Sussex. Young Cerdic was only their sounding board. They will be back, again and again and again. And still the tide comes in each spring from Germany, bringing ever more of them to try to push us off our land."

Merlin could see the blazing blue eyes of the young Prince of Dyfed all the way across the room. He was staring at Uther with rigid intensity. Uther continued: "We must stand fast against them! They are not like the Goths or the Visigoths or the other peoples throughout the empire, who are Christian and thus civilized. These Saxons are indeed the wolves we call them: barbarians, pagans, dark shadows that would put out all the civilized lights in Britain should they ever get control here."

Uther's eyes commanded the room. "We *must* hold together. That is why the high kingship was established. There must be one man to lead, otherwise we fall into small pieces. And in small pieces the wolves will devour us."

"You speak true, Uther." It was Lot's hearty, ringing voice. A murmur of agreement rose from the benches, but across from him Merlin saw how the Welsh kings were frowning.

Uther waited for silence to fall once more. "As you all know, my family has served Britain for many years. My father, Constantine, was the last Roman-appointed war leader, the *Comes Britanniarum*. My brother Ambrosius was the first man elected high king." The room was deathly silent. "I am not a well man," Uther said. "And the time has come to name my heir." Next to him on the bench, Merlin heard Cai's indrawn breath. Near the door Lot made a sudden move, as if he would speak, and then did not.

Uther raised his voice. "Sixteen years ago, the queen and I had a son. He was born three months after our marriage, and because we feared there would be doubts about his paternity, we sent him away. When it became clear that the queen would bear no more living children, Prince Merlin undertook the education of this boy. That he is my son, there can be no doubt. You will see this for yourselves as soon as your eyes fall upon him. My lords, this is the heir I propose for Britain. Arthur," and his voice rang suddenly with strength and vigor, "will you come forth?"

Chapter 10

A FIGURE moved from out of the shadows behind the dais. Even Merlin, who had known the plan, had not seen the boy slip in the door, so effectively had Uther commanded the room's attention.

It was an entrance, Cai was to say later, that beat Lot's by a Roman league. Suddenly Arthur was there, standing beside his father, erect yet perfectly natural, perfectly comfortable. He looked out at the assembled council of men.

There was a commotion of sound in the hall. Over it all, Lot's voice sounded, shouting angrily, "What kind of trick is this, Uther?"

"No trick," Uther replied, but his words were lost in the noise of the chamber. Lot was standing, and a number of other men also began to get to their feet.

"*Quiet.*" The word was not shouted, but its biting edge ripped easily through the babble of noise. Silence descended abruptly. Arthur said, "I believe the high king desires to speak," and turned to his father.

Merlin stared at his grandson. The boy's black hair was neatly brushed away from his brow and he wore his best tan wool breeches and white tunic. On his shoulder was a brooch that Merlin recognized as belonging to Uther. Every man present must recognize it, he thought. Uther was seldom without it.

"I know I gave it out that he was dead," Uther was saying to Lot. "What king of sound mind would leave a potential heir vulnerable for his enemies to perhaps use against him?"

"Enemies?" Lot shouted. "What enemies? You have no enemies, Uther. Our enemy is the Sea Wolves, and I say we need a trained war leader to be high king, not an untried boy, whatever his parentage may be."

"He wears his parentage on his face." It was Ban of Dyfed speaking, a big man with shaggy blond hair. "You have only to look at the boy, Lot, to see he is the high king's son."

Under the thick blond eyebrows, Lot's blue eyes were hot with anger. "Perhaps he is Uther's son. But he is a boy. I repeat, we need a trained leader for this fight against the Saxons."

"Like you?" Ban shot the words across the room in a hard, angry voice.

Lot had not resumed his seat and now he drew himself up to his impressive height. "Yes," he returned defiantly. "Like me!"

"The King of Lothian makes a valid point." Every head in the room whipped around to look at the speaker. Arthur had rested a hand lightly on the back of Uther's chair, but otherwise he stood as before. The sun, slanting in through the high windows, glinted off the brooch on his shoulder. Arthur continued. "The high king is, above all else, the war leader. The survival of us all depends upon his effectiveness in that role." He removed his fingers from Uther's chair and stepped away from his father to stand alone. He clasped his hands lightly behind his back and looked slowly around the room, his gaze going from face to face as he spoke, making each man feel as if he were being addressed personally.

"The King of Lothian says I am untrained in war," Arthur told them. "That is not so. For the past seven years I have been trained, quite relentlessly I assure you, by my grandfather, Prince Merlin. I would match my knowledge of war against any man's in this country."

The gray eyes came to rest upon Lot's face. "Shall I tell you, my lords, what is the most important lesson I have learned during all my years of study?" Arthur's clear, flexible voice held the room's absolute attention. "It is what my father has just said to you. Above all else, we must be united. The Christian Bible tells us that a house divided against itself cannot stand, and so it is with Britain." He stared at Lot. "The ambition of princes must not be allowed to divide us against ourselves," the black-haired boy said to the king.

Lot flung back his leonine head. "You are not a one to speak of the ambition of princes," he jeered.

"Perhaps not." Arthur took a step forward, and the sunlight from the window fell full upon him. "I am ambitious," he said. "I am ambitious for Britain. I want to see her whole and prosperous once more, not cowering in fear of the Saxon darkness. I want to see our towns thrive as once they did, our fields teem with the harvest. I want ships filled with gold, iron, silver, tin, hides, and wheat once more sailing out of British ports. I am ambitious for peace, my lords, for only in peace can a nation grow and prosper."

As Arthur was speaking, Merlin looked around the room. Every man's eyes were on Arthur, none on Lot. Cador of Dumnonia was nodding as if in agreement.

"We all want peace!" Lot was shouting now as he felt the momentum slipping away from him, as he felt the attention of the room centering on the boy who was facing him down. "But the only way to peace is to beat the Saxons," he said to the men who had gathered here today to decide the future of the high kingship. "And the only way to beat the Saxons is to elect a proven war leader, not an untried boy who has yet to grow a beard."

"To beat the Saxons, we must be united," repeated Arthur, "and for that you need me." There was a sharp line between his black brows, and he did not look young at all. "You need me because I am Uther's son and Constantine's grandson; because I have no ties to the north or to the south or to Wales, but only to Britain. In choosing me to be high king, you are not choosing Lothian, or Dumnonia, or Dyfed. You are choosing a Comes Britanniarum. And I promise you, my lords, that I shall lead you to victory."

They believed him. Merlin could sense it as he looked around the room for what seemed the hundredth time that afternoon. It was a quality in Arthur he was to see over and over again, yet always it amazed him, that ability to move and inspire men. He did not do it by his words; other men could speak the same words and have no effect at all. It was something in him, some quality in his very existence, intangible yet absolutely commanding. Constantine had had it to some degree; in Arthur it was paramount.

Cador of Dumnonia was getting to his feet. He was a short, heavyset man with a powerful neck and deep-set dark eyes. "My lords," he said in his deep, rumbling voice, "I propose that we accept the high king's nomination of Prince Arthur as his heir."

When the vote was over, Lot went back to his camp and began to gather his men. He sent word to the praetorium that Morgause was to make ready to depart.

This message was brought to Uther as he was consulting with his wife and his father-in-law in the reception room of his private chambers. Uther told the man to wait outside for a reply, and the three of them looked at each other as the messenger left the room.

"He is angry," Merlin said to Uther and Igraine as soon as the door had closed. "Angry enough to storm Avalon and demand the return of his wife and his sons."

"I don't think so," Uther replied. "I sent a whole cohort under Claudius with orders to surround Avalon. He won't risk Morgause or the boys getting hurt."

Merlin still looked worried. "I wouldn't put too much faith in Lot's tender heart."

"Nor would I." Igraine's voice was dry. "But Morgause is his tie to the high kingship. And his sons. Without them he has no more claim than any other of the Celtic kings."

"Igraine is right," said Uther. "I will send a reply to him that Morgause is at Avalon and does not wish to return to Lothian just yet. He won't tarry for her."

"True." Merlin's face had relaxed. "Things have not fallen out as he had expected."

"They did not fall out as I expected, either," Uther said frankly. "I never expected Lot's to be the sole dissenting vote."

The king was looking exhausted and Igraine said to Merlin, "Where is Arthur? It was his idea to send Morgause to Avalon. Let him deal with Lot."

"The last I saw of Arthur," Merlin replied dryly, "he was flanked by Cai and a blond-haired giant from Wales and was listening with admirable patience to contradictory advice from five different kings and princes."

Uther's thin, sallow face broke into a smile. "I wish you could have been at the council, Igraine," he said to his wife. "The boy was magnificent."

"I'm glad." She gave her father a hard, meaningful look before she continued, "I'm glad you have such a competent son, my love. I am quite sure that between Arthur and Father they can deal with matters here while you take a little rest. You look tired."

Merlin stood up. "Igraine is right, Uther. You must save your strength. I'll have the message sent to Lot."

"All right." The king's skin looked gray and his breathing was audible. His half-closed eyes turned to Merlin. "Tomorrow," he said, "I will present Arthur to the army."

Merlin nodded. "I'll speak to him. Get some rest now, Uther." As he turned to leave the king's chamber, he saw Igraine bend over her husband. She said something to him, and her voice was heartbreakingly tender. Merlin's mouth set hard; then he went out into the hall to speak to Lot's courier.

*   *   *

When Lot learned of the disposition of his wife and his sons, he ranted and stormed and threatened, and in the end turned his men north and went back to Lothian. As Merlin had remarked, things had not fallen out as he expected, and he was anxious to reevaluate his plans.

The mood in Venta was triumphant. The question of the succession had hung like a cloud of doom over the country for the last few years and the introduction of a young prince gave heart to everyone. Arthur's formal presentation to the army the following day was an occasion for unabashed celebration.

Uther had arranged a parade down the main street of Venta, to be led by himself and Arthur. The army regulars and low-ranking officers lined the street on either side to catch a glimpse of the new prince; the kings and princes of Britain, along with Uther's chief captains, rode in procession behind them.

Merlin was not in the parade but had been delegated to welcome the high king and his son on the portico of the praetorium. He stood there now, looking past the courtyard to the street up which the parade would come. Not that he needed to see Arthur to know what he looked like today. He personally had helped the boy to dress early this morning, putting a new leather tunic over his white one, and a new coat of mail over all. The mail coat was circled at the waist by a leather belt that had been specially made at Avalon to hold his sword. Merlin himself had placed the sword with Hadrian's ruby into its holder, and had handed Arthur his oval shield on which was emblazoned the red dragon Uther had chosen long ago for his emblem. Arthur today was dressed like the soldier-king he had sworn he would be.

The cheering was moving up through the town along with the procession, and Merlin heard it long before the parade came into his sight. At first it was just a roaring noise, like a roll of thunder coming down a river valley. Then it was Arthur's name he could hear being shouted, over and over again.

The noise was coming closer and at last Merlin could make out the figure of his boy, riding in the lead beside Uther. The sun reflected off the shining ebony of Arthur's unhelmeted head and off the metal of his mail coat as well. He was riding a magnificent black horse which had been presented to him yesterday by Bedwyr, the big blond son of King Ban of Dyfed. The horse was sweating with excitement but the boy controlled him without visible effort. Behind the two leaders rode the kings of Gwynedd, Powys, Dyfed, Elmet, Rheged, and Dumnonia, and behind them an assortment of minor princes and chiefs. Edun of Manau Guotodin, Merlin saw immediately, was not present.

The horses finally reached the courtyard of the praetorium and Merlin went down the steps formally to welcome them. Arthur's face was studiously grave as he replied to his grandfather, but his eyes were brilliant.

Wine was being served in the audience chamber of the praetorium, and as servants took their horses, the various participants in the procession made their way into the house. It was not long before every square foot of mosaic floor was occupied by a king, a prince, a chief, or an army officer. And they all wanted to talk to Arthur.

Merlin stood a little to one side and watched the scene before him. Uther was sitting in his chair on the marble dais at the far end of the room, yet it was not the high king who was the center of interest today. People spoke to Uther, to Merlin, to each other, but all the time they were listening for the voice of the slender black-haired boy who moved among them with such quiet confidence.

"The boy is doing splendidly." It was Ector who had come up beside him, and Merlin turned with a smile.

"That he is." He looked back toward Arthur again. "And it seems as if Cai and the Prince of Dyfed have constituted themselves his personal bodyguard."

It was something Merlin had noticed almost immediately; wherever Arthur was, the tall, broad-shouldered bulks of Cai and Bedwyr were right behind. Both boys watched the crowd constantly. "They have not overstepped themselves, though. It would be all too easy for someone to use his dagger on Arthur in a crush like this."

"I know," said Ector. "That's why I told Cai to keep close to him."

Merlin put a hand on his steward's arm. "Good man." His face suddenly looked older. "I've aimed him for this moment for the last seven years, Ector. Why do I suddenly wish he was a boy again, and safe at Avalon?"

"I know," Ector replied. "I remember so well the first day I took them out on the practice field and showed them how to hold a sword."

They looked at each other with rueful humor. "We're growing old, my friend," Merlin said, and Ector sighed.

"My lord Merlin," said a voice behind them, and both men turned with relief to the King of Elmet, who had come to speak to them.

Chapter 11

ARTHUR had been given his own room in the praetorium, with a soldier to guard his door. Merlin thought the boy had gone to bed and was himself preparing to retire when there came a knock at his door, and Arthur's voice requesting to speak to him. Merlin dismissed his servant and bade the boy come in.

The hanging lamp swung a little as the door opened and closed; then Arthur was inside, dressed in the same white tunic he had worn all day, an air of coiled tension about him. Merlin frowned in concern. "It's late. You should be in your bed. What is so important that it cannot wait until tomorrow?"

"There is something I must speak to you about, sir," Arthur answered tensely. "As it has become a trifle difficult to see you alone, I came tonight."

"I see." Merlin pulled his cloak about him more closely and sat on a straight-backed wooden chair. He gestured Arthur to the other chair, but the boy shook his head.

The air of tension was becoming more pronounced, but when Arthur spoke at last his voice was steady. "I want to speak to you about Morgan."

A shiver of apprehension ran along Merlin's spine. "What about Morgan?" he asked.

"We want to marry," said Arthur, and Merlin knew that the sword that had been hanging over him for weeks had finally fallen.

"Arthur," he said heavily. He closed his eyes, then forced them open. He looked at his grandson. "You cannot marry Morgan. Surely you must see that for yourself."

All the blood seemed to leave Arthur's face. "No," he replied quickly, breathlessly. "I don't see it. Why not? If you are concerned about our relationship, we are no closer in blood than if we had been cousins."

"Your mother is Morgan's sister."

"Her half-sister!"

Merlin rubbed his temple as if it were throbbing. The boy had thought it all out. "It is not as simple as that, Arthur," he said after a minute. "Half-sister or full sister, it would still be seen as incest. You cannot marry your mother's sister. The church would not permit it."

"The church has allowed such things before. You know that, sir." Arthur's eyes were glittering in his white face.

"You don't understand, boy. Think. You have just been proclaimed Uther's heir, but your title is not secure. There are men other than Lot who would be glad to see the end of you, no matter what they may say in public. You cannot give them a lever to use against you! And that is exactly what such a marriage would be, Arthur."

The boy was breathing as if he had been running. "I don't care."

"You don't have just yourself to consider in this matter. There is Britain. You said yourself yesterday that Britain needs you. Don't fail us before you have even set your hand to the wheel."

"*You* don't understand," Arthur replied. His face was stark. "Without Morgan . . . I cannot live without Morgan."

Merlin looked away. Never had he thought he would wish to see Arthur's still, shuttered look; but anything was better than this.

"Arthur . . ." He spoke to the lamp hanging beside him. "Do you remember what once I told you, that a leader is a public thing, that he cannot ever consider his affairs as private, because they are not. Believe me, boy"—he forced his eyes back to his grandson—"I would do anything to spare you this sorrow. I know how close you are to Morgan. I wish to God I had known which way things were tending between you two, but I thought . . ." His voice ran out. The flesh on Arthur's face seemed to be pressing back against the bones of his skull. "Arthur!" he said desperately. "Boy, don't look like that."

Arthur's eyes were wild and glittering. "I will go to the king."

"Uther will tell you the same thing I just did. You cannot risk the whisper of incest. It is impossible for you and Morgan to marry."

Arthur's hands opened and closed at his sides. Then he turned, pushed open the door of Merlin's room, and without a backward look went out into the corridor. Merlin watched the door close behind him and lowered his face into his hands.

Best let the boy be alone for now, he thought. Slowly he rose from the chair and went over to his bed. Never, Merlin thought wearily as he lowered himself to the mattress, never had he felt so old.

*   *   *

Merlin was awakened the following morning by a servant of Igraine's, who brought an urgent summons from the queen. He dressed in reasonable haste and went along the corridor to her room. He was admitted immediately and found her alone.

"Arthur is gone," Igraine said to her father the moment the door closed behind him. "When his servant went into his room to wake him this morning, he found the bed unslept in. Then we discovered that his horse is missing from the stable. Where in the name of God can he have gone, Father? If he wanted a girl, we could have got one for him . . ."

"You can't get him this girl," Merlin replied, and sat heavily in a chair.

Igraine was still standing. "What do you mean, Father? Do you know where he has gone?"

"Yes," Merlin replied, and stared bleakly at Arthur's mother. "He has gone to see Morgan."

"Morgan? Why Morgan? Father, what is the matter? You are frightening me. You look terrible."

"I feel terrible," Merlin returned. He rubbed his forehead and said, his head bowed, his whole posture bespeaking defeat, "Arthur came to me last night and asked to marry Morgan. I said he could not."

"*Marry Morgan*! He cannot marry Morgan. Morgan is my sister."

"That is what I told him." Merlin looked up. "I think he means to have her anyway, Igraine."

"He can't do that." Igraine's voice was shrill. Finally she too sat down. "I think you had better explain all this to me, Father."

"It is not difficult to explain. Arthur has been attached to Morgan ever since he first came to Avalon. They have been inseparable since childhood. I would say that Arthur loves Morgan more than anything else in the world."

Igraine was rigid with outrage. "Were you mad, Father, to allow such a thing to happen? You knew what their relationship was!"

"Not mad, Igraine, just blind. You see, I assumed all along that Arthur thought he was my son. I thought he regarded Morgan as his sister."

"And he did not think he was your son?"

"No. It seems Malwyn often told him he resembled his father. He does not look like me, so he never thought he and Morgan were related."

Igraine's beautiful high cheekbones looked more prominent than usual as she sat slowly back in her chair. "It is too bad that this had to happen," she said slowly after a moment's reflection, "but if you and Uther refuse your permission, they cannot marry. That is the end of it."

Merlin looked at her from under his brows. "It is not so simple as that. I saw Arthur's face last night. He will toss everything aside if he must—Uther, the high kingship, Britain—before he will give up Morgan."

"No priest will marry them without your permission," Igraine insisted.

"That is so. But they may settle for something less than marriage." Merlin's shoulders were slumped against the back of his chair.

Igraine stared at him. "Have they slept together?"

"I don't know. They have certainly had every opportunity."

Igraine catapulted herself out of her chair and began to pace the floor. "We cannot allow this to happen," she said as she prowled up and down the room. "We cannot allow an adolescent love affair to ruin everything Uther has striven for all these years. They must be separated. Send Morgan away, Father. God knows there are hiding places enough in Britain."

But Merlin was shaking his head. "Do you think Arthur would stand for that? You don't know him very well, Igraine, if you think he would. He would tear the country apart looking for her. The only way you could stop him would be to chain him up."

Igraine halted in her pacing. "Such a stupid, self-indulgent thing to do," she said. "To throw away a crown and a nation . . . for a girl!"

"He is your son, after all, Igraine." As her angry eyes flew to his face, Merlin smiled bitterly. "I seem to remember that once you threw away husband, home, religion, and family honor . . . for a man."

Igraine had gone very white. "That is true," she said in a low voice. "And if it is like that with him . . . God, Father, what are we to do?"

"There is nothing we can do. We must leave it to Morgan. He has gone to her, and he will tell her everything I said to him." Merlin's voice had lost its bitterness. "More than any of us, Morgan knows what Arthur is," he said, "what he has it in him to be. And she is more my daughter than either you or Morgause, Igraine. I think she has it in her to send him away."

There was a twist to Igraine's voice as she answered, "We must pray that she does, Father. We must pray that she does."

Morgan got Morgause and her sons to Avalon with little trouble. The Lothian children were tireless horsemen, even the youngest, four-year-old Agravaine; and Morgause herself rode competently and uncomplainingly. In fact, she seemed to enjoy the hot dusty ride, pointing out landmarks to her sons and chatting easily with Morgan.

Of all his daughters, Morgause was the one who looked most like her father. Her hair was more red than his had been, but she had his features and his clear blue eyes. But the trace of austerity that hung always about Merlin was completely absent in Morgause. She was rich and vibrant and warm. Her figure was lush, her hair luxuriant, her lips and cheeks brilliant with color. Her smile and laughter were always good-humored. She was far more likable, Morgan thought, than Igraine.

The apple orchards of Avalon rose before them, and Morgan, who had been listening tensely the whole ride for the sound of hooves pounding in pursuit, finally relaxed. They rode through the sweet-smelling orchards and came at last into the colonnaded courtyard of the villa.

The Lothian children stared at the stone house with big-eyed awe. "Was *this* where you lived when you were a little girl, Mother?" Gawain, the eldest, asked.

"Yes." Morgause sighed with happy nostalgia as she looked around. "Half of Britain is lying in ruins," she said to Morgan, "yet nothing at Avalon has seemed to change."

"The outside world doesn't trouble us much here," Morgan replied. "The villa is virtually self-sustaining."

"What does that mean?" Gawain asked curiously. "Self-sustaining?"

"It means that everything we need we make right here, Gawain," Morgan answered her nephew. "Our food, our clothing, our furniture, our tools. Everything is made right here at Avalon. The only things your grandfather must buy from the outside world are wine and oil." She smiled at all the children. "If you like, I'll take you around tomorrow and show you the farms. And the kiln where we dry our wheat. And the blacksmith and the carpenter and the weaving houses. Would you like that?"

"Yes!" Gawain and Gaheris chorused in reply.

Morgan looked from the two eldest boys to the youngest, who had remained silent. Gawain and Gaheris were handsome boys, big like their father, with Morgause's hair and eyes, but Agravaine was beautiful. His hair was the color of ripe corn and the eyes that looked up at Morgan were the darkest blue she had ever seen. "And you, Agravaine?" she asked gently. "Would you like to see the villa too?"

"Oh, yes." He gave her a charming, little-boy smile. "But I would like to see the house first."

Morgause put a caressing hand on his golden hair. "And so you shall, my love." She smiled at all of her sons. "What fun we shall have," she said with infectious enthusiasm. "Wasn't your father clever to think of sending us to Avalon?"

Morgan felt a distinct twinge of guilt.

When Arthur fled from Merlin's bedchamber, the only thought in his head was to get away. His feet had taken him halfway back to his own room before he realized he had somewhere else to go. The thought quickly became a fixed idea. He had to see Morgan.

Morgan was at Avalon, safely behind the shield of Claudius Virgilius and his cohort of soldiers. No matter, Arthur thought instantly. He could get through to her. If it cost him his life, he would get through to her. With no further hesitation, he swerved in his path and made for one of the back doors of the praetorium.

He walked that night like one who is cloaked in darkness. Neither the guards at the praetorium nor the guards at the stables saw him. The army had been celebrating the election of the new prince that day, and the sentries were drowsy with wine and too much food.

Arthur threw a saddle on the new horse Bedwyr had given him, one of Sodak's colts, and led him out of the stable. He did not mount until he was at the main street; then he swung into the saddle and put the horse to a trot. They rode out of Venta and turned toward the road to Avalon. Dun Loaghaire, the horse Bedwyr had given him, was eager to go, and Arthur touched him to a canter as soon as they reached the Roman road.

It was a moonlit night and he rode on steadily, the three-beat rhythm of his horse's hooves the only sound in a silent world. He had no thought of what he would do when he saw her, of what he would say. There was only this necessity driving him forward, like an arrow hurtling through the night toward its final homing.

He veered off the main road and approached the villa through the fields. No one saw or challenged him. He woke up one of the slaves who slept over the stables and told him to see to Dun, and then, on silent feet, he made his way to the house. The sky was beginning to lighten with the approaching dawn.

The shutters to his room were open, and he entered through the window. He stood for a moment, looking around the dim bedroom at the familiar furniture. It seemed a hundred years now since he had first seen this room. Morgan had been the one to show it to him, he remembered. He moved on stealthy feet out into the corridor and then through the door of the bedroom next to his.

She was asleep, her brown hair spilling across her arm and her pillow. He looked at her with wordless longing, at the faint hollow of her temple, at the long brown lashes lying so peacefully on the soft curve of her cheek. At her mouth. Her lashes lifted and she was looking back at him.

"Arthur!" Her brown eyes reflected the breaking dawn light from the unshuttered window. "What are you doing here?" she asked, pushing herself up on her elbow.

How to explain to them, he thought. How to make them understand that the touch of her hand, the expression of her eyes, the feel and smell of her hair, the sound of her voice, all these were as necessary to him as the air he breathed, the water he drank. "Morgan," he said. His voice was strangely hoarse. She sat up and pushed the hair off her face.

"But what is it?" she breathed.

He could not answer. He came to sit beside her and take her tightly into his arms. He held her against him, his cheek against her hair, and closed his eyes. Her hair felt like warm silk against his face. It smelled, as always, of lavender. He felt her quiver within his embrace and forced himself to speak. "I asked Merlin if we could marry and he said we could not." He tightened his arms as he spoke, pressing her flexible young body close to him in a spasm of possessiveness.

"Arthur." Her voice seemed very far away. "What did Father say? Tell me."

Reluctantly he loosened his hold. He looked down into her eyes. "A lot of nonsense," he said huskily. "We must simply do as we want without him."

She moved away from him. Her hair streamed down over her thin cotton bedgown, her brown eyes commanded him. "Tell me," she said again, and he did.

When he had finished she bent her head. "I was afraid of this." Her voice was barely audible. "I tried not to think about it, but I was afraid."

"Morgan." His voice was low but urgent. "It doesn't matter what he says; it doesn't matter what anyone says. You and I, we don't need them."

She was pale as a ghost in the gathering light from the window; her eyes were somber. "No priest will marry us without your father's permission."

His eyes glittered like silver under their long black lashes. "Do you need a priest to feel married to me?"

"No." Her lips formed the word, though no sound came.

His face relaxed very slightly. "We'll go away together. Across the sea to Armorica, perhaps, like so many other Britons have done. I can keep us. I can always sell my sword if I have to. We don't need much to make us happy, you and I."

There was a long moment of silence as she stared up into his face. Then she reached out and touched the lock of hair that had fallen across his forehead. Tears began to slip down her cheeks and she shook her head. "No," she said in a constricted voice. "No, Arthur. I cannot let you do it."

He put his hands on her shoulders. "Listen to me, my love." He was gripping her so tightly that his fingers would leave bruises. "None of this matters to me if I cannot have you. I would rather be a nameless mercenary with you at my side, than High King of Britain without you. You know that!"

"Yes, I know that." Her voice was barely a thread of sound. The tears had ceased to fall but her face was still streaked with wet. "And if we two do as you say, Arthur, what will become of Britain?"

At that he got to his feet and walked to the window. He stood staring out, his back rigid. "Britain has managed very well without me up till now," he said over his shoulder. "It will continue to manage in the future."

She had got herself under control. "And if it does not?" she said to his resistant back. "If, after Uther dies, Lot takes the throne? You know what will happen then as well as I. There will be civil war. And the Sea Wolves will come pouring in." Her voice beat against him relentlessly. "How will you feel, Arthur, sitting in Armorica, when you hear about that?"

He swung around to face her, the conflicting emotions that were tearing at him clearly visible on his face. "Don't you understand, Morgan? I cannot do it without you. I simply . . . cannot."

"You can," she said. "You must."

He took a step toward her, then another one. "No! Morgan, no. You must listen to me."

From somewhere deep within, she found the courage to say what must be said, to do what must be done. Her head high, her spine straight, she said, "And how do you think I will feel? Britain is my country too."

He did not answer. He felt suddenly numb, as if a great blast of icy wind had frozen him to his very marrow. This could not be happening. . . .

Her eyes were so dark they looked almost black. "You are too precious a commodity for me, Arthur," she said. "You were meant for greater things." And closed her eyes to blot out the look on his face. "We can still stay friends," she added unsteadily.

There was a frightening silence. Then: "Don't be stupid as well as cruel." His voice was corrosive with bitterness. "I could never think of you as a friend." He wanted, with a violence that frightened him, to touch her, to kiss her, to force her to understand what he was feeling.

She opened her eyes. He could see that she was trembling. Perhaps, if she truly understood what she was doing . . . "It seems, then," she said, "that there is no way for us at all."

Pain stabbed through him like a knife thrust in the gut. "If you send me away tonight, I will not come back." He did not recognize his own voice. He was breathing with difficulty, through narrowed, pinched nostrils.

She had to clench her hands to keep herself from reaching for him. What was there to say? That she would always love him? But he knew that already. "Be the king you were born to be," she said at last.

He stood for a moment, poised and taut as an arrow, then turned and left her room as silently as he had come.

He went to the stable and took one of the ponies. He was at the river before he realized where he was heading. He dismounted, tied the pony to a tree, and went to stand along the bank, gazing into the slowly moving gray water.

The dawn was streaking the sky with red. The birds were riotous in the trees. All about him was the fresh pungent smell of dew and of woods. The river bottom here was rocky, with boulders worn smooth by the moving water.

This can't be happening, he thought. Morgan cannot mean it.

Instead of the water, he saw her face, saw it as it had looked when she said, "You are too precious a commodity." She meant it. She was going to sacrifice them both for the good of Britain.

She was wrong. *He* had meant it when he said he could not do it without her. She was the very heart of him. Without her . . . without her . . . He shut his eyes and the desolation was so great that he was dizzy with it. He felt as if he were falling down a dark and endless well of despair, with no help, no hope, no escape.

He opened his eyes and looked at the river.

Escape.

The Camm was deep in the middle here, deep enough for him to do it. He would wade out until he was over his head and then let the river take him.

Escape. Escape from this pain that froze his skin to his bones and turned his very marrow to ice. This pain of aloneness. He stepped into the river. The water at the edge was up to his ankles. It was warm from the summer sun, pleasant almost. He walked a little forward. The river splashed about his legs and filled his shoes. He looked down and watched it darken the woolen cloth of his breeches.

If he did this, Morgan would know it was because of her.

He stopped. She had done this as a great act of unselfishness, to save him for Britain. If he walked into this river now, he would be throwing her gift back into her face. He would be condemning her to live with his death on her conscience.

He could not do that to her.

He stared out at the deeper water. Not now, he thought. Not here. Later perhaps, in battle, when she would never know the cause. . . .

He raised his hands to his face to stifle the sound of his own crying.

Chapter 12

THE twilight was fading when Arthur returned to Venta that evening. He said nothing as he dismounted in front of the praetorium and handed his reins to the sentry. He had not been in his room for more than ten minutes before his grandfather was announced by the guard at his door.

"Come," Arthur called sharply, and Merlin entered to find him bent over a basin of water. He straightened as his grandfather came in, and reached for a towel. Arthur was stripped to his short underbreeches and as Merlin watched him dry his face, he studied the boy's half-naked body. Despite its slim build, narrow hips, and flat belly, the shoulders and chest were well-muscled, as were the long, horseman's legs. Arthur, as Merlin knew, was very strong. The boy finally dropped the towel and let his grandfather see his face.

He looked exhausted.

"When did you last sleep?" Merlin demanded.

The boy shrugged. "Two nights ago, I suppose." The gray eyes held an unmistakable warning. "I was about to go to bed when you came in."

"I won't keep you, then." Merlin knew, without a word being spoken, where Arthur had been and what had happened. And Arthur knew he knew. The man would have liked very much to offer a word or a gesture of comfort, but he understood from Arthur's eyes that that would not be permitted. The best thing he could do for the boy was to leave him alone to sleep. And so, with a brief good night, he turned and left the room.

Arthur, dimly, was grateful for his grandfather's tact. He felt sodden with fatigue. He went to the bed, lay down, and in less than two minutes was asleep.

He did not know that Merlin came back later to check on him. The old man stood for quite a long time looking down at his grandson's sleeping figure. He settled a blanket over the boy gently. Arthur never moved. Finally Merlin went to the door. Tomorrow would begin Arthur's new life as Prince of Britain. It was a thousand pities that it would have to begin on such a note as this.

The following morning Arthur met with Uther and Claudius Virgilius and proposed expanding the existing cavalry units. Claudius, who was not anxious to have the young prince meddle with his own foot command, supported him. After Uther had agreed also, Arthur made a list of all the present cavalry commanders and went off to discuss them with Bedwyr and Cai.

It was not the men, but the horses, however, that were the problem. "The present cavalry horses won't do," Cai said. "Most of them are too small to carry a fully armed man into battle. Uther has used the cavalry mainly as auxiliary troops. The horsemen carry swords but no lances."

"The Romans never fully learned the use of heavy cavalry," Arthur explained to Bedwyr. "For one thing, the Roman cavalry never used stirrups. It is impossible to keep your seat under the shock of a heavy lance thrust if you do not have stirrups."

Bedwyr frowned. "What are stirrups?"

"Foot supports," Arthur replied. "They hang from your saddle. The people of the steppes have used them for years. The Goths, however, have improved on the old rope stirrups and made theirs out of leather and iron." He looked at Cai. "Do you remember the engineer Merlin engaged to teach us how to build bridges and roads?"

"I do," Cai replied promptly. "I was interested in the bridges and roads. You kept asking him about stirrups."

"Bridges and roads?" Bedwyr asked in bewilderment.

"Half of war is a knowledge of military engineering," Arthur replied matter-of-factly. "Well, that engineer was in Rome when Alaric invaded, and he knew all about the way the Goths used stirrups. I got him to draw me some pictures and then Cai and I put some together and practiced in secret."

Cai grinned. The three of them were gathered in Arthur's bedroom, the one place in all of the praetorium where they could find privacy. Arthur had had a table brought in and he sat behind it now, the light from the window coming across his shoulder, a roll of paper before him, a stylus in his hand. Cai and Bedwyr sat before him on two straight chairs. They were both too big to fold themselves comfortably onto stools. Cai turned now to Bedwyr and said, "Merlin did not set any store in stirrups or heavy cavalry. He would never admit that the Goths were in any way superior to the Romans."

There was a touch of contempt in Bedwyr's voice. "Rome is finished," he said. "It's only a fool that holds to a dying world."

Arthur's face was very grave. "My grandfather is many things, but he is not a fool."

"Well, he is wrong," Bedwyr persisted.

"Not necessarily."

Bedwyr's golden eyebrows rose. "*You* certainly don't consider yourself Roman, Arthur. Why, I have never even heard you speak Latin!"

"He does when he speaks to Merlin," Cai put in humorously. "We all do."

"I speak Latin when I talk to my grandfather," Arthur agreed, "but that is not the point, Bedwyr. It is not a language we are talking about, and not an empire either. It is the idea of Romanitas: What Rome stood for. Rome stood for law, for civilization, for peace. Tacitus wrote that the task of Rome was to induce a people hitherto scattered, uncivilized, and therefore prone to fight, to grow pleasurably broken in to peace and ease.

"We have two jobs before us in Britain today. One is to push back the Saxons. The other is to teach the British to live together in peace."

There was a wry look in Bedwyr's blue eyes. "The first task may be the easier."

"Perhaps." Arthur put down the stylus and laced his fingers. "But the Saxons are no easy business. Uther was a good war leader, and even with all his effort, the Sea Wolves have encroached ever farther into Britain. If we are to hold them, we must develop effective cavalry." He held them a moment with his eyes. Then he leaned back in his chair, his voice becoming brisk and businesslike.

"First, the horses. There must be some bigger horses among the cavalry mounts, Cai. I want those singled out. And the men we mentioned earlier as well." As Cai nodded, Arthur turned to Bedwyr. "Can we take some horses from your father's runs?"

"Yes," Bedwyr answered instantly. "And men to ride them, too."

Arthur gave him a faint smile. "Good. The rest of the horses we shall have to buy in Gaul."

"Buy with what?" Cai asked baldly. "Coined money hasn't been in use in Britain for years. What can we possibly use to trade for horses?"

Arthur's face did not change, although the knuckles of his laced hands showed suddenly yellow with pressure. "Morgan has a collection of pearls she will let me have," he said tonelessly. "They were her mother's."

Cai let out his breath. "Morgan's pearls! But they were from Maximus."

Arthur nodded.

"Does Merlin know she has promised them to you?"

"It is not his affair," said Arthur. "The pearls are Morgan's to do with as she likes."

"What pearls are you talking about?" Bedwyr asked.

"The pearls the Emperor Maximus sent home from Gaul when he rode to conquer Rome," Cai answered. "They have come down to Morgan through her mother."

Bedwyr looked at Arthur. "Will they be enough?"

"They will buy us the beginnings of a cavalry." Arthur's eyes were absolutely impersonal. "They are extremely valuable."

"You'll need a breeding farm as well," Bedwyr said.

"I know. And our own riding school." Arthur looked at the two faces in front of him. "I want young men for this unit," he said. "An elite group of officers who, when we are finished with them, will be able to go out and train others."

Bedwyr's eyes were like sapphires. "I will bring you half the princes of Wales," he said, "all mounted on magnificent horses and ready to die for you, Arthur."

"Not for me," Arthur replied soberly. "For Britain."

After a week had passed, Morgause began to wonder why she had not heard from Lot. Morgan sent a message to her father and asked what she was supposed to tell her sister. In response, Merlin came to Avalon.

He had been a week with Arthur and had seen what the separation from Morgan was doing to the boy. He realized bleakly, as he talked to his daughter in the library shortly after his arrival, that Morgan was not faring any better.

Her eyes had always been large but now they seemed to engulf her face. The sleepless shadows beneath them were duplicates of the marks on Arthur's face. "I am so sorry, Morgan," he said to her helplessly. Then, as she looked away from him, "It was an act of great courage."

"Yes. Courage." Her lips were white. "How . . . how is he?"

"He is managing. Cai and Bedwyr are with him. He is planning his precious cavalry unit."

She nodded. Her eyes were unfocused, her lips pressed together. Nothing could have made clearer the fact that the bond between them was severed than this, that she had had to ask her father how Arthur was. Before, she would have known. But that link of feeling that had always been between them, even if they were separated, was broken. Arthur had broken it, and she must respect his wishes.

Merlin cleared his throat. "Uther is not well," he offered, and at that she returned to awareness.

"And what of Lot?" she asked.

"I have every expectation that Lot will go to war," Merlin said bluntly. "He did not even wait for the end of the council before he gathered his men. And Edun was not long after him. They will challenge Arthur. It is all too clear that Uther's war days are over. Lot is not going to relinquish his dream of the high kingship without a fight."

"And what are we to do with Morgause and the children?" Morgan's eyes were shadowed. "I feel such a traitor, lying to her like this."

Merlin straightened his fine blue tunic. "I will tell her the truth. I will tell her that we got her here by a trick and against her husband's will. It was a tactic designed to gain us time, and as such it has succeeded. If she wishes to return to Lothian now, I will send her."

Morgan sighed. "Yes. I suppose that will be best."

Morgause, however, surprised her father and her sister by having a very different idea. "If Lot were there, then of course I would return to Lothian," she said to Morgan later in the afternoon. "However, according to Father, he will not be there; he will be away somewhere fighting. You have no idea of how tedious life is when Lot is away, Morgan. I shall enjoy myself more at Avalon."

Morgause had come out to the small garden where Morgan grew the herbs she used for medicines. The herbs used for seasoning food were grown in the kitchen garden along with the vegetables and were attended to by slaves. The herb garden was Morgan's domain. Now she put down the small digging tool she was holding and looked in amazement at her sister's vivid face. Then she got to her feet and brushed the earth from the skirt of her old brown gown. "But won't Lot think you disloyal if you remain here?" she asked.

Morgause looked puzzled. "Why should he think that? If there were something I could do for him in Lothian, of course I should return. But there is nothing. I see no point in making that great journey only to sleep in an empty bed."

Morgan brushed a strand of hair that had escaped its tie away from her face. Her fingers left a smudge of dirt on her cheek. "Morgause," she said with infinite kindliness, "perhaps Father did not make it clear. Lot will probably be fighting Arthur."

Morgause reached out with a mother's capable hand to brush the dirt off her sister's cheek. "Lot is always fighting someone," she said.

Morgan stared. "And do you usually reside with his enemies during the hostilities?"

Sarcasm was lost on Morgause. She merely smiled. "If Lot wins," she explained, "he will come to Venta to be named high king. It will be much more convenient for me to wait for him here at Avalon than it would be for me to return to Lothian and then have to come south again."

"I see," said Morgan little acidly. "And if Lot loses?"

"Lot never loses," his wife replied with simple faith.

Morgan bit her tongue to keep from answering with the words that leapt to her lips: But Lot has never fought Arthur. Instead she made herself kneel once more and pluck an herb from a cluster. "Here," she said a little desperately, "I believe you were interested in how I extract oil from thyme for dressing wounds."

The days went by. Merlin went back to Venta and Ector came home to Avalon to take up his job of supervising the farms. He had no knowledge of what had passed between Morgan and Arthur, and so talked of Arthur and his plans freely and enthusiastically. Morgan clung to his every word. News of Arthur was like water to her drought-stricken soul.

She had sacrificed her happiness to make him high king. It was necessary for her to hear that he was succeeding in his new life. She was not succeeding very well, she thought dully, in her own.

But Arthur would find fulfillment, and eventually some measure of happiness, in the work he had taken on. Once he got over the initial pain of losing her, his brain would take over from his heart. He had studied the use of cavalry for so long, had fought so many hypothetical battles, had trained his body so relentlessly. He was bound to find satisfaction in doing at last what he had longed to do for so many years.

Cai would stand by him. Cai loved him too. He would not be alone. Whereas she . . .

The days were almost unendurable. It was Morgause and the boys who kept her going. She had to dissemble before them, force herself to show some semblance of normality.

At night she dreamed of Arthur. It was almost more unbearable that all her dreams were happy ones: they would be children again, playing in the tree house; or they were older, and he was holding her in his arms. She woke with a smile from dream to nightmare. For it was a nightmare she was living, and every morning when she opened her eyes it was to find with anguish that the nightmare had not gone away.

She began to feel physically ill. She was nauseated and could not eat. Fatigue seemed to permeate her very bones. It was an almost unendurable effort to arise and dress in the mornings. Justina clucked over her like a mother hen, and made her possets, which Morgan threw away when Justina wasn't looking. She knew what was wrong with her. She lacked Arthur.

It was her sister who first suggested there might be another cause for her sickness and her fatigue. She and Morgause were sitting together in the small family chamber one evening after dinner when Morgause brought the subject up. She put down the harp she had been playing, and which Morgan had been pretending to listen to, and asked gently, "Do you need help, Morgan? You can talk to me, you know. We have not met very often, it's true, but I am your sister. I would like to help you."

Morgan's eyes had been half-closed, but at Morgause's words they opened wide. "Need help?" she echoed. "Whatever do you mean?"

"I've borne three children," said Morgause. "I know what pregnancy looks like, and unless I'm very much mistaken, my dear, you are pregnant."

Morgan felt the blood drain from her head. She felt suddenly cold. The room swayed before her. She made herself sit upright. I will not faint, she told herself furiously. I will not faint.

Morgause was standing beside her holding a cup of water. Morgan took it and raised it to her lips. Her hand was shaking. When she gave it back she said, her voice as shaky as her hand, "I don't know if I am pregnant or not. I hadn't thought about the possibility."

"*Could* you be?"

Morgan's fine nostrils flared. "Yes."

"Let me ask you a few questions," Morgause said, and at the end of them neither sister was left with much doubt about Morgan's condition.

Morgause's advice was immediate and practical. "Well, we had better see about getting you married."

Morgan bent her head. Seated in the big wicker chair, her fragile figure looked like a child's. "I'm afraid that is impossible."

Morgause looked at her with pity. "Why?" Then, as Morgan did not answer, "Surely you haven't been sleeping with some slave?"

Morgan shook her head.

"He is married?"

Again Morgan shook her head.

"Then why cannot you marry him?" Morgause sounded very patient.

"Father has forbidden it," came the whispered reply.

Morgause shrugged. "Father will have to change his mind."

"No, you don't understand." Morgan pressed clenched fists against her temples. "It is impossible."

"It is impossible. It is impossible. Is that all you can say?" Morgause's patience was slipping. When Morgan made no response, she went on, "Then, if one marriage is impossible, Father will have to arrange another."

"No!" Morgan looked up, her frozen misery edging into panic. "No, I could never marry anyone else! It's not to be thought of, Morgause."

"Bearing a bastard child is not to be thought of either."

Morgan bowed her head once more so that her hair swung forward to hide her face. Morgause was right, but not for the reason she was thinking. The disgrace to herself mattered not at all; what mattered was that there was danger to Arthur in this pregnancy of hers.

He would never keep silent. Once he knew she was having a child, he would step forward immediately. He would never allow her to face this by herself.

Arthur must never know.

"You know the use of herbs," Morgause was saying. "Perhaps you could get rid of it."

Get rid of it: Kill it. Her child and Arthur's.

"No! I can't do that!" She looked at her sister out of huge shadowed eyes. "Oh, God, Morgause. You said you would help me. What am I going to do?"

Morgause came to sit beside her and put a comforting arm around her shoulders. Morgan let herself be drawn against the soft shelter of her sister's breast. "Hush now," Morgause said. "We'll find a solution, never fear. Don't make youself ill, Morgan. I'll send for Father, shall I?" She stroked Morgan's hair and, mutely, Morgan nodded.

Morgan was sleeping when Merlin arrived at the villa late in the afternoon three days later. Morgause had been making Morgan take a nap in the afternoon, and Morgan found herself obeying her sister quite as if she were Gawain or Gaheris. Consequently it was Morgause Merlin talked to first. He was drinking a cup of wine in the family chamber when she came in. The ride from Venta had put color in his cheeks and his eyes were the exact shade of blue as the summer sky. His tall body still had not an ounce of fat on it. He was sixty-three years old and looked ten years younger. Morgause smiled when she saw him and said admiringly, "I hope I wear as well as you, Father."

Merlin's response was rueful. "It's an illusion. This ride back and forth from Venta is aging me by the minute." He put down his wine cup. "Now, Morgause, what has happened that you felt it necessary to summon me so peremptorily? Have you changed your mind? Do you wish to return to Lothian after all?"

Morgause chose a wicker chair and folded her hands in her lap. She was twenty-eight and the bloom of ripe femininity was still upon her. "No, it's nothing to do with me, Father," she replied. "It's about Morgan."

Merlin looked instantly alert. "What of Morgan? Isn't she well? Marcus said she was lying down."

"She is with child," said Morgause, and watched as all the blood drained from her father's face.

There was a catastrophic silence.

"She did not realize it herself," Morgause said finally, just to break the quiet. "I noticed it first."

"*You* noticed it?" Merlin still had not regained his color. "Has anyone else noticed?"

"I shouldn't think so. She hasn't got a belly yet, if that's what you fear. But she has that big-eyed, thin-cheeked look." Morgause looked complacent. "I know it well," she added.

"You can't be mistaken?" He stared at her fiercely.

"I don't think so. All the other signs are there as well. And she says it is a likely result of her . . . ah . . . activities."

Merlin buried his face in his hands. "This is terrible," she heard him groan. "Terrible."

Morgause leaned back in her wicker chair and watched her father with a mixture of amusement and curiosity. Finally, when he looked up once more: "It is not the end of the world, Father. All it needs is a little shrewd management on our part."

Merlin looked at his middle daughter. She was very lovely as she sat across the room from him, her long auburn hair touched with fire by the sun. "Did she tell you who it was?" he demanded.

She shook her head. "All she would say was that you would not allow her to marry him."

"Marriage is out of the question." The illusion of youth had quite fallen from Merlin. He looked every one of his sixty-three years.

"If she cannot marry the child's father, then she must marry someone else." Morgause sounded very practical.

"Marry someone else," he repeated.

"Good heavens, Father. Surely it is the obvious solution. There must be someone you know who would be willing to take her and give her child a name in return for the honor of being connected with our family."

Merlin gripped his hands on the arms of his chair. "If I could get her to marry . . . You are right, Morgause. That would answer the problem."

"It is certainly a good thing I was here. You are almost as useless as Morgan, Father. Now, think. Do you know anyone who would be willing to marry her?"

"Yes," said Merlin. "I do."

"Good. I must warn you, however, that she is likely to prove difficult." Her blue gaze was frankly speculative. "She evidently loved this man very much. I suggested she try to get rid of the baby, and she refused instantly. She would not feel that way if she did not love him."

Merlin would not meet her eyes. "Yes. I believe she loves him."

"Then, if she refuses to consider marriage to someone else, tell her this. Tell her that her only alternative is to go away, have the child in secret, and give it to someone else to rear. It is done all the time, as you know."

Merlin was looking like an eager student receiving advice from a knowledgeable teacher. "Yes. I will tell her that, Morgause."

"Father." Her voice was very soft. "Who is this man whom Morgan cannot marry?"

Blue eyes looked into blue eyes. "I cannot tell you that, Morgause," Merlin said finally.

And Morgause replied, even more softly, "Never mind. I think I know."

Chapter 13

MERLIN knocked softly on the door to Morgan's bedroom. When there was no answer he pushed the door open and entered the room on quiet feet.

She was curled on the top of her bed like a kitten, fast asleep. Her short-sleeved, round-necked gown showed him the thinness of her arms and neck. Her long brown lashes looked very dark against the pallor of her cheeks. He did not awaken her, but went to the chair by the window and sat down to wait.

It was another ten minutes before her lashes lifted. When she saw his figure silhouetted against the window, her whole body went rigid. "It's Father, Morgan," he said quickly, and knew from the look on her face that she had thought for a moment he was someone else.

After a minute she sat up, her bare feet not quite reaching to the floor. "Hello, Father." She pushed her loose hair off her face. "Have you spoken to Morgause?"

"Yes."

"Well then, you know." The brown eyes that met his held the faintest of challenges. She was so thin, he thought. It hurt him to look at her.

"I know well that this is my fault, Morgan," he said to her. His voice was harsh with feeling. "I should have told Arthur who he was. I should not have given you two the freedom I did. But, by the cross of Christ, I had no idea that you regarded each other as aught but sister and brother."

At that she turned her head away and shut her eyes, a gesture that so clearly begged for silence that he fell quiet. Finally she said, her face still averted, "What shall I do?"

He drew a deep breath and said the words he had been thinking since he spoke to Morgause. "Marry Cai."

Her head snapped around. *"What* did you say?"

98

"I said to marry Cai." He leaned a little forward in his eagerness to persuade her. "Cai loves you, Morgan. I have seen that for a long time. In fact, once I even thought that if you ever wished to marry him, I would agree. He is not of princely birth, but he is a good boy and I am fond of him. He would take care of you."

Her fine lips curled a little in derision. "And do we inform him about Arthur's baby?"

He did not back down from her stare. "He would marry you anyway. And he would be a good father to the baby."

She was the one to finally look away. "No. It won't do, Father. Arthur can count, you know."

"What would that matter if you were married? He would not expose you, nor would he hold Cai up to ridicule. He would keep silence. He would have to."

"No," she said again. "I will not marry Cai . . . or anyone else for that matter. You will have to think of something else."

He could feel himself beginning to lose his temper. He had just offered her the perfect solution. "Well then, you must go away and have this child in secret. I will find someone to take it."

She went, if possible, even paler. "Yes," she answered at last, and her voice was hard with bitter gall. "You're very good at that, aren't you? Perhaps Esus would be willing." And she turned away.

"Morgan!" He was on his feet and moving toward the bed before he stopped himself. "Contrary to what you think, I do not enjoy giving away my grandchildren."

There was a long silence. Then: "I suppose not. I'm sorry I said that."

He put a hand on her shoulder and for the first time saw what she had been at pains to conceal from him, the tears that were pouring down her thin white face. "Dear God." He sat beside her and put an arm around her rigid shoulders. "Do you want me to send for Arthur?" he asked.

He felt the shudder that went through her at his words. Everything was wrecked, he thought bleakly. All the years of hard work, of preparation, the years he had so carefully and painstakingly trained the boy to succeed Uther. He had not just made a king, he thought. He had made a great one.

All for naught, because of one small girl and her baby.

Morgan's voice was barely a whisper. "No."

Hope stirred in his breast. "You give me little choice, Morgan."

She slid off the bed, pulling herself away from his embrace. There was a jug of water on the table beside the bed and she went and splashed some on her face. Then she turned to him once more. "I am not being difficult merely for the sake of being difficult, Father. I could marry Cai, yes. And perhaps that would be best for me. Cai is kind and caring. I like him. Perhaps we could make a family." Her brown eyes were level now on his face. "And you are right too in that Arthur would do nothing. But how, Father, do you think he would *feel*?"

Merlin made a gesture, then looked away from her.

"He would feel I had betrayed him," she went on, "and he would be right." She walked to the window and looked out at the September sky. Still looking at the sky, "I know him better than anyone living," she said, "and I know that if I did that to him, you would lose him. Britain would lose him. It is difficult enough for him as it is. Then . . . it would be impossible."

Merlin looked at her slight figure outlined against the window and in his mind's eye he saw Arthur's face as it had looked when he returned from his last visit to Morgan. He let out his breath. "You may be right," he said. Then: "What are we to do?"

She turned to face him. "If I give my child up, it must be to someone I can trust to take care of it. And I must be able to verify that for myself. I will not have Arthur's child brought up as he was."

The relief was so great it almost took his breath away. "Of course," he said after a minute. "Do you have anyone in mind?"

She smiled crookedly. "Morgause would be perfect, if it were not for Lot."

"Morgause?" He looked at her in surprise.

"Morgause is a good mother. I have seen that for myself these last weeks. But I cannot turn Arthur's child over to the tender mercies of Lot."

Merlin's face took on an abstracted look. "Lot could be made to think the child was his. His and Morgause's. He has not seen her since Venta." He raised his brows. "Why should Morgause not be the one to be pregnant?"

She bit her lip and did not reply.

"The more I think of it, the more pefect a solution it seems." Merlin rubbed his hands together. "And Lot is going to war. The chances are good he won't return to ask any awkward questions." He would have a private word with Cai, Merlin thought, and make certain Lot did not return. Morgan was right. It would be best not to put a child of Arthur's into those particular hands.

"All right," Morgan said from the window. "If Morgause will agree to take the child as hers, then I will give him up."

The very quietness of her voice caught at him. Her face was expressionless, but Merlin could feel her pain all the way across the room.

"I am so sorry, my dear," he said in a gentle voice, able to be gentle now that he had got his way. "But it will be for the best, believe me."

She turned her back once more to look out the window, and after a moment he left her to the solitude she so clearly wanted.

Word came to Venta that the King of Lothian was gathering his forces.

"Give me an army and I will march for Luguvallium," Arthur said to his father. "Lot has made a treaty with the painted people and they are joining his standard. They must not be allowed to pentrate beyond the wall."

There was only one wall in Britain that was universally referred to as "the" wall—the fortification built by the Emperor Hadrian across the north of Britain more than three hundred years before. The wall was eighty miles long, crossing Britain from the Tyne to the Solway, a continuous stone structure which had, in the days of Roman occupation, taken some ninety-five hundred legionaries to man. Uther had a detachment of five hundred men stationed in Corbridge and a garrison in Luguvallium to do the job.

The wall had long been regarded as the dividing line between the civilized and the uncivilized parts of Britain. North of the wall dwelt the Picts and the Scots, the tattooed tribes referred to by the British as the painted people. North of the wall also were the Celtic kingdoms of Lothian and Manau Guotodin, which now, it seemed, were determined to expand their influence to the south by means of the high kingship.

"There is word also of a Saxon push in the east," Uther said to his son now. "I cannot give you the entire army, Arthur, and leave the south unprotected."

Father and son were alone in the audience chamber of the praetorium. Uther was seated in his chair on the dais and Arthur was standing before him, his head bare, his thin, muscular hands hanging empty by his sides. He had just come from a meeting with Claudius Virgilius and so Uther's words were no surprise.

"I realize that, my lord," he replied. "Give me two thousand foot soldiers and the cavalry unit I have been forming."

Uther never had enough breath anymore. "Two thousand?" he almost whispered. "Lot is said to have twice that number."

Arthur smiled. "If you can give me more than two thousand, I'll gladly take them."

"No." Uther's face was like a mask. "I cannot spare you more than two thousand."

"I will raise the garrisons at Corbridge and Luguvallium as well," Arthur explained. "And we may gain some more recruits as we march north."

Uther tried to smile. "You are taking Prince Bedwyr and his men, I gather? And your friend Caius?"

"They wouldn't miss this chance for the world," Arthur replied lightly. He hesitated and then stepped up onto the dais. He knelt and bowed his head. "Thank you," he said. "Father."

Uther put his hand upon the shining black hair. "I wish it was all to do again," he said achingly.

He felt the quiver that ran through the boy's body. Then Arthur looked up. "I will do my best," he said, and his gray eyes were clear and fearless. He picked up his father's hand, kissed it, and rose to his feet. "Good-bye, Father."

Unable to answer, Uther merely nodded. Arthur turned and walked out of the room.

"We march in two days," Arthur said to Cai and Bedwyr later in the afternoon. He had summoned his lieutenants to his room as soon as he had had further speech with Claudius Virgilius. Both Bedwyr and Cai were in the leather tunics of army dress, although they were not wearing their mail coats. Arthur wore his usual white wool long-sleeved tunic with the leather belt Morgan had made for his fifteenth birthday. The table in front of him was piled with papers. Cabal, the hound puppy, lay at his feet, his tail occasionally thumping as he responded to a change in the tone of his master's voice.

"The king has given me the Eighth, Ninth, Twelfth, and Fifteenth foot regiments. And we can take our cavalry." Arthur looked at Bedwyr. "That is the one hundred and fifty from Wales as well as the fifty from the King's units."

Bedwyr nodded. He was lounging in his chair, his long leather-covered legs stretched out in front of him. "How many men is Lot reported to have?" he asked.

Arthur's reply was matter-of-fact. "At least three thousand from Lothian and Manau Guotodin. I don't know how many tribesmen."

Bedwyr grinned. "It should be fun."

Cai was not smiling. "We may be able to raise more troops in Elmet and Rheged."

Arthur lifted a black eyebrow. "Reports are that the kings of Elmet and Rheged are waiting to see who comes out the victor before declaring themselves."

"Cowards." Bedwyr's blue eyes were full of contempt.

"They call it prudent," said Cai.

"Well, whatever one chooses to call it, I'm afraid we can't rely on much help there. I have better hopes of the garrisons at Corbridge and Luguvallium. We should be able to pick up additional troops there, troops who know the country." Arthur's voice was businesslike. "Now," he went on, "I have here the rosters of all of the companies we will be taking, with their officers." He touched one of the neatly stacked rolls before him. "And a list of all the supplies we shall require." The pointing finger touched another roll. Bedwyr stopped lounging in his chair and sat up as Arthur began to issue a list of instructions. When the two young men left the room twenty minutes later they had enough to do to keep them busy until they marched.

Waiting in the corridor outside Arthur's door was a soldier they both recognized. He gave them a friendly grin. "Finished right on time, I see," he said cheerfully, "I'm next in line. The prince wants to know all about the terrain in the north."

Both Bedwyr and Cai watched as Uther's mapmaker, Gerontius, knocked on the door of Arthur's room. At the command to enter, his attitude changed magically from breezy insouciance to respect. Bedwyr and Cai exchanged an amused glance before they went off to carry out their respective commands.

Arthur finished with his interviews and his paperwork at midnight and, exhausted, finally permitted himself to go to bed. He awoke two hours later, his limbs still leaden with weariness but his brain infuriatingly active.

It was like this every night. He slept like a man drugged for two hours and then lay awake counting the hours until dawn, when he must rise and face another day.

He thought again of his lists, of the plan of march he and Gerontius had mapped out, of the officers who must be spoken to and encouraged. His brain raced and the blood pounded feverishly through his tired body. Sleep was impossible. He could force his mind to go blank and his limbs to lie quietly, but still sleep would not come.

He could not continue to live like this. He put his hand down and let it rest on the warm head of the hound who slept beside his bed.

He was trapped. It was like living in a dark cave from which escape was impossible. The weight of the pain was too much. No one could be expected to bear it.

The weight of her absence. It was not getting better, it was getting worse.

He could not continue to live like this. Beside him, the puppy snorted in his sleep. Arthur got out of bed and went to light the lamp on his table. He would go over the list of supplies once more.

Chapter 14

"WHERE is she?" Arthur, with a wild look in his eyes, burst into Merlin's room at the praetorium. It was almost midnight and Merlin was in bed; Arthur's army was due to leave Venta the following morning.

Merlin, who had not been asleep, stared up at the figure of his grandson looming over him. The oil lamp held in Arthur's hand clearly illuminated the boy's face. Merlin felt a stab of fear. He struggled to a sitting position and shoved a pillow behind his back. "Do you mean Morgan?" he managed to say with an assumption of calm.

"Of course I mean Morgan! I sent a courier to Avalon and he just returned with the news that she is not there. Where is she? What have you done with her?"

Merlin's eyes closed, an involuntary reflex of relief. It was all right. Arthur did not know. He looked at the boy once more and answered, "I sent her into Wales for a change of scene. This has been difficult for her too, Arthur. You have your work and the distraction of a new place and new faces. Morgan has been at Avalon surrounded by memories."

The boy's slim frame was shaken by the force of his breathing. "Why didn't someone tell me she was going?"

"I was supposed to, but I'm afraid, in all the excitement of the army preparations, I forgot. I'm sorry."

He had not forgotten, of course. He had never had any intention of telling Arthur. He looked now at his grandson's tense face. He might have known Arthur would keep some sort of surveillance on Morgan.

Arthur's brow was still lined. Merlin's easy answer had not completely reassured him. The danger, Merlin realized, had not yet been averted. "Why Wales?" Arthur asked.

"Morgan's mother brought some holdings in Wales as her dowry," Merlin answered with elaborate patience. "Since the property will be

Morgan's one day, I suggested she go and look at it. Morgause went with her. They were both in need of something to do, and this seemed to be a good solution." He made himself stop talking. If he talked too much, he would only increase Arthur's suspicion.

In the little silence that followed, Merlin studied his grandson's face. There were hollows beneath the high cheekbones, and the shadow of a coming man's beard on his upper lip and jaw. The outward marks of fatigue were unmistakable.

"You will never survive the march north if you don't get some sleep!" Merlin exclaimed. "You're driving yourself too hard, boy."

Arthur's smile was not pleasant. "Where in Wales?"

"Powys. The holding is called Dinas-Cymri."

Arthur nodded slowly. Merlin refrained from letting out his breath in relief. Even if Arthur sent someone to Wales to check on her, as he undoubtedly would, it would be all right. Morgan and Morgause were to exchange identities on the way to Dinas-Cymri. If news reached Arthur that one of the sisters was pregnant, the name he heard would be that of Morgause.

"When will she come home?" Arthur asked.

"In the spring. I don't want them traveling through the mountains in winter. And it will be as well to have Morgause out of the way until we can make some arrangements about Lothian." He added after a moment, "The boys are still at Avalon."

Arthur's expression became slightly more friendly. "You are very confident, sir."

"Yes. I am." Merlin allowed something of what he was feeling to color his voice. "I wish I were coming with you, but that is for my sake, not yours. You will do very well without me. However, about Lothian . . ."

He spoke his mind and Arthur listened with his usual courteous attention. When his grandfather had finished, Arthur nodded. "I will remember what you have said. I am sorry as well that you cannot come, but . . ." Gray eyes held blue in perfect comprehension. "I fear you will be needed more here in Venta," Arthur concluded.

"Yes," said Merlin. Unspoken but perfectly understood between them was the knowledge that Uther would not live to see his son again. With Arthur away in the north, it would be left to Merlin to deal with the government at Venta. Merlin ran a hand through his still plentiful gray locks and frowned. "Now, get yourself to bed, my boy," he ordered gruffly. "You need sleep—"

"Yes," returned Arthur. "I will." And turned away too quickly for Merlin to see the bitterness that twisted his mouth.

It was gray and overcast when the line of troops marched out of Venta the following morning and headed north. In leaving Venta, they were leaving Rome. There would be no more square forums surrounded by colonnades containing shops and offices. No more public baths, or inns offering good food and beer to the traveler or to the farmer come to market his goods. Venta was one of the last functioning cities in Britain, held that way solely because it had been the center of government under both Ambrosius and Uther. Luguvallium, their destination, was but a legionary fortress with none of the amenities they enjoyed at Venta.

Their march north, however, would be greatly facilitated by one of Rome's greatest legacies to all her outposts of empire. They would march on Roman roads, first north to Calleva, then west to Glevum, where they would take the road that led directly north to Luguvallium, the last British stronghold before the wall.

The foot soldiers marched four abreast, wearing their leather tunics and mail coats and carrying weapons that shone with careful polishing. The cavalry led the way, with the supply wagons and camp followers bringing up the rear. Arthur, mounted on Dun, rode up and down the line of men, assessing the mood, his sharp eyes checking the equipment and the readiness of the weapons.

It rained, but they were British and used to the rain. The mood in the tents when they camped for the nights was cheerful. The food was hot and plentiful and the young prince appeared to know what he was doing. The soldiers all found themselves unaccountably cheered whenever they caught sight of their commander's black head, white tunic, and scarlet cloak. He knew just what to say, too, to make a man laugh.

They marched into Rheged, through the humpbacked bare uplands that were its chief feature, and saw no sign of the king or any of his followers. The only people besides themselves they encountered were a smattering of hill farmers whose holdings overlooked the road.

They were within twenty miles of Luguvallium when Arthur called a halt to the day's march. They camped in a small valley called Glein and had finished putting up tents and were eating their dinners when scouts brought Arthur the news that the garrison in Luguvallium had declared for Lot. As had the five hundred men at Corbridge.

It was not news Arthur had expected to hear. He was not happy.

"They are all men of the north," Cai said slowly as they sat in Arthur's tent discussing the unwelcome report.

"They fought with Uther in the spring campaign!" Bedwyr said angrily.

"Presumably because Lot fought for Uther also." Arthur's voice was cool. "It's a pity, but it seems we will have to do without them."

"More than that." Cai's normally calm face was looking extremely worried. "We will have to fight them."

"How many men does that give Lot now?" Bedwyr demanded of Arthur.

"By all the accounts we can discover, about forty-five hundred," Arthur replied.

Bedwyr swore. It was more than twice their own strength. Arthur looked at him and raised a black eyebrow. "But we have the cavalry."

Bedwyr ran an impatient hand through his hair, dislodging some golden strands to fall across his forehead. "The cavalry is not trained," he said. "You know that, Arthur."

Arthur looked into the arrogant face of the man he had chosen to be his cavalry leader and replied, "You will be able to do what I need." Bedwyr's nostrils flared, and then he nodded.

"You'll think of something," Cai said to the companion of his youth. The worried frown had lifted from his brow. "You always do."

Arthur produced a shadow of his old grin. Then he said, "I need to talk to Gerontius." He rose to his feet as his two commanders stood up. They looked down on him from their superior height and he said to Bedwyr reassuringly, "If all else fails, I'm very good at ducking and hiding. Ask Cai."

"Shall I send Gerontius?" Cai asked him in return.

Arthur shook his head. "I rather think he must be waiting," he replied, and indeed, as Cai and Bedwyr left the tent, they saw the little mapmaker waiting outside.

All of Arthur's careful planning with Gerontius was in vain, however, as he was awakened the following morning with the news that Lot had made a secret march through the night and was now but seven miles away. Arthur swore and called for his horse.

As the horns roused his army and his officers prepared their men for battle, Arthur reconnoitered the local terrain. Then, when the troops were drawn up and ready to march, he called in Bedwyr and Cai to look at the map he had drawn.

"Here," he said, pointing to a place on the map, "this is where we'll put the center. It's a relatively strong position; there are a lot of bushes and rocks to shelter behind." He looked at Cai. "The center will be your command."

Cai was deeply surprised; traditionally the center was the commander's post. "I am honored—" he was beginning when Arthur cut in.

"Don't be. I've given you the worst job of all. You will have the Twelfth foot."

Cai and Bedwyr stared at him in stupefaction. The center was also traditionally the position of the greatest strength. "Five hundred men and my banner," Arthur continued grimly. "I want Lot to deliver his chief attack against you, Cai. I want him to think that is where I am. And I want you to hold him for as long as you possibly can."

Bedwyr recovered his voice. "Those are eight-to-one odds."

"I know." Arthur turned to the Celt. "Bedwyr, the cavalry will be stationed here, in this hollow. The landscape will screen you from Lot's view." The finger pointed to another mark on the map. "I will be here, with the rest of the foot. Behind the hill." The gray eyes scanned both faces.

"From your position, Bedwyr, you will be able to see me. When I give the signal, you are to ride like devils out of hell and smash into Lot's forces." Bedwyr nodded and Arthur continued, "But not until I give the signal. Understood?"

Bedwyr looked down his arrogant nose. "Understood."

Arthur turned to his oldest friend. "The brunt of this is on you, Cai. You must draw them on. And you don't have enough men to do it properly."

Cai grinned. "Well, when you see me sinking, you can ride to the rescue."

Arthur smiled back. "I will."

It was one of those cobalt-blue mornings you sometimes get in the north, but Arthur would have preferred mist and rain. The entire success of his plan hinged on Lot being made to think that the bulk of Arthur's forces were in the center with Cai.

He knew he had affronted several of Uther's officers by putting Cai in command of the center. Cai had been only a junior officer under Uther, and Arthur's policy had been to be as conciliating as possible toward army veterans, but still he had put Cai in command. He knew Cai, knew his mind and his capabilities. Cai had the fortitude to take punishment and not retaliate. It was something Bedwyr, for example, could never do. There might perhaps have been someone among Uther's senior officers who could have commanded the center successfully today, but Arthur did not know any of them well enough to be sure. He knew Cai and he knew Cai could do it.

Arthur had all his men in position by the time the skirling sound of the Lothian pipes came echoing down the glen. From his vantage point on higher ground, Arthur could see Bedwyr and the cavalry hidden in the hollow further up the glen. Lot should march right past him, leaving his rear exposed to Bedwyr's surprise attack. Arthur could not see Cai, who was to the right of both his command and Bedwyr's, on the other side of the hill that was screening Arthur and his men from Lot.

There was a shout of triumph as Lot's forces spotted Cai's banner. The war pipes skirled even louder. Then the noise began to move down the glen in their direction. The pipes and the roaring from thousands of throats came even closer. Lot was attacking the center with the full force of his army.

In the moment before the battle was enjoined, Arthur had time to remember what everyone else had apparently forgotten: he had never yet been in a battle himself, let alone commanded one.

The deafening noise from the far side of the hill was suddenly augmented by the sound of sword clashing upon sword. Then, more horribly, came the shrieks of the wounded. Arthur turned Dun over to a subordinate to hold while he went to lie on his stomach at the top of the hill to watch.

Cai could scarcely see for the sweat that rolled down his face and into his eyes. The fighting around him was hard and vicious. He had a plan of retreat in his mind, and as it became impossible to hold one line, he fell back, sheltering behind bushes and rocks, shouting encouragement to his men, who were being overwhelmed by the superior numbers pounding against them.

Backing up, Cai stumbled over a prone figure. The man moaned, and Cai, thrown off his balance, began to go down. Out of the corner of his eye he saw a sword coming toward him.

The training of Avalon saved him. As he fell he automatically swung his own sword up in a maneuver drilled into him by one of Merlin's imported journeymen years ago. Blood spurted, and it wasn't his.

A hand under his elbow dragged him to his feet. "This is madness!" the Twelfth's chief officer screamed in his ear. "Send for the reinforcements!"

"No!" Cai shouted back from a raw throat. "We can hold out a little longer!"

The stench of blood was in his nostrils. God, he thought as he saw the colors on his left, the bastards are surrounding us. "Back!" he shouted to his men. "Fall back!"

"By all the gods of the underworld," Bedwyr said savagely between clenched teeth. "When is he going to give the signal?"

Bedwyr would have charged five minutes ago. In fact, he had sent a courier to Arthur to ask if he could attack. The answer had been uncompromising. "Don't move until I give the signal." So Bedwyr waited and fumed and swore. Cai, poor bastard, was being murdered out there, while he sat here . . .

"My lord!" Peredur, who was closest to him, pointed toward the hill. He could see Arthur mounting his horse. Then the figure on the big black looked his way, put an arm above his head, and brought it down decisively.

Bedwyr laughed with savage elation. "This is it!" He turned, giving Peredur a brief glimpse of white teeth and blazing blue eyes. He stood in his stirrups then, and turned to his men. *"For Arthur!"* he shouted and, wrenching his horse around, drove him straight up the slope of the hollow and at the massed forces of the Lothian rear.

Arthur sat his horse on the top of the hill and watched Bedwyr's mad charge. The cavalry smashed into the Lothian lines, and Lot's men gave way before them. Arthur turned to his own command.

"Are the Twelfth and the cavalry to have all the glory of this day?" he shouted.

"No!" came the resounding reply, and Arthur put Dun into a brisk trot and began to move down the hill. The Eighth, Ninth, and Fifteenth foot came pouring behind him.

The Lothian forces, certain the day was theirs, were staggered by the dual assault. Bedwyr's horses were trampling them down in the rear when the fresh troops under Arthur smashed into them from the left. For a moment the battle wavered in the balance.

Arthur thrust Dun through the ranks of men in checkered cloth, slashing a path for the soldiers who followed him with a sword that was bloody up to Hadrian's great ruby. The time for strategy was over. Now it was a matter of who could fight the hardest.

The noise at Bedwyr's end of the battle abruptly changed. Arthur looked and saw, with almost unbelieving eyes, that the Lothian forces had broken and were running from the field. He turned back to his own men and urged them on with greater ferocity.

As the brunt of the battle was taken off his shoulders, Cai drew breath and took the time to look around him. There, to the right of the field, was the standard he was looking for. With his keen, farsighted eyes, Cai could make out the figure of the King of Lothian. Calling a few men to him, Cai began to make his way across the battlefield.

It was fifteen more minutes before Arthur could be certain that the battle was won. Lot's forces were disengaging everywhere on the field and melting away into the surrounding hills. Arthur paused for a minute in the center of the field to assess the situation, and it was then that it happened.

A man in checkered tartan, who had been lying in front of Dun, apparently dead, was on his feet with sword drawn and aimed directly at Arthur's exposed throat. It was a picture that froze itself into Arthur's brain even as his hand automatically went to his sword to respond.

No, his mind suddenly said. *Let it be.*

He saw very clearly the other man's face, the dirt and the blood and the eyes full of hate. This will solve it all, he thought, and let his sword hand drop to his side, empty. He did not look away as the enemy's blade came driving toward him.

There was a blaze of silver in the sun, and the Lothian was on the ground again, this time unmistakably dead. Arthur turned and met Bedwyr's furious blue eyes.

"What in Hades do you think you are doing?" the Celt shouted at him. Then he began to curse.

Bedwyr made an awesome sight as he sat his big black stallion in the middle of the battlefield. He had lost his leather cap and his golden hair shone like a helmet of bronze in the sun. His shoulders under his mail tunic were enormous. His arms and his leather breeches were covered in blood.

The smaller, slimmer black-haired figure on an almost identical black stallion looked at him somberly and did not reply. Arthur waited until Bedwyr had run out of words and then said, "Call the men back. I don't want the Lothians pursued. And find out what has happened to Lot." With still no word of thanks, Arthur turned and galloped his horse off the field.

Chapter 15

THE army was in high heart as it poured back into camp early in the afternoon. They had acquitted themselves with distinction and beaten an enemy twice their number. The names of the young men who had led them to victory were in every conversation as the soldiers sat around the cook fires and ate and drank the ration of beer Arthur had ordered.

The aftermath of battle was handled quite as efficiently as the actual fighting had been. The wounded, mainly from the Twelfth foot, were tended by one of Uther's surgeons and some of the camp followers. The dead were taken off the field and buried. Still wearing his leather tunic and bloody leggings, Arthur visited every hospital tent and spoke to every wounded man personally.

Bedwyr saw to his men too, and his horses. As he moved around the camp, his massive blond-haired figure was pointed out with awe. His cavalry charge had been the stuff of which legends are made. But Bedwyr was not satisfied.

"They backed off from the horses, of course," he told Cai as they shared a jug of beer in their common tent at the end of the day. "But we should be more effective with the heavy lances. It will take many more months of practice, for myself as well as for the men." His blue eyes gleamed. "These stirrups of Arthur's are wonderful."

Cai grunted and took a long drink of beer. "Trained or no," he said, "I was damn glad to see you."

"I'll wager you were." Bedwyr put his own cup on the ground next to him and looked at Cai, broodingly. "I wanted to charge earlier, you know. He waited for so long . . ."

"He had to."

"I know, but gods . . ."

Cai's dirty face split into a grin. "He had it judged to perfection. Just when I knew I couldn't hold on for one more minute, there he was."

Bedwyr's answering smile was rueful. "He judges everything to
perfection. He judged you and me down to our very marrow." Both he
and Cai were sitting cross-legged on rugs on the grass floor of their
tent, and now Bedwyr drew his legs up and rested his chin on his
knees. His bright hair was dulled and matted with sweat. Neither he
nor Cai had yet found the energy to bathe. "I could not have done
your job," said Bedwyr the Lion.

Cai looked at him. "Nor I yours."

"And neither of us could have done Arthur's." Bedwyr was not
returning Cai's look, but staring steadily at his own feet.

"You and I are good," said Cai. "But Arthur is a genius."

"Cai . . ." Bedwyr's voice was low and strained. "Something happened today. At the end of the battle."

Cai stared frowningly at Bedwyr's bent head. "What happened?" he
asked when it appeared that Bedwyr was not going to continue.

"It was toward the end of the battle," Bedwyr repeated finally. "One
of Lot's men drew a sword on Arthur, and he just . . . sat there. He
saw it, saw it coming, but he did nothing. If I had not been there, the
bastard would have chopped his head off. And then, when I screamed
at him for not defending himself, he looked at me as if he hated me."

There was a very long silence. The air in the tent was pungent with
the smell of sweat and beer. Finally Bedwyr raised his eyes and looked
at Arthur's oldest friend.

Under the layer of dirt, Cai was very pale. "I did not think he would
go that far," was all he answered.

Bedwyr ran a big hand through his grimy hair. "But *why*? Why,
when the day was won, the victory was his? Why would he do such a
thing?"

"No one has told me this," Cai replied slowly, "but I have eyes and
ears and I know Arthur." His eyes were shadowed by an indefinable
sadness. "You met Morgan, I believe."

"Yes." Bedwyr sat up straighter.

"Well, you see, Arthur and Morgan . . ." Cai could not seem to find
the proper words.

"Yes," said Bedwyr again. "I remember about Arthur and Morgan. It
was not something easy to miss."

"Merlin missed it. Otherwise he would certainly have told Arthur
who he was." Cai rubbed his thumb along the rim of his cup. "Not
that he could have changed things," he added, his eyes on his own
broad, callused finger. "I could have warned him, I suppose, but by

then it was already too late. Arthur and Morgan weren't going to change their feelings."

Even in the dimness of the tent, Bedwyr's eyes looked blue. "I don't understand," he said.

"It's simple. They cannot marry. The relationship between them is too close."

Bedwyr drew in a long breath.

"Yes," said Cai, and poured himself another cup of beer.

"Do you mean that is why he did not defend himself today? Because he cannot marry Morgan?"

"I think so," said Cai, and drained his cup in one draft.

Bedwyr sat for a few moments in silence, his golden brows knit. "He did change. After the council he was all lit up, on fire almost. Then . . . he changed."

Cai's hand went up to his forehead, as if to shade his eyes. "He disappeared for almost a full day. I would wager my soul that he went to Avalon to see Morgan."

"I remember her," Bedwyr said slowly. "A small girl with big brown eyes. She walked up to my father's vicious brute of a stallion, and he let her rub his nose."

Cai's mouth twisted. "That's Morgan." He poured more beer into his cup.

"If it's that important, then he should marry her," said Bedwyr.

"And put the cry of incest into all of his enemies' mouths?"

There was a long silence. Then Bedwyr said in a different tone altogether, "Then he must put her behind him. He has too great a responsibility to allow a disappointment in love to destroy his life."

Cai gave Bedwyr a sardonic look over the rim of his cup. "And you are going to tell him so?"

They were still sitting in silence when a voice at the flap of their tent informed them that the prince wished to see them immediately.

Unlike his captains, Arthur had found the time to wash and change his clothes. They found him sitting behind the small table that was his tent's chief furnishing, writing on a scroll. He waved Cai and Bedwyr to the stools that were placed in front of it, finished writing, put down his stylus, and with the paper still unrolled before him, favored them with his attention.

"It appears," he said, "that the King of Lothian is dead." He looked at Cai.

Out of the corner of his eye Bedwyr could see that Cai was looking very stoic. There was a distinctly uncomfortable note in Arthur's voice. Bedwyr tried to draw some of Arthur's attention to himself. "Good," he said. "That is one less problem to deal with."

Cai flicked him a glance. "My feelings exactly," he murmured.

There was a long, nerve-racking silence. The air in the tent was cool, but both Cai and Bedwyr could feel sweat starting to bead on their foreheads. Then Arthur looked down at his report and slowly began to roll it up. Cai let out his breath in careful relief. For whatever reason, Arthur was not going to pursue the subject. Although, Cai thought wryly as he watched the thin brown hands dealing with the scroll, he had taken care to make clear that he knew Lot's death had been a virtual execution.

Arthur finished rolling the paper and looked up. His face had changed and there was unusual warmth in his voice as he said, "You both were magnificent today. The battle could not have been won without you. I thank you both."

Why was it, Bedwyr found himself thinking, that a word of praise from Arthur meant so much? Beside him he heard Cai answering gruffly, "It was our pleasure."

Now, thought Bedwyr suddenly. Now was the time. And being Bedwyr, he followed his instincts and plunged straight in. "We will always be there for you, Arthur. The question I should like to have answered is, will you be there for us?"

All the warmth left the fine-boned face before him. The marks of sleeplessness beneath the gray eyes that were regarding him so coldly were as dark as bruises. Bedwyr's hands, hidden by his tunic, clenched themselves into fists. But he was not Bedwyr the Lion for nothing. "Will you?" he asked again.

The gray eyes looked to Cai and saw that he knew also. Then they moved to the scroll on the table before him. "Yes," Arthur said then, mildly. "All right, Bedwyr."

The mildness surprised them more than an explosion would have. Cai spoke into the suddenly quiet room. "You are needed," he said. Without emphasis.

Arthur rested his forehead in his hands. "Yes." His voice held only weariness. "I know."

Bedwyr was opening his mouth to say something more, when Cai's hand on his arm halted him. "How do you plan to deal with the regiments at Luguvallium and Corbridge?" Cai asked matter-of-factly.

Arthur raised his head. "That is what I wished to discuss with you." There was the faintest flush of color under his tanned skin. He drew a deep, steadying breath.

But Bedwyr was not content to leave matters so unresolved. He gave Arthur a piercing blue stare and said ruthlessly, "No need for bodyguards?"

Arthur looked at Cai. " 'Tact' is not a word in Bedwyr's vocabulary." He did not sound as if he had quite enough breath to speak.

Cai gave him the time he needed. "You should hear the stories they are telling about him already," he said humorously. "The men think he is Ysbaddaden himself, chief of the giants."

Arthur gave his oldest friend a faint smile. Then he was able to turn to Bedwyr. "No need for bodyguards," he said. "I promise."

The following day Arthur moved against the garrisons at Luguvallium and Corbridge. Over the protests of both Bedwyr and Cai, he rode out of Glein with only Gerontius and a small escort of four men. He went first to Luguvallium, and then followed the wall through rolling, desolate moors and hills until he came to Corbridge. In both garrisons he was in time to catch most of the men before they had packed their belongings and fled—those, that is, who had somewhere else to go.

They had expected a large force to come against them. If they fought, they expected to be crushed. If they surrendered, they expected to be executed.

Instead, the prince whom they had betrayed rode in, alone, and raked them over the coals, verbally, for their desertion. He then inspected the garrison and pointed out every flaw in its maintenance. He checked every man's weapons. He informed them that in the future they would fight for him, without question and when called upon. Then he left.

"It was a scene," Gerontius reported reminiscently to Cai and Bedwyr when they returned to Glein. The little mapmaker's wizened face was mellow in the light of the tent's single oil lamp. "What he said to them! Both the officers at Luguvallium and at Corbridge told me they would have rather he whipped them with a lash than with his tongue the way he did."

Gerontius took another draft of beer. "By the time he left, they would have died for him," the mapmaker added, and then rose to his feet. He smiled at Cai and Bedwyr ironically. "Which, of course, was what he intended all along." He made for the door. "Thanks for the beer," he said, and departed.

*   *   *

The problem of how to deal with Lothian was not so easy to resolve as that of the renegade army regiments. Lot was dead. Arthur, remembering his grandfather's advice on the evening before he left for the north, had very good reason to suspect who had given Cai the orders for that particular execution. Merlin had seemed very certain that Lot would not survive a battle with Arthur.

Merlin's advice had been explicit. "You must name a king to take Lot's place," his grandfather had said. "Someone who is both acceptable to Lothian and loyal to you."

Such a paragon, however, was not easily come by. Nor was Arthur ready to disinherit his cousins, Lot's sons. Merlin had been adamant that Gawain, at eight, was too young to be installed as king. "He will be fair game for any strong man to manipulate," Merlin had said. "You must put someone in Lothian who can keep the north in order." Then, when Arthur had still proved reluctant: "Name a new king and marry him to Morgause. That will give Gawain his proper position as heir, and your new man more power than if he were appointed merely regent."

Arthur remembered he actually had been shocked by the suggestion that Morgause would marry the man she must consider Lot's usurper. But Merlin had smiled ironically. "Pick a man young enough, and strong enough, and handsome enough, and she'll have him. Morgause is not one to be long content with an empty bed."

So, after he returned from Corbridge, Arthur made plans to move his army north of the wall to winter in Lothian. He needed time to meet and to judge the men who had fought with Lot. He needed to meet with and judge Edun, the King of Manau Guotodin, who had fled from the battle of Glein still alive. He needed to see how serious was the threat posed to the south by the Caledonian tribes Lot had raised. And, finally, he needed to make certain of the loyalty of Gwyl of Elmet and Urien of Rheged.

Arthur gave the order for his army to march for Lothian exactly five days after his first battle had been fought and won. On the night before they were to leave for Lothian, a courier reached him from Venta with news from Merlin. Arthur took the report and waited until he was alone before he broke the seal to read it. It could not be a response to his own message about the battle; there had not been time for that. He took the scroll to his desk and read it in the light of the oil lamp that burned there. Then he rolled it up again and placed it carefully in a chest on the floor. He put his elbows on the desk and rested his forehead on his hands. The oil was almost gone in the lamp when finally he rose and made his way toward the pile of skins that was his bed on campaign. Cabal yawned in huge relief as his master prepared to go to bed. The hound had dutifully maintained a watch at Arthur's feet for the last several hours, but he was anxious to curl himself up in the warmth of the skins and blankets.

Arthur looked down at the dog. "You didn't have to wait for me," he said astringently.

Cabal slapped his tail against the floor, then leapt enthusiastically into the bed. Arthur stepped over the dog's recumbent body and wedged himself between the hound and the wall of the tent. Cabal licked his face and then wiggled down into the nest of wool and fur. In a minute he began to snore.

"Some bedmate," Arthur remarked to the darkness above him. In answer, Cabal snored again. Arthur smiled a little painfully.

He was tired, but the tiredness was normal weariness from a day of hard physical and mental labor. He would sleep tonight, he knew. His bed was no longer the enemy; not, in fact, since the day of the battle when he had invited death and Bedwyr had staved it off.

He had given Bedwyr his promise, and he would keep it. He would not seek that way out again. He would do the job he had been freed to do. He would try to make her proud of him.

Nothing, for as long as he lived, would ever lessen for him the weight of her absence. But the overwhelming blackness of soul that had threatened to engulf him had lifted.

Be the king you were born to be, she had said.

I'll try, Morgan, he answered now, deep in the blackness of the northern night, with the dog she had given him snoring at his side.

He was king. The message from Merlin had been to tell him that Uther was dead.

II

GWENHWYFAR
(462–465)

Chapter 16

THE rain was falling steadily. Bedwyr could hear it drumming on the roof of the praetorium, beating against the glazed window of his bedroom and dripping down the walls of the building into the muddy garden below. He ran his fingers through his still-damp hair, took another drink of wine from the cup he was holding, and looked warily at his father.

Father and son had not met in more than three years. Ban of Dyfed rarely left his own hills, and Bedwyr's fighting had kept him far from Wales. The fact that his father had made the journey to Venta was unusual enough to put Bedwyr on his guard. His mind was not made easier by the fact that Cador of Dumnonia and Dubricius, the archbishop of all Britain, were lodged in the praetorium along with the King of Dyfed.

Bedwyr himself had arrived in Venta only hours before. Arthur was bringing the army to winter in the city and had sent Bedwyr on ahead to prepare the shelters and arrange supplies for the influx of men. It was a job that would ordinarily have been Cai's, but Cai had been wounded earlier in the autumn and was at Avalon recuperating.

So Bedwyr drank his wine and watched his father over the rim of the cup. He had an unpleasant feeling he knew what was on Ban's mind. The king, in his turn, regarded his son's large figure with distinct disapproval. Bedwyr was sprawled in a carved wood chair, his long legs thrust out in front of him, his massive shoulders slumped against the cushioned high back. He had changed his wet, muddy clothes for a clean, dry tunic and his leather breeches for ones of soft wool. He looked very much at home in the comfortable bedroom, which indeed was home to him whenever he was at Venta. Prince Bedwyr was one of the few to rate permanent quarters in the praetorium.

This evidence of his son's favor, however, did not seem to be pleasing King Ban. "I imagine you can guess why I am here," he said now, his eyes pale and cold.

Bedwyr's eyes, of a much more brilliant blue, glinted, but he did not reply.

"He must marry," Ban said. "I have written you on this subject numberless times. Since it seems that you are so reluctant to broach the subject to the high king, I have come myself."

Bedwyr took another swallow of wine. It was his third cup in the last hour. "Have you any suggestions for our future queen?" he asked flippantly.

King Ban's disapproving frown deepened. "Yes. Maelgwyn's youngest daughter. Gwenhwyfar."

"I didn't know Maelgwyn had any daughters left," Bedwyr said over his wine cup. "How old is she?"

"Seventeen."

Bedwyr's golden brows rose half an inch. "Seventeen and still unwed? What's wrong with her, Father?"

"Nothing is wrong with her," Ban snapped. "She was contracted to wed Magach's son when she was fifteen, but then he got himself killed fighting with Arthur. At present there are no other unwed Welsh princes"—Ban's frown became positively formidable—"except, of course, you."

Bedwyr finally put down his cup. "I have no wish to marry."

"You can please yourself," Ban replied shortly. "I have grandsons enough by your brothers." The pale blue eyes bored into Bedwyr's resistant face. "But the king cannot please himself in this matter. He must marry. Gwenhwyfar is wellborn. I have never met her, but I understand she is very beautiful. She is acceptable to Cador as well as to Wales. And . . ." He paused meaningfully before adding, "Maelgwyn will give one hundred horses from Gaul as her dowry."

"One hundred horses." Bedwyr's eyes were like sapphires.

"Yes."

"Well," said Bedwyr, "Arthur will be in Venta within the week. Good luck to you. And to Gwenhwyfar and her one hundred horses." He reached once more for his wine cup.

King Ban put his hands on his knees, leaned forward, and fixed his son with his most piercing stare. "Will you kindly explain to me why you are so reluctant to broach the subject of marriage to Arthur?" he asked. Bedwyr said nothing. "He has been king for ten years," Ban went on. "He is twenty-six years of age. It is more than time for him to wed."

Bedwyr once more put down his cup and rose from his chair. "He has been rather busy these last ten years," he said to his father over his shoulder from his new place by the window. He could hear that the direction of the rain had changed. Through the translucent, rain-smeared glass Bedwyr could dimly see the lights from the lanterns hanging on the front of the stable.

"It does not take long to get a son," said Ban, King of Dyfed.

"I suppose not." Bedwyr turned back to face the room. "It looks as if the Saxons are finally contained," he offered, hoping to change the subject.

Ban's lined face lightened. "Is it so?"

"It seems so, at any rate. Offa has drawn all his forces back into Kent. And Cynewulf and Cerdic are back in their lairs as well. We may actually have a few seasons of peace before us."

"The Sea Wolves have been driven back to the Saxon shore," Ban said in wonder. "It is a thing that neither Uther nor Ambrosius was able to accomplish."

Bedwyr straightened his shoulders and seemed to come to a decision. "Perhaps this *is* the right time to speak to Arthur about marriage." He began to stride up and down the floor, his long lion's prowl of a walk making the room seem small. "He had a perfect excuse to avoid taking a wife while Igraine ruled for him here in Venta. It would have been difficult for her to give precedence to a younger queen. And Igraine and Merlin did an excellent job of keeping some sort of civil government in place while Arthur was in the field. He could not have done without either of them. But Igraine has been dead for more than a year."

"Bedwyr." The King of Dyfed's voice held a note that halted his son's pacing. "There is nothing . . . wrong with Arthur, is there?"

It was a moment before Bedwyr realized the import of the question. Then: "No!" The violence of his feeling was reflected in the blazing blue of his eyes. "What swine has been telling you that?" he demanded fiercely.

Ban mastered an impulse to back away from his son. It was said that Bedwyr was the most feared man in Britain and right now his father could see why. "No one," he answered hastily. "There has been no breath of scandal, I assure you. It is just that I find his reluctance to marry so odd . . ."

The blue blaze slowly died out of Bedwyr's eyes. "Gods," he said, and ran his fingers once more through his already disordered hair. "There is nothing wrong with Arthur's appetites," he said then in a quieter voice. "In fact, I understand there is a veritable cat fight among the camp followers if a woman is requested for the king's tent. And it would be the same were he not the king, or so they say. No"—Bedwyr's face now looked stern instead of angry—"there is no need to worry on that head, Father."

"Very well then." King Ban was not completely successful in hiding his relief. "When the king arrives in Venta, we will approach him on this matter."

"Not *we*," said Bedwyr instantly. "I want no part in this particular discussion. You and Cador are welcome to the job. And the archbishop, of course. I presume that is why he is here, to talk to Arthur about his 'duty.'"

"The king is a Christian," Ban said stiffly. "I understand Christians are supposed to be guided by their bishop. Dubricius was Cador's idea," he added after a minute.

"Well, I wish you and Cador and the archbishop luck," Bedwyr said cordially. "But leave me out of it. I am his commander of cavalry, not his political or marital adviser."

The King of Dyfed got to his feet and stared at his son irritably. It annoyed him that he, a large man himself, had to look up. "You are supposed to be more than his commander of cavalry. From what I hear, you are supposed to be his friend."

"Oh, I am," came the cheerful reply. "And I should like to keep it that way. Which is why I have no intention, now or ever, of talking to Arthur about marriage."

King Ban gathered his cloak about him and left the room in silent dignity.

Three days later, Arthur the King rode into Venta. The townspeople lined the main steet of the city to welcome him. Bedwyr, waiting on the front steps of the praetorium, could hear the noise of their enthusiastic greeting rolling down the street as the procession came closer. Then the rider on the big black horse came into sight. Behind Arthur rode a picked contingent of heavy cavalry and light horse. The foot soldiers would have been left in their camps outside the city gates.

Bedwyr watched him come and tried, for perhaps the thousandth time, to fathom the secret of Arthur's appeal. He sat relaxed and at ease in the saddle and scarcely seemed to notice the people who were shouting his name. Nor was his preoccupation feigned. He really was not noticing his admirers. He was probably planning the jobs he would give to the army to keep the men busy and out of trouble for the winter.

He never seemed to make any effort to charm, yet no one had been able to move and inspire men as he did. He had taken men from all over the country and welded them into a single fighting unit. Before him, men had fought for their tribes, for their chiefs. They had fought for Rome. These last ten years, they had fought for Britain.

Or they had fought for Arthur. For most of them, there was no difference between the two.

The small procession had almost reached the praetorium, and Arthur's cavalry commander went down the steps officially to greet his king.

Bedwyr was present at the first meeting between Arthur and the kings of Dyfed and Dumnonia. It was the temporary absence of the archbishop that gave Bedwyr the confidence to attend. He reckoned the kings would not raise the one topic he wished to avoid while they were missing one of the most persuasive of their number.

They met in the audience chamber of the praetorium. Arthur, as was his custom, did not use the chair on the raised dais, but joined the men in a circle of chairs placed comfortably close to the brazier that glowed against the cold November air. Arthur did not need a state chair to demonstrate his authority, Bedwyr thought. The quality of his presence was enough.

The meeting was clearly to center on military matters. Cador, who had led Dumnonian troops under Arthur in several engagements, wanted to know the king's future plans. "You have been successful in driving the Sea Wolves back to the coast," the King of Dumnonia said. "That is a great thing. But what are we to do now?"

Arthur looked thoughtfully back at Cador. Then: "I would like to make a treaty with them," he said.

"What!" Ban's voice rang out over Cador's milder protest. "A treaty! You don't mean to push them back into the sea?"

There was a pause. Then Arthur said, quietly and definitely, "We cannot."

In the sudden silence, Bedwyr could hear his father's heavy breathing. Arthur laced his fingers together and waited.

"Will they honor a treaty?" Cador asked. "They are savages," he added with loathing. "Barbarians. They have no honor."

"They are from a race of raiders and destroyers, certainly," Arthur agreed. "But many present-day Saxons were born and bred in Britain. They know no other place. They will not be dislodged. You and I, my lords, must accept the fact that there will always be Saxon kingdoms within Britain."

"Well I, for one, will never accept that!" It was Ban again, looking red in the face and breathing heavily down his nose. "I will never rest content until we push them back across the Narrow Sea to the place from which they came."

"I will be happy to release to you the men of Dyfed," Arthur replied cordially. "You are, of course, welcome to make the attempt."

There was a reverberating silence.

"We will make a treaty with them," Arthur continued, as if Ban's interruption had never occurred, "and clearly define the borders of their land. Then it is our task to make certain the boundaries of these kingdoms are secure and held to."

"They won't stay on the coast forever," said Ban.

Bedwyr stopped breathing. He knew Arthur's thinking on this subject, and he did not think it was wise to share it with his father. *Don't, Arthur,* he said to the king silently.

Arthur's long, slender fingers unlaced themselves and he answered, "It is my job to see to it that they do. You asked about my military plans. I must tell you, my lords, that for the next few years military matters will become secondary. What is needed in Britain is a strong central government." Bedwyr began to breathe again.

Cador frowned ominously. "What do you mean?"

"I mean that the high king must become more than just the war leader. With a season of peace before us, he must become the central civil authority in the country."

Cador's bull-like head was pushed far forward on its thick neck. "You want to make yourself emperor?" he said dangerously.

"No." Arthur's face was perfectly calm. "I want to be High King of Britain, not just Comes Britanniarum. I want to build a capital for this nation that will not be Roman, as is Venta, but purely British. The capital must have barracks for the army, but it is not to be merely an army garrison. It must be a place of government." The light gray eyes looked from Cador to Ban and then back again to Cador. "If we are to be one nation," Arthur said, "then we must have one heart. If we are to treat with other nations, then we must speak with one voice. If we are to rebuild Britain from the devastation of war, then we must have one architect."

"You would cut down the power of the regional kings," said Cador.

"I agree that we need a war leader," Ban put in. His pale eyes raked the slender figure of that war leader from head to toe. "And you have done a good job, I grant you that." Arthur raised a straight black eyebrow and Ban added reluctantly, "You have done what no one else could do. Be content with that. We are perfectly capable of ruling our kingdoms without you."

"Indeed?" Arthur's voice changed note infinitesimally and both kings looked wary. "Have you noticed what has happened to Britain since Rome left, my lords? Most of the towns have fallen into decay, villas have been abandoned, industry has collapsed. The army effort of the last ten years has rebuilt the iron industry, at least, but it must be expanded beyond the mere manufacture of weapons. The roads are in need of major repair. Agriculture has fallen to a sustenance level; it must be revived to a scale that will enable us once more to export wheat. Ships need to be built."

Arthur rested his hands on the arms of his chair. "I do not mean to wrest all authority from the regional kings. You know your tribes and your people's needs. But this country must be restored to a money economy if we are to take our place among the nations of the world. It is economic strength that will ultimately win the fight against the Saxons. And we cannot gain economic strength without a central government."

"Would you use the regional kings as a council?" Cador asked.

"Of course," Arthur replied promptly. "I am *not* planning to make myself emperor. But I think it is essential that we begin to undertake a major rebuilding of our resources, and I think that I am the best person to direct it."

"The roads are in disgraceful condition," Ban said reluctantly.

Cador looked searchingly at the young high king. "Do you really think we are going to have peace?"

"Yes," said Arthur. "I do."

Bedwyr stayed after the two kings had retired for the night. "You certainly knocked them between the eyes," he said to Arthur half-humorously after the door had closed behind his father. "First a treaty with the Saxons, then a new capital with yourself reigning in state over the whole of the country."

"They will have to get used to the idea," Arthur said a little impatiently. "Cador is the best-informed of all the kings. I think he will come to see that what I have proposed is only sensible."

"And then he can convince the others?"

A black eyebrow rose. "Something like that."

"You were very encouraging about the Saxons."

Arthur shrugged and stretched his legs out before him. "If we are lucky, we will have perhaps a hundred more years. But that should be enough."

"You didn't tell them that."

Quite suddenly Arthur grinned. His smile was so rare that when it came its effect was quite extraordinary. "No," he said. "I didn't."

"Good thing." Bedwyr smiled back. "My father, for one, would not appreciate your views on that subject."

"I meant everything else I said, though." Arthur's face was sober once more. "The stronger we are, the longer we will stave off the inevitable. And the inevitable, when it comes, need not be a thing of devastation and terror. The strength of the empire always lay in the influx of new people into it."

"The Saxons are not the Goths," said Bedwyr.

"Give them a hundred more years and they will be as civilized as the Goths. You yourself are not a Christian, but you must see the tremendous civilizing influence of the church. In a sense, the civilizing mission of Rome that my grandfather used to talk so much about has been passed to the church. There was a Patrick for Ireland; there will be an apostle for the Saxons too. And that will make the difference."

"Given time," said Bedwyr.

"That is our job." Arthur leaned back in his chair, looked at Bedwyr from under his lashes, and asked, "What is your father doing in Venta?"

Bedwyr was annoyed to feel the blood rise in his cheeks. "I don't know," he mumbled.

"Ban and Cador. And Archbishop Dubricius too, I understand. They wish to meet with me tomorrow. All three of them."

Bedwyr wished he had a drink in his hand.

"Have they someone particular in mind, Bedwyr?" came the cool voice of the king. "Or is it to be just a general discussion?"

Bedwyr's eyes jerked up.

"I see," said Arthur. "Who is she?"

"One of Maelgwyn's daughters," Bedwyr said reluctantly. "Gwenhwyfar."

There was the faintest of pauses. Then: "A princess from Gwynedd. What else are they offering?"

Bedwyr stared at him. "One hundred horses from Gaul."

The long lashes lifted. "They are serious, then."

"Very serious." Against his better judgment, Bedwyr continued, "You could do worse. She is seventeen and of good blood. Maelgwyn is Christian, so that is all right. My father and Cador clearly approve." He stopped abruptly, aware of the amusement in Arthur's eyes.

"And there are the one hundred horses," the king said.

Bedwyr frowned in perplexity. "I shall never understand you. You have spent the last five years deftly avoiding all mention of marriage. On the one or two occasions when someone dared to raise the subject, you almost took their heads off. Now you are suddenly ready to settle for one hundred horses."

Arthur shrugged. He appeared perfectly relaxed as he lounged back in his chair, but Bedwyr, who knew him very well, could see the tension in his fingers as they clasped the chair's carved arms. "As with the Saxons, one can delay the inevitable for only so long," Arthur said. "I suppose Gwenhwyfar will do as well as anyone. And if I am to create the sort of stable central government I want to, I will need an heir."

The room was very silent. In the light of the oil lamp, Arthur's face looked suddenly tired.

"I have never heard you talk about building a new capital," Bedwyr said slowly. "When did you decide to do that?"

"I have been thinking about it for some time now. Venta is not adequate for the kind of building I have in mind. There is simply not space enough here. And the praetorium is too small to contain the kind of government I have in mind."

Bedwyr was looking worried. "If you do this, Cador won't be the only one to accuse you of trying to make yourself emperor," he warned.

"I don't care what they call me," Arthur returned. "But I will tell you this, Bedwyr." His gray eyes were as cold as ice. "Whether the Celtic kings like it or not, I intend to rule."

Chapter 17

HE would have to marry. As he had told Bedwyr tonight, one could delay the inevitable for just so long. He needed a wife. To give Britain an heir, he needed a wife. To give Britain a queen, he needed a wife.

The king knew he had to marry. It was the private man who recoiled from the thought.

A Welsh princess from Gwynedd. As Bedwyr had said, it could be worse. Such a marriage would ensure the support of Wales. And outside of Dumnonia, Maelgwyn's court was the most cultured and Romanized in the country. This girl would understand very well that she was making a dynastic marriage. She would know what her role in his life was to be.

"Is that all, my lord?" It was Gareth, his body servant, who had finished putting away his clothes. Arthur turned from his brooding contemplation of the scrolls on the desk and gave the boy a faint smile.

"Yes, thank you, Gareth. You may seek your own bed now."

The boy's returning smile was radiant. "Good night, my lord."

"Good night," Arthur replied, and stood looking at the door for a few minutes after it had closed behind the boy. Gareth was . . . what . . . sixteen now. Arthur was conscious of deep surprise. It seemed almost yesterday that the twelve-year-old boy had appeared out of the northern mist and begged to join the army. He remembered quite vividly the look on Gareth's bruised and dirty face as he had clung to the high king's stirrup and refused to be dislodged by Cai.

Sixteen. At sixteen Arthur had been high king. Gareth was too old to continue as his body servant; the time had come for him to take his place among the men. He would ask Bedwyr to take him in hand. Cai already had enough to do.

Cai. He had been wounded in the leg in their last engagement with Cerdic. The wound had not healed and so Cai had been sent to Avalon.

132

Lucky Cai.

Gareth had left a cup of wine for him on the marble table near the brazier, and Arthur moved to pick it up. Cabal, who was sleeping on the rug in front of the glowing coals, lifted his head at his master's approach and then stretched out again, his eyes closing.

Avalon. Avalon of the apple trees. The one place in the world he longed to be, and the one place he could not go.

The Lady of Avalon, that was what she had come to be called these last ten years. She was famous throughout Britain for her healing arts. Half of his injured officers had spent some time at Avalon, and she had returned them all to him in perfect health.

He knew all about her. He knew when she left Avalon to go visit her sister Morgause in Lothian, and when she returned. He had not seen her since the night he had stormed out of her bedroom and almost walked into the river Camm.

He had written to her twice in ten years. Once was to thank her for the pearls she had sent to him before his coronation. And he had written to her when Igraine died and asked her once again to marry him. She had refused.

His grandfather, ill and living now at Avalon, was no longer the chief obstacle standing between them; it was Morgan herself. He had read that clearly in her letter. She had told him, in no uncertain terms, that he must marry elsewhere.

He might as well marry Gwenhwyfar.

The message from Avalon came two weeks after Cador and Ban and the archbishop had left Venta. It was Cai who came riding through the cold winter dusk to tell the king that his grandfather was dying.

"Morgan thinks he has a week or two left at most," Cai said when he and Arthur were alone in the private reception chamber that had belonged to Uther. Cai smoothed the folds of his tunic and straightened his leather belt and refrained from looking at Arthur's face. "He wants to see you."

"I shall go tomorrow," said Arthur. Cai looked at him at last, and seemed relieved by what he saw.

"He is in no pain," he offered. "The seizure, or whatever it was, seems to have passed. He is just very weak. He's . . . old. All of a sudden, Arthur, he is so old."

"He is over seventy," said Arthur. "I suppose we could not expect him to go on forever."

"No, I suppose not."

Arthur went to the table near the window and poured two cups of wine. He brought one back to Cai and handed it to him. As Cai smiled his thanks, Arthur said, "How is the leg? The last time I saw you, you were being carried away in a litter."

Cai's smile turned into a grin. "I remember your face hanging over me. You looked worried and I thought: God, I must be dying for him to look like that."

"I thought you were going to lose the leg," Arthur said grimly.

"So did Morgan, at first. She says it is nothing short of a miracle that the infection cleared."

Arthur seated himself and took a drink of his wine. The room they were sitting in was the room where he had first met his father, more than ten years ago. It looked exactly the same as it had when Uther was alive. Arthur had not spent enough time in Venta to change things. And, too, there had always been Igraine's feelings to consider. He said now, with the careful steadiness he always employed when speaking of her, "Morgan is the miracle. She's healed every man of mine who managed to make it to Avalon alive."

"The local people say she knows magic," Cai said with amusement. "Morgan thinks it's funny."

Arthur was looking at his cup of Samian ware as if he had never seen it before. "Does she still run an infirmary for wounded animals?" he asked, his voice sounding a little muffled. He very rarely permitted himself to talk about Morgan.

"Oh, yes," came Cai's easy reply. "The dog she has now makes Horatius look like a purebred."

At that Arthur looked up, his gray eyes unusually bright. "Do you want to come with me tomorrow?"

Cai shook his head. "I said my good-byes to Merlin. And I am needed here, I hope."

"You are needed." Arthur put down his wine cup and came to place a hand on Cai's broad shoulder. "I missed you," he said. "It's good to have you back."

Arthur left Venta early the following morning, and he rode alone. Bedwyr had protested that decision, had pressed Arthur to take an armed escort. Arthur had refused.

"It is insane for the High King of Britain to be riding along open roads with no protection," Bedwyr raged to Cai the night before Arthur's departure. "Suppose he is attacked by a band of thieves? We can't afford to have him killed or injured because of a foolish whim."

"I pity the poor band of thieves that attacks Arthur," Cai replied humorously. "He may not be as flamboyant as you, Bedwyr the Lion, but he is fully as dangerous. You know that." Then, when Bedwyr merely grunted and continued to look worried: "There are times, Bedwyr, when we must give him room to breathe." The humorous note had disappeared from Cai's voice. "He needs to be alone. Don't harass him."

"I wouldn't dare," Bedwyr retorted. "He got that very still look on his face while I was talking to him and I had sense enough to make a hasty retreat before I had my head taken off. But I still don't like it, Cai." He frowned. "Do you think we could send a small escort to follow him at a discreet distance?"

"Are you serious?" Cai asked incredulously. "Against his direct orders?"

"No, I suppose we can't," Bedwyr agreed with obvious regret. "If he ever found out . . ."

"Exactly. Leave matters as they are, Bedwyr. Arthur is perfectly capable of getting himself to Avalon safely." He sighed. "It's what happens *after* he arrives that concerns me."

"He has promised to marry Gwenhwyfar. My father and Archbishop Dubricius have gone to bring the good news to Gwynedd."

"Good news," repeated Cai. "Yes, I suppose it is good news. Come on," he said then a little desperately, "let's you and I go somewhere and get drunk."

Arthur was not thinking of either of his commanders as he traveled the road to Avalon that morning. He was remembering the last time he had made this journey, when Dun had been merely a colt and they had cantered through the night as if their very lives had depended on reaching Avalon before dawn.

Ten years ago.

He was not the boy he had been the last time he had ridden to Avalon. Part of him would always belong to Morgan, but he had made his life without her. As she had made hers without him. Perhaps it was time for them to meet again, to meet as adults come into the fullness of their powers, no longer desperately unhappy children fearful of facing life alone.

The bare apple trees looked forlorn in the thin winter sunlight. For some strange reason, he had expected to find them in bloom. In his memories of Avalon, the apple trees were always in bloom. Which was ridiculous, of course. He set his mouth at his own sentimental stupidity and lifted Dun into a canter. He was suddenly eager to see the villa before darkness should begin to creep in.

They slowed pace as they came down the avenue and so walked sedately into the villa's courtyard. Arthur looked around, at the stone so clearly etched against the pale sunlight, at the light reflecting off the glazed windows. He remembered with amazing vividness how the villa had looked to him the first time he had ridden into this courtyard behind Merlin.

The front door of the house opened and two people came out. The first he recognized immediately as Marcus. The second was Ector. The door closed and they started across the courtyard toward him. He closed his eyes briefly. Thank God he was not going to have to meet her again in the mercilessly public view of the courtyard.

"Arthur!" Ector was exclaiming with a delighted smile. Then, remembering: "My lord king."

Arthur grinned, dismounted, and gave the old man a rare embrace. "It's good to see you, Ector," he said, and unthinkingly went on, "It's good to be home."

They took him immediately to see his grandfather.

"Arthur?" Merlin said from where he lay on the bed.

"How are you feeling, sir?" Arthur asked. He took the fragile old hand, so white and blue-veined, into his own strong grasp. He had not seen his grandfather since Merlin had suffered a seizure in Venta in the spring and Morgan had brought her father home to Avalon. Arthur was suddenly glad that his grandfather had got to see the apple trees in bloom.

"I'm feeling old," said Merlin. One side of his face looked stiffer than the other and his speech was slightly slurred.

Arthur brought a chair close to the bed and sat down. He told his grandfather the one piece of news he thought would cheer him. "I am going to marry the princess Gwenhwyfar."

Merlin's blue eyes flickered with gladness. "A good choice," he said after a minute. "Maelgwyn is a good man."

"Yes," agreed the king.

There was a pause as Merlin collected his thoughts. "I am leaving Avalon to Morgan, Arthur. She will never marry and she must have her own property. I look to you to safeguard it for her."

"Of course," Arthur answered steadily.

The pale, blue-veined fingers plucked at the red wool blanket. "I wish I had something to leave to you, my boy."

Arthur's reply was measured, but the feeling he was holding in check was still visible. "You leave me a kingdom," he said, "and the skills with which to lead it. You leave me a dream. I only hope, Grandfather, that I can bring it to fruition for you."

Merlin's eyes searched the carefully disciplined face of his grandson. At last he said in his slow, slurred speech, "I never expected you to forgive me."

Arthur bowed his head. "It was not your fault," he answered with difficulty. Merlin said nothing, just looked at the top of that ink-black head. This was a subject that had not been raised between them for ten long years.

"All my life, for almost as long as I remember, you have been there behind me," Arthur finally said in a muffled voice. He raised his head and the emotion he had been so carefully guarding was naked in his brilliant eyes. "What am I going to do without you?" he asked. And Merlin, holding out his arms to receive the slim, hard-muscled body of his grandson, was suddenly, fiercely, happy.

Morgan returned to the villa shortly after dark and was met by Ector with the news that Arthur had arrived

"He was with your father for almost an hour," Ector told her. "Merlin looked . . . very peaceful after the king left."

"Where is Arthur now?" she asked.

"In his room, changing for dinner." Ector grinned. "The cook is turning out the kitchen for him."

Morgan forced a smile, said, "Well, I'd better change too," and began to walk slowly toward the bedroom wing of the villa.

It was hard to breathe and she unpinned the brooch that fastened her cloak as she approached her bedroom door. She had known, of course, that he would come. She had just not expected him quite so quickly. She might have known, she thought a little ruefully. He was famous for the speed with which he moved his army. It was one of the reasons for his success against the Saxons.

Morgan stopped in front of her door and looked down at her old tunic. She had been visiting several of the farmworkers' children who were ill, and her clothing reflected the nature of her business. She should wait, change into her best clothes, brush her hair . . . She walked briskly to the next door on the corridor and knocked.

There was no noise from within, but suddenly the door opened and he was there.

"Ector told me you had come," she said without preamble. "I thought it best to get our initial meeting over in private."

"Come in," was all he said. She walked to the middle of the room and heard him close the door behind her. She took a deep breath, and then turned.

He had not moved from the door. The lamps in his room had been filled and lit, and they cast a warm glow of light by which the two of them could take stock of each other.

He was different, Morgan thought immediately. The thick black hair was the same—it had even fallen across his forehead in the way she remembered. The eyes were the same light gray, the nose was as before, the bones of cheek and jaw had not altered, but he was different. Not just older either. Harder. More powerful. Infinitely more powerful. She felt it immediately.

He shook his hair back from his brow in an achingly familiar gesture and said, "You haven't changed at all."

She thought she smiled. Her hair was clinging to the wool of her tunic and she put up a small, capable hand to smooth it back behind her ears. "I know," she said. "Untidy as ever."

The gray eyes were searching her face. He ignored her attempt at humor and said in a totally different voice, "How are you, Morgan?"

The hard knot that had been lodged in her stomach ever since Cai left for Venta dissolved. This time she knew she smiled. "I'm fine," she said. "Most of the time."

He did not return the smile. Instead he drew a short breath and said in an abrupt voice, "I have promised to marry the princess Gwenhwyfar."

"Good," she answered immediately. "I hope you told Father. He will be delighted."

"Yes, I did." Finally he left his post at the door and came toward her. "Almighty God," he said. "Morgan. How I have missed you."

"I know." He was holding her so tightly that her ribs hurt. Her cheek pressed into the hollow of his shoulder. He was taller than he had been at sixteen.

"I couldn't come here," he was saying over her head. "I was afraid to come here."

"I know," she said again. "I always understood."

"Of course you did." His arms finally loosened and he looked down into her upturned face with hungry eyes. After a minute: "Thank you for Cai. I thought I was going to lose him."

The large brown eyes looked back at him as only Morgan could look. "The leg was very bad. I think it was prayer more than art that saved it."

"Or magic," he added gravely.

The brown eyes brimmed with amusement. "Have you heard that rumor? I'm thinking of adopting some appropriate garb—a druid's gown perhaps. What do you think?"

He grinned and suddenly looked sixteen again. "I'll make you the official king's magician." They were both laughing when Justina knocked on the door to tell Morgan she was going to be late for dinner.

Dinner was just the two of them and Ector. At first the old steward was very careful to call the king "my lord." Then Arthur said plaintively, "In this whole world I can number but five people who call me Arthur. Surely you are not going to reduce the count to four?"

Ector beamed. After a minute Morgan said sadly, "It is going to be reduced to four shortly enough, Arthur."

An identical shadow marked all their faces. "I know," Arthur answered. "I saw him this afternoon."

"Eight months ago he was running things in Venta," said Ector. "It happened so . . . quickly." He stared broodingly at his own big hand before him on the table. "He is ten years older than I," he added.

Morgan and Arthur exchanged a glance and said nothing.

Ector looked up. "I always thought he would go on forever."

"I think we all thought that," Arthur replied.

Silence fell. Morgan toyed with the oysters on her plate. They were one of Arthur's favorite foods and had been served tonight in his honor. "Eat them," Arthur said to her, "or your cook will be very insulted."

She looked up and the shadow lifted from her eyes. Defty she transfered the oysters from her plate to his. "They were served for you," she said. "You eat them." She had always given him her oysters. They smiled at each other and Arthur began to eat.

During the main course, which consisted of roast boar, another of Arthur's favorites, and venison with apple sauce made from the Avalon apples, and vegetables from the Avalon kitchen garden, the topic of conversation turned to Arthur's war against the Saxons.

"We heard that you have driven Offa back to Kent and Cynewulf to Sussex," Ector said. "Is it true? And will they be willing to keep to their own boundaries in the future, Arthur?"

"I think so," Arthur replied. He was clearly enjoying his roast boar. "I hope so. But I am not about to dismiss my army just yet."

"The Saxon bretwaldas have never joined forces, have they?" Morgan asked. "They have always fought separately."

Arthur put down his knife and looked at her. "You have just exposed my worst nightmare. One of the reasons we have won is that we are united and they are divided. If they ever decide to forget their rivalries and join together, then there will be serious trouble." He forced himself to look away from her small, serious face. After a minute he turned to Ector and said, "Cai has been one of the main reasons for our success these past years."

Ector's weather-beaten face lit with pride. "I am glad he has been useful to you," he answered modestly.

"*Useful!*" said Arthur, and Ector abandoned his attempt at modesty and glowed unrestrainedly. Arthur continued, "It is Cai who has done all the engineering work for the refortification of the old hill forts around the country. And that, let me tell you, has been a major reason for our success. If it were not for the key forts and for the iron forges we set up in them in order to produce the weapons we need, Offa and Cynewulf and Cerdic would not be penned on the Saxon shore today."

"Half of all warfare is engineering," Morgan said. She wrinkled her nose. "I think I remember someone saying that to me once. Or twice."

His eyes glimmered with amusement. "What a boring conversationalist I must have been. If it was not engineering, it was cavalry."

"You couldn't help it," Morgan said philosophically. "It was Father's fault, really. All those experts he used to import for your instruction! My favorite was the one who absconded with the statue of Venus from the garden."

"He was the engineer," Arthur replied promptly. "Only an engineer could have moved that statue."

Ector chuckled. "Do you remember . . ." he began, and the two of them looked at him with identically startled eyes. For a moment they had forgotten that he was there.

Chapter 18

GLASTONBURY Abbey, the foremost monastery in Britain, was situated not far from Avalon, and the following day two of its most important monks arrived to visit Merlin. Gildas, the abbot, was the son of a prince and famous throughout Britain for his shrewd administration. Brother Iltud, the son of peasants, was almost equally famous for his simple holiness. Merlin had always been a generous patron of the monastery and evidently Glastonbury felt that all possible attention was due him in his illness.

They had come to see Merlin, but Morgan thought that Gildas had also hoped to meet the king. The abbot was a sharp-faced man in his middle years, and he was ambitious, both for himself and for his monastery. Arthur, however, was not in a mood to be approached. Morgan gave the monks three minutes before she took them to the bedroom wing to see her father.

Arthur was waiting for her when she returned to the family salon, and he persuaded her to come out with him for a ride. He wanted to see the estate again.

Morgan sent word to the stables that they would require horses; then she and Arthur changed into outdoor clothing. They met again in the clear cold air of the courtyard, and Morgan's dog, a shaggy orange-brown mongrel with crooked ears and a distinct limp, joined them as well. Arthur looked at him in wonder. "Cai warned me," he said. "You have outdone yourself, Morgan."

"His name is Gwyll," she replied tranquilly. "He's very smart."

Arthur snapped his fingers and the dog came to him immediately. Arthur looked up at Morgan and saw that she too was remembering his first meeting with Horatius. They smiled at each other and Arthur bent to rub the dog's ears.

"You didn't bring Cabal with you," Morgan said after a minute.

He shook his head. "He's getting old. He rides in the wagons now most of the time. It would have been too much for him to follow me down here."

Morgan looked for a moment at the bent black head and didn't say anything. Finally Arthur looked up from the dog. "Are those still my breeches?" he asked.

She laughed. To ride out in the cold weather she always wore wool breeches, and she had inherited all of Arthur's outgrown pairs when they were children. "No," she said. "I had to have some made. Yours all wore out."

He was going to reply but at that moment there came the sound of horses' hooves and they looked up to see two ponies being led across the courtyard. Arthur was giving Dun a day of rest and so he too was riding a pony.

The slave who was leading the horses knew Arthur from the old days, and his seamed old face was bright with pleasure. Arthur spoke to him for perhaps five minutes, with far more attention than he had accorded the abbot, Morgan thought with amusement, and then they mounted and rode out of the courtyard together, with Gwyll trotting at Morgan's pony's heels. They wore several tunics under their cloaks for warmth, but in true British fashion, they were both bareheaded. Their breaths hung white in the cold clear air.

"Let's ride around the farms first," Morgan suggested, and Arthur agreed.

It was pure joy to be with her again, Arthur thought, their ponies walking side by side, the winter sun shining on her lovely long hair. The hard ground crunched under the ponies' hooves and Gwyll went on occasional expeditions in chase of a bird or a squirrel. Without his having to ask, she told him all about herself, about the villa, about her animals and her study of herbs and flowers, about the people who came to see her. He listened hungrily. He wanted to know everything.

One thing she did not mention, and he brought it up himself after they had been out for an hour. "You go to Lothian every summer." Their ponies were picking their way single file along the river. Arthur was in front and had made the remark over his shoulder, so did not see the frightened look that flared briefly in her eyes.

"Yes," she answered after an infinitesimal pause. "Morgause and I became quite close that winter you were fighting Lot. I try to go north to see her once a year."

The track widened and he waited for her to come abreast of him again. "It has worked out well," he asked when she was beside him once more, "this marriage of Morgause and Pellinore?"

"Yes." She knew immediately that something was disturbing him and fear stabbed at her heart again. "Why do you ask?" Her voice sounded slightly breathless.

"I just wondered. It has been to my benefit, certainly. Pellinore has kept Lothian loyal to me for all these years. I have been able to fight the Saxons without worrying about a knife in my back." He shrugged very slightly. "I suppose that is my justification."

She frowned. "Justification for what, Arthur?"

"For killing Lot, of course."

She searched his face. "You had no choice. He raised an army against you."

"I know that," he answered, "and you know that. But it is a hard thing to explain to a woman and her children."

Finally she understood. "Is that why you have not gone to Lothian for all these years?" she asked. His absence was a fact of which she was well aware, and for which she had been profoundly grateful. The youngest Lothian child, Mordred, bore a startling likeness to the high king.

"I cannot be overly popular with Morgause or her sons," Arthur answered her. "And I did not think it fair to put Morgause into the position of having to receive me."

Morgan's fine brows lifted in irony. "Arthur. Morgause's sons are all mad to leave Lothian and come fight with you."

She could see how that stunned him. He stopped his pony and stared at her. "I thought they would hate me," he said.

Irony curled her lips. "They adore you. Gawain most of all. His chief aim in life is to ride with your cavalry." Then, as he continued to look bewildered: "Don't you know that every wellborn boy in Britain dreams of riding by your side?"

His hair had slipped down over his forehead and he pushed it back with his hand. She looked away from him to where Gwyll was chasing a squirrel. Mordred's hair grew in exactly the same way. "Morgause, of course, finds their enchantment a little difficult to understand," she added. "It was thoughtful of you not to make her receive you."

It was a lie. Morgause was perfectly happy in her new marriage. Morgan doubted that she spared a thought for Lot or the manner of his death. But at all costs, Arthur must be kept from Lothian. From Mordred. Morgan continued to watch Gwyll. She did not think that she had ever lied to Arthur before. She could feel him watching her; he knew something was wrong. "Don't be surprised, however, if your cousin Gawain should appear someday in Venta," she said with an attempt at lightness. "Pellinore is trying to teach him to be King of Lothian, but Gawain's heart is with you."

"I would be happy to see him," he answered. He was still watching her. She called to Gwyll and touched her pony into a walk once more. "You didn't kill Lot," she said abruptly. "Cai did."

"It's the same thing. Cai is my man."

"I think, in that particular thing, he was Father's man."

That surprised him. He had long thought Merlin was the one who gave Cai the order to kill Lot. But how did Morgan . . . ?

Finally she looked at him. "I'm a witch," she said. "Didn't you know?"

Her eyes were a clear, limpid brown and he grinned. "I think you may be, after all."

"Do you want to go to the valley next?" she asked, and he said that he did.

When they returned to Avalon later in the day it was to learn that Merlin had suffered another seizure.

It took him two more days to die. He never fully regained consciousness, but his fingers would return a slight pressure if someone held his hand, so Arthur and Morgan and Ector took turns sitting with him. Both Morgan and Arthur were with him, holding a hand on either side of the bed, when he died.

The day they buried Merlin, it was raining. Father Gildas and Brother Iltud had both stayed at the villa, and so were there to recite the prayers for the dead. Afterward the small group by the grave walked through the winter-sodden day back to the warmth of the house.

Dinner was silent. Everyone was tired, and everyone was painfully conscious of the empty seat at the head of the table where Merlin had always sat. The seat had been empty for a long time, of course, but now its emptiness was permanent. The abbot, who had been hoping to have a private word with the king, took one look at Arthur's preoccupied face and decided to wait for a more auspicious time. He and Brother Iltud excused themselves immediately after dinner and went to their rooms.

Ector joined Arthur and Morgan in the family salon, but he looked exhausted. When Morgan suggested that he go to bed also, he gave her a grateful look and took himself off without further persuasion.

Morgan and Arthur sat on in silence, listening to the rain drumming on the roof. Finally Arthur said, "I'm glad he came back here in the spring. I'm glad he saw the apple trees in bloom again."

"Yes," said Morgan softly. She was sitting on a stool in front of his chair and now she bent her head forward and covered her eyes with her hand. Her hair parted and through the silken strands Arthur could see the white nape of her neck.

His defenses were down, or perhaps it wouldn't have happened. But he was tired and heartsore and he looked at her neck and he could feel its soft tenderness under his hand, could feel the shining brown hair falling over his wrist. Suddenly it was more than he could bear. He thought he had closed that particular door behind him, but he knew now that he had not.

"Morgan," he said. "This is no good. I can't do it. I thought I could, but I can't."

Her head swung around. She looked into his eyes and knew instantly what he meant. He saw her swallow. "You have to, Arthur." Her voice was not nearly as steady as his had been. "You . . . have to."

"Why?"

She stared at him like a dumb animal and did not answer.

"I wrote to you when Igraine died," he went on in the same careful, steady voice, "and again asked you to marry me. You were quite emphatic in your refusal." She could hear from the very carefulness of his voice how that refusal had hurt him. "I thought I had accepted that. But I haven't. And you never told me why."

"You know why, Arthur. We went through all that once before."

"That was ten years ago. Things have changed. My position has changed. No one is likely to raise a rebellion against me now. So why can't I marry whom I please? If there is any talk of incest, it will quickly pass over. The church will give us its blessing. I've saved enough monasteries these last ten years for it to owe me something."

She tried to look away from him and could not. He was training the full force of his will upon her, and she could not look away. "I can't marry you, Arthur," she said. "I can't."

He was relentless. "Why not? Tell me why not."

She drew a long shuddering breath and told him the truth. "Because I cannot bear children and you need sons."

That shocked him, as she knew it would. There was a line deep as a sword cut between his brows. "How do you know that?"

She pushed her hair behind her ears. "Oh, I have seen doctors. And

I know enough about these matters myself now. I cannot bear children, Arthur. That is why I will not marry you."

She could see him assimilating this information. His frown became less deep. "There is Gawain," he said thoughtfully. "I could name Gawain as my heir."

"No!" She was on her feet now. The stool rocked with the violence of her movement. "No," she repeated in a quieter voice. "You must have your own sons, Arthur. And I cannot give them to you."

"Morgan." He too was on his feet. The frown was completely gone and she could see that he was preparing to deal with her, to convince her, to win her over. He thought he could reassure her. He was wrong. He took her two cold hands into his and looked down into her eyes. "My dearest love"—his voice was very gentle—"can't you see? Don't you understand? I don't care."

Her voice was full of the bitterness that filled her heart. "But I do, Arthur," she said. "I do."

Still he did not understand. "Britain is filled with princes who can succeed me," he said reasonably. "The next high king does not have to be of my getting."

She let her hands lie lax in his. "*You* are Britain. And if you do not leave an heir by right of birth, we will be back to chaos and dissension and the tribal kings fighting among themselves while Britain goes down to the dark. I told you once before, I will not be responsible for that."

He dropped her hands. At last he understood. She looked away from his face. "I wish I were a farmer or an innkeeper," he said with a bitterness that matched her own. "You would marry me then."

She shook her head. "Don't wish to be other than what you are. It is you I love."

He turned away from her and walked to the empty wicker chair where Merlin had been accustomed to sit. "Marry Gwenhwyfar," she said to his back, "and have a dozen sons for Britain."

He ran his fingers over the high back of the chair. "I am not married to Gwenhwyfar yet." He turned to look at her, his face white and very set.

She could feel herself begin to tremble. The intensity of his look was like a blow. "Arthur . . ." she said. Her knees would scarcely hold her up. "Would it make it better?" she asked. "Or worse?"

His hair had fallen forward over his forehead. His eyes were terrible. "Nothing can make it worse."

She bent her head to hide from that look.

"Morgan." No one ever said her name as he did. She heard him move and then he was holding her against him, holding her and kissing her as if she were life itself to him. She swayed against him, every part of her being, body and soul, responding to that kiss.

Right or wrong, wise or foolish, she didn't know. And she no longer cared.

The last time they had lain together on her bed, they had been boy and girl, with the world opening before them like a flower waiting to be plucked. They were ten years older now, and this was not the joyous, almost carefree lovemaking they had shared before. This was intense, hungry, driven. And yet, after the almost desperate passion there was still the one thing that they had always found with one another and with no one else. Peace.

Arthur held her against him and gently kissed the top of her head. Her hair always smelled like lavender.

This was his home, his mooring place, his land of heart's desire. Here in her arms, and nowhere else. It was such perfect peace, such infinite happiness, to be able to hold her, to be still with her, to be simply and wholly together.

All those other times, when his young male body had driven him to take some other woman to his bed, there had been only physical relief and then an intense desire to be alone.

He felt her lips against his throat, his shoulder. He slid his hand under her hair and ran it down the length of her back and over her hip. The feel of her skin, her small, perfect bones, was the most beautiful thing in the world to him.

He turned her over, unfolded her, kissed her eyes, her mouth, her throat. To have her . . . to love her . . . He sank into her slowly and her breath was deep and slow next to his ear. He said her name and she answered and then they were lost in each other again.

The rain had stopped by early morning when it was time for him to return to his own room. As he tore himself away from her and walked to the door, he knew he had been wrong in what he had said to her earlier in the family salon. He had made it worse, for both of them.

Chapter 19

ARTHUR was unapproachable for two weeks after he returned to Venta from Avalon. His captains attributed his vile mood to natural grief for the death of Merlin, and did their best to keep out of his way. This tactic was made easier by the fact that the king spent most of his time in his rooms, working at his desk.

At the end of two weeks he sent for Cai and handed him a scroll. "Here are the plans for our new capital city," he said. "I want you to look them over."

Cai looked at Arthur, then bent his head over the drawings that were on the scroll. Minutes passed. Finally Cai looked up. "When you said you were going to build, you meant it."

The king's still face never changed. "I want it done in two years."

"Two years." Cai went back to looking at the scroll. "Where is this capital to be located?" he asked, his eyes still on the drawings.

Arthur got to his feet. "Go and get your cloak," he said, "and I'll show you."

They left Venta within the hour, with an escort of five men, and took the road to Amesbury. When they turned south, on the Roman road to Durovarium, Cai glanced at Arthur but said nothing. Except for a few brief comments, the king had been silent ever since they took horse. It was when they veered west, off the Roman road and onto a narrow, rutted track, that Cai could not help an exclamation.

Arthur gave him a cool look. "We are not going to Avalon," he said. "We're going to the old hill fort."

The old hill fort. Cai's hazel eyes widened. He pictured the drawings Arthur had shown him. "Of course," he said slowly. "It's the perfect place."

"We'll see," said Arthur briefly, and put his horse into a canter.

The place they referred to was an old Celtic fort which had been abandoned shortly after the Roman occupation of Britain. It was but twelve miles from Avalon, and Cai and Arthur had occasionally ridden their ponies there when they were children.

The track they were following took them right to the hill in question, which rose about five hundred feet before leveling off to a plateau on top. There were still earthwork defenses mounded around the hill's circumference. They had played on those defenses when they were boys.

"We can reinforce the earthworks," Arthur said as they walked slowly around them. "But I want a wall built as well. An unmortared stone wall, sixteen feet thick, with blocks of Roman masonry to reinforce it." He picked up a stick from the ground, and as they walked, he pointed. "Guard towers to go here"—they walked some more—"here . . . and here." They came to the point of easiest ascent. "The gate will be here," he said, "with a gatehouse."

They left their horses and the escort and began to climb the hill. "I want a cobbled road to go from the gates to the plateau," Arthur explained. They topped the steepest part of the hill. The ground here was uneven, but buildable. "Here will be the barracks"—the stick pointed—"and here the houses for the officers." Cai nodded. "The stable blocks will be on the far side of the hill, with paddocks and a riding school."

They reached the plateau. The wind was very cold on the top and Cai pulled his cloak around him. The view of the surrounding country was excellent. To the northwest Glastonbury Tor, that strange hill which jutted out of the island where the monastery was situated, was clearly visible. To the southwest stretched the lands of Avalon.

"I always thought this hill was the perfect location for a fortified city," Arthur said.

Cai had been here as many times as Arthur, but the military possibilities of the place had never been one of his preoccupations. He looked around now, not with the eyes of a boy but with the eyes of an engineer. He looked at the ancient earthworks heaped around the edges of the plateau, at the uneven ground below where Arthur had planned the military enclave, at the steep hill below that. The plateau here at the top would easily hold a great hall, a variety of smaller buildings, and gardens. He looked back at the king. "You were right," he said.

"Can you build it in two years?"

"The buildings are to be of timber?"

"Yes."

"And I can conscript as many men as I need from the army to work on it?"

"Yes."

Cai looked again, this time calculating drainage. At a little distance from the foot of the hill, on the west, flowed the river Camm.

"Yes," he said. "I think I can do it in two years."

Arthur smiled at him. It was the first smile Cai had seen since the king returned from Avalon. "I'll get Gerontius in from Luguvallium to help you," he said. "And I'll keep Bedwyr out of your way."

Cai raised his eyebrow, an imitation of Arthur's own look that had been unconsciously adopted by all his officers. "And how do you plan to do that?" he inquired ironically. When Bedwyr was not fighting, he tended to organize ferocious games that often left half the cavalry incapacitated.

All the humor left Arthur's face. "I'll send him into Wales," he said, "to collect the Princess Gwenhwyfar for me."

When her father had first told her she was to marry the high king, Gwenhwyfar had been happy. For too long she had been an unmarried daughter, and she was weary of her single state. There was no honor in being a princess and unwed. It was flattering of course that her father valued her too highly to offer her to a man whose rank was less distinguished than her own, but you could not take your rank to bed with you at night. Gwenhwyfar was more than ready for a husband.

The court of Gwynedd was delighted that they were to give Britain a queen. The women, in particular, went immediately to work. The wedding was set for the spring, and all through the long, dark winter the women wove and cut and stitched and sewed, making clothing and blankets and pillows and wall hangings to send to Venta when their princess went east to wed the king.

At first Gwenhwyfar had been happy, but as the sewing piled up and the snow melted from the mountains, the reality of the marriage began to set in. She had never been more than twenty miles from home, and now she was to go out of Gwynedd completely, to a place that was not even Wales. She was to be queen of all Britain. What had sounded marvelous in the fall was fearful in the spring.

Her father was very explicit about her duties. "Arthur needs sons," he said. "That is your role, Gwenhwyfar. Give him sons, and all will be well."

Arthur. She had heard the name for as long as she could remember.

Arthur. The king. What was he like? she wondered. He would be her husband and she did not even know what he looked like. She asked Peredur, her brother, who had fought under the king for several years. It was a mild afternoon and the wet, heavy snow was falling from the trees and the brooks were rushing down the mountainside. Soon now the passes would be open and she would be able to travel to Venta for her wedding.

"He's more Roman than Celt," her brother answered. "Very dark, not overly tall . . ." Then, when she looked disappointed, "I'll tell you this, Gwenhwyfar, he may not be a big man, but when he is present, you don't look at anyone else."

"But is he handsome, Peredur?"

At that he grinned and put out a finger to flick her cheek. "He's as beautiful as you are," he answered teasingly. Which told her nothing at all.

A messenger came to Gwynedd at the end of March. The high king sent word that he was sending Prince Bedwyr, with a suitable retinue, to escort the Princess Gwenhwyfar and her wedding party to Venta. The marriage ceremony itself would take place in mid-May, with Archbishop Dubricius officiating.

Gwenhwyfar's women were almost as excited by the prospect of seeing Bedwyr as they would have been if Arthur himself were coming. Bedwyr's exploits were already legend in Wales.

It was Olwen, one of the young girls who companioned Gwenhwyfar, who was the chief source of their information about Bedwyr. Olwen's brother had ridden with the cavalry for four years past, and in the two quick visits he had made home during that time he had been full of stories. Olwen, herself a born storyteller, never tired of recounting Culwych's exploits with Bedwyr.

The favorite tale of all the girls was the story of the cavalry's escape from Cerdic the previous winter. Olwen's voice would take on a mesmerizing cadence when she told that story, and the rest of the girls would sit big-eyed and attentive while their busy fingers stilled on loom and needle.

"Prince Bedwyr and his men were trapped in the wild mountains by the whole of the Saxon host under Cerdic," Olwen would invariably begin. "There was not food enough for man or beast, and the winter was deadly cold. There was nowhere for them to go, with the mountains at their back and the Saxons, with ten times their number, guarding the only route of their escape." Olwen's slim fingers gestured, conjuring up a Saxon camp. "The Sea Wolves were settled comfortably in their warm camps, do you see, just waiting for Prince Bedwyr to surrender or to die of starvation and cold."

They had heard this story many times before, and still it caught them. As Olwen's voice deepened, they all sat up, listening with breathless attention. "Then, one terrible winter night, when the mountain coldness was at its fiercest, and the hunger was sharp in their bellies, and the Saxon fires were burning bright and cheerful in the darkness, Prince Bedwyr gathered his men about him. They must break through the Sea Wolves, he said, or they would die. And so they mounted their horses, now thin and savage from lack of food, they grasped their weapons, and they charged down the snowy mountainside."

Olwen's dark gray eyes went around the circle of faces. "There were ten times their number in the Saxon camp, but they slashed their way through it, killing men with their lances, their axes, their heavy swords. The Saxons fought back, but they could do nothing against Prince Bedwyr. Our men stampeded through the camp, leapt their horses over the twenty-foot river that backed it, and were free in the world."

A general sigh of contentment ran around the circle of girls. They picked up their neglected work.

"Culwych says that no man in Britain but Prince Bedwyr could have led such a charge," Olwen concluded. "They were three hundred against three thousand. And two hundred of them got through."

"They say he is the most feared man in all Britain," one of the other girls contributed. "There is no one who has his physical strength, his prowess in arms."

A tall dark-haired girl looked sideways at Gwenhwyfar, who had been very quiet for the last half-hour. "Not even the king?" the girl asked.

"Ah, the king." It was Olwen who answered. She looked at Gwenhwyfar as well.

The flames picked out the fire in the princess's glorious hair. She looked back at Olwen and said coolly, "Yes, Olwen. What does your brother say of the king?"

Olwen smiled. "My lady," she said. "He says they admire and fear Prince Bedwyr. But they would walk barefoot over hot coals for the king."

It was a cold and blowy March day, with racing clouds periodically darkening the sun, when Bedwyr and his party rode into Dinas Emrys, Maelgwyn's chief stronghold in Gwynedd. Earth and timber ramparts surrounded the entire enclosure of Dinas Emrys, and anyone seeking admittance had to go through the gate. Olwen happened to be near the gatehouse on an errand when Bedwyr and his troop arrived, and she ran all the way back to the women's house to tell the princess.

"They are taking him to your father's hall, of course," she reported breathlessly to Gwenhwyfar. "I do not know when they will be sending for you, but you should make ready, Princess."

There was the usual circle of girls around the hearth, sewing, and every face lit with anticipation. "What does he look like?" one asked, voicing the thought that was in everyone's mind.

Olwen, the storyteller, drew a long, preparatory breath. Before she could begin to speak, however, Gwenhwyfar cut in. "We do not want a saga, Olwen. We just want to know what he looks like. Briefly, please."

Olwen's face fell. "Well, he is big," she began reluctantly, hating to part with the list of giants she had been ready to cite. "The biggest man I ever saw. His hair is bright as the sun." A little warmth crept into her voice. "His eyes are blue as—" Gwenhwyfar cut her off again. "That will do, Olwen. Doubtless we will all get a chance to see him for ourselves shortly." She stood up and looked pointedly at her ordinary gown and tunic. "Perhaps someone would help me to change?"

She was dressed and ready when the summons came. She was to come to the king's hall in order to be presented to Prince Bedwyr, the high king's emissary who had come to escort her to her wedding.

Gwenhwyfar smoothed her embroidered tunic and adjusted her soft leather belt. She did not once glance in the polished metal that served her as a mirror. Gwenhwyfar had never had to be concerned about her appearance. For as long as she remembered, she had known she was beautiful. Olwen laid a cloak around her shoulders and, head held high, she went out to meet her future.

He was standing on her father's hearth, surrounded by smaller men, and she understood immediately Olwen's desire for embellishment. Seeing him, one believed instantly every tale one had ever heard about him. He was the sort of man who could ride down an entire army.

He was walking toward her, her father by his side. When Maelgwyn finished speaking, she gave Bedwyr her hand. "Welcome to Dinas Emrys, Prince," she said. And looked, with unmaidenly candor, into his face.

It was a handsome, arrogant face, with vividly blue eyes and a strong, sensual mouth. He was looking at her the way men always did and she slowly lowered her lashes to screen her long green eyes. He had forgotten to return her hand and she gently withdrew it from his enormous grasp.

"Thank you, Princess," he answered her at last. His voice was very deep. She was a tall woman, but he towered over her. He cleared his throat. "The roads are muddy, but passable," he said. He was talking to her father now.

"Good," said Maelgwyn. "We will be ready to leave within the week."

The day before they were to leave for Venta, Gwenhwyfar and Bedwyr went for a ride together. Maelgwyn's stronghold might be a defended fort, but life in Wales was actually very peaceful. Outside the gates of Dinas Emrys there were extensive farmlands, worked by free farmers and Maelgwyn's tenants. There were pastures, with sheep and cattle grazing placidly under the brightening spring sun. Two of Maelgwyn's retainers rode behind their princess and the king's man, but at a discreet enough distance so as not to impede conversation.

Gwenhwyfar and Bedwyr had sat next to each other at dinner for the last four evenings, and thus far that was the extent of their acquaintance. Polite conversation, in the midst of a large roomful of people, had not given Gwenhwyfar the opportunity she craved to question Bedwyr about the king, and so she had engineered this quiet ride together through the Welsh countryside.

"Is the fighting really over?" was her first question as they walked their horses across a soft, muddy field just outside Dinas Emrys.

"It seems so," he replied. "For the first time in my memory there is no war host outside the Saxon shore. And there has been no activity so far this spring that would indicate they intend a move. Arthur is hopeful of making a treaty with them."

Bedwyr sounded regretful. Gwenhwyfar looked at him curiously. "The thought does not please you?" she asked.

He gave her a sideways blue glance. "If we have peace," he answered, "I shall be bored to death."

She regarded his profile and thought he was probably right. She said, "We have heard all about you, Prince Bedwyr. You are a great hero in Wales." He looked amused, and that annoyed her. "The story of your famous escape from Cerdic has enlivened our hearths all winter," she added, in a voice that was noticeably cooler.

He looked at her. "Culwych," he said. "Am I right?"

"Yes, Culwych."

He nodded. "He's a good lad. A good fighter."

"So he says." Bedwyr's mouth quirked with humor. A faint line creased Gwenhwyfar's smooth brow. "One thing has always puzzled me, though." She looked at him. "Where was the king? How could he have left you in so vulnerable a situation?"

She got the full force of his blue stare in response. "Well, now," he said, and rubbed the back of his head. He raised a golden eyebrow. "Arthur was not happy with me about that particular escapade."

She was astonished. "Why not?"

"It makes for a good winter's tale around the fire, I grant you, but I never should have let myself get trapped like that in the first place. The truth is, Cerdic outgeneraled me, and I wound up losing a third of my men and my horses."

"You were outnumbered ten to one," Gwenhwyfar protested.

He shrugged. "It never would have happened to Arthur."

She was silent, digesting this new information. She slid her hand up and down the rein, then said on a faint note of inquiry, "My brother Peredur says he is a very great general."

"He is," came the immediate reply. Bedwyr grinned at her, very blond and blue in the March sun. "I, on the contrary, am only a very great leader of cavalry."

She smiled back. They rode on in silence for another few minutes before he said half-humorously, "Was that what you wanted to ask me?"

She was startled. "Ask you?" she repeated.

"I thought, when you arranged this little outing, that you must want to ask me something."

"Oh." She wasn't looking at him now. "It wasn't anything in particular," she said a little breathlessly.

"Anything in general, then?"

At that she turned to him. His eyes were as brilliant a blue as the sky, and they looked sympathetic. She smiled ruefully. "In general," she answered, "everything. It is not precisely easy, you see, having to marry a man you have never met. And when that man is the high king . . . well, it is almost intimidating."

He nodded. She had the strangest feeling that she had known him for quite a long time, and it was that feeling that prompted her to say, "What will he think of me, Bedwyr?"

He looked surprised. "You have a mirror. What do men always think of you?"

"But the high king is different."

"How do you know that, if you have never met him?"

"When people talk about him," she answered, "their voices change."

The blue eyes registered comprehension. They had left the open field and were riding around the perimeter of a stone-edged farm. "I don't know if I can explain it to you," he said.

"Try."

Bedwyr frowned a little in concentration. "He is a king, Gwenhwyfar. He was a king when first I met him, when he was fifteen years old and an obscure fosterling of Merlin's, with no parents and no position." The frown smoothed out. "You could feel it in him, even then. He was nobody and I was a prince, and I pledged myself to him on that day."

"I see," she said.

He watched her face. She was the most beautiful woman he had ever seen. Her cheekbones were high and perfectly sculptured, her mouth full and generous, her eyes like long green jewels. But the thing about her you saw first, and always remembered, was the color of her hair: not red, not gold, but a beautiful blend of both. Every time he saw her, he was stirred anew.

What in the name of all the gods was Arthur going to make of her? Not only was she beautiful, it seemed she was intuitive as well.

He wouldn't like that at all, Bedwyr thought instantly. "He is a very private man," he said. "That comes with being a king, I suppose."

She thought about that for a minute before she brought up the other thing that had been worrying her. "He has taken a long time to marry. I have heard my father discussing it with the others."

Bedwyr looked distinctly exasperated. "I know. It never seems to occur to anyone that Arthur was spending all his energy fighting the Saxons. He had neither time nor thought for anything else. And when you come down to it, the man is only twenty-six years old!"

Gwenhwyfar bestowed upon him an extraordinarily sweet smile. "You care for him a great deal, don't you?"

"Yes," said Bedwyr. "I do."

Chapter 20

*I*T took two weeks for Bedwyr to get the Princess Gwenhwyfar from Gwynedd to Venta. All the cushions and hangings and embroidered chairs had to be transported by litters, as it was still too muddy to get wagons over the mountain roads. Gwenhwyfar's wedding party consisted of her father, her brother Peredur, an assortment of men who had at one time or another fought with Arthur, and four of her women. Olwen, Elaine, Cara, and Ruta traveled in litters. Gwenhwyfar had a litter as well, but she spent several hours each day in the saddle, riding next to Bedwyr. Bedwyr's men were not accustomed to such slow going, but the prince showed none of his usual impatience.

"If I had the Princess Gwenhwyfar riding beside me, I wouldn't be in any hurry either," murmured Gwynn to Lionel as they paced decorously behind the women's litters one gray afternoon.

Lionel gave his companion an expressive look. "One of the Welsh girls, the dark one, made a comment about that last night."

Gwynn looked at him with raised brows and he continued, "She wondered if Arthur had been wise to send so splendid a man as Prince Bedwyr to escort the princess."

Gwynn's eyebrows dropped and he shrugged. "It's not the princess I'm worried about."

"Bedwyr?" Lionel shook his head. "Don't worry about Bedwyr. He would never touch anything that belonged to the king."

Gwynn looked impatient. "Of course he wouldn't. I never meant to suggest such a thing. But you know the prince and women . . . and *that* is a woman, Lionel. After weeks of such noble restraint on his part, can you imagine what Bedwyr is likely to think up for us once we get back to Venta?"

Lionel groaned. "The king will be in residence," he said after a minute. "That is our only hope. Arthur will pull the reins in on Bedwyr if he gets out of hand."

"That's true." Gwynn sighed and looked ahead over the women's litters to where a red and a gold head were riding side by side. "She is . . ." He groped for a word.

"I know," said Lionel.

"God," said Gwynn. "Are they stopping already?"

It appeared that they were.

Gwenhwyfar enjoyed her hours with Bedwyr. He made her feel safe. It had to do, she thought, with his size, his lazy grin, the way his most casual command was instantly obeyed by his men. Even her father, who was a king and an older man, never challenged Bedwyr's right to direct their journey. When she mentioned something of this to the prince, he had given her his beguiling grin and said, "After all, I'm accustomed to moving far larger parties than this one, Gwenhwyfar. And across far rougher ground."

It crossed her mind, treacherously, that she would be happier by far if it were Bedwyr she was going to wed.

The closer they came to Venta, the more nervous she became. It was not a state with which she was familiar. She was Gwenhwyfar the fair, Gwenhwyfar the jewel of Gwynedd; men had been begging to marry her since she was thirteen years old. She had always rested secure in the knowledge of her own desirability.

But the king was different. He *is* a king, Bedwyr had said. Gwenhwyfar did not want to marry just a king; she wanted to marry a man. A man who wanted her. She looked once more at the shining gilt head and massive shoulders of the man riding beside her. If only her father had chosen Bedwyr!

It was midafternoon when they finally arrived in Venta. Gwenhwyfar had never seen a Roman city, and she looked with curiosity and wonder at the public bathhouse, at the forum, and then at the colonnaded front of the praetorium. Bedwyr smiled at her reassuringly and said, "I'm going to have you and your women taken to your private chambers. Then I will inform the king of your arrival."

Gwenhwyfar smiled back gratefully. She did not wish to meet Arthur for the first time while she was wearing her travel-stained riding clothes.

An elderly woman conducted her to Igraine's old rooms, which had obviously been put in order for her coming. There was fresh paint on the walls. The bronze of the lamps had been polished, and the mosaic floor was spotless. Another servant brought her heated water and

Olwen helped her to wash and to change. She had a golden gown with an embroidered tunic ready for this very occasion. After it was on, Olwen brushed the road dust from her hair and dressed it with two golden combs. Then she was ready. She sat down in a high-backed chair by the window to wait.

The summons was brought by a very tall, broad-shouldered man who introduced himself as Cai. Gwenhwyfar recognized the name immediately. After Bedwyr, he was said to be the most important man in Britain. After Bedwyr and after the king. Of course.

Cai gave her a pleasant smile and said, "The king would like you to come to the audience hall, my lady."

"Certainly," Gwenhwyfar replied. She fixed her most serene expression on her face as she placed her hand on the arm Cai offered her. He was almost as tall as Bedwyr, she thought as she walked with him down the hall, half-listening to what he was saying. They left the hallway and entered another. Finally they stopped in front of a door. Cai gave her an enigmatic look and threw it open.

"My lord king," he said formally, "the Princess Gwenhwyfar is here." She drew a deep, steadying breath and walked into the room. Bedwyr was there, standing a little behind the king, and she threw him a quick look before her eyes went to the slender black-haired figure of Arthur. He was wearing a simple white tunic of beautifully woven wool, and no jewelry. Even his dark hair was bare of any identifying gold circlet. It seemed to her he hesitated, and she walked steadily forward, across the mosaic floor, and stopped directly in front of him.

"My lord," she said in her charmingly husky voice, bowed her head, then raised it and looked directly into his face.

He was dark, as her brother had said. And not overly tall; the top of her head was perhaps two inches below his. As her eyes scanned the still, reserved face of her future husband, she saw one other thing. Peredur had not been teasing after all when he said that Arthur was beautiful.

He was making her a friendly, courteous speech of welcome. The friendliness, however, was not reflected in his surprisingly light eyes. Nor did those eyes hold anything like the glow Gwenhwyfar was accustomed to see in the eyes of men when they looked at her.

He finished talking and she gave him her loveliest smile. "Thank you, my lord. It is good to be here."

The guarded look in his eyes did not change, nor did he return her smile. "Come sit down and take some refreshment," he said. He had a beautiful speaking voice. "You must be weary after such a long journey." As she walked slowly toward the circle of chairs, she saw Bedwyr and Cai coming to join them. Arthur, it seemed, did not want to be alone with his future wife.

There was a great banquet in her honor that evening. She sat next to the king at the high table, with Bedwyr beside her and her father beside Arthur. The food was excellent, but she was not hungry. The king was unfailingly polite and pleasant. Most of the time she talked with Bedwyr.

The following day her things were unloaded from the litters, and she and her ladies settled into their new quarters. From her window she saw Arthur ride away from the praetorium on a big black horse. She did not see him come back, but he was present at dinner. She sat between him and Bedwyr once more and was polite to them both.

There was a great hunt the following day, and all the men disappeared until late in the evening. Dinner was served to Gwenhwyfar and her ladies in her private rooms.

Cai appeared at her door the following day with a scroll under his arm. He was there to discuss the wedding plans, and she sat beside him and smiled and nodded and agreed to everything he said.

She appeared at dinner that evening with her usual serenely beautiful face, but behind the smile there was growing anger. Never, in all her seventeen years, had the Princess Gwenhwyfar been treated the way Arthur was treating her now. She was a princess, the king's intended wife, not a necessary nuisance. She pushed the food around on her plate all through dinner, and listened to Arthur making conversation with her father. When finally he turned to say something to her, she said, without pausing to consider the wisdom of this course of action, "I should like to speak with you alone, my lord."

There was a startled pause. Then: "Of course." His voice held only the careful courtesy she so resented. "If you will go into the small audience room? I will join you there in a few moments."

She nodded and swept off to murmur an excuse into Olwen's ear. She went to the room he had indicated and sat in one of the circle of chairs that edged the mosaic. Anger was beginning to die and some other emotion, unnervingly like fear, had lodged itself in the pit of her stomach. What had she done? And what, in God's name, was she going to say to him? She clasped her hands together tightly and at that moment he came in the door.

"Sit down," she said, and bit her lip. He walked toward her slowly and chose the chair directly opposite hers in the circle. If he had sat next to her, she might have found something else to say, she might have held her tongue. But he sat as far away from her as he possibly could. "If you didn't want to marry me," she said, her voice huskier than usual, "you shouldn't have brought me here."

His face never changed: the straight black brows, the guarded eyes, the unsmiling mouth. "I never said I did not want to marry you," he answered.

"You didn't have to. Your feelings are quite obvious." Her hands were freezing and she gripped them together even more tightly. Her heart was pounding with tension and with fear. "What is it?" Even to herself her voice sounded hard. "Don't you like women?"

That surprised him. The gray eyes widened. "You certainly don't like me," she said. In spite of herself, her mouth trembled.

"Gwenhwyfar." He was looking at her now, really looking at her. She bit her quivering lip. "Oh, God," he said, the careful courtesy quite gone from his face. "I'm sorry. I didn't think . . ." A lock of black hair had fallen across his forehead. He looked more human than she had ever seen him look before.

She sniffled. "Didn't think what? That I would notice?"

The gray eyes were rueful. "I didn't think of you at all—which was inexcusable, and I apologize." He pushed the hair back off his brow. "I've been so nervous about meeting you. That's why I've behaved like such a boor. And of course I want to marry you."

She felt as if a weight had been lifted from her chest. "Nervous of meeting *me*?" She stared at him incredulously. He didn't look like a man who knew the meaning of the word "nervous."

"Well," he replied reasonably, "it is rather nerve-racking, the thought that you are to marry a total stranger."

"You don't need to tell me," she said, and at that he smiled.

"I've been a selfish brute, Gwenhwyfar. Shall we try to start again?" He rose from his chair and came to stand before her.

It was not the same smile he had given to her father. She felt suddenly shy. "I'd like that, my lord." Her voice was very soft.

"Arthur," he said.

"Arthur," she repeated, and smiled back at him.

There were three more weeks to wait until her wedding, and Gwenhwyfar was happy. Restored to her old confidence, she spread the radiance of her beauty about the entire court. Arthur went out of his way to make up to her for the neglect of her first few days in Venta. He took her riding. He showed her the small Christian church where their vows would be exchanged. He was friendly and charming, an utterly different man from the guarded stranger she had first encountered.

A week before the wedding there was some minor commotion about a mock battle that Bedwyr had arranged, and the Prince disappeared from Venta. When she questioned Arthur, he told her blandly that he had sent Bedwyr out with a hunting party to bring in fresh meat for the wedding. Culwych, Olwen's brother, had another story. He said that Arthur had put a stop to the mock battle and got Bedwyr away from Venta to keep him out of trouble.

"The prince gets bored when there's no one to fight," Culwych said. It was evidently a fact about Bedwyr that everyone knew and accepted.

The prince returned the day before the wedding. The praetorium was filled with guests and Gwenhwyfar had been busy all day greeting people. Arthur had not been in the praetorium and she did not see him until dinner that evening, when he came into the dining room with Bedwyr.

The company was not yet seated, awaiting the entrance of the king. Arthur came first through the door, then Bedwyr followed, his massive frame filling the doorway. He had to duck his golden head in order to keep from hitting it on the frame. Gwenhwyfar watched the two men as they crossed the floor toward the high table, and remembered her brother Peredur's words. They were true, she thought. When Arthur was present, you did not look at anyone else.

Chapter 21

*F*OR Arthur, his wedding day was less a personal than a state occasion. He understood very well the significance to Britain of his taking a wife. It meant the founding of a dynasty; it meant the establishment of a stable government; it meant peace for the country. With all these things in mind, he had called in Cai from his work on the new capital and asked him to create a wedding day that few would forget.

Five kings were coming to Venta for the occasion, and numberless princes and chiefs. The one thing Gwenhwyfar found strange, however, was the absence of any member of Arthur's own family. His parents, of course, were dead. And Merlin, his grandfather, as well. But he had two aunts. Morgause lived in the far north and Gwenhwyfar supposed one could understand her reluctance to undertake such a journey, but the other lived quite nearby, at Avalon. Gwenhwyfar wondered at her absence.

"My aunt?" Arthur said blankly when she asked him. Then, when she elaborated: "Oh. You mean *Morgan.*"

"Yes," replied Gwenhwyfar a little diffidently. Physically Arthur had not moved, but she had the distinct impression that he had just retreated a hundred miles beyond her reach. "I just thought, since she is so close . . ." Her voice ran out.

"Morgan is in Lothian at present, visiting her sister," he said. "Otherwise I am sure she would be present."

Gwenhwyfar thought it extremely odd that Arthur's aunt should choose such a time to travel to Lothian. The roads would be better later in the year, and she would not have to miss the marriage of her nephew. There was evidently an unfriendly feeling between Arthur and this aunt. His face was wearing the remote, austere look she dreaded, and she hastily changed the subject.

* * *

"Morgan isn't coming?" Bedwyr asked Cai the evening before the wedding. They were sitting in Cai's bedroom in the praetorium and sharing a jug of wine.

"No," said Cai. "She went to visit Morgause in Lothian. It meant that Morgause and Pellinore couldn't come to Venta, of course. However"—Cai shrugged—"all in all, it seemed the best solution."

"I suppose so." Bedwyr looked at Cai over the rim of his cup. "Gwenhwyfar was curious. I told her that Morgause had no love for Arthur because of Lot, and that Morgan had gone to Lothian out of loyalty to her sister."

"Good." Cai's chin was sunk into his chest. "It may go well enough after all, this marriage." He watched Bedwyr pour himself another cup of wine. "Gwenhwyfar might be just what he needs."

"He needs something." Bedwyr drained half his cup. "He was hell to live with all winter."

Cai grunted. "So were you."

Bedwyr grinned crookedly. "I get bored. That's not Arthur's problem, though. If anything, he has too much to do."

"He needs a woman," diagnosed Cai. "I pushed a few into his bedroom this winter, but it only made him angry." He stared into the glowing coals of the brazier. "I think this girl will be good for him."

Bedwyr's reply was strangely brooding. "But will he be good for her?"

Cai looked at him, surprised. "He's made an effort to please her. It was disastrous as first, but he's been much better lately. Gwenhwyfar handled him just right."

"Yes. She did."

"What's the matter, then?" Cai asked. "She can't have expected to find a love match, after all. And Arthur has apparently decided to make the best of it. Why shouldn't it turn out all right?"

Bedwyr drained his cup. "No reason." He pushed himself to his feet. "If we drink any more of this wine, we won't make it to the great day tomorrow. Good night."

"Good night," replied Cai, and watched, frowning, as Bedwyr walked out of his door.

The day of Arthur's marriage dawned bright with sunshine and May flowers. Cai was enormously relieved. It was physically impossible to fit all of the guests into the dining hall of the praetorium, and so tents had been constructed for those of less importance. Dining in a tent in the sunlight was pleasant; in the rain and the mud, distinctly less so. Admittance to the small church was only for the select few, and after the actual ceremony was over, everyone repaired to either dining hall or tent for a sumptuous banquet.

Arthur had taken the pageantry of the day very seriously. There was a formal procession to and from the church, and the king wore a gold circlet on his brow and a cloak of imperial purple. Gwenhwyfar looked impossibly beautiful in a glimmering gold gown that was not as brilliant as the cloud of bronze hair that fell around her shoulders and down her back. The street was lined with hundreds of guests and townspeople to watch them go by.

The cooks had outdone themselves with the dinner, which was grandly Roman in style. The first course, the gustatio, consisted of eggs and oysters washed down with honey-flavored wine. The main part of the meal was roast boar, venison, beef, and mutton served with a variety of vegetables and breads. Cai had imported the wine from Italy. For the final course, the mensae secundae, Cai had ordered puddings, pastries, cakes, sweetmeats, fresh and dried fruits, and more wine.

The gustatio was served and Arthur sat toying with the oysters on his plate. He looked over at Gwenhwyfar, seated beside him at the high table, and saw she was eating her oysters with obvious pleasure while she talked to the archbishop.

He felt suddenly sick. Sweat stood out on his forehead and he clenched his teeth.

"Are you well?" It was the voice of Gwenhwyfar's father, seated on his other side. Maelgwyn's handsome face bore a look of concern.

He forced the nausea back down. "I'm all right. I don't think the oysters quite agreed with me." He put down his knife. He didn't think he would ever eat oysters again.

The feast went on for a very long time. Finally Gwenhwyfar's women rose to take her away. She caught his eye before she left the table, an apprehensive, fleeting look. She was a virgin, of course. She would be afraid.

He thought of another time, when the rain had been beating down, and the air had smelled of grain. Morgan had not been afraid.

Not now, he told himself fiercely. Forget it for now.

The men around him were laughing and joking. He forced himself to smile and make a reply. They all roared.

He had to pull himself together or he would mishandle tonight. He did not want to hurt her or frighten her.

He hadn't been with a woman since Morgan.

That had been a mistake. Tonight, what he needed was control. But he had not been able to bear any of those other women . . . All the men were looking at him. Abruptly he realized that it was time. Well, he would do the best that he could.

He would not allow anyone to leave the banquet when he went. The last thing he needed right now, he thought with bitter humor as he walked down the corridor to her rooms, was an audience.

She was sitting up in bed when he came in, her glorious hair loose around her shoulders. She wore some sort of thin linen shift. He crossed the room to her side of the bed.

Her face was flawless, with a suggestion of great sweetness in the curves of her lovely full mouth. She was intelligent, he had discovered, and she had faced him bravely when he had not given her the attention she felt was due her. It could have been much worse, he thought. There was a good chance that they could become friends. If he didn't mishandle things now.

He smiled at her. "A crowd of them wanted to come too, but I wouldn't let them."

"Thank goodness for that." The apprehension had left her eyes as soon as he smiled.

He sat down beside her on the bed. "You are very beautiful," he said, and put his hands up to cup her face. He held her gently and then bent his head toward her mouth.

She gave him an almost instant response. He let his hands travel down her cheeks, to her throat, then to her shoulders. He pulled her closer and her arms came up to circle his neck. After a minute, without releasing her mouth, he pressed her back to the bed.

Gwenhwyfar could sense that he was fighting to control himself. Far from frightening her, however, his obvious need only brought her gratification and joy. He wanted her. All her doubts vanished, and she arched up against him, abandoning herself to the feelings his touch was arousing, her blood answering strongly to the call of his.

There was pain when first he came into her, but she had been prepared for that. She had not been prepared for the explosive pleasure that followed. It astonished her and elated her and humbled her all at once. She nestled into his arms and laid her cheek against his shoulder, listening to the slowing beat of his heart. He smoothed her damp hair off her forehead with a gentle hand. That gentleness was a surprise to her, and a profound joy.

She went to sleep cradled in his arms. He waited until he was quite sure she was asleep before he disentangled himself and got out of bed to go to the window. He stood there for a long time, his forehead pressed against the cool glass, staring at the blurry lights of the lanterns on the forum. Then, finally, he returned to the bed.

He was asleep when Gwenhwyfar awoke the following morning. She opened her eyes slowly and saw the sun shining through the translucent glass of the window. The coals in the brazier had gone out, and the air in the room was cold, but she herself was warm under the woolen blankets that she had brought with her from home. The man next to her did not stir and, a little cautiously, she turned her head to look at him.

All she saw at first was a bare brown shoulder and a tangle of black hair on the pillow. Carefully she raised herself on her elbow so she could see his face. That was when she first noticed the scars.

They were obviously old, but the thin white lines were still clearly visible on the smooth brown skin of his shoulder. Gwenhwyfar frowned. They looked like lash marks. Her eyes moved from his shoulder to his face, relaxed and defenseless-looking in sleep. He seemed to sense her regard, however, for his lashes lifted almost immediately.

She thought, at first, he did not recognize her. Then he pushed himself up, shaking the hair off his forehead, giving her a warm and friendly smile. "Well now, my lady," he said, and there was warmth in his voice as well. "Did you sleep well last night?"

Her anxiety vanished. "Yes." She was very conscious of his bare, lean torso, of her own nakedness under the blankets. He had discarded their clothes with flattering haste last night.

He read, easily, what was in her eyes and responded by putting out a hand to touch her hair. It was so fine it floated, a cloud of red and gold about her white shoulders. "This is the one morning of my life," he said, "when I can be sure no one is going to come knocking at the door to wake me." His hand moved from her hair to her arm. "Come here," he said softly, and she went.

* * *

Spring changed into summer. The work on Arthur's new capital was progressing. The Saxon shore was quiet and Arthur entered into tentative negotiations with Offa, Cynewulf, and Cerdic. Morgan was back at Avalon once more.

Summer turned into autumn. It was October when Cai went to Avalon to see her.

His father was the one to greet him, and Cai was appalled by how much Ector had aged in the months since Arthur's marriage.

"Are you ill, Father?" he asked almost as soon as he had stepped back from Ector's embrace.

"No, no," Ector reassured him heartily. A little too heartily, Cai thought. He frowned as he scanned his father's seamed face. Ector seemed smaller than he used to, and distinctly less massive.

"You should have let me know if you weren't well," Cai said severely. "I would have come sooner."

"I am perfectly well. And you've been busy with the king's work, I know." His face glowed with simple pride.

Cai felt a pang of guilt. He had been busy, yes, but for most of the summer he had been only twelve miles away. He should have come to Avalon before this. He would have, had it not been for Morgan. He had wanted to wait, to give her time . . . Ector was putting an arm around his shoulder. "Come along now," the old man said. "I want you to tell me all that you've been doing. What is this new city that Arthur is building?" They went to the family salon and were still there talking when Morgan came in an hour later.

She smiled with pleasure when she saw Cai, and came immediately to kiss his cheek. He raised his head and looked down into her face. Her eyes were searching his, and he knew she saw how disturbed he was about his father.

No one looked at you like Morgan, he thought. She saw right through into your soul. Which meant, of course, that she saw, had always seen, other things too. But he had always known he had no secrets from her. He smiled a little crookedly and said, "It's good to see you, Morgan."

They had no chance to speak alone until much later in the evening, when Ector had gone to bed. Then they pulled their chairs closer together and lowered their voices.

"Father looks terrible," he said.

She sighed. "He's lost weight, I know." She looked at him sadly.

"He misses Merlin, you see. He's never been the same since my father died."

"But is he sick?"

"He's just getting old, Cai. And it seems to be happening very quickly."

"I should have come to see him."

"Well, you are here now. And he is so proud of you, of how Arthur depends on you."

The name, dropped so unobtrusively into the conversation, seemed to reverberate between them. He said it again. "Arthur."

There were lines of tension around her eyes. "How is he?" she asked.

"He is well." He was not sure what she wanted to hear but he had come to give her the truth. "I think this marriage has been a good thing for him," he said deliberately.

The brown eyes closed. There was a pause that seemed to Cai like a small eternity. Then: "Thank God," she said. "I have been so worried."

Cai realized he had stopped breathing. He drew in a long breath and let it out again. "I was worried too. When Gwenhwyfar first came, it was . . . dreadful. You know how he can be, Morgan." She gave him a shadowy smile. "But somehow she managed to break through the ice and ever since, they have done very well. He's much more relaxed than he was." He looked at her gravely.

"I'm so glad." Her eyes were bright with unshed tears but there was no mistaking her sincerity.

He stared at that small face with its great luminous eyes. "Morgan," he said. The brown eyes blinked and then looked at him with sharpened attention. "Morgan," he repeated, unaware of how vulnerable he suddenly sounded, "now that Arthur has married, have you ever thought of marriage for yourself?"

It was out, the thing he had waited to say to her since last May. He continued doggedly, determined to say it all now that he had begun. "I love you. I have always loved you. You know that. And I know that all I can expect from you is kindness . . . but that would be enough for me."

His words filled her with such deep sadness. "Cai," she said, and gazed up into his dear, familiar face, "if I were to marry anyone at all, it would be you."

"Then why not?" he asked. "Marriage has been good for Arthur. Why shouldn't it be good for you?" He leaned over, picked up her hands, and held them tightly.

She looked down. His hands were so large they engulfed her own. They were wonderful hands, she thought: strong, steady, competent hands. Hands one could trust. "I have little doubt that marriage to you would be good for me," she said, still looking at their clasped hands, "but I don't know how good it would be for you."

Her words were a strange echo of Bedwyr's comment about Gwen-hwyfar and Arthur. "Why do you say that?" Cai asked.

Her lashes were long on her peach-brown cheeks. She was outdoors so much that her skin was lightly tanned even in October. "It is not an easy thing," she said, "to love more than one is loved."

His voice was harsh as he answered, "I know I can never take his place, Morgan. I wouldn't expect to. I know you don't love me—"

"Of course I love you," she interrupted. "After Arthur, you are dearer to me than anyone. But Arthur comes first, Cai, and because of that I can never marry. Not you, not anyone."

He was trying to understand. "Because you couldn't bear to marry anyone who wasn't Arthur?"

"Because he couldn't bear it," she answered, and looked up into his face.

A faint flush reddened his cheeks. "Arthur would never grudge you happiness, Morgan."

"Of course he wouldn't."

"But then . . ."

"Cai." Her brown eyes were kind. "If you think he was difficult to live with this winter, you would not want to see him if I married you."

He frowned. "I don't believe . . . Nonsense."

"It is not nonsense. I know Arthur."

He dropped her hands. "*He* married."

"He had no choice. And I was the one who forced him to it, Cai. I would not marry him."

She was pale beneath the light tan, but her voice was composed. This was clearly a subject she had thought out long ago. "Why, Morgan?" He asked the question that he had long wondered at. "Why wouldn't you marry him? Ten years ago, I could understand it. But now . . . Arthur has the church in his pocket. There would have been no trouble."

The faintest quiver passed over her face, but her voice was steady. "I cannot have children," she said.

"Ah . . ." It was a long, drawn-out note of comprehension and compassion. "I see," he said, and drew her to her feet and then into his arms.

She rested against him, the top of her head not reaching as high as his shoulder. "You know him too, Cai." Her voice was a little muffled by his chest. "He is a king. About some things he is intensely possessive. He can't help it; it's in his nature."

Cai held her close, felt the warmth and tenderness of her body against his, thought of Arthur, and knew she was right.

Chapter 22

*T*HERE was the flare of torches in the courtyard of the praetorium and then the clatter of hooves on stone.

"The king is back!" Word ran like wildfire through the house and the stables, and men came running to take the horses. The December night was cold and breath hung white in the air as the men moved into the house. The horses were led away and quiet fell on the courtyard once more.

Inside the praetorium, servants ran to and fro. Food was ordered to be served in the king's private rooms for Arthur and Prince Bedwyr. Then Gareth went running to summon Lionel and Valerius from the army encampment. Cai had already joined the king and Bedwyr. The food was removed and the five men sat down to talk.

Gwenhwyfar paced her room impatiently. News of Arthur's return had reached her, but he had not come to greet her. The servants had said he wanted to see Cai and Lionel and Valerius.

Gwenhwyfar told herself she understood. Arthur and Bedwyr were returning from a meeting with Offa of Kent. They had met to discuss the terms of a treaty that would carve distinct boundaries for the Saxon kingdoms within Britain. It was a meeting of momentous importance for all of Britain; of course Arthur would want to inform his men about what had happened.

He had been gone for weeks. He would come to her as soon as he finished with the men. She knew that. Suddenly, however, she could not wait.

"Olwen, get me my cloak," she said in her most imperious voice. Olwen looked surprised but made no comment as she handed the queen a deep green cloak and watched as Gwenhwyfar flung it around her shoulders. The queen turned to take a quick, cursory glance in the mirror.

"Shall I come with you, my lady?" the girl asked.

"No." Gwenhwyfar swept regally to the door. Then, over her shoulder: "I am going to the king." The door closed behind her.

The four girls left behind looked at each other. Then Elaine said, "Bedwyr is back too." She went to look in the queen's mirror.

Olwen sighed. "I hope the king's return improves my lady's temper."

"She has missed him," Cara said softly.

"Yes." Olwen turned her head. "Elaine, get away from that mirror. No matter how much you preen, you'll never be as beautiful as the queen."

"But the queen already has a husband," Elaine said complacently as she came back to pick up her sewing.

"Stay away from Bedwyr, Elaine," Olwen warned. "The prince has no mind to marry."

Elaine smiled secretly. "We shall see," she returned.

Cara said, "Olwen, tell us a story."

The guard at Arthur's door admitted Gwenhwyfar immediately. She stood for a moment on the threshold, looking at the lamplit room with the five men seated in a circle at the far end of it, and her poised exterior masked inner uncertainty. Perhaps she ought not to have come.

Five male heads turned to her. Arthur recognized her first and, with the courtesy Merlin had drilled into him, rose to his feet. The rest of the men followed suit immediately. "Gwenhwyfar," her husband said, the faintest note of surprise in his voice.

She came one step into the room. "I heard you were home . . ." Her voice trailed away and then he was smiling and holding out his hand, and she knew it was all right.

"Come join us and hear all about our momentous meeting with the bretwalda." There was no extra chair in the room, so he moved a stool close to his own chair and Gwenhwyfar sat down. She looked around the circle of faces and smiled.

Bedwyr's eyes held hers for the longest, and he gave her the sweet lazy grin she was so fond of. The smiles of Lionel and Valerius were slightly fatuous. Only Cai appeared to be unmoved by her presence. He nodded to her with calm courtesy and looked again at Arthur.

"As I was saying," Arthur recapitulated for the benefit of his wife, "there was a great deal of discussion about the safest place to meet. We decided at last upon the Isle of Wight." The faintest amusement colored his voice. "That way, neither of us could have armies bent on assassination hidden in the woods."

Cai grunted. "Makes sense."

"Yes. Both parties crossed to the isle by separate boats and we met in a tent on the shore."

"Whom did Offa bring with him?" Cai asked.

"Three of his brothers. And a bodyguard of five other warriors. They were all unarmed, of course. I only had Bedwyr, but he was more than sufficient."

There was a pause. Cai looked from Arthur to Bedwyr. "All right," he said resignedly. "What happened?"

Arthur's face was very grave. "Offa challenged Bedwyr to arm-wrestle with him."

"Arm-wrestle?"

"You're familiar with the sport?" Arthur asked. He was obviously enjoying himself.

"Yes," Cai replied, and looked sourly at Bedwyr. The prince's blue eyes held a distinctly wicked sparkle. There was not a man in the army, Cai included, whom Bedwyr had not beaten in arm-wrestling. Many times.

"It seems that Offa had heard of our hero's prowess," Arthur continued smoothly, "and was anxious to test Bedwyr's reputation himself." Arthur looked at his wife's wondering face. "Offa," he explained, "is built like an oak tree."

"He is indeed." Cai had seen the bretwalda in battle many times. He stared at Bedwyr. "Well," he demanded, "did you beat him?"

Bedwyr raised a golden eyebrow. "Of course I beat him. I beat his brothers too. I offered to take on the bodyguard, but at that point they were convinced."

Cai began to laugh. "Precisely," said Arthur, and his own voice was filled with amusement. Gwenhwyfar looked from Cai to Bedwyr and then turned her head to regard her husband. It was only when he was with these two friends that she saw this easy, humorous, approachable side to him.

"So then," Arthur continued, "having established the most important point of business, we proceeded to discuss a treaty."

"So that's why you took Bedwyr!" Cai suddenly exclaimed, enlightenment dawning in his hazel eyes. Arthur's choice of the prince to accompany him to the treaty negotiations had bewildered a great number of people, Bedwyr not precisely being famous for his diplomatic talents.

Arthur grinned. "Of course. I didn't know about the arm-wrestling, but I did know that Bedwyr is the single most feared man in all our army. Offa has been on the receiving end of too many of Bedwyr's mad-dog cavalry charges not to know just how dangerous our prince can be." The gray eyes looked with affection at the big golden man sitting next to him. "Just having him there, looming beside me, was a potent reminder to Offa that it was in his best interests to negotiate a treaty."

For the first time Lionel spoke. He said to Bedwyr, "It's a good thing you didn't lose."

Bedwyr was unperturbed. "I never lose," he replied, a statement which no one challenged, as it was all too depressingly true.

Cai returned his attention to the king. "All right," he said briskly. "What happened next?"

The men began to talk about boundaries and accesses and safeguards, and Gwenhwyfar leaned her shoulder against Arthur's knee and thought dreamily of how glad she was to have him home again. She did not begin to pay attention until the tones of the men's voices changed.

"No," Arthur was saying, "I don't trust him." Gwenhwyfar turned her head to look at her husband. He was frowning slightly and seemed to be completely unaware of her presence. He was talking to Cai. "We did all our negotiating through a translator. I did not tell them I spoke Saxon. And there were a few things said that I did not like."

"Do you think he wants to lull us into a false sense of well-being?" Cai asked.

"I think that is a distinct possibility."

"They were almost too accommodating," Bedwyr said.

There was a little silence. Gwenhwyfar clasped her hands tightly in her lap. She had been so sure the fighting was over.

"The army is to be kept in complete readiness," Arthur was saying. "Having come so far, I don't want to lose all now."

"God no!" said Lionel.

"Full drill, Valerius, for as long as the weather holds," Arthur said. "And I will send messages to all the kings, to warn them that there is a possibility that we may be calling on them for troops once more."

"Yes, my lord." Valerius, son of Uther's old general Claudius Virgilius, was in charge of the foot soldiers.

"Lionel. I want spies in Kent. More men than we have already, and deeper within the country. If there is any sign of an army being gathered, I want to know about it immediately." Over the years, Lionel had become Arthur's chief scout.

"Yes, my lord," he replied promptly. "I'll see to it."

The men were beginning to get to their feet. Gwenhwyfar smiled courteously as they bade her good night. Then, at last, she was alone with him.

"I hope you didn't mind my coming in on your meeting," she said. "It's just . . . it's been so long since I've seen you."

"Of course I didn't mind." His voice sounded a little absent. He was still thinking about the meeting, she thought with annoyance.

"Well"—she let her annoyance show in her voice—"I'll say good night then."

That got his attention, she was pleased to see. "Just one moment." He reached out and put his hands on her shoulders. She stared into his face, which was now concentrated on her.

It was a face she knew so well: the light eyes, the thin, straight nose, the severely beautiful mouth. Yet she was never quite sure of what he was thinking. It was the Roman side of him, she often thought, that made him such an enigma to her. The Celts showed their feelings far more openly.

"Did I ignore you?" he was saying, and apology mingled with amusement in his voice. "I'm sorry. It's my grandfather's fault: he drilled it into me that duty must come before pleasure."

"I missed you," she said softly.

"I missed you too," came the prompt reply. Too prompt, Gwenhwyfar thought. He sounded as if he were merely returning a courtesy. There was no love in his voice. Of course, love had not been one of the factors in their marriage arrangement. Only she . . .

"It has been a long time," he was murmuring. His fingers brushed her cheek. "Too long." He bent his head and kissed her. "Let's both go to your room," he said then, and she nodded mutely in response.

She walked beside him with studied decorum, and when they reached her rooms she dismissed her women. Then, finally, she was in his arms.

It was only at moments like this, she thought, that she was sure he needed her as much as she needed him. Please, God, she prayed as his clever hands began to arouse her to the pitch of passion, please, God, let me conceive a child.

Two weeks later, Arthur's cousin Gawain came to Venta. Arthur was down at the cavalry school with Bedwyr, addressing some new recruits, so Gwenhwyfar received Gawain in the small official reception salon.

He was a handsome boy, she thought as she smiled at him and bade him be seated. His hair was auburn and his eyes a clear sky blue. Those eyes held a distinctly dazzled expression as he looked at her, and he was clearly feeling very shy. Gwenhwyfar, who was the same age as her husband's eighteen-year-old cousin, had long since learned the art of putting tongue-tied young men at their ease, however, and in short order she had him talking comfortably.

"I expect you'd like to see the cavalry school," she said finally, and rose to her feet.

Gawain's face lit. "Oh, yes!"

Gwenhwyfar smiled. It had not taken her long to discover that all young men who visited Venta wanted to see the cavalry school. "I'll have some horses brought around for us," she said. "In fact, the king may even be there."

The queen wrapped herself in a thick woolen cloak and led Gawain out into the sunshine. They rode down the main street of Venta and Gwenhwyfar pointed out places of interest along the way. The cavalry encampment was located several miles beyond the city gates, and Gwenhwyfar took Gawain directly to the big dirt ring where she thought there might be some activity for him to watch. There were indeed horses working and Gwenhwyfar directed Gawain to pull his own horse up near the rope that fenced the ring off from the surrounding area.

On the side of the ring nearest to them there was a group of young men on horseback, all of them trotting their mounts in small circles. There was another group of horses on the far side of the ring, performing some other exercise. Arthur and Bedwyr were watching from the center, both of them mounted on their own black stallions.

"These must be the new cavalry recruits," Gwenhwyfar remarked to Gawain. "That is the king with Prince Bedwyr." Both black stallions were standing with remarkable quietness. "The king is the one with the black hair," Gwenhwyfar added kindly.

"I know," said Gawain. As he spoke, one of the horses on the far side of the ring exploded out of the bending exercise he was supposed to be doing.

"Oh, dear," said Gwenhwyfar as the horse threw its head back and reared. The man on its back swore and then used his whip. The horse, a bright chestnut, bucked. Then he bucked again, and the rider went sailing through the air. The riderless horse began to gallop around the ring.

All the other horses halted. The thrown rider got slowly to his feet. "Come here," said the king.

The rider limped over to stand forlornly before Arthur. "Are you all right?" Arthur asked.

"Yes."

"You are too rough. I have been watching you for the last fifteen minutes and I am only surprised that the horse did not rebel sooner." Arthur looked around the ring. "Nor are you the only one at fault. Your horse was just more sensitive than the others." The king was now addressing the entire group of recruits. "You must make work pleasant for a horse, or he will not want to work for you. And in the cavalry, a willing, obedient, well-trained horse is, quite literally, essential for life."

Arthur dismounted from Dun and gave his reins to the horseless rider to hold. He then proceeded to walk up to the chestnut, which was standing now in the middle of the ring. The horse backed away but the king talked to him quietly, and when he reached for his reins the chestnut let himself be caught. There was perfect silence in the ring as Arthur mounted.

"I know you have all been exposed to the teaching of Xenophon," Arthur said as he began to walk the horse around the center of the ring. The chestnut was still excited and pranced instead of walking quietly. Arthur patted his neck. "For a horse to be effective in battle," Arthur continued to the ring at large, "you must have command of his haunches. Xenophon is quite explicit on that point. And in order to have command of the haunches, the horse must be completely tractable at all times. A horse that becomes excited in battle will kill you." The chestnut was beginning to walk quietly. As he turned in their direction, Arthur for the first time noticed the presence of his wife. He lifted a hand and she waved back.

"What does Xenophon mean by command of the haunches?" Arthur asked the men in the ring.

Hesitantly someone answered, "The horse must be balanced enough to go sideways as well as forward."

"That is partly it," Arthur agreed. "Prince Bedwyr will demonstrate what it means for you."

Gawain watched with open mouth as Bedwyr and Sluan moved into the center of the ring. The muscles of the black stallion gleamed in the sun as he leapt in the air, kicking out with his hind legs. The demonstration took five minutes and left all the recruits, as well as Gawain and Gwenhwyfar, in a state of speechless wonder.

"Of course, not all horses are as talented as Sluan," Arthur said pleasantly after Bedwyr had finished. "Nor are many riders as proficient as Prince Bedwyr." The chestnut was walking with complete calm now and Arthur asked him to trot. The horse went forward freely and softly.

"Did anyone see Prince Bedwyr use his hands or his legs?" Arthur asked as he made the chestnut trot large circles.

"No, my lord," came the uniform response.

"You will achieve nothing by force," Arthur said. "Xenophon knew that four hundred years before Christ was born. Look at this chestnut. Is he resisting me?"

"No, my lord," came the chorus back.

"Be soft," said Arthur. "Never hard. Always soft. Now, let us go back to what you were doing before."

The limping rider took Dun off to the stable and the rest of the riders returned to work. Arthur continued to ride the chestnut in ever-smaller circles as he watched the recruits. Bedwyr came over to Gwenhwyfar.

"That was a very impressive demonstration," she said to him admiringly.

He grinned. "Arthur and I do this with every new batch of recruits. We wait until the first horse blows up, then Arthur gets on and gets him to behave like a lamb, and Sluan and I do our fanciest maneuvers. It always makes its point."

Gwenhwyfar had begun to laugh. "Do you mean you've done this before?"

"Every winter for the last eight years," Bedwyr replied amiably.

Gwenhwyfar transferred her gaze to her husband, riding so unconcernedly in the center of the ring. "I did not realize he was so closely involved with the training," she said. "I thought he . . ."

Her voice ran out as Bedwyr gave a deep, rich chuckle. "You thought he just gave orders."

Gwenhwyfar looked at his amused face and smiled. "Yes, I suppose I did."

"This army is Arthur's," Bedwyr said emphatically. "From the bottom up. And there isn't a man in it who doesn't know that."

Gawain made a small sound and Bedwyr looked at him. "I'm so sorry, Gawain," Gwenhwyfar said contritely. "Bedwyr, this is Prince Gawain of Lothian. He arrived in Venta only an hour ago."

"Gawain?" Bedwyr's blue eyes sharpened. "Lot's son?"

"Yes." Clearly Gawain saw nothing amiss in being Lot's son. "I have come, Prince Bedwyr," he announced proudly, "to join the army."

Bedwyr was surprised. "Does Pellinore know about this?"

The ready color flushed into Gawain's cheeks. "Yes. In fact, I have a letter from him to the king."

Bedwyr made up his mind. "The king will want to see you," he said and, turning, trotted his stallion over to Arthur. The two men conferred for a moment, and then Arthur moved in their direction while Bedwyr stayed to supervise the recruits.

"Morgan told me I might expect to see you one day," Arthur said as soon as he reached the fence. "Welcome to Venta, cousin." And he gave the boy his rare, warm smile.

Gawain's eyes were wide and startled as he took in the king's face at close range. Some of the warmth left Arthur's eyes. "Is something wrong?" he asked.

The light dappling of freckles on Gawain's cheeks vanished in a flood of red. "No, my lord," he stammered. "It's just . . . just . . . you look exactly like my brother Mordred!"

"Oh." Arthur's smile returned. "I look very like my mother," he explained. "I expect Mordred looks like her too. After all, my mother and your mother were sisters."

The confusion lifted from Gawain's eyes. "Of course," he said. "That must be the reason."

"Bedwyr tells me you have a letter from Pellinore to me?"

"Yes, my lord. It is with my things at the praetorium."

Arthur turned to his wife. "I'll ride back with you now, if you like."

"All right," she replied slowly, and Arthur began to walk the chestnut around the rope fence. Once he joined them on the other side, they all three turned and began to retrace the way to Venta. "So you have come to join my army?" Arthur asked Gawain, and his cousin grinned in delighted response.

Gwenhwyfar urged her mare to keep pace with Arthur's bigger-striding horse and watched her husband's profile out of the side of her eye. He was clearly delighted to see Gawain. Just as clearly, his cousin's arrival had not been the shock to him it had been to Bedwyr.

"Morgan told me I might expect to see you. . . ." Gwenhwyfar had been under the impression that Arthur was not on speaking terms with his aunt. Obviously she had been mistaken. There was the faintest of lines between her perfect brows as she rode in silence beside the two men and listened to them talk.

Chapter 23

*I*T was a time of waiting. The king waited for news of the Saxons, which came in sporadically and was ambiguous in nature. Messengers were going back and forth among the three bretwaldas, and in March Offa, Cynewulf, and Cerdic met for two days in Sussex.

"They might be meeting about the treaty, or they might be planning something else," Arthur said to Bedwyr when this piece of news came in from one of Lionel's spies.

"Wouldn't it be ironic if our peace proposals were the very thing needed to make them unite in opposition to us," Bedwyr said.

Arthur's straight black brows rose faintly. "Very ironic." His tone was extremely dry.

Bedwyr grinned.

The two men were returning to the praetorium from the cavalry schooling ring. Bedwyr was riding Sluan and Arthur was on the chestnut, Ruadh, he had first ridden during the training session that Gwenhwyfar and Gawain had witnessed a few months ago. Arthur liked the horse and was using him as a second mount. The horses walked slowly side by side and Bedwyr looked again at Arthur's lean, dark face. "You think they're coming, don't you?" he asked.

"Yes," said the king, "I do." There was no irony now in his voice.

"If Kent and Sussex and Anglia combine," Bedwyr said soberly, "they will come against Dumnonia."

"Yes."

Bedwyr drew a long breath. "Ambrosius' wall has held them before." The wall he referred to was one built by Arthur's uncle, Constantine's oldest son, in order to protect Dumnonia's vulnerable east from attack from the Saxon shore. The rest of Dumnonia was effectively guarded by natural obstacles: the south and west by the sea, the north by the Aildon hills. Ambrosius' wall, a fifty-mile-long bank with a ditch, had done for Dumnonia what Hadrian's wall had done for several centuries in the north—held back the barbarian invaders.

"They will have to come over the wall," Bedwyr went on. "It is the only feasible access into the southwest from the Thames valley. We shall have to concentrate our defense there. We've held them before. We can do it again."

Ruadh shied at something on the side of the road and Arthur absently patted his neck. He stared in silence for a moment at his own hand on the horse's bright coat, then said, "Actually there are two ways into Dumnonia from the Thames valley."

"Two ways?" Bedwyr looked at him in puzzlement. "Do you mean by sea?"

"No. One way is the way you have named, the Roman road to Calleva. In order to get through to Calleva, however, they would first have to breach Ambrosius' wall and the forts that guard it. Not an impossible task, but difficult."

"And the second way?"

"The Roman road to Corinium."

Bedwyr continued to look puzzled. "The Aildon hills are between the Corinium road and Dumnonia. And they are high in the west, up to a thousand feet. No army could get through there."

"They could if they took the Badon pass." He looked from his hand to Bedwyr's face. "Cut off the Corinium road, break south through the pass, and you'd find yourself right on the Roman road to Venta."

"Gods," said Bedwyr. "So you would."

"If we were all at the wall, facing east, Offa could come in behind us. We would be between the Saxons and the wall, with more Saxons beyond."

Bedwyr's blue eyes blazed. "Gods," he said. "I never gave a thought to that pass."

"I want to look at it," Arthur said.

"I'll go with you."

"Very well, but I don't want anyone to know where we are going, Bedwyr."

Bedwyr nodded. "When do you want to leave?"

"In two days. I'm not going to bother to call Cai in from Camelot." This was the name they had chosen for Arthur's new capital. "Gwenhwyfar is perfectly capable of seeing to things in Venta in my absence."

There was a short silence. Then Bedwyr said slowly, "Why do you want to keep where we are going a secret? Surely the one way to keep Offa from using the pass is to let him know we are aware of it."

"But I don't want to keep Offa from using the pass," came the prompt reply.

Bedwyr stared at the king. "The sides of the Badon pass are very steep, Arthur. You cannot use cavalry there."

"I don't need the cavalry."

"*What*! Your whole success against the Saxons has been based on the use of cavalry."

Arthur gave him a level gray look. "Bedwyr, an army caught in the Badon pass, if it is as I remember, is an army caught in a death trap. If I can lure Offa into Badon, we won't need cavalry. All we will need are shovels to bury the dead." And as Bedwyr stared, the king put his horse into a trot up the main street of Venta.

The queen's wait was far more personal than the king's. She waited from month to month, hoping desperately that this time there would be no blood, that this was the month she would have conceived a child.

It was most cruel when she was late, when her hopes had begun to rise, when she had begun to imagine that she felt unwell in the mornings . . . and then, there it would be, the hated sign of failure.

A barren woman was always tragic, she thought despairingly, but at least her tragedy belonged to herself and her husband alone. When a queen was barren, the tragedy belonged to a nation.

Arthur was always reassuring. Every month, when she had to report to him she was not yet with child, he would tell her not to worry, that she would conceive eventually. But Gwenhwyfar was beginning to fear that she would not. More, she was beginning to fear that, in his heart, Arthur was not as confident as he made himself appear to her.

He had married her in order to get heirs for Britain. What would he do, she wondered, if she could never have a child? Would he put her away? Take another wife?

No. That would not happen. It could not happen. Surely God would not be so cruel.

Mary, she prayed. Mother of Our Savior. Help me. Let me conceive a child.

"You are not taking a bodyguard?" Gwenhwyfar asked Arthur worriedly. He had just informed her that he and Bedwyr were going to visit Camelot for a few days to see what progress had been made in the last month. He was not telling anyone at all about the Badon pass. "Is that wise, Arthur?" his wife continued. "Surely it wouldn't hurt to take an escort of cavalry."

Arthur's face lit with real amusement. "Bedwyr would be extremely insulted if he could hear you, Gwenhwyfar. He considers himself the equal of a whole troop of cavalry. And what's more, he is. We shall be perfectly safe, I promise you."

She sighed. "Very well. It's no use arguing, I can see."

His amusement deepened. "No use at all."

"Who is going to be in command here while you are gone? Valerius?"

"Valerius will see to the army, of course. But I am leaving you in charge of the praetorium." She looked pleased. "I don't think anything unusual will arise," he added. "Prince Meliagrance is supposed to be coming to Venta to talk with me, and he could possibly arrive in my absence. If he does, just entertain him until I get back."

"Meliagrance," said Gwenhwyfar thoughtfully. "Isn't he the new chief of the Verica Tribe?"

"Since his father died in January. Old Col was never much use to me, but I think Meliagrance might have a different point of view."

Gwenhwyfar gave him a long green look. "He might provide some soldiers for you, you mean."

Arthur's reply was cheerful. "Precisely."

There was no answering humor on Gwenhwyfar's lovely face. "You think they are coming, don't you?" she asked, echoing Bedwyr's earlier words.

He gave her the same reply he had given to Bedwyr. "Yes, I do."

She nodded, trying to conceal the shiver of fear that ran up her spine. "All right," she said. "I will look after things here for you and entertain your prince should he arrive."

"That's my girl." He gave her an approving smile and a comradely pat on the shoulder before he left to see to other things.

The dark storms rose within her. She did not want his approval. She did not want to be his comrade. She wanted to be his love. But she had learned to tread carefully with him, not to show him too clearly how she felt. The few times she had tried to step across the invisible line he had drawn between them, he had withdrawn so quickly he had frightened her.

She had his confidence. She had his friendship. She had his passion. She did not have his love.

If only she could have a child! That was what was standing between them, she was certain of it. He could not commit himself to her completely, because if she were barren . . . if she were barren . . . he might have to put her away.

Surely this month, she prayed. Surely this month she would conceive.

Meliagrance came to Venta while Arthur was gone and Gwenhwyfar kept him entertained until the king returned. In the process, the young chief of the Verica fell madly in love with her, but Gwenhwyfar was so accustomed to men falling in love with her that she scarcely noticed.

It was early evening when Arthur and Bedwyr rode into Venta three days after their departure. Arthur spent an hour with Meliagrance and then went to seek out his wife. She had retired early, he was told, as she was not feeling well. The guard at her door opened it for him and he entered the private reception salon that had at one time belonged to Igraine.

He was surprised to find Gwenhwyfar alone. She was sitting on a stool by the brazier. No, he thought, she was huddled by the brazier. "What is wrong?" he asked sharply as he crossed the floor to her side. "Are you ill? Where are your women?"

"I sent them away," she replied dully.

"Are you all right?" He had reached her now and he sank on his heels to look into her face.

She avoided his eyes. "Yes." There was unmistakable bitterness in her voice. "I'm perfectly fine."

He knew then what was the matter. She had found out once again that she was not with child.

Arthur closed his eyes, blocking out the sight of his suffering wife. He had not wanted to have to deal with this, but now it seemed he would have to.

The irony of it was almost too much for him to bear. Morgan had refused to marry him because she could not have children, and now it seemed that Gwenhwyfar . . . He opened his eyes and looked at his wife's averted profile. She needed comfort from him. The problem was, he did not know if he had it in him to give to her. There was too much emptiness in him. He managed in his role as king. He could even find it within himself to return friendship. But what Gwenhwyfar needed from him . . . wanted from him . . . he did not have.

He would have to try. It would be cruel to leave her like this.

"Gwenhwyfar," he said very gently. "My dear. Don't. Don't. I can't bear to see you so unhappy."

She raised her head, looked at him, and then she was in his arms. They sat on the floor together before the brazier and she buried her face in his shoulder and sobbed—deep, wrenching sobs that hurt him to hear. He held her lightly and stroked the beautiful hair that drifted across his chest and shoulder, and made inarticulate sounds of comfort.

When the force of her grief had been spent, she lay exhausted against his shoulder and listened to the quiet beat of his heart. "I'm not pregnant. Again." Her voice was still thick with tears.

He smoothed the hair back from her hot forehead. "Next month," he said.

But she shook her head. "What if it's not next month, Arthur?" She had been so afraid to say this, but now, with the comfort of his arms around her, she found the courage. "What if I am barren?" He didn't answer and she pressed her face against him. "I don't think I could bear it if you put me away," she whispered.

She could feel the surprise that ran through him. "Put you away? Who said anything about putting you away?"

His white wool tunic was wet from her tears. She huddled close and said in a small fearful voice, "You must have a son. Everyone knows that. It's why you married me. And if I cannot . . . if I cannot . . . perhaps you should take another wife."

He put his hands on her shoulders and held her away so he could look at her. This, at least, was one point on which he could reassure her. "*You* are my wife." Even when it was swollen with crying, her face was beautiful. "Nothing can change that. I have no intention, now or ever, of putting you away."

It was as if twin candles lit behind her eyes. "Do you mean that? I have been so afraid."

"Of course I mean it. And it takes two to make a child. The fault could as easily be mine as it is yours."

That thought had never occurred to her. Her eyes widened.

He smiled and gently touched her wet cheek. "You are the Queen of Britain. No one will ever take that away from you."

"Oh, Arthur." She burrowed back into his arms. "I don't care about being queen. I only care about losing you."

Arthur stared at the beautiful red-gold hair that clung to his arm and hand, and the expression on his face was bleak. He should have foreseen this happening, he thought. She was young. He was the man who had awakened her body, had taught her the meaning of passion. And he was the high king, the most powerful man in Britain. Of course she would fancy herself in love with him.

He liked her. He was grateful to her. She was honest and passionate, and she had helped to relieve some of the terrible tension in his body, even if she had been unable to fill the emptiness in his soul.

He supposed he had been a fool to think he could be just friends with her, as he was friends with Bedwyr and Cai. The dynamics between a man and a woman did not allow for uncomplicated friendship. He, of all people, should have known that.

The problem was, friendship was the best he could offer her. And loyalty. He owed her that and he would keep to his word. Besides, the last thing he needed was another wife.

And perhaps, in time, friendship and loyalty would be enough. She hero-worshiped him, really, like so many of his men. She couldn't love him. She did not know him well enough to love him. Only one person knew him well enough for that.

Gwenhwyfar felt the shudder that ran all through him. "What is it?" she asked, raising her head.

His face wore the remote, austere look she dreaded. "Nothing," he answered. His mouth smiled at her, but his eyes remained aloof. "Are you as hungry as I am?" he asked.

An absurdly surprised expression crossed her face. "Yes," she said in astonishment. "I believe I am."

His smile became more natural. "Good. Why don't you send for some food and we'll have supper here together?"

She smiled back, radiantly beautiful. "All right," she said. "I will."

Chapter 24

BY the end of May it was clear that a Saxon army was gathering in Sussex. For the first time in history, the three Saxon bretwaldas were combining forces for a concentrated attack against Dumnonia, the heartland of Romano-Celtic rule in Britain. This was not going to be like the campaigns of the past; that was clear too. This time, instead of a spread-out action fought on many fronts, the two armies were heading for a single confrontation, strength against strength, with the reward for the winner to be Britain itself.

In early June Arthur sent Valerius with two divisions of foot to garrison the forts along Ambrosius' wall. He also sent Bedwyr with the entire cavalry. Arthur himself was staying with the main body of the foot at Calleva.

"I am giving you the worst part of this battle," he told his two commanders soberly. "I have little doubt that Offa will attack the wall. He will want to test our strength. It is up to you to convince him that he cannot break through the wall without tremendous cost to himself. And you must do this with only the cavalry and two divisions of foot. It is up to you to force the Saxons to take the option of the Badon pass."

Bedwyr's eyes became midnight blue, but he said nothing.

It was Valerius who answered Arthur. "What if Offa does not back off, my lord? What if he decides to make one great thrust and keeps on coming?"

"Then," came the king's measured reply, "you must hold him back until I can get the remainder of the foot to you."

Bedwyr grinned. "Don't worry, Arthur. We'll hold the bastards."

Arthur's eyes, so light in his deeply tanned face, met Bedwyr's. He knew, and he knew that Bedwyr knew, that if Offa threw his whole army at the wall, Bedwyr would have to sacrifice his entire command to hold them. In a rare gesture of affection, Arthur put his hand on his cavalry captain's arm. "Bedwyr the Lion," he said. Bedwyr laughed.

* * *

Ambrosius' wall was always garrisoned; there was a series of manned forts running along the whole of its fifty-mile length. Bedwyr and Valerius did not try to protect the whole wall, but concentrated their forces along the sloping hill where the wall met the Roman road to Calleva. A week after their command was in place, the Saxon army made its appearance.

Gareth, whom Bedwyr had taken under his wing at Arthur's request, brought the news to the prince. Bedwyr's white teeth flashed in a satisfied grin. "Good," he said. "Now we shall see some action." Gareth, who had never been in battle before, stared with wonder at Bedwyr's pleased face. The report was that the entire combined forces of Offa, Cynewulf, and Cerdic were out there. And Bedwyr was smiling! It was a misty, foggy morning when the Saxons decided to make their move. The British foot soldiers, among whom were a number of Meliagrance's men, who had not yet seen the Saxons in battle, were lined behind the protection of the great earthen wall. Many of them could not see the enemy, but they could hear the bloodcurdling yells of the Saxon warriors and then the sound of the horns. The noise began to move closer. The first line of men at the top of the wall raised their arrows. As soon as the Saxons were within range, Valerius gave the order and a murderous spray of death shot toward the oncoming Saxon ranks. Men fell but the oncoming wall of screaming warriors simply climbed over their own dead and continued their forward rush. Bedwyr gave the order for the cavalry to charge.

He had all three kinds of horse under him today: his own heavy horse, so effective in smashing lines of Saxon foot; the medium horse under Peredur, faster than the great horses from Gaul, but lighter; and the light horse under Gwynn. All had followed Bedwyr into battle before, and all knew what to expect. In total they numbered just under a thousand horses and men. It seemed to Gareth, who was watching the oncoming horde with a dry throat and slamming heart, that the Saxons had ten times that number.

Bedwyr saw immediately that this was not a tentative strike. This was dangerous, and if he did not turn it back almost immediately, they were going to be in very serious trouble. With a roar that carried even over the shrieks of the Saxon masses, Bedwyr launched Sluan down the slope of the banked wall, leapt the ditch beyond it, and charged straight into the wall of the oncoming enemy. His men followed.

Bedwyr had always been awesome in the field; his great height and tremendous physical strength gave him advantages few other men enjoyed. Never, however, had he fought as ferociously as he did today. He almost decapitated the first man he swung his sword at, and he took the hand right off the man behind him.

Gareth kept his horse close behind Bedwyr's and prayed. Even in his worst nightmares he had never believed anything could be as awful as this. The noise . . . the smell . . . the blood. The only safety in the world seemed to be behind the broad back of the big blond man on the black stallion. Bedwyr himself seemed not to know the meaning of fear as he slashed through the line of Saxons, scattering them in panic with his slicing blade, bloody now up to its hilt. Gareth swung his own sword and fought to keep up with the prince. The rest of the cavalry, ablaze with their leader's reckless, raging courage, came pouring behind him.

It was not battle lust that was driving Bedwyr, however, but the clear, coolheaded conviction that if he did not turn the Saxons back in the first ten minutes of fighting, they could not be turned back at all. And there were only two divisions of foot to hold them once they got past the cavalry. So he drove men to their knees with his bloody sword, then trampled them underfoot with the equally bloody hooves of his stallion. He forged on relentlessly, a pitiless instrument of terror and death, and after five minutes the Saxon line began to waver. Then there came the sound of a horn. Offa was calling a retreat.

It took the Saxons another five minutes to disengage. During that time, the British cavalry never let up its attack. Gareth watched Bedwyr continue to drive his sword through the remaining front line of warriors, killing, crippling . . . and then it was over. The Saxons turned their backs and ran, and Bedwyr called the cavalry to return to the wall.

Once they were behind the welcome protection of the ditch and great bank, Bedwyr slid from his saddle. Gareth had a brief glimpse of blazing blue eyes before the prince turned away to speak to Valerius.

"Send me a courier," he said. "I have a message for the king." Then, leaning against his stallion's massive sweaty, bloodflecked shoulder, he began to laugh.

The message Bedwyr sent to Arthur was brief: "They sent their whole force against us and we turned them back. All is well."

Arthur listened to the courier recite the simple words and then he turned to Cai. "Bedwyr the Lion," he said, and his eyes were very bright.

Cai grinned. "The Saxons say he is a demon."

"The Saxons may be right." Arthur regarded his orderly camp of foot soldiers. "I do not think Offa would have pulled back so quickly if he did not have another plan in mind." He thrust a hand through his thick, smooth hair. "We shall soon see. Lionel has scouts posted on the Corinium Road. If Offa makes a move, we shall know about it."

The scout they were waiting for came galloping into Calleva at noon the following day. The news he brought was that Offa and Cerdic had put three-quarters of the army on the road to Corinium, leaving Cynewulf to hold the line at the wall. Once Arthur heard this, he began to move his own men north. The British were at the Badon pass within hours.

The pass in question was a deep valley that ran between the heights of Mount Badon and Mount Dal. It was extremely narrow and the sides of both mountains were steep; there were places where only two men could walk abreast. The entire pass, from beginning to end, was five miles long.

Before dark Arthur had archers and crossbowmen hidden all over the heights of Mount Badon and Mount Dal. Their orders were to remain hidden until the king gave the signal to shoot.

The British stayed on the mountainsides all night long. Arthur had stationed Cai at the beginning of the pass, on the Mount Dal side, while he himself was on the heights of Mount Badon, about two and a half miles into the pass.

When the sun rose the following morning, Arthur's men, who had huddled under their cloaks for warmth all night and who had only bread to eat for breakfast, came to attention. The sun illuminated the higher slopes of the mountains and moved slightly westward in the sky. It was two hours after sunrise before the Saxon army made its appearance, coming from the direction of the Corinium road.

It was eight o'clock in the morning when the first Saxon entered the pass. The British archers lay still. Arthur wanted Offa fully committed before he opened fire.

The Saxons laughed and talked as they marched along. When the line of warriors first came into Arthur's view, he recognized them as Cerdic's men. The line passed below him and Arthur let it go. He looked at the sky, estimating time. Another half-hour, he thought, and they would be strung out nearly the whole length of the pass.

When the sun told him it was time, Arthur rose to his feet and, with the voice trained by Merlin for just such a situation, called to his archers to open fire. On either side of him, up and down the valley, his commanders heard his call. The first arrow whispered through the air, and a Saxon fell.

There were perhaps seven thousand Saxons strung out along the length of the pass and death was raining down upon them from out of the skies. They scrambled to find shelter, but there was no shelter. The overhanging rocks of Mount Badon could be penetrated by the archers stationed on Mount Dal. The Saxons were dying every inch of the way, climbing over their own dead as they tried to go forward to reach the safety of the plain beyond the pass.

Once Offa realized what had happened, he had to make an immediate decision: pull out and save as many men as he could, or go on and try to break through the pass. If he could somehow get his army through this valley of death, he would be between Arthur and his supply base, between Arthur and his cavalry. The whole outcome of this ambush could be turned completely around.

His men were dying, but he outnumbered the Britons by a significant margin. Offa ordered the provision wagons into the pass to give his men protection under them, and he continued to send his army forward. He also ordered his own scouts into the heights of the mountains to seek out and kill as many of Arthur's archers and crossbowmen as could be found. Fifteen of his finest men he sent on a special mission: find the High King of Britain and cut him down.

The British attack was murderous. Arthur had no intention of leaving Offa enough men to launch an effective counteroffensive from the plain beyond. When the king learned that Offa was using the supply wagons for shelters, he ordered fire arrows used on them. Soon the pass below was filled with smoke.

The sun hit the floor of the Badon pass only when it was directly overhead. By the time its first rays shone down between the heights of the two mountains, the slaughter had been under way for several hours. While Offa's scouts had accounted for some of the British bowmen, they could not seriously affect the steadiness of the murderous barrage. Arthur had thousands of bowmen hidden on the heights above the pass. The Badon pass was a charnel house beyond anything anyone in the two participating armies had ever seen.

Offa, however, remained hopeful for almost another hour that he could reach the end of the pass and turn the course of the day. His own scouts scrambled back and forth across the mountains bringing him news of what was occurring below. At just about the exact time that Offa realized he had lost, that he would not have enough men left alive to mount an effective counteroffensive, one of his specially commissioned scouts was aiming his arrow at the unprotected back of the High King of Britain.

It had not been difficult to find Arthur. His voice rang up and down the valley, seeming to the dying men below to be coming straight out of the sky. Offa's man had tracked it easily enough, and now, hidden behind a boulder and unseen by the Britons who flanked their king, he raised his bow, his eyes fixed unwaveringly on the black-haired man before him.

At the very last minute, Arthur sensed danger. He whirled to face it and received the arrow in his chest rather than in his back. The arrow, shot from so close a distance, penetrated his leather tunic. The king fell without a sound.

Gawain, who had been standing at Arthur's side, turned also and, without pause, drew his own sword and ran for the assassin. He killed him with vicious pleasure.

There was a circle of men kneeling around Arthur when Gawain returned to the king's side. They made way for him. "Send for Drusus," Gawain said as he dropped to his knees beside his cousin.

"Bors has gone for him," came the instant reply. Then they all fell quiet as Arthur's lashes moved on his cheek. They lifted, and pain-filled gray eyes looked up into Gawain's. "Cai," said the king. It was hard to hear him, so Gawain bent his head low, next to Arthur's lips. "Tell Cai to finish this out."

"We will, my lord," Gawain said strongly, and Arthur's eyes closed once again. Gawain thought he was still conscious, however, as there were lines of pain between his brows and around his mouth.

Someone ran to bring the news to Cai, and in a few minutes Drusus, the army physician, was at the king's side. He looked horrified when he saw the prone figure of Arthur, with the arrow still sticking out of his chest. They had been afraid to remove it. Too many of them had seen that death often followed that particular procedure. But, of course, it had to be done.

Drusus, muttering under his breath, took out the arrow. Arthur went, if possible, even whiter, but the terrible gush of blood they had all feared did not follow. Drusus said, with relief very evident in his voice, "It must have hit the breastbone."

There was a loud release of sound from the encircling men.

Drusus looked up. "He must be got off this mountain."

The men exchanged grim looks. They were two and a half miles into the pass.

It was Gawain who took charge. "Bind up the wound as best you can," he told the physician. "We will make a sling out of a cloak and carry him out that way."

As Drusus began to assemble his bandages, Gawain dropped back to his knees beside Arthur. Once again the long lashes lifted. "I got the murdering bastard, my lord," Gawain said fiercely.

The faintest glimmer of approval appeared in the heavy gray eyes. "You are doing very well, little cousin," Arthur murmured. And, mercifully, lost consciousness.

They brought Arthur to Calleva, a Roman city that had been used most recently as a place to quarter troops. At one time Calleva had been a thriving market for the agricultural district that surrounded it; today it was merely a shell of its former self, its small permanent population spread out behind the walls built hundreds of years before by Roman legions.

The county hall was in good repair and it was there they carried the injured king. Drusus cleaned and bandaged Arthur's wound once more and then sat down to keep vigil.

He was still there when Cai arrived in Calleva shortly after midnight. Drusus met him at the door of Arthur's room. "How bad is it?" Cai demanded.

"There has been some tearing," Drusus replied in a low voice. "The arrow hit the breastbone and then veered off. But I don't think any vital organs have been damaged, Commander. We must just hope that no infection sets in."

Cai nodded. "Is he sleeping? May I see him?"

"Yes, you can see him. He hasn't been sleeping. I think he's been waiting for news from you."

Cai's sunburned face was somber as he crossed the floor to the bedplace where they had laid the king. Arthur's eyes were closed, but when Cai spoke his name, they opened.

"The Saxons are finished," Cai said. "The few who made it to the end of the pass were met by Antonius and the Sixth foot, as you planned, and were completely routed. Offa pulled out what men he could and retreated toward the coast. He left eighty percent of his army at Badon, Arthur. It will be many years before the Saxons fight again."

The heavy eyes registered comprehension. Then in a low but clear voice Arthur said, "Send word to Bedwyr that he is to remain where he is until Lionel is certain the Saxons have retreated from the wall as well."

"I will," said Cai.

The faintest flicker of a smile crossed the thin drawn face on the pillow, and then the gray eyes closed once more.

Late the following afternoon Gwenhwyfar arrived in Calleva. Word was out that the king had been injured, but not seriously, and the mood in the country was jubilant. This was their day of deliverance. A whole generation of Saxons had fallen at Badon; for the first time since Vortigern had invited Hengist and his people to settle in Britain, the Saxon threat was lifted.

Gwenhwyfar had not expected to find Arthur so ill. He was semiconscious when she went in to see him, and he did not seem to recognize her. She turned to Drusus, who was standing beside her. "They said it was only a flesh wound!"

"We thought it best not to alarm the country, my lady. And, truly, the wound is not serious. But it will take time to heal."

Gwenhwyfar put a slim hand on her husband's forehead and was relieved to find it cool. She smiled at Drusus. "I'll sit with him for a little. You look tired, Drusus. Get some rest."

After the physician had left, Gwenhwyfar took her place in the chair that had been drawn up beside the bed. Arthur seemed to be sleeping and Gwenhwyfar studied his unconscious face with hungry eyes. He was unshaven and his suntanned skin looked sallow and his hair fell in a tangle across his forehead and, still, he was beautiful. She loved him so much. If anything should happen to him . . . Her throat ached and she reached out to pick up the hand that was lying lax on the blanket. She was alone and so she bent her head and pressed her cheek against the thin, strong fingers. "Don't worry, my love," she whispered fiercely. "You'll get better. I'm going to take very good care of you, I promise." The face on the pillow did not change.

Chapter 25

"*I* DON'T like it at all," Drusus said to Cai as they conferred outside the king's bedchamber three days later. "He is not improving."

Cai had forced himself to keep a cheerful face in front of others, but he did not like it either. "Has an infection set in?" he asked worriedly.

"No. That is what I don't understand. There is no fever. The wound is clean. It's as if . . . it's as if he's not trying, as if he doesn't want to get better. I may sound foolish, but I'm afraid if things continue to go on as they are, we will lose him. And I don't understand why!"

"Christ in heaven," said Cai. "We cannot lose him."

Drusus looked harried. "Well, it is my duty to inform you, Commander, that we are in very grave danger of doing just that. I can get no response from him. The queen can get no response from him. He is, quite simply, going away from us."

Cai had grown very pale. "I didn't realize," he said. "I thought it was the wound."

"I wish to God it were," Drusus cried in frustration. "The wound I could do something about. This . . . this is beyond me."

"There is only one person who can deal with this," said Cai. "The Lady of Avalon."

Drusus shook his head. "She is a great healer, I will grant you, but it is not the king's flesh that is our present problem."

"I know. That is why we need her." He looked over at the still figure on the bed. "I'm leaving right now," he said to Drusus. "Don't dare let anything happen to the king until I return!"

Gwenhwyfar was at her post by Arthur's bedside when Cai came to the door the following afternoon with Morgan by his side. The queen heard the door open and turned to see the two in the doorway. She rose from her chair and went quietly to speak to them.

When Drusus had told her yesterday that Cai had gone for the Lady of Avalon, Gwenhwyfar had been glad. She had no idea if Morgan could help or not, but her reputation as a healer was great. And Arthur was dying. Gwenhwyfar sensed that quite clearly as she sat by his still figure for hour after endless hour. He was dying, and they were all helpless to do anything to save him.

So now she looked hopefully from Cai to the small figure beside him, but the words she had prepared to say died on her lips. Surely this was not Arthur's aunt! This girl did not look any older than she herself.

Cai was speaking. "Any change?"

"No," Gwenhwyfar managed to answer. She looked at Morgan's small, empty hands. "Are you the Lady of Avalon?" she asked.

Huge brown eyes looked gravely back. "Yes, I am," came the composed answer. "May I see Arthur, please?"

"Of course." Gwenhwyfar turned as if to lead her to the bedside, but Cai's hand grasped her arm.

"Wait here," he said imperatively. "Leave them alone."

Gwenhwyfar's eyes widened; then she nodded. The two of them stayed in the doorway and watched.

For days now Arthur had been sinking deeper and deeper. It was so peaceful here in the warm dark. So restful. Far in the distance he could still hear the dim sound of voices, but he had gone deep enough now that they did not disturb him. He was floating in the dark, down, down, down. . . .

Arthur. Someone was calling him. *Arthur.* It came again, clearly. *Arthur.* It was insistent, urgent, and he knew who it was. He would answer that call were he at the very door of death, and he had not gone that far yet. He half-opened his eyes.

She was there. He could see her face floating above him, could see her eyes. *No,* she said to him. He could hear her voice in his brain, even though her lips had not moved. *No, Arthur. You cannot do this.*

Why not? His own answer was like hers, silent, mind to mind. They had never done this before, communicated in words without speech. It was surprisingly easy.

I won't let you, she said.

Morgan. He had to make her understand. *I am so weary. So weary of it all. So weary of being alone. Let me go.*

No.

He could feel the strength of her will, and he sought to evade it. *My job is done. Britain is safe. Let me go.*

No, she said. *Not yet. There is work still for you.*

What work? But she was putting a block between them, hiding her thoughts. *What work, Morgan?*

She switched to the plea she knew could not fail. *Don't leave me, Arthur. Don't leave me.*

He felt her fear. *I can't—* he started to say.

Don't leave me, Arthur. Don't leave me.

It was panic now. Morgan in fear. It was something he could not allow. *All right. All right.* He tried to reassure her. *Don't be afraid.* He gathered his forces, made a tremendous effort, and struggled up through the dark. He closed his eyes, then opened them fully. He could see her clearly now, could see the tears on her face. "Morgan." His lips moved, although only a thread of sound came out.

Her great dark eyes searched his face. She had been sitting on the edge of his bed and now she leaned forward and buried her face in his sound shoulder. He turned his head slightly so his cheek could touch her hair. It smelled of lavender.

He was suddenly exhausted. *It's all right, my love.* Even in the full light he could still hear her in his mind. *Now you can sleep,* she said. And he closed his eyes.

Gwenhwyfar felt cold fear strike her heart when she saw Morgan raise her head and turn away from the bed, weeping uncontrollably. Drusus, who had joined Cai and the queen in the doorway, moved instantly into the room. Gwenhwyfar, crying "Arthur!" in a sharp, panicked voice, reached the bedside before him.

He was breathing; she saw that immediately. Breathing normally, not the shallow slow breathing that had so frightened her these last days. His face had a little color; it did not look so sallow as it had. Drusus bent his head to listen to the king's heart and when he looked up at Gwenhwyfar his face was amazed. "He's sleeping naturally," he said. "He seems . . . better."

The queen and the doctor both turned at the same moment to look at the small weeping figure who was being held now in Cai's arms.

"I know," the big man was saying in a voice Gwenhwyfar had never heard him use. "But it had to be done, Morgan."

"Yes," came the choked reply, barely audible to the two by the king's bedside. "But . . . oh, Cai . . ."

"Come along." Cai picked up Arthur's aunt as if she had been a child and carried her out of the room.

Arthur slept for hours and then woke up normally, looked at his wife, who was sitting by his side, and gave her a faint smile of recognition.

"Oh, Arthur." Gwenhwyfar's voice trembled with relief. "Thank God. We have been so worried about you."

His face looked so thin, she thought. The hollows under the beautiful cheekbones were painfully deep, but his eyes were clear and focused directly on her face. "Could you drink a little broth?" she asked.

"Yes," he said. "Thank you."

He let her feed him, which pleased her immensely. She was returning the empty bowl to a table in the corner of the room when Morgan came in the door. The Lady of Avalon did not seem to notice that the queen was in the room; her eyes were all for Arthur. Gwenhwyfar stilled her greeting, stood quietly and watched.

Morgan crossed to Arthur's side and stood there for a long moment. They simply looked at each other, neither of them speaking a word. Then Morgan slipped her hand in the thin muscular hand that was lying so quietly on the top of the blanket. From where she stood, Gwenhwyfar could clearly see his fingers close tightly.

She put the bowl down sharply upon the table and two pairs of eyes looked at her with identically startled expressions. Then Morgan smiled. "I'm sorry, my lady. I did not see you."

Gwenhwyfar came slowly back toward the bed. Morgan had withdrawn her hand from Arthur's and was looking with approval at Gwenhwyfar. "Oh, good," she said. "You've got him to eat."

"Yes." Gwenhwyfar looked from Morgan to her husband. "He had a little broth."

"I object," said Arthur in an astonishingly clear voice, "to being discussed as if I weren't here."

"You're in no condition to object to anything," his aunt told him astringently. "You just do as you're told."

Gwenhwyfar stared. No one spoke to Arthur like that.

"It's the secret of her success as a healer," Arthur said to his wife. "She bullies her patients back to health." Incredibly, he sounded amused.

"What is it?" Morgan asked. He was searching the room with his eyes, as if he were looking for something.

"Cabal," he said. His black brows drew together. "Where is Cabal?"

"We had to take him out," Gwenhwyfar replied in a constricted voice. "When you were so ill . . . he kept crying . . ."

Arthur's lashes screened his eyes. "Ah," he said. "Well, you can let him back in now. I'm going to be all right." He raised his lashes and looked at Morgan.

"I don't understand how you did it," Gwenhwyfar said to Morgan later in the evening before they both retired for the night. They had previously moved beds into the county hall for Drusus and the queen, and Cai had just had another one set up in one of the old offices for Morgan. "You used no medicine," Gwenhwyfar went on.

Morgan smiled at Arthur's wife. "The simple folk say I have magic. I don't believe in magic, of course, but God did give me a special power to heal. I don't always understand it myself." Her large brown eyes were wide and innocent. Morgan had no intention of telling Gwenhwyfar of what had passed between Arthur and herself.

Gwenhwyfar's long green eyes were regarding her husband's aunt skeptically. There was intelligence behind that beautiful face, Morgan realized. And Gwenhwyfar loved Arthur. Morgan had seen that very quickly. She would have to be careful.

"I did not realize you were so young," Gwenhwyfar said.

"I'm not so young really," said Morgan. "I'm twenty-six."

Gwenhwyfar looked surprised.

"Arthur and I were children together," Morgan went on. "We both grew up at Avalon, you know."

Gwenhwyfar did not know. Arthur rarely spoke about his childhood. "Well, I am very grateful to you for your . . . assistance," she said, and even to herself she sounded stiff and ungracious. She made an effort to unbend. "He . . . I . . . I was afraid I was going to lose him."

The great luminous brown eyes seemed to understand what she was feeling. Morgan laid a small chapped hand on Gwenhwyfar's sleeve. The queen smiled. "Good night."

"Good night," Morgan replied, and both women went off to their respective rooms.

They were returning to Venta; Drusus and Gwenhwyfar wanted Arthur to travel by litter and he wanted to ride. Both the queen and the physician appealed to Morgan, who appeared to be the only person Arthur ever listened to.

"Let him ride," Morgan said. "It's not that far. Besides, you'd have to tie him down to get him in a litter, and I don't think anyone quite has the nerve to do that."

They did not have the nerve, and consequently Arthur rode the few hours it took to get from Calleva to Venta. His wife rode beside him, watching him worriedly every inch of the way. Morgan and Cai rode behind them and chatted unconcernedly as the miles dropped away. Arthur was silent and Gwenhwyfar, considerately, did not try to initiate conversation. She thought he needed his energy to stay on his horse.

They were waiting for him in Venta: his soldiers, the town merchants, the local farmers who had come into the city. They lined the main street of the city ten deep, and all the way it was *Arthur! Arthur! Arthur!* Gwenhwyfar was deafened by the noise. The king looked from one side of the road to the other, recognizing faces among the screaming crowd. The mood of the city was that of ecstatic adoration.

"They love you," Gwenhwyfar said when finally they reached the courtyard of the praetorium. "You are their deliverer."

"For the moment," he replied. He shook his head at Cai's offer of help and dismounted by himself.

"What do you mean, for the moment?" Gwenhwyfar asked sharply. "I thought the Saxons were destroyed, that we were finally free."

He gave her an odd, slanting look. "Oh, we are free," he replied. "But freedom brings burdens of its own, Gwenhwyfar. And peace its own problems." He shrugged. "Let them savor this moment of sweetness. It will probably never be equaled again." He turned away from her to mount the steps of the praetorium.

Bedwyr returned to Venta a day after Arthur, and had to hear the whole story of Badon first hand. He was also reintroduced to Morgan, whom he had not met since the harvest fair at Glevum so many years ago.

"I remember you very well," he said. "Sodak let you rub his nose. I've never forgotten that." He gave Arthur a sideways blue glance before he asked, "What brings you to Venta after all these years?"

There was a distinct pause. Then Gwenhwyfar said quietly, "Arthur was far more ill than we let out, Bedwyr. We must thank Morgan and her healing arts for his life."

"*What?*" Bedwyr turned an accusing stare on Cai. "You never told me. You said it was just a flesh wound."

"It was a flesh wound and I am feeling perfectly well," said Arthur. His tone was cool. "And I am becoming extremely weary of discussing the state of my health."

"What shall we discuss then?" Morgan said affably. "The weather?"

Arthur looked down at her, raising his brows.

"Not the weather." She looked off into the distance, contemplating. "I know. We can talk about your new capital. What is it called? Camelot?"

Gray eyes met brown. Then Arthur turned to Cai. The five of them were sitting in Arthur's room, with the summer sun streaming in the open window. "My new capital," he said softly. "How is it coming, Cai?"

"Well, I've been busy with other things lately," Cai replied. Bedwyr grunted. "However, I hear from Gerontius that the building is almost finished." He looked at Morgan. "It should be habitable by late fall."

Morgan smiled at him, then turned to the queen. "Are you looking forward to your new home?" she asked. Gwenhwyfar looked from Morgan to her husband and then back to Morgan again. She forced herself to make a civil reply.

Morgan remained in Venta for a week before she returned to Avalon. It was a disquieting week for Gwenhwyfar. She was jealous of the relationship between her husband and his aunt, and she was ashamed of herself for being jealous.

Morgan and Arthur had grown up together, she told herself. They were like brother and sister. It was selfish of her to begrudge him the pleasure he so obviously found in Morgan's company.

But he was different when he was with her. There was no disguising that. He was more relaxed than she had ever seen him, more . . . happy.

She walked in on them two days before Morgan left Venta. They were in Arthur's room, and Cabal had got something he was not supposed to have. Morgan was trying to get it away from him. Gwenhwyfar opened the door to find Arthur dissolved in laughter as he watched Morgan and Cabal tussling on the floor before his desk. Gwenhwyfar stopped dead and looked at her husband's face. He looked like a boy.

The dog was the first one to sense her presence, and he gave a sharp bark. Arthur's dark head turned toward the door. His face did not alter when he saw his wife. "Come in, Gwenhwyfar," he said in a shaking voice.

"Got it!" came a triumphant cry from the floor, and Morgan stood up. Her brown hair was ruffled and there was the glow of healthy color in her cheeks. In her raised hand she was brandishing a shoe.

"Morgan Victorious," said Arthur in Latin. Gwenhwyfar was unsure of the words, but she understood the look in his eyes, and a blade twisted in her heart.

It was as well for the queen's peace of mind that she did not witness the scene that took place between Arthur and Morgan the following afternoon. This time, however, Arthur had made sure that they would be alone by taking her out of Venta completely, to the open countryside beyond the army encampment. They said little as they rode along through the summer sunshine, and when they moved off the road Morgan simply followed Arthur's lead as they wound down a rutted track toward a small stream. There was no sign of any human habitation, and Arthur pulled his horse up and said, "Here."

They dismounted, still in silence, and picketed their horses to graze. With one accord they moved to a patch of dried grass in front of a large boulder and sat down side by side, leaning their backs against the sun-warmed smoothness of the rock.

Morgan picked up his hand. "I did not know it was so bad," she said, her eyes on the fingers lying so relaxed in her own. "Cai told me you were doing all right, that you and Gwenhwyfar were . . . all right."

He watched her down-looking face. "No," he said.

She looked up. "It is like being at the bottom of a well," he told her. "With no hope of ever being rescued."

He saw the pain in her eyes. "You should have let me know."

"You knew. You had to know. Was it any better for you, Morgan?"

Slowly she shook her head and he turned his hand and pulled her closer. "I didn't want to know, I suppose," she said in a muffled voice.

"It was Badon," he explained. "I could keep going for as long as I knew I was necessary, but after Badon I thought it would be . . . safe."

There was a long silence. Then: "I always used to know what you were feeling," she said. "But I never before knew what you were thinking."

He rested his cheek against her hair. "We were always together then. You didn't have to know."

"That's true."

"You should have married me."

"Yes." Her voice sounded constricted. "She cannot have children?"

"It seems not."

She rested against him. "We don't need a priest to feel married to each other, you and I."

He raised his head and looked down into her face. "What am I thinking?" he asked softly.

Her brown eyes glazed a little, looked off as if into a far distance. Then she smiled. "The grain barn," she said. "And a rainy day."

He smiled back. "When I move to Camelot, Avalon will be but twelve miles away."

They looked at each other in perfect comprehension. Then she said, simply, "We tried."

"God knows, we certainly tried." The note in his voice was grim. "Gwenhwyfar need never know," he added. "Avalon is my childhood home. You and I grew up togther. It will not seem strange for me to visit."

He slid his hands into her hair, loving the familiar feel of its silky texture, loving the shape of her head under his fingers.

"What am I thinking?" she asked.

He smoothed his thumbs across her delicate cheekbones. "I love you too," he replied a little shakily, and then his mouth was on hers and he was kissing her in an intense, starving anguish. Morgan's arms went up around his neck and he laid her back on the summer-dry grass.

Chapter 26

*T*HE summer progressed. Arthur sent the auxiliary troops raised by the regional kings home to their clans and kept in Venta only his own standing army with its officers. By early October the troops were moving into their new quarters in Camelot.

Arthur left the furnishing of their new home, called by the British word for palace, to his wife. Gwenhwyfar threw herself into the project with all her considerable energy. She was happy to have something to think about.

She still was not pregnant. Arthur had returned to her bed, but he was not the same. In matters that involved him, she was too closely concerned to be fooled. The passion, the need, were gone. In their place was kindness, but kindness was not what she wanted from him.

If only she could have a child! She hated the assessing way people looked at her waistline, hated the speculation she was certain she saw in their eyes. If she saw a woman in town holding a baby, she had to fight not to burst into tears.

The single person she felt comfortable with was Bedwyr. His blue eyes always held a glint when they looked at her, and it was not a glint of speculation. He teased her and joked with her and she was happy when she was with him. They were of the same stock, after all, both Welsh, with none of the troubling enigmatic Roman streak in their makeup. She was actually more comfortable with Bedwyr than she was with her own husband. She understood Bedwyr. She was beginning to think that she would never understand Arthur.

Then one morning she discovered Elaine being sick in a basin. It did not take long for the girl to confess she was pregnant.

"I told you to stay away from the prince," said Olwen. "You know what his reputation is. But you wouldn't listen . . ."

Gwenhwyfar was furious. She did not think she had ever been so angry in her life. She went to Arthur.

"Elaine?" he said. "The black-haired one?"

"Yes. The black-haired one." She had caught him coming in from the schooling ring. The day was hot and his hair and tunic were drenched with sweat. There was a smear of dirt across one elegant cheekbone. "Bedwyr has got her with child," she said again, looking at him out of flashing green eyes.

He sighed. "What do you want me to do about it?" he asked patiently.

She had waited for him in his room and they were alone. She stared at him for a moment in angry frustration. She was not quite certain what she wanted him to do, but she wanted him to do something.

"Did he say he would marry her?" Arthur asked.

"No." Gwenhwyfar turned her back, suddenly not wanting him to see her face. "No, but surely he should. After all, there is going to be a baby . . ." Despite her best efforts, her voice quivered.

"Gwenhwyfar." She could not bear the pity in his voice. "I'm so sorry, my dear. But this is best left to Bedwyr to handle. And to be honest, I don't think this is mainly his fault. The girl was pursuing him. Anyone could see that."

Gwenhwyfar had not seen it. She had always thought that she was the one that Bedwyr . . . "He ought to be horsewhipped," she said.

"I never whip my horses," Arthur replied gravely. "And I am certainly not going to whip Bedwyr. I will talk to him, however, and if he does not want to marry Elaine, then I will send her home to Gwynedd. You will not have to have the baby around you."

It was not to be borne. Gwenhwyfar pressed her fingers to her trembling mouth. Elaine did not even *want* this baby, whereas she . . .

Her husband's arm encircled her. "Don't fret so," he said softly, and she turned her face into his shoulder and wept.

Bedwyr did not want to marry Elaine and, weeping and miserable, she was sent home to Wales. Gwenhwyfar had one interview with Bedwyr on the subject of Elaine and it did not leave either of them in a good temper.

"You wicked seducer," she said.

"Don't be ridiculous, Gwenhwyfar," he answered. "If anything, *I* was the one who was seduced. The girl came to my bedroom. I only gave her what she asked for. I'm sorry there were . . . other consequences, but she should have thought of that before she slipped into my bed."

Other consequences! This was not a subject upon which Gwenhwyfar was rational, and she flared up at him with bitter, hurtful words.

"You sound like a jealous shrew," he told her coldly.

"Jealous!" She was shouting by this point. "You flatter yourself, Prince. I would never be jealous of Elaine because of you!"

"Not because of me." His eyes were cold blue ice, his mouth thin with anger. This was a Bedwyr she had never before seen. "You're jealous because she is having a baby and you're not. That's what this is all about."

She could hardly see, she was so furious. She picked up a goblet of Samian ware and threw it at him. He ducked and it shattered all over the mosaic tile.

Bedwyr laughed. "Your aim is rotten, my lady," he said. "Like your temper." And he walked out of the room.

The following day Meliagrance, chief of the Verica, arrived in Venta. The Verica had been one of the most important Celtic tribes in eastern Dumnonia before the arrival of the Romans, and the chief of the Verica had at one time been a very important person. In recent years, as the power of the high king had increased, the importance of the chiefs had declined. Meliagrance's father, Col, had never raised troops for either Uther or Arthur because he had refused to recognize the position of High King of Britain. Meliagrance himself had sent a troop of men to fight for Arthur during the last great Saxon attack, a concession that had pleased Arthur, for he had seen it as a sign of reconciliation between the tribe of the Verica and the high king.

So when Meliagrance appeared now in Venta, Arthur greeted him graciously. It soon became apparent, however, that it was not the king Meliagrance had come to see.

Gwenhwyfar was accustomed to men falling in love with her, and usually she did not pay them much heed. But she was feeling shut out from Arthur, and betrayed by Bedwyr, and Meliagrance's adoration was like balm on an open wound. Consequently she was kinder to him than she would ordinarily have been. She let him ride out with her in the mornings, and she seated him next to her at dinner and listened with flattering attention to his every word. She was tired of listening to Arthur and Bedwyr; all they ever talked about anymore was the administration of the army once it was moved to Camelot.

Arthur and Bedwyr did not seem to mind Meliagrance monopolizing her time. In fact, to Gwenhwyfar's extreme irritation, they appeared to find the chief of the Verica's infatuation distinctly amusing. Their lack of concern only provoked Gwenhwyfar into being even nicer to the besotted young man.

The move from Venta to Camelot was accomplished over a period of six weeks. The foot soldiers moved into their barracks first; then, at the end of October, Bedwyr moved the cavalry into its permanent quarters. By the second week in November, the palace was ready for occupation.

Gwenhwyfar was enjoying the prospects of arranging and decorating her new home, and she chose with care the furniture she wanted to go to Camelot from the praetorium in Venta. Arthur had given her the sketches of the palace and it was almost three times the size of the praetorium, so a great deal of additional furniture would be needed. Arthur had stayed in Venta with her, and for a few blissful weeks she had him to herself. Finally, however, the last of the packing was done, the last of the wagons had rolled away toward Camelot, and the king and queen were ready to make the official move themselves.

Then Arthur decided to make a series of short visits to the various forts along the Saxon shore before the winter set in. Gwenhwyfar assured him that she did not need his escort to get safely to Camelot, and he promised to meet her there in a week. He left an escort of ten cavalrymen for her and rode out himself with five others for an inspection tour.

Gwenhwyfar did not leave Venta right after Arthur, as she had originally planned. Olwen was ill with a severe cold, and as the weather was miserable, Gwenhwyfar decided to wait until her serving woman was feeling better.

Four days after Arthur's departure, Gwenhwyfar's party finally left Venta. The November day was damp and chill, and Olwen huddled inside her cloak and shivered. Gwenhwyfar chatted to Gareth, who was one of her escort, and when they reached Amesbury she stopped at the monastery for food and to give Olwen a chance to get warm.

It was early afternoon when they reached the place where they would turn off the western road and veer south onto the Roman road to Durovarium. As they arrived at the crossroads, however, there came the sound of galloping hooves thundering down the road just ahead of them. Gareth and the rest of Gwenhwyfar's escort drew their swords and formed a wedge around the queen and Olwen.

"We're friends! Friends!" The shout came from the leader of the oncoming horsemen. "Thank God I have found you, my lady! I was on my way to Venta. It's the king . . ."

Gwenhwyfar had recognized Meliagrance after his first shout. She said now, sharply, "Let him through!" She was very pale. "What is this about the king?" she said as Meliagrance's horse drew up to hers.

"He's had a fall, my lady. Coming by here late yesterday on his way to Camelot. His horse tripped. His men brought him to Clust, as we are so near."

"Oh, my God." Gwenhwyfar looked distraught. "Take me to him," she demanded. "Immediately."

"Of course, my lady. If you and your escort will follow me . . ."

"My lady," Gareth said. There was a deep line between his eyebrows. "Perhaps I should go with the chief of the Verica and you continue on to Camelot." There was something about this encounter that did not ring true to Arthur's former body servant. The king never came off a horse.

"Don't be ridiculous, Gareth," Gwenhwyfar snapped. "If the king is injured, of course I must go to him." She urged her horse forward and Meliagrance followed her lead. Gwenhwyfar turned to him and began shooting questions: "How badly is he hurt? Have you sent to Camelot for Drusus? Is he conscious? . . ."

Gareth brought up the rear as the entire party began to canter up the road. He still did not like this, but there was nothing he could do to change the queen's mind. He watched the Verica horseman who was riding by his side and when the man was not looking, he deftly transferred the dagger he was wearing from its sheath at his belt to a concealed place beneath his tunic.

When the legions had ruled Britain, the Verica had been one of the more Romanized of the Celtic tribes. It was during this period of their history that the chief had built Clust. At first the villa had merely been the country residence of the chiefs, but for the last fifty years, as the civil disorder in the country took its toll on the cities, Meliagrance's family had made the villa their main place of residence. Clust still operated as a working farm, although on a much-reduced scale from former times.

The house itself was no more elaborate than a simple farmhouse; it had none of the Roman splendor of Avalon. A ditch and a wall separated the cultivated lands and the livestock from the road, and the courtyard was not cobbled. As the queen's party rode into the dirt courtyard, men came running from the house to take their horses. The Verica men were smiling and courteous, but Gareth looked behind him and saw that the road out of the courtyard had been effectively blocked by their escorting horsemen. He thought for a moment of trying to charge through the line of horse, hesitated, and by then someone's hand was on his bridle. The man was smiling, but he had a death grip on Gareth's horse. Slowly Gareth slid to the ground.

The queen had gone into the house with Meliagrance and the Verica men were herding her escort toward another door. Gareth watched in which direction they were taking the horses before he was pushed, none too gently, in the path of his fellows.

When Gwenhwyfar realized she had been tricked, her initial reaction was fury. "Are you mad?" she asked Meliagrance. "Just what did you hope to accomplish by this extraordinary behavior?"

They were alone together in a small bedroom. Gwenhwyfar had rushed in the door, expecting to find her injured husband, and instead the door had closed and she had found herself alone with Meliagrance.

"I love you," the chief of the Verica answered her with frightening intensity. "You have become an obsession with me, Gwenhwyfar. And you care for me too. I saw that clearly enough in Venta last month. You care for me more than you do for that cold Roman husband of yours."

Gwenhwyfar opened her mouth to tell him how very wrong he was, and then thought again. Meliagrance was not above medium height, but he was strongly built. And there was a glitter in his widely set brown eyes that she did not like at all. Abruptly Gwenhwyfar realized she was in danger.

She swallowed. "Of course I care for you." Her voice was milder than it had been. It took great effort to keep it steady. "But was it really necessary to get me here by trickery?"

He smiled, pleased with her response. He waved his thick hand. "Please sit down, Gwenhwyfar. Make yourself comfortable."

Gwenhwyfar sat cautiously on the very edge of the bed. Meliagrance looked at her, and the glitter in his oddly set eyes seemed even more pronounced. His voice, however, was reasonable. "How else was I to get you here?" he asked.

Gwenhwyfar clasped her hands and did not answer for a moment. Then she looked him in the eyes and said bravely, "What do you want, Meliagrance?"

He smiled and a chill ran up her spine. "I want you."

She would have to try to reason with him. "Meliagrance, think. If you keep me here overnight, Arthur is sure to find out about it. I am not worth getting killed for. Let me go now, and I will swear to keep quiet . . ."

Her voice trailed off. He was smiling very strangely. "You don't understand, Gwenhwyfar. I am not afraid of Arthur. I don't at all mind his finding out about us." Gwenhwyfar gripped her hands together more tightly to keep them from visibly shaking. "You see," the chief of the Verica continued with perfect confidence, "I am going to be the new high king. And you will be my queen."

Gwenhwyfar stared. He was surely mad. "I don't understand . . ." she managed to say faintly.

"Arthur's task is finished," Meliagrance answered. "He was a good war leader, I will grant him that. He has thrashed the Saxons soundly. But he overstepped himself, Gwenhwyfar, with this new capital. He is a fool if he thinks we will allow him to rule over us in peace as he did in war."

"We?" Gwenhwyfar said tentatively.

"We. The Celtic leaders of Britain. It is time to banish this Roman usurper."

"Meliagrance," Gwenhwyfar said, "Arthur has the army."

"He has part of the army," came the ready reply. "The rest of it, the tribal troops he trained so efficiently, he sent home to their rightful chiefs."

For the first time Gwenhwyfar felt a fear that was not purely personal. Could it be possible? she thought in horror. Could Meliagrance actually be the leader of a Celtic conspiracy against Arthur? Were the rest of the kings and princes of Britain part of this?

"Who is joined with you?" she asked.

"I expect troops from all over the country to be joining me very shortly. I sent out the word as soon as I had you."

"I can't believe it," she said incredulously. "I can't believe they would do this to Arthur. After all he has done for them, for Britain." Her green eyes were like emeralds in her beautiful, pale face.

Meliagrance was frowning. "He is a Roman. Of course they will heed the call of one of their own."

Gwenhwyfar searched his face. He was not an ill-looking man, she thought, but those widely set eyes gave a strangely unstable expression to his face. Why had she not noticed that before? She would have to be very careful. He was looking at her now with suspicion. "What you say is true, of course," she said, and his frown smoothed out. "But have you got . . . ah, assurances that the rest of the country will join with you against Arthur?"

"I have only just informed them of my actions," Meliagrance said complacently. "But I have no doubt they will answer my call. Believe me, Gwenhwyfar, no one likes this Roman setting himself up as emperor over us."

Gwenhwyfar almost sagged with relief. There was no conspiracy; it was all in the head of this deluded fool. Arthur was safe. Meliagrance took a step toward her and she realized with a stab of fear that while Arthur might be safe, she was not. "Meliagrance," she said urgently, "Arthur will most likely get here before your followers. He's closer."

"Ah, but he does not know where you are." He reached out a thick-fingered hand to touch her hair. Gwenhwyfar repressed a shudder. "I have all your men in close confinement, my love. Never fear. He won't find you."

Gwenhwyfar froze with fear. He was going to rape her. She stared up into his strange glittering eyes and knew that this was what he had brought her here for. What a stupid fool she had been to let him think . . . Abruptly her brain began to function again. He was not thinking rape. He thought she loved him. She would have to play up to him. "Meliagrance," she said softly, "how very clever you are." He beamed. His hand continued to caress her hair. "But I am so dirty and weary," she went on. "Is it possible for you to have my things sent to me? I would so like to wash and change my clothes."

His eyes seemed to clear a little. "Of course," he said after a minute. He stepped back, and his hand left her hair. His arms were abnormally long. He looked like an ape, Gwenhwyfar thought. "Forgive me, my dear. In my excitement at seeing you, I have forgotten my duties as a host."

He was completely mad, Gwenhwyfar decided despairingly as she smiled and thanked him. The only thing she could do was play for as much time as she could. And pray to Jesus and his blessed mother that Arthur would come to her rescue.

Chapter 27

IT was not Arthur but Bedwyr who rode to Gwenhwyfar's rescue. Gareth used his dagger on the guard who was bringing him food and managed to get to the stables unseen by any of Meliagrance's men. By the time the dead guard was discovered, Gareth had half an hour's start. He rode straight to Camelot.

Bedwyr took a troop of light horse and galloped through the night. By daybreak he was at Clust. Once Meliagrance realized the alarm was raised, he had posted his men behind the ditch and wall that separated his land from the road. When Bedwyr and his men galloped up in the morning mist, the Verica archers raised their bows.

Bedwyr pulled Sluan up at a distance of twenty feet from the wall. The road behind him was crowded with men and lathered horses. Bedwyr said in a voice that carried like a trumpet through the heavy morning air, "I have come for the queen. Put down your weapons or I will cut you to pieces."

The majority of Meliagrance's archers had been with Bedwyr at Ambrosius' wall when he had turned back the Saxons with just the cavalry. And here he was now, a massive figure on his huge black horse. They could see the brightness of his hair even through the heavy mist. "You have one minute to put down your weapons," came that voice, and the first bow dropped to the ground.

Bedwyr galloped through the gates followed by the company of light horse. The dirt courtyard was empty but there was a line of men massed in front of the house, swords drawn. Bedwyr pulled up Sluan. "Meliagrance!" he shouted, ignoring the Verica guard as if it did not exist. "Meliagrance, come out of there!"

The courtyard was filled now with horses. Some of the Verica men before the house had been with Bedwyr at the wall; others were seeing him for the first time. All were quaking in their shoes. The prince dismounted and strode to the door of the villa; the guard fell away from him in white-faced terror. Not a man of them even thought of using his sword. Bedwyr wrenched open the door with such force that it came off its hinges. They could hear him in the hall shouting "Gwenhwyfar! Where are you?"

They did not hear the queen's breathless "Here." Nor did they see Gwenhwyfar come running into the hall to throw herself into Bedwyr's arms.

"Bedwyr. Oh, Bedwyr." Her voice was trembling. "Oh, thank God you have come." She was shaking uncontrollably, and she clung to him tightly. He was so big. So safe.

"Did he hurt you?" Through the storm of emotion racking her, she heard the words. Heard the tone, actually. She released her hold on him enough to allow her to look up into his face. He was white with fury. "Did he hurt you?" he repeated.

"No." She stared at him, fascinated. "No, Bedwyr. I managed to play for time. But if you had not come when you did . . ." She moved closer to him again and pressed her face into his massive shoulder. His arms came around her at once, crushingly. Over her head she heard him speak. Two words only. "Find Meliagrance."

There were footsteps in the hallway. Then he said to her, "Come, Gwenhwyfar. Let us find someplace where we can talk. I want to know what happened."

"All right." She hated to move away from the safety of his arms, but she forced herself to step back. "This way," she said. "The bedroom he gave me."

"I told him I had got Olwen's sickness," she was saying fifteen minutes later, when there came a knock upon the bedroom door.

Bedwyr called and the door opened. "We've found him, Prince," the cavalryman who stood there said. "He was hiding in the cellar."

"The weasel," said Bedwyr contemptuously. "Lock him up someplace secure."

"We have, my lord."

"And his men?"

"They are all in the courtyard." A look of scorn crossed the cavalryman's fair Celtic face. "They are wetting their breeches, they're so frightened." He looked at Gwenhwyfar. "Beg pardon, my lady."

"I'll come in a minute," Bedwyr said. After the door had closed once more, he turned to the queen. "Will you be all right?"

"Yes." She managed a wavering smile. "What . . . what will you do to him, Bedwyr?"

"What I would like to do," Bedwyr replied through his teeth, "is cut his heart out of his living body. But I can't. I must wait for Arthur."

"Is Arthur coming too?" She sounded out of breath.

"I've sent riders out to find him." He looked down on her from his magnificent height. "Wait here. I won't be long."

When he left, Gwenhwyfar went to the window and stared blindly out. It had begun to rain. Her bedroom was at the back of the house, so she could not see what was happening in the courtyard. It seemed to her that Bedwyr was gone for a very long time.

Then there was a knock on the door and he was there. His shoulders filled the doorway. He smiled at her. "Everything is quite secure."

She smiled back and he came into the room. "Can you bear to spend another day in this house?" he asked. "It's raining hard now. I don't think you would enjoy riding for hours in this weather."

"I can stay," she replied, "so long as you are with me." He closed the door and stood there looking at her out of eyes that were intensely blue. "What would you have done," she asked, "if Meliagrance had raped me?"

"Killed him," came the instant response.

"Without waiting for Arthur?"

"Without waiting for Arthur."

He began to walk toward her, filling the room with his huge masculinity. Both physically and emotionally, she was at the end of her tether, and when he put his arms around her she collapsed against him like a broken reed. He smoothed her hair, and, feeling his touch, she turned her face and put it against his hand. His other hand closed hard on her shoulder.

His powerful body was taut against hers as he turned her face up. She had a glimpse of blazing blue eyes and then his mouth came down on hers. The kiss seared her to her soul. Gwenhwyfar closed her eyes, breathless and dazed. His whole enormous masculine strength bore down upon her and she gave way before it.

All the emotions of the last two days seemed to her to have been leading up to this moment. Nothing mattered now except this intensity of physical passion that blazed up between them. She locked her arms around his neck, and when he lifted her to lay her on the bed, she made no sound of protest.

*   *   *

Gwenhwyfar lay still and listened to the rain. It sounded so dreary, she thought. So desolate. She looked down at the tousled gilt head that was buried on her breast and it seemed that the desolation of the rain crept through into her soul.

What had they done?

Her hand moved, instinctively to touch his hair, but she stilled it. His great weight was pressing her back into the bed. Suddenly she was afraid to see his face. She did not want to see the look in his eyes. No one loved Arthur as much as Bedwyr. He would hate himself for this. He would hate her.

The rain beat even harder against the roof. "Bedwyr," she said tentatively. Then, when he still did not stir, "I don't know how this happened . . ."

The gilt head finally moved, lifted, and he was looking down at her. Gwenhwyfar stared. His eyes were full of blue, lit-up laughter. "You don't?" he said. "Gods. I have been wanting to do this ever since first I saw you, Gwenhwyfar. You must know that."

He had taken his weight off her, leaning it on the hands he had braced on either side of her. The great muscles in his bare shoulders and arms stood out clearly under the fair skin. She did not reply, only continued to look at him in astonishment. He smiled, a warm and tender look, lowered his head to kiss her gently, and said, "Don't look so worried."

"But Bedwyr, what about Arthur?" She was completely bewildered.

The laughter fled from his face, leaving it perfectly serious. "True. I had better not stay here any longer. Although"—his eyes devoured her—"I'd like to stay all day."

The thought flitted through Gwenhwyfar's mind: *Arthur can't wait to leave me.*

She watched Bedwyr dress. When he had put on his belt he came back to the bed, bent, and gave her a lingering kiss. "Don't worry about it," he said again. His blue eyes commanded her. "If there is any blame in this, it is mine. You were in need of comfort, and I took advantage." He straightened up and grinned. "I can't say I regret one minute of it, however." He moved to the door. "You would do best to stay in here, Gwenhwyfar. I'll send Olwen to you in fifteen minutes." He raised his golden brows. "Get dressed," he commanded softly, and left.

Gwenhwyfar watched the door close and sat still staring at it for several minutes, trying to understand what had just happened. One thing was certain, however. Bedwyr was not suffering from remorse for having gone to bed with his best friend's wife. As for her . . . She was not sure what she felt. It had never even entered her mind as a possibility that this could happen. How was she to face Arthur?

The door remained securely closed, but in her mind's eye she saw Bedwyr's figure once more. Bedwyr had got Elaine with child, she thought. Perhaps, perhaps . . . She lay back against her pillow and continued to stare at the door, her eyes wide with thought.

Arthur rode into Clust just after dawn. Like Bedwyr the previous day, he had ridden through the night. The sound of horses in the courtyard did not awaken the queen, as her room was at the back of the house, but the sound of feet and voices in the hall did. Gwenhwyfar got out of bed and went to open the door of her room to listen.

There was the deep rumble of male voices; then Arthur's voice cut through, quite clearly. "Where is he?" the king was asking. Gwenhwyfar shut her door and went to crawl back into bed.

He was here.

How was she going to face him? Since last they had met, she had almost been raped by Meliagrance, and she and Bedwyr had . . . There was a lump like lead in the pit of her stomach and she curled into a ball under the blankets. She was shivering with cold and fear.

He came half an hour later. She heard her door open and half-opened her eyes to see him slowly pressing it shut behind him. He was looking to see if she was awake. The room was still quite dark. She forced herself to sit up and say, "Come in."

He crossed the floor to the bed, moving with his distinctive fluid grace. He sat down on the side of the bed and looked at her gravely. His eyes were very light in his lean, unshaven face. "Bedwyr tells me you took no hurt," he said.

She shook her head. All her nerves were on end. "I told Meliagrance I was sick."

He was holding a candle and now he got up and lit the lamp that was on her bedside table. "Smart girl," he said approvingly.

"It was all my fault, Arthur," she said in a rush as he sat back down beside her. "I was too nice to him. I should have had more sense."

"My dear, if you stopped speaking to all the men who fell in love with you, you'd soon find yourself with no one to talk to at all."

Her eyes fell away from that amused gray gaze. He knew perfectly well she had been more than merely polite to Meliagrance. She bit her lip.

"Gwenhwyfar." He leaned toward her. "Bedwyr says there was more to Meliagrance's plot than his lust for you."

"Yes." She nodded vigorously. "He had some mad notion of making himself high king, Arthur. For a few minutes he actually had me convinced that there was a Celtic conspiracy against you."

"Tell me about it," he said.

He listened to her intently and when she had finished he got up off the bed and went to stand at the window. She watched him in silence. She knew the look of him so well, she thought: the set of his collarbone, the austerely beautiful cut of his mouth, the long sweep of lashes against the high bones of his cheek. He was so familiar—and so unfathomable.

He had made up his mind. He turned to her and said, "Well, we must thank God for Gareth."

"Yes," she replied fervently. "He didn't want me to come to Clust, Arthur. But Meliagrance said you were hurt. What else could I have done?"

He nodded absently, as if he were not thinking of what she was saying but of something quite different. "Meliagrance had this whole plot quite carefully thought out."

"Yes," she replied. "It would seem so."

He came back to the bed and stood there looking down at her. "I am so very sorry you were frightened, my dear. But you proved yourself a queen indeed. You handled him brilliantly."

There was a rare warmth in his voice. The tone, the words of praise, had their intended effect. Her whole face lighted. "What will you do to Meliagrance, Arthur?" she asked.

"I'll have to kill him."

"Kill him?"

"Yes." His black brows were drawn together in thought. "And it had better be done this morning. I want word to get out of his fate before the other Celtic leaders have a chance to think about his summons."

"They wouldn't. Not against you! Not after all you have done for them."

His gray eyes were bleak. "I told you once, Gwenhwyfar, that peace has its own problems, and this is one of them. We no longer have the war against the Saxons to unite us. With a little encouragement, Britain would fall right back into its old pattern of tribal squabbling."

"Do you know, Arthur," she said, "I really think Meliagrance is a little mad."

"Well, mad or not," came the grim reply, "by the time this morning is over, he is going to be dead."

"How?" she asked as he moved toward the door.

"In the traditional fashion. Single combat."

"Will you choose a champion?" she asked breathlessly.

"No. You are my wife. I'll do it myself." And he was gone.

Chapter 28

WITHIN an hour the courtyard at Clust was filled with spectators. Unmounted cavalrymen lined the right side of the courtyard
while the exit to the road was blocked by a line of horse. Meliagrance's
men, unarmed in contrast to the troops from Camelot, were lined up
silently on the left side of the courtyard. Among the Verica tribesmen
was Meliagrance's cousin Kile, heir to the chiefdom after Meliagrance.

The faces of the tribesmen were sober but not bleak. If Meliagrance
defeated the king in single combat, they would perhaps have a future.
And Meliagrance was an exceptionally good swordsman.

The rain had passed over and the sky was clear. The watching men
stood in almost perfect silence, their eyes on the door of the villa. It
opened at last and Meliagrance, followed by Gwynn, captain of the
Light Horse, came out into the chill sunshine. Meliagrance was carrying a sword. They moved to the center of the courtyard, stopped, and
waited.

At the last minute, Gwenhwyfar and Olwen had run to one of the
rooms with a window that faced on the courtyard, and they were just
in time to see the king, accompanied by Bedwyr, come out the front
door of the villa and move to join the two men in the center. Bedwyr
appeared to be urging something on Arthur, but they could clearly see
the king shake his head and motion the two extra men away. Bedwyr
and Gwynn moved to join the cavalrymen on the sidelines, and Arthur
and Meliagrance were left facing each other, alone in the center of the
yard.

Gwenhwyfar drew a deep, unsteady breath. She was almost certain
that Bedwyr had wanted to fight Meliagrance for Arthur, and she
wished that Arthur had let him do so. Bedwyr, she knew, was always
victorious in the various training exercises the army indulged in. She
had never seen Arthur wield a sword, but she was certain he could not
be as good as Bedwyr. He had not Bedwyr's size, for one thing. She

looked now at Meliagrance, and fear shivered through her. The chief of the Verica was not much taller than Arthur, but he was considerably broader through the shoulders and chest. And he had those long, simian arms. A long reach was a distinct advantage in swordplay, as Gwenhwyfar well knew.

"He should have let Bedwyr do this," she said. "He should not take a chance with his own life."

"He wants to avenge you himself, my lady," Olwen said in response. Her dark gray eyes were glowing with the romance of it all. She seemed to have quite forgotten her cold.

Gwenhwyfar threw her serving woman an impatient glance before concentrating once again on the scene before her.

Meliagrance raised his sword first and began to circle around the king. He looked exactly like an ape, Gwenhwyfar thought, and shivered again.

Arthur lifted his own sword, the ruby flashing in the sun, and stepped sideways to his right. He was two years older than Meliagrance, but from her post by the window Gwenhwyfar thought he looked no more than a boy, with his light, slender frame and his black hair blowing in the chill November wind. He moved like a boy too, lithe and graceful, his weight perfectly balanced on the balls of his feet.

Meliagrance feinted, and Arthur moved away.

"Meliagrance's arms are too long," Gwenhwyfar said despairingly. "The king cannot reach him."

Meliagrance had evidently come to the same conclusion, for he began to smile. He struck at Arthur, and the king parried, moving back away from the other sword, unable to get within its circle to go on the attack. He backed away further and Meliagrance followed, slashing again and again while Arthur parried.

Gwenhwyfar's nails cut into her palms. As she watched in helpless horror, Meliagrance's attack pushed Arthur off balance, and the chief raised his sword for the final blow. With the full weight of his body, he drove it at the king.

It did not bury itself in living flesh but landed instead on immovable steel. Then, with a movement that had nothing to do with weight and everything to do with the wrist, Arthur flicked Meliagrance's sword aside and drove his own blade, one-handed, into the momentarily unprotected chest of the chief of the Verica. Meliagrance fell. Arthur pulled out his blade and stood looking down at the man lying crumpled at his feet. Then he looked up at the line of Verica tribesmen.

There was no doubt in anyone's mind as to Meliagrance's fate. Arthur's sword had driven straight at his heart.

Inside her window, Gwenhwyfar began to shake. Olwen dragged her eyes away from the king long enough to ask her if she were cold. Gwenhwyfar shook her head and leaned a little forward to hear what was being said in the courtyard.

One of the Verica men was bending over Meliagrance and he looked up from the chief's body long enough to announce what everyone already knew. Meliagrance was dead.

Arthur looked up and down the line of tribesmen. The fear in the courtyard was so thick that Gwenhwyfar could smell it. "The chief of the Verica was guilty of treason," Arthur said to the assembled men, his voice perfectly calm. He was not even breathing hard. "And so shall I deal with all who are guilty of the same crime."

Gwenhwyfar thought she could see a shudder run through Meliagrance's men.

"Kile," said Arthur.

A brown-haired boy of no more than eighteen stepped forward. "Yes, my lord," he said bravely. He stood bravely too, faultlessly erect, shoulders back and chin up.

"Since the fall of Vortigern the tribe of the Verica has refused to acknowledge the power of the high king." Arthur's voice was soft but implacable. "Your chief has just attempted to kidnap the queen and raise a revolt against me. Can you think of any reason why I should spare your lives?"

"My lord," the boy replied, "Meliagrance was our chief. Like it or no, we were bound to follow him."

"And you, Kile." The king's voice was now very quiet although it could be heard in the furthest reaches of the courtyard. "If you were chief of the Verica, would you seek to raise a rebellion against me?"

"Oh, no, my lord!" The reply was immediate, breathless, and vehement. "If I were chief of the Verica, I would be proud to be your man."

Arthur leaned the point of his sword into the ground and regarded Kile thoughtfully. Gwenhwyfar could see the boy's face, but not her husband's. "The queen," Arthur said, "tells me she is convinced Meliagrance was not in his right mind."

"My lord," said Kile instantly, "I do not think he was."

Arthur's eyes went from the boy to the line of men behind him. Afterward, every Verica man in the courtyard would swear that the king had looked directly at him. "From this time forward, you are to consider yourselves British first and Verica second. Is that understood?"

"Yes, my lord." Kile's reply was echoed loudly by the men massed behind him.

Arthur looked up and down the line once more. "If word ever again comes to me that the Verica are plotting treason, I will not rest until every last one of you is begging for death." The words were like the slash of a whip. There was not a man listening who doubted that the king meant every syllable.

"You will never again hear of treason from the Verica, my lord," Kile said. "I swear it on the grave of my father."

"Very well." Arthur turned his head slightly. "Bedwyr. See to it these men have their weapons returned to them. They may bury Meliagrance however they choose."

The wave of relief that went through the courtyard was palpable. Bedwyr moved forward. "Yes, my lord."

"Kile." Arthur sounded perfectly friendly; the whip had been withdrawn. "Come into the house with me. We must talk." The boy's face was bright as a candle flame as he moved to the king's side.

At the window, Gwenhwyfar began to breathe normally again.

"Oh, my lady," said Olwen with a long sigh. "Is he not wonderful?"

He was so clever, Gwenhwyfar thought as she went slowly across the hall to her small bedroom. He knew exactly how to bind men to him. Young Kile would adore him, as did all his men. He had turned this potentially disastrous situation into a triumph. He would have no trouble from the Verica from now on.

He had thought this all out when he had decided to kill Meliagrance. As always, his reaction had been that of a king.

It was Bedwyr of the blazing blue eyes who had said, "I would like to cut his heart out of his living body." And Bedwyr would have done it for her.

Arthur left Bedwyr and Gwynn at Clust and rode to Camelot with Gwenhwyfar and an escort of light horse. The sunshine of the morning had given way again to low gray clouds, and as she entered through the gate of Arthur's new city and her horse began to climb the steep hill to the palace at the summit, all Gwenhwyfar could see stretching around her was grayness and mud. She was cold and tired, with a weariness of soul as well as of body. She shivered when she saw the huge timber building that was to be her new home. She wished with all her heart that she was back in Venta looking at the graceful colonnade of the praetorium.

Cai took them on a tour of the building. Most of the rooms were empty as Cai, not knowing where she wanted things, had simply put them all in the great hall for her to sort out. The elegant Roman furnishings looked dwarfed by the hugeness of the hall, Gwenhwyfar thought. The whole building was so huge. Never would she grow accustomed to living in such a place. Room followed room, and even though she had seen the plans of the building, she was too tired to follow where they were going.

No beautiful Roman plasterwork on the walls. No marble. No colorful mosaics on the floor. Just bare, unpainted wood.

"It still needs painting," Cai said cheerfully as he took them through a smaller hall that was larger than the main audience chamber at Venta. "But it's weather-tight and all the smoke vents work."

"Well," said Gwenhwyfar with her sweetest smile, "as long as the soldiers and the horses are comfortable, what does it matter that we may have to suffer for a while?"

This was Cai's own view and he smiled at her approvingly. Arthur's look was shrewder and after she was in her own rooms and finally getting ready to sleep in her own bed, he made an appearance. Olwen ran the comb one more time through Gwenhwyfar's hair, put it down, and wished the queen good night. Husband and wife were alone.

"At least they put your bed in the right room," Arthur remarked. He was looking around the bedroom, at the bare floor, the sparse furniture, the jumble of wicker baskets containing clothing and hangings. The only cheerful thing in the whole place was the glowing charcoal brazier.

"Well, don't you expect to share it tonight." The words were out before she even knew she was going to say them.

She had surprised him. Sometimes she thought the only time she ever got his full attention was when she surprised him.

She wished he would come and put his arms around her, hold her, and comfort her. She was so tired . . . she had scarcely slept at all last night.

Of course, he hadn't slept either. He had been in the saddle riding to Clust.

"I'm sorry." His voice was quiet. "I'm sorry, Gwenhwyfar, that you had to come here to an unfinished house. I know how tired you must be."

He was standing in the middle of the big room, with emptiness all around him. She was seated in front of a small table, her chair turned to face him. She wore her night robe with a cloak over it for warmth. Arthur had changed out of his riding clothes, and he had shaved.

He had been planning to sleep with her.

She longed for him, longed for him to push aside her objections, longed to bury her weariness in his warm strength, to be comforted and forgiven and loved.

There was empty space all around him and he stood there watching her, his hands at his sides. There was always a space around him, she realized sadly. And he was happiest when no one tried to breach its boundaries. He had come to her tonight because he thought she might need him, not because he needed her.

She looked at her hands. "I don't mean to complain. You're right, Arthur. I'm tired. I need a good night's sleep."

Finally he came to her side. "Things will go better in the morning," he said comfortingly. "I'll put a crew of men at your disposal, and you can do what you want with the house." She gave him a shadowy smile and he bent and kissed her gently on the mouth. "Good night, my dear."

"Good night." She watched him walk out of the room, bowed her head into her hands, and cried.

The following day the sun shone, Gwenhwyfar's women began to unpack, and Bedwyr arrived back at Camelot. He looked in on the queen late in the afternoon as she was having furniture moved into her private salon.

He seemed to bring the sunshine with him.

"Bedwyr!" Gwenhwyfar greeted him with a warm smile.

He looked from her to the men who were busily moving tables, to Olwen, who was telling them where to put the tables, and said, "Come out with me for a while. The sky is beautiful."

The sun would set within the hour. "A little air would do me good," Gwenhwyfar agreed. "Olwen, get me my cloak."

They walked slowly around the side of the palace, where the gardens would go in the spring. The ground was muddy but Gwenhwyfar did not seem to notice. The sky was streaked with rosy fire and the setting sun was like a great red ball of flame hanging just above the horizon. Gwenhwyfar looked at the sky and let out her breath in a long, melancholy sigh. The beauty of the dying sun made her feel suddenly very lonely, and ineffably sad.

From just behind her shoulder came Bedwyr's soft voice. "Tell me."

She answered, her eyes still on the sky, "Do you remember when you came to Gwynedd to fetch me for my wedding, and I asked you questions about Arthur?"

"Yes."

"You said to me then, 'He is a king.' And you said also, 'He is a very private man.' Well, it was not until just recently that I finally realized what you meant."

Bedwyr did not answer and she turned to look at him. "I cannot reach him, Bedwyr. He keeps a space around himself, always, and if you try to walk into that space, he puts up a wall. I used to think that if I could have a child, then he would change. But I don't think even that would make a difference now."

"It's not you, little bird." His voice was very quiet. "It's the way he is with everyone."

She stared at the sky once more. "He was not that way with Morgan."

Bedwyr felt as if he had just stepped onto treacherous ground. Gwenhwyfar's profile was rigid. "He and Morgan were children together," he said at last. "That makes a difference."

A picture flashed before her eyes: Arthur, helpless with laughter, watching Morgan tussle with Cabal.

"I have brothers, but they are not the only people I can be happy with," she said bitterly.

He reached out and turned her to face him. "You weren't abandoned and brutalized when you were a child, either," he said. "You've seen the scars he carries. He got those before he was nine years old, Gwenhwyfar. Avalon must have seemed like heaven to him after that. Morgan was probably the first person he could ever trust."

There was silence. Then: "I didn't know." Her voice was muffled. "He never would tell me about the scars." Bedwyr's face was as harsh as his voice, his eyes the deep blue that strong emotion always turned them. She had spoken angrily because it hurt so much, that picture of Arthur and Morgan. And now here was Bedwyr, the only person who cared about her, staring at her with those hard blue eyes. "I'm sorry," she whispered.

The eyes softened. "I didn't mean to shout. And he would never tell me about the scars either. I got it from Cai."

Arthur had grown up with Cai as well as with Morgan, but he did not look at Cai the way he did . . . She wouldn't think of it. "You love Arthur very much, don't you?" she said instead.

"Yes," came the simple reply. "I do."

He was so blessedly uncomplicated, she thought. So easy to understand. "I know you do. That is why I expected you to be appalled by what happened between us at Clust. But you weren't. At first, I couldn't understand it. But now I do." She looked up, meeting his eyes, not letting him look away. "You knew it would not matter to Arthur," she said.

"Gwenhwyfar . . ." The admission was in his eyes, in the helplessness of his voice.

She buried her face in his shoulder. "Bedwyr." It was a cry of pain. "Oh, God, Bedwyr. I am so lonely!"

His arms came around her, warm, strong, loving. "Don't, little bird. Don't. He does love you, you know. But his way is the way of a king. Mine is just the way of a man." At that she took her head away from his shoulder and looked up. His eyes were like sapphires.

The words, the look, fell like balm on her scalded heart. When he bent his head to kiss her, she reached up in instant, desperate response.

They thought they were sheltered from the house, and they were. Neither of them saw the figure of the king silhouetted against the hill behind them. Arthur too had come out to watch the sunset.

He stood for perhaps five seconds, motionless. Then he turned and walked quietly back to the palace.

Two days later he left for Avalon.

This time it was Morgan who came to meet him. She stood beside Dun's shoulder while he slid to the ground. Then he was beside her, his gray eyes looking down into the face that he loved. "Welcome to Avalon, Arthur," she said, and smiled. "Welcome home."

III

MORDRED
(467–470)

Chapter 29

*T*HE morning air was clear when Arthur left Avalon, with a fresh wind blowing white clouds across the blue summer sky. He took his time, ambling along the familiar track that led through the fields and back to Camelot. The larks trilled high in the sky and the breeze ruffled the hair on his brow, and he was happy.

His mood had been quite different two days earlier when he had ridden through the gathering dusk in the opposite direction. The memory of what had precipitated his hasty visit to Morgan crossed his mind and he frowned, the serenity of his mood marred by the thought.

Urien, Prince of Rheged, had asked him for permission to marry Morgan. Urien had spent the previous month at Avalon because of a case of boils that Drusus could not cure. Morgan had cured the boils, and Urien wanted to marry her.

There had been nothing wrong with the request. Urien was Morgan's equal in birth. He was young, younger than she, handsome, stalwart, a perfectly acceptable candidate for the hand of any princess in Britain.

Arthur had wanted to kill him.

He hoped now, in retrospect, that he had not made an enemy. He was afraid he had been brutally rude to the boy. He had not been thinking of prudence; he had been thinking of how he would like to get his hands around Urien's neck for even daring to . . .

He had ridden to Avalon at a pace that was too fast for his beloved old stallion. Morgan had been quite cross with him. But she had made it perfectly clear that she had no intention of marrying Urien, or anyone else.

Arthur patted Dun's neck. The birds sang louder. In five minutes the walls of Camelot became visible in the distance and the king regarded them with pleased proprietorship. A great flag bearing the red dragon of his house was flying over the gate, brilliant in the bright sunshine.

Gwenhwyfar had made that flag for him, surprising him with it one day early this spring. He remembered that she had asked him where he was going when she saw him leaving the palace two days ago. He was afraid he had been rude to her as well. He would make it up to her, he thought. On a morning like this, he was at peace with the whole world.

There were permanent shops inside the city gates, but a sort of bazaar had sprung up outside the gates as well, with everything being sold, from food to jewelry, weapons, cloth, eyeglasses, pottery, and fortunes. As Dun threaded his way through the colorful confusion of booths and wagons and merchandise, the word went round: The king is here! The king is here!

Arthur acknowledged the cheers with a nod and a raised hand, and then he was at the gate, which was kept open during the day. The guards on duty saluted and the king rode through.

The road that led from the gate to the plateau and palace at the top of the hill had been graveled last spring. Grass had been planted as well, and Arthur's eye was gratified by the rolling green landscape that fell away from him on all sides. He and Dun topped the steepest part of the hill and the road branched off in three directions. Arthur continued on the path that would take him to the palace, but he could hear the sound of muffled shouts and the clash of steel coming from the left path, which led to the training grounds for the foot.

Good, Arthur thought. The men were working. The cavalry quarters were off to the right, out of view and out of hearing, but he was certain there was as much activity there as in the foot camp. Bedwyr had been driving his men relentlessly these last few weeks. Arthur had planned a great festival to show off his new capital, and the army was to present several demonstrations to the guests.

He continued up the hill to the level plateau at the top. There, at the end of the road, fronted by a wide graveled courtyard, was the palace of Camelot. There were flags flying from the roof, made also by the queen and her women. The glazed windows, with all their shutters wide open, gleamed in the bright summer sun. Arthur checked Dun for a moment and regarded his home with pleasure. If he had not been a king he would have liked to be an architect, he thought, and laughed at his own self-satisfaction.

He had reason for pride, however. The palace was a brilliant example of Roman architecture adapted to the harsher British climate. Arthur and Cai had spent many hours poring over Merlin's copy of

Vitruvius' *De Architectura*, looking at floor plans, discussing theory, trying to decide what would be functional for Arthur's needs and what would not.

They had ended by keeping the basic Roman floor plan which utilized a peristyle, or central court, with most of the main rooms arrayed around it. The Roman peristyle, however, was an open court-yard surrounded by a colonnade. This feature, so pleasant in a south-ern house, was not practical for a colder, wetter climate, and so the peristyle had become a great hall, and the colonnade a series of deco-rated wooden pillars. One more British addition had been made to the basic Roman plan: hearth places for burning wood were built into most of the rooms. The charcoal brazier was inadequate to heat rooms of the size they had constructed, and a Roman-style hypocaust was beyond their means.

Arthur handed Dun over to one of the guards on duty in the courtyard and entered the palace through the main door. The door led into a vestibule, with another guardroom off it, and from the vestibule Arthur passed into the main public room of the palace: the great hall. This room was always busy with traffic: servants passing through on errands, people waiting to see the king, or Cai, or the queen. The floor of the great hall was tiled and it was decorated with some of the best statues from the praetorium in Venta. It was a huge room, with a floor space of five-thousand square feet, and most of the public reception rooms of the palace opened off it. Behind the pillars of the indoor colonnade were the doors to the dining room, the council room, the king's office, Cai's office, and several reception salons.

Arthur walked through the hall unhurriedly, scarcely noticing the groups of people gathered there. At the far side of the great hall was a corridor which led to the second part of the palace, the little or private hall, which was the center of the family part of the house. The little hall was only three-thousand square feet in size, and off it were three separate suites of rooms. One belonged to the king, one to the queen, and the other was shared by Bedwyr and Cai. Extra bedrooms opened off the corridor, and these were used as guestrooms for important visitors. Corridors ran off to the left and the right between the two parts of the house, and these led to other rooms and to the kitchens. The servants, of which there were many, slept in various places. Personal servants slept near their masters and mistresses; most other servants slept in the attics.

The little hall was as crowded as the great hall, but mainly with women. Arthur went directly to the anteroom that led to the queen's suite, down a small corridor, and into her office. It was in this room that Gwenhwyfar interviewed her staff, and in general ran the complicated mechanism of the palace's private functions. Most public functions were delegated to Cai, but both of them had been working together on the upcoming festival.

Gwenhwyfar was seated behind her desk, a stylus in hand, frowning thoughtfully at the scroll before her, when Arthur came into the room. "Working on the festival?" he asked lightly as he crossed to the chair opposite hers. He sat down. "There's ink on your chin," he added.

Gwenhwyfar stared at her husband. "You're back early," she said. He had ridden out of Camelot two days ago in an ill-concealed fury. Now he was making jokes about ink on her chin.

"The abbot from Glastonbury is coming to see me this morning," he reminded her.

"Oh, yes." She looked down at her scroll. "I've been trying to sketch out the field for the games."

"Let me see." He came around the desk to stand behind her, leaning forward over her shoulder to see the paper spread on her desk. "What is wrong?" he asked after a minute "It looks perfect to me."

She could feel the heat from his body, smell the faint male aroma of sweat and leather and horse. "I don't know if there is enough seating," she said. "I was wondering if perhaps I could squeeze some more benches in here." She pointed.

"No." His answer was quick, decisive. "That would make the entry to the field too small. It wouldn't be safe, not with the horses." He straightened. "If we're short of seats, some people will have to stand."

"There are just so many people!"

He laughed. "Is anyone in Britain staying at home?"

"I don't think so." She watched as he returned to his seat. "It's what you wanted, after all. You can't impress the country with the splendor of your new capital if no one comes to see it."

He quirked an eyebrow. "True."

The last time she had seen him, the look on his face had been enough to congeal her blood. Now he was smiling at her with that rare small-boy grin that was her favorite of all his expressions. Gwenhwyfar put two and two together. "I gather that Morgan is not going to marry Urien."

He shook his head and his hair fell across his forehead. "No," he answered with mendacious regret. "I'm afraid Morgan will never marry,

Gwenhwyfar. She is too dedicated to her work." His voice warmed with real enthusiasm. "She has begun to write a compendium of herbal medicine. Isn't that a marvelous idea? There has been nothing done on the subject since Dioscorides wrote the *De Materia Medica* four hundred years ago."

Gwenhwyfar schooled her voice. "It should be a very valuable work, considering her success as a healer." She looked away from his face. "Morgan is fortunate to have resources few other women possess. I know I have been wishing more and more frequently that I knew how to read and write. It's such a nuisance, always having to rely on Marius to be my scribe."

"Merlin had advanced ideas about the education of women," Arthur said. "All his daughters learned to read and write. But it's not too late for you to learn, Gwenhwyfar. I agree that it would be an advantage to you. I'm afraid I have given you a great many responsibilities. You shouldn't be so competent—you would have less to do."

It was how he got them all to kill themselves for him, Gwenhwyfar thought. A few measured words of praise, a carrot for the workhorse. And it worked. "I don't know," she said a little sulkily. "I suppose I could get Marius to teach me."

"I'll teach you," came the prompt reply.

"*You?*" She had never expected this. "You wouldn't have the time, Arthur."

"I'll make the time." He rose to his feet. "I wonder what complaint Gildas has for me this morning."

"He wants you to keep a priest in the palace and he wants more money for his grain," Gwenhwyfar replied.

"I wouldn't bet against you."

The door closed behind him and Gwenhwyfar began to roll up her scroll. When she had finished she placed it neatly in a basket beside her, straightened, and sat back in her chair, her eyes wide and unfocused as she stared at the door.

She had thought he no longer had the power to hurt her. It was frightening, and humiliating, to discover that she was still so vulnerable.

All of Britain thought he loved her. She was childless and he had refused to put her aside. He had been approached to do so, she knew. But he had refused. They thought he loved her. It was only the very few, the people who lived with them, who served them most closely, who knew the truth. The truth that it was Bedwyr, not Arthur, who went to her bedroom at night.

Arthur and she had never exchanged a word on the subject. He had known about her and Bedwyr almost immediately, though. He had not slept with her since.

And yet . . . he trusted her. She had joined Bedwyr and Cai in that inner circle of friends with whom he could simply be Arthur and not "the king."

It was a very great deal. She had thought it was enough. Until she had seen Arthur's reaction to Urien's request for Morgan's hand.

Morgan. That small brown-eyed witch who held Arthur's heart. She never came to Camelot, but a week rarely passed without Arthur making a visit to Avalon. The farms and orchards of Avalon supplied a great deal of the food consumed at Camelot, and since Ector's death the previous autumn, Arthur had supposedly been helping Morgan run the estate.

Gwenhwyfar had not even bothered to suggest that Arthur appoint a steward to replace Ector. She knew well enough why her husband went to Avalon.

He would never let anyone marry Morgan. But she . . . He had been happy enough to hand her over to Bedwyr.

She felt a dark understirring of jealous hatred and tried desperately to push it away. She had found happiness with Bedwyr. She must not lose that now.

There came a knock at the door. "My lady." It was the head carpenter. "You wished to see me?"

"Yes," said Gwenhwyfar, and forced her mind to the matter of benches for the festival.

Gildas not only wanted more money for his grain, he wanted to be the one to bless the festival. Arthur told him pleasantly that Archbishop Dubricius had already been requested to open the festival with a blessing, but that the abbot could bless its conclusion. Gildas, who thought Glastonbury should be the premier church in Camelot because of its proximity, was not happy.

"He's never happy," said Bedwyr half an hour later when Arthur had gone down to the cavalry school to watch the men practice. "In fact," the prince went on, "he's one of the reasons I've never been tempted to become a Christian. He's such a censorious, sour-faced old bastard."

"I can't dispute that with you," Arthur returned with amusement.

Then, more seriously: "But any religion would be found lacking if judged solely by its human servants."

Bedwyr looked curiously at the king's suddenly grave face. "I suppose that's true." The two of them were leaning on the wooden fence that encircled the cavalry training ring. Inside the ring a group of horses and riders was going through the timed exercise they were performing for the festival. "What do *you* believe, Arthur?" Bedwyr asked abruptly.

Arthur's face did not change. "Do I believe in anything beyond the church's civilizing mission?"

"Yes."

Arthur rested his elbows on the fence. "I think I do," he answered thoughtfully.

Bedwyr looked from Arthur's profile to the men in the ring. "I don't need religion," he said. "I've got the cavalry."

The austerity left Arthur's face and he laughed. "We are not all so singlehearted as you, Bedwyr."

Silence fell as the two men stood side by side in companionable silence, watching the maneuvers. The riders, aware of the king's eyes, strove for perfection. The horses trotted in pairs down the center of the ring, separated, and then began to cross the ring on different diagonals, meeting and crossing precisely in the center. Arthur watched them thread through each other with perfect cadence and timing and said to Bedwyr, "Very nice."

"Yes. This festival has proved to be a boon. The men have been working very hard for it."

A faint smile touched Arthur's mouth. He did not answer, however, but continued to watch the drill. The horses all curved in a great arc and returned to the center to form a circle within a circle, each circle trotting in a different direction. Bedwyr watched intently. "We've just put that in. I like it."

"I like it too." Arthur turned away. "Well, I must get on over to see Valerius. He has a group of men who can put up a whole camp in half an hour."

"Are they going to do that at the festival?"

"I think so. Valerius says it is very impressive."

"Well," Bedwyr returned, "that's what we want to do. Impress."

"Precisely." Arthur pushed away from the fence. "Much as I would like to stay and admire your drill, Bedwyr, I had better get on over to admire Valerius' men." He threw Bedwyr a humorous look as he signaled for his horse. "The foot get jealous if I spend too much time with the cavalry."

The sun beat warmly on Arthur's bare head as he guided Ruadh toward the level field they had dug into the hill for the foot to practice drilling. If the busy, purposeful atmosphere in the foot camp was the same as it was here with the cavalry, he would be well-assured that the festival was indeed doing what it was conceived to do: keep the army busy.

The idea had come to him one rainy January evening when he and Morgan were in the library at Avalon with the lamps lit and the brazier glowing and the rain beating hard as sand against the closed shutters. He had been telling her about the army. "I must keep a standing army, there's no way around that," he had said. "An army is my only insurance against rebellion by one of the lesser kings. If I keep an army, we will have peace. If I disband the army, there will be rebellions and Britain will lose its only chance to regain its former prosperity. The only problem is"—he had raised his brows half in frustration and half in amusement—"the army has no one to fight."

"I see your difficulty," Morgan had murmured. "The whole purpose of having an army is to fight." She had thrust out her lower lip a little, the way she did when she was thinking hard. "Are the men restless?"

"Not yet. But it will come if I don't do something to channel their energies."

He was never quite certain which of them first made the suggestion to have a great festival to commemorate the building of Camelot. Their minds were so in tune that sometimes it was difficult to separate one's thoughts from the other's.

He had presented the idea of the festival to his circle of captains as a way of impressing the regional kings and princes with the continued readiness of the army. The only person besides himself and Morgan who understood his chief motive for going to all this trouble and expense was Cai, who had guessed.

Even if the festival itself proved less than spectacular, it still would have done its job, Arthur thought. The entire population of Camelot had been busily employed in preparing for it since February. The great occasion itself was to be held the third week in July.

As Arthur listened to the sound of purposeful activity humming through the warm June air, he thought ruefully that when this festival was over he would have to think of something else.

Chapter 30

I N late June the King of Lothian, Pellinore, had a fall down some stone stairs, broke his neck, and died.

Gawain, as Lot's eldest son, was next in line to be king, but Gawain had been away from Lothian for years and had never shown any inclination to return. It was Gaheris, Lot's second son, who had acted as Pellinore's heir. The prevailing sentiment in the country was for Gaheris to become king.

"Gawain must be given a choice," said Morgause to her sons the afternoon after they had buried Pellinore. The four of them were sitting in the stone hall of the king's house, where it was chill even on a sunny day in June. "If he wishes to come home to take Pellinore's place, that is his right," she continued.

"But if he does not, then he must hand the kingship over to Gaheris."

"He won't come," said Agravaine. "He would be a fool if he did."

Gaheris stared with dislike at his golden-haired brother. "There are worse places in the world than Lothian," he said.

"Name one," came the instant, malicious reply.

"Now, Agravaine," Morgause said placatingly. She was always stepping in between these two sons. "You may not be happy in Lothian, but that does not mean others don't find it pleasing."

Gaheris' blue-gray eyes were hard. "You are leaving, I presume?" he said to Agravaine.

"I would have left years ago if the old man had let me. You know that."

They all knew that. What they didn't know was Pellinore's reason for keeping Agravaine tied to Lothian: "I don't trust him," Pellinore had said to Morgause. "He is not as innocent as Gawain. He will see immediately the resemblance between Arthur and Mordred, and he would not be put off with a story of a likeness to Igraine. No. Agravaine must stay in Lothian."

239

And so Agravaine had stayed, and had hated Pellinore for keeping him.

Gaheris' eyes became even harder. "Just where were you, brother, when Pellinore fell down those stairs?" he asked in a voice to match his eyes.

"Gaheris!" It was Mordred's shocked voice. Then, to Agravaine: "He did not mean it, Agravaine. He is just upset by Pellinore's death."

"He meant it, all right." There was a white line around Agravaine's mouth. He looked at Morgause. "I will leave in the morning, Mother."

"Leave for where?" she asked.

"For the center of the world." His dark blue eyes gleamed. "Camelot." There was a pause as he looked at Mordred. Then: "Why don't you come with me, little brother?"

Morgause shifted her weight on her hard wooden chair and looked worriedly at her youngest son. It was Mordred who was the cause of Pellinore's deliberate severing of Lothian from the rest of Britain, although the boy certainly did not know that.

Pellinore had guessed that Mordred was Arthur's son when the boy was but two years of age. The child's face even then had borne an uncanny likeness to the high king's. Pellinore was the only one in Lothian who had been familiar enough with Arthur to see the resemblance, however, and he had made certain that no one else from the north was likely to come into contact with the king. And Arthur himself had, for whatever reason, stayed away from Lothian. So the secret had been safe. But if Mordred went with Agravaine to Camelot . . .

"We were invited for the festival, after all," Agravaine was saying. "It is not too late, if we leave immediately."

Mordred's face was alight at the thought. It had gone hard with him when Pellinore had refused the invitation to the festival. Mordred was content in Lothian, but that did not mean he would not like to see Camelot and meet the king. "Would you really take me?" he was saying now to Agravaine.

Agravaine smiled and answered lightly, "Why not?"

Mordred was the only one of his brothers for whom Agravaine had any affection. Morgause thought it was because Mordred was beautiful. Agravaine demanded beauty in the people he surrounded himself with. It was because he was so beautiful himself, his mother thought as she looked at her third son's smiling face and brilliant eyes.

"Do you want to go to Camelot, Mordred?" she asked.

"Could I, Mother?" The light gray eyes turned to her with sparkling anticipation. "Just for the festival, you know. And I could go to Avalon to see Morgan. She says it is not far from Camelot. I wouldn't stay. I would come home before the winter."

Morgause stared at Morgan's son. If Mordred went to Camelot, the secret she had kept so well for fifteen years would be out. Or then again, it might not be. Gawain had believed Arthur's explanation that Mordred must look like Igraine. Why should that not suffice for others as well?

Morgause also had been disappointed by Pellinore's refusal of the invitation to the festival. "I think I will go too," she said. "It would be best for me to see Gawain personally and find out what it is he wishes to do." She looked at Gaheris. "If he does not wish to come home, I will get him to execute a document formally relinquishing his rights to you."

Gaheris of the plain freckled face and steady eyes smiled. "Thank you, Mother."

"We shall make a family party," said Agravaine with amusement. Then, with a touch of malice: "Won't Gawain be surprised?"

It was the first time in his life that Mordred had been out of Lothian. The occasion of their journey, Pellinore's death, was sad, of course, but Mordred had never been close to his mother's husband and felt no sense of personal loss. His spirit was free to enjoy the prospect of a visit to the court of the hero of his childhood and to the home of his favorite relative.

They took the old Roman road that went down the west coast of Britain, through the Kingdom of Rheged, and south into Dumnonia. There were few inns along the way; most of the time they fixed a tent for Morgause, and Mordred and Agravaine slept with the rest of their escort under the stars.

Agravaine was in a good mood, and when Agravaine was in a good mood, no one was better company. Mordred had always felt sorry for his brother, who had been like a prisoner in Lothian under Pellinore. He had never understood Pellinore's refusal to allow Agravaine to leave.

"Are you as excited as I am?" he asked Agravaine as they rode out of Glevum early in the morning.

Agravaine gave him an amused look. "I doubt it. You look as if you are about to jump out of your skin."

Mordred laughed. "I feel as if I could jump out of my skin. Just think, only two weeks ago we never thought we would be able to go to the festival in Camelot."

"Two weeks ago the old man was in charge. Not any longer, though." There was a kind of savage pleasure in Agravaine's last words and Mordred looked at him in wonder. But his brother's face was expressionless. "If you join the cavalry," he said to Mordred, "you won't be able to spend all your time watching birds and playing your harp."

"I am not going to join the cavalry," Mordred replied. "I just want to see Camelot and the king. And I want to go to Avalon to visit Morgan. Then I shall probably go home to Lothian."

"You're such a solitary little mouse," his brother said with careless amusement. "Perhaps Morgan will teach you all about herbs."

"I would like that," Mordred answered serenely. "Thank you for taking me with you, Agravaine."

"For some reason even I can't fathom, I'm fond of you." Agravaine turned in his saddle. "We shall have to hurry Mother up if we're to reach Camelot before they shut the gates."

"I'll go ride next to her and push her along," Mordred offered, and trotted his horse back to Morgause.

Morgause complained at the pace, but agreed that she would rather not spend another night on the road. She was getting too old to sleep in lumpy beds, she said, or worse yet, on the ground.

"You're not old at all, Mother," Mordred said loyally, and Morgause had indeed kept her auburn hair and her beautiful creamy skin. She had put on weight with the years, but the extra pounds only made her look more voluptuous. Igraine at the same age, though more beautiful, had looked older.

It was early evening when the small group from Lothian finally reached the gates of Camelot. They were closed.

Morgause drooped in her saddle and Mordred's heart sank. They were all tired and now it seemed that they would not be able to enter the city until the morning after all.

Agravaine was not so easily daunted. "Hey there!" he shouted. "The Queen of Lothian is here. Open these gates immediately!"

A man appeared on the ramparts behind the wall. He was wearing the scarlet of the foot under his leather tunic. "We can't open the gate until the morning," he shouted back.

"You had better open it now," Agravaine returned brazenly. "The king will not be happy to learn that his aunt, Queen Morgause, and his two cousins were kept waiting outside his gate all night like common peasants."

The man on the wall turned his head and could be seen to be conferring with someone who was out of their sight. Then: "Queen Morgause, did you say?"

"Yes. And Agravaine and Mordred of Lothian. The king's cousins."

"I will admit the three of you," the guard called back after another consultation. "The rest of your party will have to wait until morning."

"All right," Agravaine returned. In a moment Mordred could hear the great bars that fastened the gate shut being lifted. He looked with admiration at his brother. He would never have had the nerve to challenge the king's men like that.

Finally the gate began to swing open. Agravaine urged his horse forward first, followed by Morguase and Mordred. Once they were inside, four men began to close the gate once again.

"We are here to see my brother, Prince Gawain," Agravaine said. "Can you tell me where to find him?"

The guards were not looking at Agravaine but at Mordred. "He'll be up at the palace just now," one of them answered slowly. "The king is giving a dinner for his officers this night."

Mordred shifted in his saddle. Why was everyone staring at him? And with such strange expressions? He looked away from the men's faces and stared at his horse's ears.

Neither Agravaine nor Morgause appeared to notice anything amiss. "We'll go to the palace, then," Agravaine said. "How do we find it?"

"Follow this road to the top of the hill. You can't miss it."

Mordred shot another look at the king's men. He wasn't imagining it. They *were* staring at him. He was thankful when Agravaine pushed his horse forward and he was able to follow.

"Do I have dirt on my face?" he asked Agravaine as their horses slowly climbed the gravelled road. The poor beasts were tired.

"Of course not. Why do you ask?"

"I don't know." Mordred knew Agravaine would only make some cutting reply if he said that the men at the gate had been staring, so he changed the subject. "The city is well fortified, isn't it?"

"Mmm." Agravaine was clearly not listening to him, so Mordred turned his own attention to his surroundings. The steepest part of the hill had been topped and now they could begin to see signs of habitation. A series of long, low buildings lay to their left. The army barracks probably, Mordred thought. The still, early-evening air was perfectly quiet. Then they had reached the plateau at the top of the hill and were riding through a terraced garden. At last they saw the palace.

The party from Lothian stared. It was far bigger than they had ever imagined; the number of windows alone was staggering. Two small guardhouses were built on either side of the road before it widened into a large circular yard in front of the palace. As they rode their horses into the courtyard, men came out the doors of the guardhouse on the right and crossed to stand in front of them.

"The Queen of Lothian has come on a visit to her son Prince Gawain," Agravaine said haughtily to the leader of the guards. "I am Prince Agravaine and this is Prince Mordred."

The four guards were looking at Mordred, and this time Agravaine noticed their stares. "My lady," one guard said courteously, his eyes still on Mordred. "If you will dismount and enter the palace, I will have someone find Prince Gawain for you."

Morgause smiled gratefully and allowed a guard to help her to dismount. Then the man who had spoken to them gestured his fellows away and turned to lead them into the palace.

They went in a double door and found themselves in a large and impressive vestibule. There was a small room to the side of the vestibule, where there was another guard on duty. The two men conferred briefly; then the house guard went through his office into the room beyond and disappeared.

"Acton will inform Prince Gawain of your arrival," the other man said to Mordred. "Please wait here."

It was Morgause who said thank you, and the three of them waited in silence until they were alone.

Mordred and Morgause looked around at their surroundings, while Agravaine looked at Mordred. "Isn't it splendid, Mother?" Mordred said.

The vestibule itself was indeed splendid, with its walls decorated with paintings from the praetorium and its red tiled floor. The room beyond was what held Mordred's attention, however. It was an immense room with graceful carved archways around its perimeter and another beautiful tiled floor. Except for a few statues and benches, the great hall was empty. The sound of talk and laughter was coming from a door that was to the left of the hall. Acton had not gone through the great hall, however, but through a door on the far side of his office.

He returned that way also, and with him was Gawain. Mordred sighed with relief at the sight of his oldest brother. The vastness and magnificence of the palace were making him feel acutely uncomfortable. Gawain belonged here. Gawain would know what they should do.

It was Agravaine who told him the news they had traveled so far to deliver. "Pellinore is dead."

"Dead?" Gawain looked at his brother in surprise. "How?"

Agravaine told him. Then Morgause said, "You will have to make up your mind what you wish to do, my son. An absent king is no good for Lothian."

"Yes," he replied. "I know that." He came to put an arm around his mother. "I'm sorry," he said. "He was a good man. You must miss him, Mother."

Morgause leaned against him and allowed a few tears to brim in her eyes.

Gawain looked at his two brothers. "Surely you all did not come to Camelot just to give me this news?"

"No," replied Agravaine smoothly. "We came to meet the king."

"Well, that is a wish shortly to be gratified. He told me to bring you back to the dining room with me."

Morgause stepped away from her son. "But he is at dinner with his officers, Gawain. That is what the man at the gate told us."

"Dinner is ending. And when I told him I must leave the dining room because you had come, he specifically requested that I bring you back with me."

"Oh, dear." Morgause smoothed down her hair. "I must look like a hag."

"You look very nice, Mother," Mordred replied, and she reached out to brush some dust from the shoulder of his tunic. Then she straightened his belt. She did not even look at Agravaine. Agravaine was always immaculate.

"Are you ready, Mother?" Gawain asked patiently, and she said that she was.

For as long as he lived, Mordred would never forget the scene that followed. Gawain took them back through the guardroom and into a smaller vestibule on its far side. The vestibule led to a door that went into the side of the dining room, the way Gawain had come out. It was a less public door than the big open archway that led from the great hall.

They came in quietly, between two tables full of men who were drinking wine and talking. A few men looked up to say something to

Gawain, saw Mordred, and fell silent. They made their way to the center aisle that led from the arched doorway to the high table, and Mordred raised his eyes and saw the king.

Silence had fallen on the front of the room. In the quiet Mordred could hear Gawain's voice introducing his mother and his brothers. Mordred could not tear his eyes away from Arthur's face. It was like a mirror image of his own.

Gwenhwyfar had seen the boy before Arthur, who was looking at Morgause. She stared at the young face in utter stupefaction. It couldn't be . . . it wasn't possible . . . the same straight nose and finely molded cheekbones . . . the same hair. He reached the table, looked up, and Gwenhwyfar's goblet slid out of suddenly strengthless fingers, hitting the table with such force that some of the wine spilled onto the wood. He had Arthur's eyes as well.

She turned her head to look at her husband and was just in time to see the naked shock on his face as he beheld the youngest Lothian prince.

"My lord king," Gawain was saying, apparently oblivious of the atmosphere surrounding him, "may I present my mother, the Queen of Lothian, and my brothers Agravaine and Mordred."

Arthur pulled himself together visibly and made some sort of welcoming comment. He was very pale but his voice was under control. The boy was staring at him with a mixture of bewilderment and fear.

She had to get the boy out of here, Gwenhwyfar thought. Away from this relentless public scrutiny. She turned to Arthur. "My lord, I am sure the Queen of Lothian and her sons must be weary after their arduous journey." Her voice sounded quite normal, thank God. "If you will allow me, I shall conduct them to some rooms for the night."

Her reward was the obvious relief in the look Arthur gave her. "Yes. That is an excellent idea, my lady. Thank you."

Gwenhwyfar stood up and came around the table. She looked at Morgause and said, "If you will come with me?" As the Lothian party began to follow her down the aisle, Arthur spoke. One word only. "Gawain."

Gawain, who had started to follow his family, stopped. "Yes, my lord?"

"Sit here for a moment."

"Yes, my lord." Gawain came to take Gwenhwyfar's empty seat. Bedwyr, who was on Gawain's other side, turned his head and began to talk to Lionel. The rest of the room quickly followed the prince's lead, picking up the conversations that had been so unceremoniously dropped at Mordred's entrance.

Under cover of the rumble of many male voices, Arthur was able to say what he wished to Gawain. "Who is that boy?" he demanded in a low voice.

Gawain stared at the king in confusion. "He's my brother, my lord. My youngest brother. Mordred."

Arthur's fingers were gripped so tightly around the base of his Samian-ware cup that his knuckles and nails were white. His face was white and still as well; only his eyes moved, strange and glittering in that pale, set face. "He looks like me," he said.

"I know, my lord. I saw that myself. Don't you remember, when first I met you I said you looked like my brother Mordred." Gawain spoke earnestly. He could not understand the reason for the king's obvious discomposure. "And you said Mordred most probably looked like your mother, as you did. Don't you remember?"

Arthur stared at Gawain's open, faintly freckled face. He did remember, vaguely, saying something of the sort. "Yes," he managed to get out. "Yes. I had forgotten about that."

Gawain smiled in relief. "My mother says that Mordred does indeed look like her sister Igraine. So you see, that explains it."

"Yes, I see." The muscles under the skin of Arthur's face tensed. "How old is Mordred?" he asked.

"Fifteen, my lord."

Gawain's face wavered, out of focus, and Arthur fought to get a grip on himself. "Thank you, Gawain," he forced out between stiff lips. "You may go."

Gawain stood up, bowed slightly, and went down the center aisle with great dignity. No one watched him go. All eyes, surreptitiously, were on the king.

Next to him Cai said, "It won't sell. The eyes, the hair: they're from Uther, not Igraine."

"Cai," said Arthur, and even to himself his voice sounded odd, "I must get out of here."

Cai grunted. "Give me ten minutes, and then you can leave."

Arthur nodded mutely and sat in anguished silence as Cai had the final course served and then almost immediately removed.

It was in fact thirty minutes before Arthur could rise and officially close the officers' dinner that had begun what seemed to him a lifetime ago.

Chapter 31

GWENHWYFAR took Morgause and her sons through the great hall, down a corridor and into a smaller hall that was also encircled by a colonnaded gallery. Mordred was too confused to do more than look around in bewilderment. Then they went through a door into an anteroom, through another door and into a room where three girls were sitting, sewing and talking. The talk stopped when the queen came in with her visitors.

Gwenhwyfar spoke to one of them. "Olwen, the Queen of Lothian has come to pay us a visit and she is weary from her long journey." Gwenhwyfar smiled at Morgause. "I shall give you a room here in my quarters for the night, my lady. Olwen will see that you have all that you need."

"Thank you." Morgause looked worriedly at Mordred. "And my sons?"

"Doubtless they will like to stay with Gawain. For this night, however, I will lodge them in the palace also."

"Thank you," Morgause said again, obviously deciding to let things happen as they would. "The guards at your gates would not allow our packhorses in, so I shall have need of your kindness, my lady."

"The men have orders not to admit anyone after seven," Gwenhwyfar replied. "I shall be sure to have your things brought up to the palace early in the morning."

Olwen came forward and Morgause, with one more look at Mordred, followed the queen's serving woman out of the room.

Gwenhwyfar turned to the two princes. The older boy, Agravaine, had a very thoughtful look on his handsome face. It was to him that Gwenhwyfar spoke. "If you will follow me?"

They went back through the little hall, to the corridor they had come along earlier. Gwenhwyfar reached for a door that opened off the corridor and went through, with the two princes following her. The room they entered was obviously an anteroom with two doors opening off it. "This is your room, Prince," the queen said to Agravaine, and opened one of the doors to reveal a bedroom. Agravaine gave her a considering look before he slowly walked in. "A servant will be here shortly to attend to your needs," Gwenhwyfar said, and closed the door firmly behind him. Then she turned to Mordred and said, "This way."

He was surprised when she turned back to the corridor. This evidently was a suite of rooms; why was he not to sleep in the room opposite Agravaine's? The answer came to him as he followed her across the corridor to another door and another antechamber. They wanted to keep him separated from his family. He did not understand why.

He entered the room she indicated and turned to look at her warily as she followed him in. He wished Agravaine were with him.

Gwenhwyfar felt pain knife through her as she met the boy's eyes. Just so must Arthur have looked when he was this age. Just so might a son of hers have looked. "You bear a great resemblance to the king," she said, and now her voice did not sound normal.

"I know." The wariness mixed with bewilderment. "Gawain did tell me once that I looked like the king, but I had no idea of how close the resemblance was."

His bewilderment was genuine, she thought. He really had no idea of who he was.

Gwenhwyfar knew. He was Arthur's son. He had to be. There could be no other explanation for such a resemblance. Nor had Arthur been prepared for it. Clever as he was at hiding his feelings, he had not been able to hide his shock at the sight of Mordred.

The boy was Arthur's son. By Morgause? Gwenhwyfar did not think so. All her feminine instincts told her that her fastidious husband was unlikely ever to have been attracted by Morgause's voluptuous charms. The knife edge of pain ripped through her once more. She thought she knew who Mordred's mother was. Not Morgause, but Morgause's sister. The witch. Morgan.

The boy was gazing at her with Arthur's eyes. There was more in those eyes than bewilderment, however. There was also the dazzled wonder that was most men's tribute to her extraordinary beauty. It was not a look she had ever seen on Arthur's face, but it was there, unmistakably, on his son's.

She forced herself to meet those uncannily familiar eyes with a semblance of equanimity. "It *is* rather a striking likeness. I wonder that your mother never noticed it."

"My mother has never met the high king," came the simple, devastating reply.

"That explains it, then," said Gwenhwyfar through stiff lips. She turned to the door. "I wish you a good night's rest, Prince. Ask the servant for anything you may need."

"Good night, my lady," came the boy's polite reply. At least he did not have Arthur's voice, she thought as she closed the door of his room behind her.

She retraced her steps to her own rooms, looked in quickly on Morgause, then sent Olwen on one last errand. She was to tell Arthur's body servant, Gereint, that the queen wished to see the king as soon as possible.

She waited for two hours, until the dinner was long finished, before she sent Olwen with another message.

The reply was from Gereint, not Arthur. The king could not come to his wife tonight. The king had ridden out of Camelot an hour ago. Gwenhwyfar knew instantly where he had gone. To Avalon.

Arthur was in as little doubt as Gwenhwyfar as to Mordred's identity. As he cantered Ruadh through the light July night, his mind was working, remembering, adding, subtracting, and coming up with its inevitable conclusion.

No child of Morgause's and Lot's would look like Mordred.

It was not Morgause who had borne a son fifteen years ago, but Morgan.

That was why she went so faithfully every year to Lothian. Not to see Morgause, but to see Mordred.

Mordred was his son. His son and Morgan's.

Why had she never told him?

The last of the lingering July sunset had faded from the sky when Arthur rode into the courtyard of Avalon. All was quiet. The household, including Morgan, rose very early. It was after eleven o'clock now; they had probably all been abed for an hour.

Arthur rode Ruadh to the stable, woke up one of the grooms who slept in the attic, and told him to take care of the horse. Then he walked back to the house.

The night air was cool and he wore only a short-sleeved tunic, but he was not chilled. His mind was conjuring up for him another night, another time he had ridden alone to Avalon. He had been sixteen then, not much older than the boy at Camelot. He was thirty-one now, and the emotions tearing at him had not changed much over the years.

It was summer and all the shutters were open. Arthur went around to the back of the house to the window he knew was Morgan's. It was slightly ajar. The high king of all Britain pulled it open, levered himself up with his hands, and climbed into the room.

He landed very softly on the floor inside, too softly to awaken any sleeper. But even though the room was dark, she was not asleep. "Arthur?" she said in a soft, worried voice.

"Yes. You knew I was coming?" He walked to the table where he knew there was a lamp. She heard him pick up a tinder box.

"I knew something had happened to distress you. A few hours ago. I didn't know if you were coming here, though." The lamp was lit and he turned to look at her. She was dressed in a thin, white round-necked gown, and her bare throat and arms were round and slender as a young girl's. A strand of hair had caught in her eyelashes and she pushed it out of the way. She had been lying down; the light cover was pulled up to her waist and the pillow was dented. But she looked wide-awake.

"Morgause came to Camelot tonight," he said. "She brought Mordred with her." He watched her face change.

There was a very long silence. "I'm sorry. I never meant you to find out this way."

His composure cracked. "How could you, Morgan? How could you have done this to me? Kept him from me? Not told me? And then to let me meet him like that, in front of everyone!"

She turned her face away as if she couldn't bear to look at him. "I didn't know, Arthur. I didn't know they were coming to Camelot."

"Well, they did." His voice was bitter. "Gawain brought them into the dining room. I saw him for the first time in the full view of all my officers."

She flinched, picturing the scene. He walked from the table to the foot of her bed. She felt his eyes on her face. He said, "I always swore that no child of mine would ever be reared the way I was."

Her eyes lifted instantly. "He wasn't! I would never have let that happen! He has been happy, Arthur. Please believe that."

"I don't know what to believe." He was dark under the eyes and white about the mouth. "I still can't believe that you did this to me."

She drew a long breath. "I did it because it was the only thing I could do," she answered steadily. "We could not marry. You know the reasons for that. Then I discovered I was to have a child." She made her voice stay quiet and dispassionate, refusing to let him see the anguish that had filled her then, that filled her now. "Morgause saw it first, actually. I was too stupid, or too unhappy, to understand the signs. She saw it and she told Father. He wanted me to marry Cai."

She saw, and perfectly understood, the look that flickered across his face. Her quiet voice continued. "I refused. I refused also to consider trying to abort the child. Father then said my only other choice was to go away, have the child in secret, and give it to someone else to rear." It was so hard to say all this. It brought back the pain too vividly. She cleared her throat. "When I refused to do that too, Father said he would send for you." She met his eyes. "He was ready to do that, Arthur. You must not blame this . . . situation on him."

"*You* wouldn't." His voice was expressionless.

"I wouldn't. I said that I would give up my child only if I could be assured he would be loved and cared for. I could see how Morgause was with her own children. When she said she would take the baby and pretend he was hers, I agreed."

The lamplight was shining up under his face, lighting it from below, making the cheekbones look higher, the cheeks more hollow than they really were. "You told me you could not have children."

"I can have no more children. Mordred's birth was very hard. It did something to my insides."

His head snapped up as if he had been punched in the jaw. "What do you mean, his birth was very hard?" Then, as she did not answer: "God. Your mother died in childbirth, didn't she?"

"Arthur—" she began, but he cut in furiously.

"Was Merlin insane? What was he thinking of? He sent you off into some remote corner of Wales. You might have died!"

"Well, I didn't. It was Morgause who got me through, actually. She was better than any doctor."

He came around the bed and sat down. "I never knew." He seemed to find that incredible. "You went through all that, and I never knew." He found he was beginning to shake.

"I didn't want you to know."

"I don't understand." Even his teeth were chattering. "That time in Calleva, when I almost died. You said there was work for me. Then you hid your thoughts. You were thinking of him, weren't you?"

"Yes."

"Why didn't you tell me?"

She looked at him out of grave brown eyes. "I didn't tell you because I knew what you would do. You would never have left him in Lothian, Arthur. You would have acknowledged him and made him your heir."

He stopped his teeth from chattering by sheer force of will. "He is my heir. I have no other son."

Her eyes closed very briefly. "I know. And I am sorry."

"Well, I'm not." His eyes blazed. "I'm glad Gwenhwyfar has no children. I want our son to be high king after me." He stared at her, his mouth hard. "Why wouldn't you marry me, Morgan? Why did you send me to Gwenhwyfar? It didn't matter that you could have no more children. We had a son. We could have had him made legitimate."

"You don't understand," she began to say.

"No," he shot back with corrosive bitterness. "I don't understand. I wish to God I did."

"It is really very simple," she replied, not giving an inch before his anger. "I was not thinking of your need in this, Arthur. I was thinking of his. It was better for Mordred to stay in Lothian. He was happy. At least I could give him that, a happy childhood."

There was silence. All that Morgan could hear was the tapping of a loose shutter as it bumped against the house in the soft night breeze.

"He would have been happy with you and me," he said at last. His narrow nostrils were still pinched with temper, but his voice was quieter.

"No." The shutter was tapping harder now. "He was better off in Lothian with Morgause. Happier. Safer. As you were happier and safer in Avalon than you would have been with Uther and Igraine."

"I was happy in Avalon because I had you."

She bowed her ruffled head. "I know."

He reached out his hand to cover hers where it lay on top of the cover over her lap. He lifted it and kissed her palm once, hard, and then dropped it. "You're right," he said. "I would not have left him in Lothian. I have never been any good at giving up what is mine."

Her hand tingled from the violence of his caress. "I have had a lot of practice," she said.

He moved then and she was in his arms. She closed her eyes and pressed her forehead against his shoulder. He put his mouth to her hair. "Was it very bad?" he asked.

She had never talked about that time with anyone, but she had never forgotten it. "Yes," she said. "Very bad. The hardest thing I have ever done in my life." His arms tightened. "Even when he was a baby," she added, very low, "he looked like you."

It was very quiet. She could feel his heart beating against her temple. Someone must have secured the shutter, for it was no longer tapping against the house.

"He must be told the truth," Arthur said.

Morgan did not reply. She had always known what would happen should Arthur discover Mordred.

"He thinks himself the son of Lot and Morgause?"

"Yes."

"Who else knows the truth?"

"No one but Morgause and Pellinore."

Her face was still against his shoulder. She turned her head a little and settled more comfortably into his arms. He cradled her easily. "Morgan," he said, his lips against the top of her head, "he must be told."

She sighed. "Yes, I know. Poor boy. He must be perfectly bewildered by you."

"Mmm." He was thinking of something else. "I will tell Mordred the truth. That is his right. But it will be best to let everyone else go on thinking that Morgause is his mother."

He felt her head move under his lips and looked down into her upturned face. "But why?" she asked in bewilderment. "Surely it can make no difference to the world whether his mother is Morgause or me."

"Think," said Arthur gently. "If the world knows that you and I have produced a son, then it will know the reason for my visits to Avalon."

Her eyes widened. "I had not thought of that."

He smoothed her hair back from her cheek. "I shall talk to Morgause before I see Mordred."

"But you have never even met Morgause. How can you expect people to believe you had a child with her?"

"Who knows with certainty that we never met?" he returned.

Morgan frowned in an effort of memory. "I suppose that is true, but . . ."

"I will not be expected to furnish the date and the time," he said with assurance. "Don't worry about it. It will be enough if I acknowledge Mordred as my son and Morgause as his mother. No one will question my word."

And no one would, she thought. You did not ask the high king anything he did not want to be asked. She looked up at him now, trying to see him as he would appear to someone who did not know him. His thick black hair was ruffled from his ride through the night and he wore no jewelry, no mark of rank save the purple border that trimmed the neck and sleeves of his tunic. Yet no one, seeing him even in this casual guise, could doubt for a moment who he was. Arthur wore power as if it were an invisible cloak. He had worn it ever since she could remember. It was stronger now than it had been when he was a boy, but even then it had been a part of him.

It was a quality his son did not possess. She would never tell him, but that was the reason she had tried to keep Mordred safe in Lothian. Mordred was the dearest boy in the world, but he would never make a king.

Now that Arthur had solved for himself the problem of Mordred, his mind turned to other things. "Were you ever tempted," he asked, "to marry Cai?"

She smiled faintly and shook her head.

The pinched look had come back to his nostrils. "You gave me to Gwenhwyfar. I fear I am not so generous."

She reached up with gentle fingers and touched his mouth. "I know."

"You should have run away with me fifteen years ago. There would have been no need for all this deception, these secrets . . ."

"And there would have been no battle of Badon, either," she returned firmly. "However the world may judge us, Arthur, at least we two will always know that we acted in the best interests of our country."

"You did," he returned. "I wanted to run away to Armorica."

"You would have been miserable. You were born to be Britain's king."

"You are more Merlin's pupil than I, Morgan," he said somberly.

The room was completely dark now, the lamp the only pool of light. Morgan glanced toward the window. "Arthur. You must return to Camelot before morning. If people know that you came here tonight, it will not be possible to keep my identity a secret."

"All right." His light eyes were narrow in his concentrated dark face. "I'll go." He reached for her and, with a swift and fluid movement, brought the two of them to lie on the bed. "But not yet."

Chapter 32

ARTHUR arrived back at Camelot before dawn. He had to go through the gate, of course, and the guards who opened it for him would tell their fellows that the king had ridden out this night, but no one could know for certain where he had gone. Nor was anyone likely to ask him.

He unsaddled Ruadh himself and put the chestnut in his stall. Then he walked from the stable to the palace, which he entered by way of the open window in his bedroom. He thought, with a flash of amusement, that he was getting rather old to be spending so much time climbing in and out of bedroom windows. Once inside, he stripped, threw his clothes on a chair, fell into bed, and went instantly to sleep.

Gereint woke him three hours later with a surprised "My lord! I did not know you had returned!"

Arthur half-opened his eyes and regarded his young body servant. "I apologize for not checking in with you, Gereint."

The boy grinned. As he began to pick up the clothes Arthur had thrown in a heap on the chair, he said, "The queen wished to see you last night, my lord."

At that Arthur opened his eyes fully and sat up. He rubbed his head, yawned, and stretched. Gereint watched with admiration as the muscles in the king's shoulders and arms flexed under the smooth brown skin. "I want a bath," Arthur said. The boy's eyes moved to the king's face. All its humor had vanished. "First a bath," Arthur repeated. "Then I will see the queen."

The palace did not have a private bath wing as did Avalon. There was no one left in Britain skilled enough to install the elaborate piping required for a traditional Roman bath. But Arthur had been brought up with the Roman ideal of cleanliness, and even in the coldest weather he insisted on bathing in the big wooden tub that had to be filled and emptied by hand.

After he had bathed and shaved and dressed, Arthur had his usual breakfast of bread and fruit. Then he sent Gereint to the queen's rooms to ask if his wife would receive him.

She would. It was still very early and the little hall was filled with servants carrying water and breakfast to the various bedrooms. Arthur crossed the hall and entered the door that led to the queen's suite of rooms. Olwen was waiting for him in the anteroom. "The queen is in her sitting room, my lord," she said, and Arthur nodded and walked down the corridor, a faint line between his brows. He hoped Gwenhwyfar was not going to ask where he had been last night.

Gwenhwyfar was alone, standing beside a small marble-topped table that held a particularly unusual brass lamp that had come from Rome. It had once graced Igraine's chambers at Venta. For a brief, vivid moment the sight of the lamp conjured up his mother for him and he could see her quite clearly: the narrow, fine-boned face, the winged brows and dark blue eyes. A hawk in a cage—that was what she had always put him in mind of. His eyes moved slowly from the lamp to the woman standing beside it.

Gwenhwyfar was dressed in a pale yellow tunic and gown and the glow of her hair was brighter than the polished brass of Igraine's lamp. She was paler than usual; she did not look as if she had slept well. She regarded him silently, waiting for him to speak first.

He felt a moment's flash of gratitude for Gwenhwyfar's practical good sense. She would never grow hard and embittered, as his mother had, no matter what her disappointments might be. She had the ability to look for happiness, something Igraine had not known. He gave her a quick warm smile. "Thank you for acting so intelligently yesterday. You saved us all from an extremely embarrassing situation."

She did not return his smile. "Who is he, Arthur?" she asked.

"Surely you have guessed." He crossed the room toward her, walking so lightly that his feet made no noise on the uncovered floor. He stopped in front of her and said, "He is my son."

She seemed to flinch and he looked away from her, looked once more at his mother's lamp. "I did not know of his existence myself until yesterday," he said, trying to give her time to recover. "Nor do I believe he knows. He thinks himself the son of Morgause and Lot."

"He doesn't know." Her voice was flat with hard-controlled emotion. "When I took him to his room last night he was obviously bewildered by his remarkable resemblance to you." Arthur's hair, still damp from his bath, had fallen forward across his forehead. "Was

Morgause insane," Gwenhwyfar went on, "to have introduced him to you in such a public fashion? *She* certainly knows who he is."

Arthur thrust his hair back from his brow and walked to the window. He put a hand up to touch the thin drapery that covered it, then turned to her and said, "I suppose she thought this was one sure way to get me to recognize him. No one in that room can be in much doubt as to his identity."

"And are you going to recognize him?"

"As I just said, I don't think I have much choice."

"You can say he resembles Igraine." She took a step toward him. "You told that to Gawain when he remarked on the likeness. Don't you remember? It was the time I took him down to the cavalry ring to meet you."

Arthur said gently, "I'm sorry, my dear, but as Cai pointed out to me last night, Mordred has my eyes. And they are from Uther, not Igraine."

Her hands clenched into fists at her sides. "So you will acknowledge him. Then what?"

"Gwenhwyfar." She heard the note of compassion in his voice, and bitter gall rose in her heart. "Try to see this from a political and not a personal point of view. You have grieved because you have no children, I know that well. And you know also the problem our childlessness has posed for Britain. This boy gives me an heir, a blood descendant who can be accepted by all the regional kings and chiefs as the next high king."

She stared at him with eyes that glittered with hostility. "You mean to make him your heir?"

"Yes."

"But he is a bastard!"

His mouth thinned and all the gentleness left his voice. "He is the only son I have got."

The bitterness spilled over into angry words. "Your son, and who else's, Arthur? Don't try to tell me that you got a child on Morgause! I know full well who bore him—your precious Morgan. And she never told you. She has kept him from you for all these years. Will you forgive her that, Arthur? Did she have a good excuse for you last night? Are there any other little bastards in hiding around Britain?"

"Be quiet." The words were spoken softly, but they stopped Gwenhwyfar instantly. "Morgause is Mordred's mother," he said in the same soft, deadly voice. "Do you understand that?"

Under the pretty primrose gown, she was shaking uncontrollably. "Yes," she managed to say. She had not meant . . . it was only that she was so hurt . . . and now Arthur was speaking to her in that cold, inflectionless voice and looking at her as if he hated her.

"I want to see Morgause as soon as she awakens," he said. He had ceased talking to her; now he was just giving orders.

Her stomach was heaving. "All right."

His gray eyes were icy. "You are Britain's queen, Gwenhwyfar. It would be well if you remembered that." Then he was gone.

Gwenhwyfar crumpled into a chair and raised her shaking hands to her face. You coward, she chastised herself. He has only to look at you with that hard face, and you shake as if you had the ague. Why didn't you stand up to him? You're right. You know you are.

But she knew the answer before she even asked the question. She was not afraid of his anger, she was afraid of being locked out from him altogether. He was perfectly capable of doing that, of denying their friendship, their partnership, of treating her like an unwelcome stranger for the rest of their lives together. He would be able to live like that, but she could not. She cared too much. She could not bear to lose the little piece of him that she had.

If she wanted him back, she would have to accept Mordred. The witch's son. She did not know if she would be able to do it.

She longed, with all her sore and aching heart, for the comfort of Bedwyr.

Arthur sent a servant to instruct both Lothian princes to keep to their rooms until they were sent for. Then he went to his office, ostensibly to read his weekly dispatches from the garrisons stationed around the country, in reality to stare at his desk and to think.

Gwenhwyfar had given him an unpleasant shock. He had not expected her to accept Mordred easily. Mordred's very existence must be a reproach to her, a proof and a reminder of her own barrenness. He had been prepared for that. He had even been prepared for her to suspect that Morgan was Mordred's mother. What he had not been prepared for was the evident jealousy and bitterness that Gwenhwyfar felt toward Morgan. He had thought she was happy with their domestic arrangements. He had thought she was happy with Bedwyr.

Of course, he acknowledged honestly to himself, he had never wanted to know the secrets of her heart. It was enough for him if the surface of their lives together was serene. All his emotions were tied up with Morgan. It had always been like that. He thought she had ceased to care.

The sword Merlin had given him, the sword he had carried throughout the Saxon wars, hung on the wall of his office. His eyes fastened on it much as they had fastened on his mother's lamp earlier. It seemed to be a day for remembering, and he thought now of his grandfather, who had saved him and taught him and made him a king. It was Merlin, not Uther, who had been his true father.

Hadrian's great ruby glittered in the sword's handle. A king is a public thing, Merlin had told him. Well, he thought now as he stared at the sword that had won him so many victories, so is a queen. Morgan had put country first, and at a far greater cost than that he was asking of Gwenhwyfar. She would have to accept Mordred. Britain needed an heir.

The war against the Saxon, was won, true, but victory was worthless unless he could secure another fifty years of peace. Britain needed time, time for the barbarians to become civilized, for the inevitable merging of Saxon and Celt to be peaceful and beneficial, just as the empire had been strengthened and revitalized by the additions of the Goths and the Visigoths.

The key to such a peace was a strong high king. That was why he had built this capital. That was why he was opening communications with the leaders in Gaul, with the emperor in Rome. That was why he needed a son.

Gwenhwyfar would have to see that. Perhaps Bedwyr could make her understand.

He put his elbows on the table and rested his forehead in his hands. In less than an hour's time he would be meeting his son. It was one of the most momentous occasions of his entire life. He had no idea what he was going to say. His fingers were pressed so hard against his forehead that the skin around them was white. Then the door opened. "My lord," said one of his clerks, "the Queen of Lothian to see you."

Arthur rose to his feet. "Send her in."

He had been surprised when first he had seen Morgause last night. She looked nothing like either Morgan or Igraine. The Queen of Lothian was a tall, full-bodied woman, with Gawain's auburn hair and slightly prominent blue eyes. Her skin was clear as a girl's, with fine lines around the eyes and the mouth. She smiled at Arthur, and he thought that the lines had come from laughter and not from sorrow.

"My lord king," she said in a rich, contralto voice.

He gestured to a chair. "Won't you be seated, my lady?"

Morgause seated herself with all the proud serenity of a ship coming into port. Her blue eyes regarded him with undisguised curiosity. "It seems strange that we have never met," she said.

Arthur resumed his own chair. "You see," he said excusingly, "Morgan told me that you had not forgiven me for Lot's death. That is why I stayed away from Lothian for all these years."

"Morgan is so clever," Morgause said admiringly. She looked down at her well-tended hands and Arthur could see the faint beginnings of a double chin. "Pellinore also insisted that we keep our distance from you. He was one of the only people in Lothian who knew you, of course, and he guessed that you were Mordred's father quite some years ago." Morgause looked candidly at the king's face. "The resemblance is quite remarkable. I didn't realize, otherwise I should never have brought Mordred to you like this."

"But why did Pellinore allow him to come?" Arthur asked. "After all these years of care, it seems strange . . ." He broke off at the look on her face.

"I had forgotten that you didn't know," Morgause said sadly. "Pellinore is dead, my lord. That is the reason my sons and I have come to Camelot, to bring the news to my eldest son, Gawain."

There was a pause. "I am sorry to hear about Pellinore. He was a good man and a good king."

"Yes," said Morgause. "I shall miss him."

Arthur picked up a stylus from his desk and began to turn it over in his fingers. "But you did not bring all your sons to Camelot?"

"No. Gaheris, my second son, has stayed in Lothian. If Gawain does not wish to return home, then Gaheris will be king. Agravaine came because he would like to join your cavalry, my lord. It has long been his ambition."

"And Mordred?" Arthur asked. "Why did he come?"

"He wanted to see the king, of course. And Camelot. But mainly I think he wanted to visit Morgan. He is very fond of her, you see."

Arthur looked down at the stylus in his hand. "I suppose you realize that I knew nothing about Mordred until yesterday."

Morgause sighed. "I know. Morgan is not going to be happy with me." He looked up. "I suppose you guessed the story as soon as you saw him."

"I went to Avalon last night to see Morgan. She told me the whole."

Morgause's blue eyes were full of curiosity. She had not meant to precipitate this moment, but now that she had, she was obviously enjoying herself. "I felt so sorry for her," she said to Arthur. "We offered to find her a husband, but she wouldn't marry. She refused to try to do away with the child. This seemed to be the best solution." Arthur's lashes fell, screening his eyes from hers. "She loves you very much, you know," she added.

His lashes flickered but he did not reply. "So we went off into Wales and changed identities," she continued briskly, "and when the fighting was over in Lothian, I went home with a new baby."

He put the stylus down and looked up at her slowly. "Morgan told me she might have died in childbirth were it not for you. I owe you a great debt, Morgause. I shall probably never be able to repay you, but if there is anything I can ever do for you, you have only to ask."

Morgause's face was radiant. "She is my sister. I was happy to help." '

"Now," Arthur said, "about Mordred."

Morgause blinked and readjusted her thoughts. "Yes," she said. "Mordred."

"I do not think it will be possible to hide the fact that he is my son."

"That is what Pellinore always said."

"He is my son and must be known to be my son by everyone who sees him. That is one fact. The second fact is that I have no other children, nor am I likely to have."

"The queen is barren, then?"

"Yes."

Morgause pursed her full lips. "Poor thing." There was more than a hint of complacency in her voice.

"It is a great sorrow to her," Arthur said levelly. "It has, as well, always posed a severe problem for the state. I need an heir to follow me in the high kingship." He held her eyes. "It seems now that I have one."

The prominent blue eyes became even more prominent. "You are proposing to make Mordred your heir?"

"He is my only son."

Morgause sat very straight. "So he is." This was evidently not a possibility she had considered.

"Morgause."

"Yes, my lord?"

"I do not want it known that Morgan is Mordred's mother," he said. "You have been a mother to him. Will you say he is your child?"

She looked at him with calculation. "But why?"

"Why not?" he countered. "It is an enviable position, that of mother to the next high king."

"I would have to say I was unfaithful to Lot."

"Yes, you would. But it was many years ago. And you are a very beautiful woman. No one will question the likelihood of an attraction between the two of us."

"What does Morgan say to this idea?"

"If you agree, she will be grateful."

He could tell from the look on Morgause's face that she understood perfectly why he was asking this of her. She might not be overly shrewd about matters of policy, but matters of sex were another matter altogether. She said after a minute, "But we have never met until now."

"You were at Avalon for some months. Who is to say I did not meet you there? I was very young, you are very beautiful—"

"Stop!" She was laughing. "You almost make me believe it did happen." Her face sobered. "All right, I'll do it. As you say, it was too many years ago for it to matter much now. And Lot has been long dead."

Arthur smiled at her. "Morgan has always told me you are wonderful," he said. "I thoroughly agree."

She was suddenly immensely glad she was doing this for him. Really, she wondered, where did he get his charm? Certainly not from his mother.

"I am going to tell Mordred the whole truth," he was saying.

She would have thought Mordred was one of the last persons he would want to know the truth. She stared at him in puzzlement. "You will tell him about Morgan? But why?"

The infectious gaiety had quite left his face. "He deserves to know who he is. I, of all people, know how important that is."

The truth of that statement struck Morgause for the first time. "Really," she said, "when you think of it, it is rather extraordinary. Both you and Mordred were unaware you were sons of high kings." Her blue eyes were wide with amazement. "Isn't that extraordinary?" she repeated.

Arthur looked back at her with a mixture of amusement and something she could not quite decipher. "Yes," he said dryly. "It is."

Chapter 33

*T*WENTY minutes later, Cai was escorting Mordred to Arthur's office. Gwenhwyfar, as promised, had had the packhorses brought to the palace, and Mordred was appropriately dressed in a tunic fine enough for any prince. Cai thought he looked very young and very lonely. He gave Arthur's son a warm encouraging smile before opening the door to the king's office. "Prince Mordred is here," he said briefly, gently urged the boy forward by a hand on his back, then closed the door on father and son.

As Cai walked away across the great hall, a long-buried memory surfaced in his mind: Arthur on the day he had first come to Avalon. He had been six years younger than the boy Cai had just left in the king's office, but even then Arthur had had defenses this boy knew nothing of. There had never been anything vulnerable about Arthur.

Left alone in the king's office, Mordred paused for a moment by the door, looking around with cautious curiosity. The room was simple, obviously furnished for work and not for show. There was a long walnut table against the window wall to Mordred's right, covered with hundreds of neatly stacked scrolls. The walls were hung with maps. The king sat behind another large walnut table in a chair with a dragon crest carved on its high wooden back. There were two other carved chairs placed in front of the king's table.

Arthur rose and came around his desk as Mordred stood in the doorway, and then he beckoned the boy forward, placing the two chairs in front of the desk to face each other. "Come and sit down, Mordred," he said.

The boy came and took the chair Arthur had indicated. For the first time since he had come into the room, he looked directly at the king.

Arthur suddenly had the strangest sensation that he was looking back in time: this boy's face was his face, and he was once again the boy he had been; that boy, and this boy, both of them meeting for the very first time a father and a king. For one dizzy moment, past and present fused and became one; then the moment passed and he was himself again.

"I want to tell you a story, Mordred," he said. His face was grave and composed; only the brilliant eyes betrayed his feelings. "It is about me, but it concerns you too, so be patient."

"Yes, my lord king," the boy replied. His voice had the uncertain note of the adolescent male whose voice has not yet reliably settled into its adult register.

Arthur linked his hands loosely in his lap and began. "When I was an infant, my parents, Uther and Igraine, sent me away and gave it out to the country that I was dead. You may perhaps be familiar with the story. I had been born too soon after their marriage, and they felt it would be best to have an heir whose birth was unblemished." Mordred nodded. Every person in Britain was familiar with the story of Arthur's childhood, he thought. The king was going on, "Years passed and Igraine bore no more living children. Then my grandfather, Merlin, took me from my hiding place in Cornwall and brought me to Avalon to be trained as a king. For reasons of safety, he kept my true identity a secret. Only he and Uther knew I was the son of the high king. I was never told, nor was anyone else.

"And so I lived at Avalon from the time I was nine until I was sixteen."

Arthur's eyes were on his hands. He unclasped them and then clasped them again. "There was another child growing up at Avalon at that time. Merlin's daughter, Morgan." The king paused. The room was so quiet that Mordred could hear the sound of his own breathing. "Morgan and I loved each other from the time I was nine and she was eight. We loved as children, and then, as we grew older, we loved as man and woman. We thought we would be able to marry. We neither of us, remember, knew who I was."

The king glanced up from his hands, and gray eyes looked into gray eyes. "Then I found out, found out that I was Prince of Britain and the next high king. I found out also that I could not marry Morgan."

"Why not?" Mordred was so held by the story that he did not feel it presumptuous to question the king. Nor did Arthur appear to mind.

"Merlin and Uther said we were too closely related," he answered. "At that time the king of Lothian was one of the most powerful of the regional kings and he was not pleased to discover that Uther had a son. He had hopes of the high kingship for himself, you see, and he would be bound to raise the cry of incest to discredit me."

"The King of Lothian," Mordred repeated. "Do you mean my father?"

"I mean Lot." A pinched look had suddenly appeared around Arthur's nostrils. "To continue, I wanted to marry Morgan in spite of my father and my grandfather. I begged her to come away with me to Armorica. She would not. My duty was to Britain and not to her, she said and sent me away." A muscle flickered along Arthur's jaw. "She gave me to Britain and never told me she was carrying my child."

The boy made a sudden movement and then was still again. To give him privacy, Arthur got to his feet and walked to the long table that held his correspondence and reports. He picked up a scroll and regarded it thoughtfully. "She knew if I found out, nothing would stop my claiming her. But Morgan is, above all, Merlin's daughter. Duty to her country is bred into her bones, Mordred. She would not step between me and the kingship she believed I was born to hold. So she went secretly into Wales, had the child, and gave it to another woman to raise as her own. " He put the scroll down and looked at his son. "I think you must know now who that woman was."

The boy was so pale he looked as if he might faint. He said, his voice an almost undistinguishable croak, "Morgause?"

"Morgause," the king confirmed gently. "Morgause was her sister. Morgause was a warm and loving mother. And Morgan would be able to see her son, to assure herself of his welfare. So you went home with Morgause and were presented to all as the posthumous son of Lot."

Two brilliant spots of color appeared in Mordred's cheeks at Arthur's use of the word "you."

"Between them, Morgan and Morgause kept the secret of your birth for fifteen years," Arthur continued. "I never knew of your existence until last night, when you walked into my banquet hall. I realized the moment I saw you who you were. You know, of course, how much you resemble me."

"So I am your son?"

"You are my son."

The color came back to the boy's face. "They all stared at me so. First the men at the gate." He looked a little dazed. "I even asked Agravaine if I had dirt on my face!"

Arthur was watching him gravely.

"Have . . . have you talked to my mother?"

"I went last night to Avalon. Morgan told me the whole."

Mordred's eyes flickered and Arthur realized he had not been talking of Morgan. "I spoke to Morgause as well," he went on easily. "So you see, Mordred, there can be no doubt."

Mordred drew a deep breath. "It does not seem possible. If you only knew, my lord, how we have admired and loved you. It seems impossibly wonderful to me that I am actually your son."

Arthur's eyes were very bright. "It seems impossibly wonderful to me too," he said.

The words were not extravagant, the voice not dramatic, but suddenly Mordred's heart was slamming and his breath was short. Before he realized what he was doing, he was on his knees at his father's feet, his lips pressed to the king's fingers. Arthur's other hand touched the thick silky black hair. "I was not so forgiving to Uther," he said.

Mordred looked up. "There is nothing to forgive, my lord. How could you have claimed me sooner? You said yourself you knew nothing of my existence. Besides"—his young face was suddenly blazing—"there is not a boy in Britain who would not rejoice to learn that he was your son."

Arthur laughed a little unsteadily and moved his hand to Mordred's shoulder to raise him to his feet. "I don't think you have understood the full implication of what this means for you, Mordred," he said more composedly when the boy was once more standing in front of him. The king was the taller by a few inches. "You are not just my son, you are my only son. You are the heir to Britain, Mordred."

The young face looked bewildered. "But you are married, my lord. Surely your lawful sons would come before me in the line of succession?"

"I do not think I will have lawful sons," Arthur replied very quietly. "The queen is barren." There was a moment of startled silence; then Arthur put a hand on his son's shoulder and steered him back to the chairs. "I understand how you must feel, Mordred," he said as the boy collapsed gratefully into his seat. "The same thing happened to me. But I am good for a number of years yet. When I was told I would be high king, Uther gave himself only six months."

Mordred looked rather dazedly at his father. "Six months!"

Arthur nodded and resumed his own chair. "And let me tell you, that was daunting."

Mordred managed a laugh. "Yes, I can see that it must have been."

"Let me explain to you what I propose to do," Arthur said matter-of-factly. "Then you tell me what you think."

"All right."

"First, I have spoken to the queen and she has agreed to accept you as my son and heir. You will like her; she is a very lovely lady. Next, there is a festival planned, as I'm sure you are aware. I am expecting a great number of the regional kings and princes to be in Camelot very shortly, and I will present you to them as the future heir to Britain. There can be few doubts raised as to your paternity. You wear your heritage on your face."

Now came the difficult part. "Last, I have spoken to Morgause, and she has agreed to continue the fiction that she is your natural mother. We will tell the world that you are my son and hers." Arthur's voice was cooler now, more commanding. It did not invite discussion. "It will be less complicated that way."

"Yes, my lord," said Mordred with the faintest of stammers.

Arthur's eyes warmed and he gave his son a smile. "Would you like to see Morgause now?"

"Yes, please," said Mordred faintly.

"Come with me and I'll take you to her," said Arthur, and Mordred rose obediently and followed his father out of the room.

The Queen of Lothian had been given a large sunny room in the queen's part of the house and it was to its comfortable privacy that Arthur brought Mordred and then left him. Mordred paused at the door, suddenly uncertain. For fifteen years he had thought Morgause was his mother. Now she was not.

He opened the door and she was there sitting by the window, basking in the sun like a cat. She smiled when she saw him. "My poor love. You look as if you have been hit over the head."

He smiled back, a little uncertainly. "I feel as if someone has hit me over the head. It is a little . . . disturbing to discover suddenly that the people whom all your life you thought were your parents really were not."

The room was decorated in rich reds and blues, a fitting background for Morgause's own vivid coloring. She stood up. "You should not have found out this way, I know. But I did not realize how closely you resembled Arthur, Mordred. I see now why Pellinore was so careful to keep you apart."

"Did Pellinore know, then?" He felt strangely disoriented in her familiar presence. He did not know what he should call her.

"Yes. Pellinore guessed when you were only a small child. He knew Arthur and of course he saw the resemblance."

They were talking so calmly and rationally. Mordred looked around the room, as if trying to convince himself of where he was. Then: "The King says that Morgan is my real mother."

"Morgan certainly gave birth to you," she said, "but *I* am your mother." She held out her arms.

Her ample breast was soft and sheltering, the smell of her so familiar, so comforting. He closed his eyes for a minute. "It is all so confusing."

"My poor little lamb," said Morgause, and patted his back.

He straightened and looked into her face. Their eyes were almost on a level. "If you hadn't brought me here this way, would Morgan ever have told him?" he asked.

"I don't know. She would have had to eventually, I suppose. You are his only son."

"She should have told him."

"Perhaps." Morgause's blue eyes were speculative. "Arthur wants us to pretend that I am your natural mother. Did he tell you that?"

"Yes. But I don't understand why."

"He wants to protect Morgan, of course."

Mordred's straight black brows drew together. "But he is protecting Morgan's reputation at the expense of yours." He still had not called her "Mother."

Morgause decided to say no more. "I don't mind," she replied placidly. "It puts him under an obligation to me, and it is not a bad thing to have the high king under an obligation to one. So we will go along with him."

Mordred's frown had not eased. "What will we tell Gawain and Agravaine?"

"The fewer people who know the truth, the better. Let them continue to believe you are their brother."

The gray eyes were unhappy. "I wish the king would let us tell the truth. I don't like living with a lie."

"Nonsense," said Morgause with the brisk good sense of one who has never suffered overly from a troubled conscience. "In your heart you must feel that I am your mother and that Gawain, Gaheris, and Agravaine are your brothers. You will be living by the truth of your heart."

"I suppose that is so." The worry had not lifted from his face. "What will they think when they hear I am the son of the high king?"

"They will be delighted." Morgause picked up his hand and squeezed it. "Why don't we go now and tell Agravaine?"

"All right," Mordred agreed—and they neither of them found it odd that they thought of the younger brother first.

Chapter 34

CAMELOT was filled to the bursting point. The great hall bustled with activity. Every bedroom in the palace held a king or a prince. One could hardly move in the family part of the house for the crush of wives and daughters accommodated there. The palace grounds were covered with tents housing the crowd not considered important enough to be lodged in the palace itself. In the barracks they were sleeping two to a bed. As Arthur had once jestingly remarked, it didn't seem as if anyone in Britain had stayed at home.

Feeding all of these people was a herculean task, and Gwenhwyfar divided her time between smiling graciously at her guests and supervising in the kitchens. Sanitation was the other main problem, but this she gratefully left to Cai. The meetings and entertainment were Arthur's responsibility.

It was the first time in years that all the regional kings were gathered together, and Arthur had planned a council meeting even before Mordred arrived on the scene. The meeting in fact was the first item on his agenda, and it occurred on the afternoon of the first day of the festival. Gwenhwyfar's father, Maelgwyn, was there, as was Bedwyr's father, Ban. Cador of Dumnonia and the kings of Elmet and Rheged and Manau Guotodin were also present. The only missing council member was the King of Lothian, and Arthur informed the rest of them first of Pellinore's demise. Then he told them about Mordred.

The meeting was held in the new council chamber, one of the palace's most important public rooms. Its main piece of furniture was a large round table made of beech that Arthur had commissioned from the palace carpenters. Always sensitive to Celtic fears that he might be setting himself up as a new emperor, Arthur had made it a point to avoid any trappings that might point to imperial aspirations on his part. They would sit around the table as equals and discuss whatever had to be discussed with a comfortable lack of ceremony.

Arthur did not feel the need of a throne or a dais to establish his authority.

After the initial surprise, and after they had met Mordred for themselves, the main reaction of the kings seemed to be relief. They none of them relished the prospect of the inevitable fight for power that would ensue should the high king leave no heir. Besides, as Ban said humorously, they were growing quite accustomed to having high kings produce sons from out of nowhere.

It was Maelgwyn who asked, "What if Gwenhwyfar should bear a son?"

Arthur looked at him from under half-lifted brows. "I do not think she will," he said softly.

Patchy color mottled Maelgwyn's face under his beard. It was very easy to tell the visitors from the regular inhabitants of Camelot: the Celts were all bearded, while the capital followed the high king's Roman style and went clean-shaven. Just now, Maelgwyn's face was almost as red as his beard. He felt his daughter's barrenness to be a personal reproach, and was not yet ready to concede that she would never present Britain with an heir. "But if she should?" he persisted.

There was the briefest of pauses. "The queen's child would be legitimate, and so take precedence, of course."

Ban and Cador exchanged glances. They had both at one time or another suggested to Arthur that he set Gwenhwyfar aside and take another queen. They were still of that mind, particularly now, when it had been proven that the king was perfectly capable of getting a child. It was clearly Gwenhwyfar who was barren, and a barren queen was of little use to anyone. They refrained from voicing this opinion in the presence of Maelgwyn, however, and the council closed on an amicable note.

There was a great banquet that night, with entertainment by a famous harper, and both hosts and guests went to bed tired but satisfied that the festival had got off to an auspicious start.

The second day started promisingly as well, with bright sunshine and a pleasant breeze, just strong enough to carry the flags that bedecked the walls and the palace and the tents. This day belonged to the cavalry. A small amphitheater of wooden seats had been constructed around the large field on which the foot drilled, and this was to be the venue for all of the military demonstrations. As Gwenhwyfar had feared, there were not enough seats for everyone, and the overflow crowd was posted on the hill above the leveled-out field and surrounding amphitheater. The mood of the crowd in both the stands and on the hill was distinctly jovial.

Gwenhwyfar sat in the front row of seats, precisely in the center of the field, with Arthur on one side of her and Mordred on the other. Bedwyr, of course, was with the cavalry, as was Gawain. Morgause was seated beside Mordred, and on Morgause's other side was her son Agravaine.

A friendly family group, Gwenhwyfar thought sardonically. Thank God that Morgan had not come. She had been expected but had sent word earlier that she had to attend to a sick servant at Avalon. Gwenhwyfar had been greatly relieved.

Mordred was speaking to her. "Where will they come in, my lady?"

"Over there." She pointed and then turned to look at him. He smiled at her and tossed the black hair back from his brow in a gesture that was Arthur's own. Gwenhwyfar's heart skipped a beat.

"I have never seen anything so splendid," he confided.

She smiled back. "I'm glad you are enjoying yourself."

She had thought she would hate this son of Arthur's, but she did not. Quite the opposite, in fact; she found herself liking him very much. He, for his part, was obviously dazzled by her. It was rather pleasant, Gwenhwyfar was finding, to have a young Arthur at her feet.

Morgause leaned a little forward and said something to her across Mordred. Gwenhwyfar replied easily. She rather liked Morgause as well. In fact, her cynical thought was well-nigh close to being the truth. However oddly they might be linked, they *were* a friendly family group.

As long as Morgan stayed away.

"What is first?" Mordred was asking.

Agravaine replied, "First is a parade of heavy horse, in full armor. Then demonstrations by the medium and the light horse. Then there will be a precision drill. That is the morning's program."

Gwenhwyfar looked toward Mordred's brother and saw only the top of his smooth golden head on the far side of his mother. Agravaine had moved in with Gawain down at cavalry headquarters and she had seen little of him since his arrival at Camelot. He was very different from both Gawain and Mordred. It was odd how three brothers could be so different. But of course, she corrected herself, Mordred was not their brother at all.

Thank God, Morgan had not come.

A horn sounded and a line of horses began to trot onto the field. Gwenhwyfar, like the rest of the audience, leaned a little forward in anticipation.

The morning demonstrations were very successful, with the precision drill the obvious crowd favorite. As the audience resumed their places for the afternoon program, Gwenhwyfar noticed that Cai, who had been on Arthur's other side that morning, was missing.

"Where is Cai?" she asked her husband.

His profile remained untroubled. "I asked him to see to something for me."

"Nothing has gone wrong?"

"No. Nothing like that." A horn sounded and a solitary rider came out onto the field. Gwenhwyfar recognized Bedwyr instantly. So did almost everyone else in the audience. The crowd roared and Arthur turned to his wife and grinned. "This will pop their eyes out," he said boyishly. "Watch."

It was the demonstration she had once seen Bedwyr give to the cavalry recruits, only the horse was no longer Sluan, but another big black stallion, this one called Sugyn, and the movements were even more impressive than she recalled.

Bedwyr wore the blue tunic of the cavalry, with no armor or helmet. The sun reflected off the gilt of his hair and the polished ebony of his horse's coat and the two of them held the audience's riveted attention as Sugyn went through his smoothly planned program.

They were both so big and powerful, Gwenhwyfar thought, so perfectly matched. The stallion was glistening all over with sweat. There was an audible intake of breath from around the amphitheater as Sugyn left the ground and then kicked out strongly with his hind legs. There was the flash of silver in the sun from the iron shoes and Gwenhwyfar realized that what she was watching was a weapon in action. Those hooves were as deadly as any sword.

Man and horse were cantering around the field now, the horse looking as if he would leap into the seats at the slightest provocation. The crowd roared its approval and the stallion leapt higher with each canter stride. Bedwyr looked perfectly unruffled.

"He is magnificent," said Agravaine with obvious sincerity, and Mordred turned to his brother with some surprise. Agravaine was not given to compliments.

Arthur leaned a little forward to answer his cousin. "He's worth more than an entire regiment when he's in battle," he said. "I doubt Bedwyr's ever been equaled as a leader of cavalry."

Gwenhwyfar looked at Arthur's face. His gray eyes were full of uncomplicated pride and admiration as he watched his cavalry commander coming down the field toward him. Bedwyr and Sugyn came to a halt just below the king's party. Bedwyr gestured for silence and it was a measure of his power that the crowd quieted almost immediately. From the entrance to the field Gwenhwyfar could see Ruadh being ridden toward them.

Next to her, Arthur said, "What in Hades . . . ?"

Then Bedwyr was speaking. "The calvary would like to invite the king to give a demonstration to the audience," he announced in a booming voice that was designed to reach even the spectators on the hillside.

The crowd roared its approval. Gwenhwyfar heard Arthur say something under his breath. She leaned toward him. "I did not know you were planning to ride."

"Neither did I," he replied with exasperation. "Damn Bedwyr."

Below them, Bedwyr was laughing. "I had Gareth warm him up, Arthur," he called over the noise of the crowd. "He's ready to go."

Arthur rose reluctantly to his feet. The crowd was shouting and clapping; there was no way he could get out of this. He put his hand on the front of the stand, looked at Bedwyr before him, and said without heat, "You bastard."

Bedwyr grinned. Arthur vaulted lightly over the barrier, landed easily, and walked to where Gareth, now dismounted, was holding Ruadh. "You were in on this too, I see," he remarked as he took the chestnut's reins into his left hand.

Gareth laughed, as obviously pleased with their ploy as Bedwyr. "It was the prince's idea, my lord."

"I'm sure it was," Arthur returned, put his foot into the stirrup, and swung into the saddle.

"It isn't fair!" Mordred said to Gwenhwyfar. "It isn't fair to make him follow Bedwyr like this. You saw how surprised he was. He isn't ready."

"Bedwyr would never do anything to discredit the king," Gwenhwyfar replied. The noise in the amphitheater had quieted and Bedwyr backed his horse to stand just before Arthur's empty seat. He glanced around once, and met Gwenhwyfar's eyes. His own were full of blue laughter.

Then he turned back to the field and Gwenhwyfar said to Mordred, "Don't worry."

It was a very different ride from Bedwyr's. If the impression conveyed by Bedwyr and Sugyn was of strength and power, the impression produced by Arthur and Ruadh was of lightness and elegance. The copper-colored horse seemed to float above the ground, turning, moving laterally, changing gaits, without any sign of a cue from his rider. Arthur himself seemed less a rider than an extension of the horse, and the two of them together more a creature of air than of earth. It was so beautiful that Gwenhwyfar felt tears come into her eyes.

Ruadh came to a perfect halt in the center of the field, and Arthur patted his neck and looked at Bedwyr. The crowd watched in breathless silence as the rider on the big black stallion cantered out to face the king. They spoke to each other briefly; then both horses, side by side, began a final canter of the field. The crowd went wild.

"Very neatly done." It was Agravaine's voice, barely audible above the noise around them. "One could almost swear they hadn't planned it."

"It wasn't planned," Gwenhwyfar replied, and leaned a little forward so she could see Agravaine around Mordred and Morgause. "The king did not know Bedwyr was going to do that."

The expression in Agravaine's dark blue eyes was unreadable. "Then the prince is either incredibly generous or a fool."

"Bedwyr is no fool," Gwenhwyfar replied.

Mordred, who had been listening to this exchange, said now, "I think they both were wonderful!"

Gwenhwyfar looked at his shining face and felt a sudden surge of affection. "Yes," she said. "So do I."

There were going to be races next, and as the field was being set up, Gwenhwyfar's mind went back to her exchange with Agravaine. Bedwyr had known exactly what he was doing when he had forced Arthur into that demonstration, she thought. She understood perfectly what must have happened. Arthur had refused to perform, and so Bedwyr had made him. She understood also Bedwyr's motive. He wanted the country's leaders to see their king the way his men saw him.

Incredibly generous, Agravaine had said. It was true, she thought. Bedwyr's love was incredibly generous. He had not minded at all sharing his moment in the sun with Arthur.

And Arthur too. "I doubt Bedwyr's ever been equaled as a leader of cavalry," he had said to them with honest admiration.

How small and petty all her own feminine jealousies and hurts seemed, compared with the feeling between Arthur and Bedwyr. She would do better in the future, Gwenhwyfar promised herself. She would strive for Bedwyr's generosity of heart.

She remained fully committed to this noble goal through the remainder of the afternoon's exhibitions. Then, as she entered the palace with Arthur, a servant said, "The Lady of Avalon has arrived, my lord."

Gwenhwyfar looked at Arthur. "I thought she was attending to a sick servant," she said, and even to herself her voice sounded hard.

"It was an excuse," he returned. "Morgan thought it would be more comfortable for everyone if she stayed away. I sent Cai to fetch her this afternoon."

Morgan had been right, Gwenhwyfar thought. She struggled to keep her face expressionless in front of the servants. "Where shall I seat her at dinner?" she asked.

Arthur's eyes met hers. "Next to me. Put Cai on her other side."

Gwenhwyfar's hands curled into fists. "Very well," she said, and turned away.

Morgan had not wanted to come. "Arthur says you must," Cai told her patiently. "It isn't like you to act the coward, Morgan."

"It isn't that. It's just that my presence will be so awkward."

"For whom?" he asked. Then, as she refused to look at him: "You have to face Mordred sooner or later, my dear."

Her eyes flew to his face.

"Arthur has said nothing to me," he assured her, "but I know you both too well to believe that Morgause is that boy's mother."

The apprehensive look was still on her face. "What does everyone else think?"

"They have no reason to doubt the king's word." He looked at her still-worried face and asked bluntly, "Does Mordred know who you are?"

"Yes, Arthur told him." She gave Cai a wry smile. "You're right. I am being a coward."

"You have to face him sooner or later," Cai repeated. "And if you don't come to Camelot with me, Arthur is very likely to drag you there himself, personally."

She sighed. "All right. I'll come. Wait while I go and pack some clothes."

The cavalry demonstration was still in progress when Morgan and Cai arrived at the palace. Morgan had seen Camelot only once, before Gwenhwyfar had come to live there. The beauty of the finished house almost took her mind off the reason for her visit. Almost.

"The palace is crowded as a fairgrounds," Cai said to her. "Arthur has saved you one of the bedrooms off the little court, though."

"Where is Mordred staying?" she asked.

"Arthur has given him a room in his own suite. I think the plan is for him to move down to cavalry headquarters after the festival, though." He looked into her face. "He is doing very well, Morgan. He's a nice lad. Everyone likes him."

"I'm glad," she said.

She had been in the comfortable guest bedroom less than an hour when Arthur arrived. She stared at him from the wardrobe where she was arranging her clothes and said crossly, "You knew I didn't want to come. Why did you insist?"

"Because you ought to be here," he returned. "Everyone else in Britain is."

She pressed her lips together and did not reply. He was right and they both knew it. "I suppose I shall have to talk to him," she said after a minute.

"I know how you feel," he returned comfortingly. "I had to face him too. But he's a warmhearted boy, Morgan. It will be all right."

Finally she smiled at him. "I'm glad you are getting along."

"Shall I send him to you? Better meet him now, before dinner."

She drew a deep breath. "Yes."

After he had gone, she went to the comfortable wicker chair by the window and sat down. It was a very large chair, and when she leaned back she was almost lost in it. She clasped her hands in her lap. The minutes went by slowly.

How did you face a child you had given away at birth? What did you say to him?

Igraine had done it, but Igraine had not cared about her son. Morgan cared, cared desperately. How could she tell him that she had yearned for him all these years? That her arms had ached for him? That leaving him to Morgause each year had been like a little death to her? How could she tell him all that, and expect him to believe her? He would want an accounting from her, not sentimental protestations.

She did not think he would be as warmhearted toward her as he had been toward Arthur. Arthur had done nothing that needed forgiveness.

There was a light knock upon the door. "Come in," she said, and watched as the door slowly opened and her son came into the room.

Mordred's emotions were in a turmoil. He had known Morgan all his life, had looked forward eagerly every summer to her visits. He had shared things with her he had never shared with anyone else. There was a kind of closeness between them that there had never been with anyone else. They understood each other.

And for all those years, she had been lying to him.

He came into the room and closed the door. She was sitting in a big wicker chair, looking at him out of those well-remembered brown eyes. "Hello, Mordred," she said.

"Hello." He hesitated. "My lady."

He saw her flinch and felt a flicker of satisfaction. "I suppose I deserved that," she said. He did not reply, only stood there, his hands clasped behind his back, the width of the room between them. His heart was hammering. He had not realized, until he saw her, how very angry at her he was.

The brown eyes, as always, seemed to know how he was feeling. "I don't expect you to understand," she said. "I shall just tell you that I felt I had to do it, and that it was very hard."

For a long moment he did not answer. Then, bitterly: "I understand why you could not keep me. But I cannot understand why you never told my father about me. Not during all these years! He never knew!"

That was the sin he would never forgive. She said, without expecting him to understand, "I thought you were better off in Lothian. You were safe there. You were happy. If the queen had had a son, your position here would have been precarious. And very unhappy, I think."

"You should have told him. You should have told *me*. I could have stayed in Lothian. I would never have wanted to come between the crown and his trueborn sons."

"Arthur would never have left you in Lothian, Mordred. I knew that, and that is why I did not tell him." She sighed. "I would have had to tell him eventually, however. As I am sure you have discovered, Arthur has no other heir."

"He . . . he has named me as his heir. I am to be high king after him." His expression was half-proud, half-uncertain.

"I know. It seems the queen cannot have children."

"But what if she does?" It was a question that had been on his mind for days, and he had been afraid to ask it.

"Would you mind that?"

"I don't know."

"Arthur will do what is best for Britain. That is all I can tell you." Her brown eyes were steady on his face. "That is what it means to be a king."

He felt better and then he was angry with himself for feeling better. He did not want her to comfort him. He looked at her suspiciously. "Why doesn't my father want anyone to know you are my real mother?" he asked abruptly. He was breathing rapidly now, the tunic over his chest rising and falling with his agitation. The chest was narrow, the arms still childishly thin. He was not nearly as muscular as Arthur had been at his age.

"Why don't you ask him?" she returned.

He drew in his breath and let it out in a great gust. "Will you be at the dinner tonight?"

"Yes." Her face was very grave. "I realize all this is quite difficult for you, Mordred. I don't expect you to feel toward me as you feel toward Morgause. She has earned your love. I have not." For some reason he felt tears sting behind his eyes, and he blinked rapidly to chase them away. "If you can bring yourself to behave toward me as you would to your mother's sister, that will be enough," she said.

"I . . ." He made a gesture, turned away, and said over his shoulder, "I will see you at dinner." Then he was gone.

As soon as the door had closed Morgan pressed her clenched fists to her temples and shut her eyes. Careful, she thought. Push back the pain. Don't feel it. Don't think about it. Careful, or you will have Arthur here in a minute, before you can get control.

She forced herself to breathe slowly and deeply, she made her mind a blank, forbidding the picture of her son's face to rise to her inner vision. Think of something else. Think of the apple trees at Avalon. Don't think of Mordred, don't think of him. . . .

She was still sitting motionless in the big wicker chair five minutes later when the door opened and Arthur came in. She turned her head as he came toward her; he was wearing the blue tunic she had seen him in earlier, but it looked rumpled and creased, as if it had lain on the floor and then been put back on in a hurry. His hair was wet. She sighed resignedly. "Where were you? In the bath?"

"Never mind. What happened? Why are you so distressed?"

"Is there no such thing as privacy?" she asked, her eyebrows fine aloof arches over her inquiring brown eyes.

"Not from me." He sank on his heels in front of her wicker chair, so that his face was just below the level of hers. "What happened?" he asked again.

She leaned toward him and put her hands on either side of his face. He looked so like his son, and they were so different. "Arthur," she asked softly, "how did you feel about Igraine?"

His eyes searched hers. "It is not the same thing."

She smoothed her thumbs along the beautiful cheekbones. "In the most important way, it is the same. I gave him away. The why does not matter, not to a child. I gave him away and, what is perhaps worse in his eyes, I did not tell you. He finds it hard to forgive me."

He put his hands up to encircle her wrists. "I will talk to him."

"You will say nothing." She stared forbiddingly into his eyes. "Do you hear me? This is between Mordred and me. I do not want you to interfere. The poor boy has enough to contend with without you bullying him to be nice to his mother."

There was a long moment's silence as they looked at each other. "I never bully people," he said, and Morgan knew she had won. She leaned forward and lightly kissed the top of his wet black head. "Go finish getting washed for dinner. I shall be all right."

He released her wrists and she dropped her hands from his face. He straightened with the ease of a boy. "Do you want to come to the dinner?"

"Yes. I shall be fine."

"I told Gwenhwyfar to seat you between me and Cai."

"Thank you. I am not much in the mood for making brilliant conversation."

"Cai and I don't care what you say." He was standing and she was still sitting and she had to tip her head back to look up at him. "He will come around, Morgan," he said.

"I'm sure he will. He has a much sweeter nature than you."

He grinned. "He must take after his mother." He touched the top of her head gently and turned toward the door. "Cai will come to escort you to dinner."

"Will you go away so I can get dressed?"

"I'm going," he said and, having reached the door, suited action to words.

Chapter 35

*T*HE tables in the dining room had been arranged along the walls for the evening meal in order to leave the center of the floor free for entertainment. Seated around the room, in an order that carefully designated their rank, were the kings and princes of Celtic Britain together with their sons and wives and daughters. The high king, with his family beside him, presided over the meal from the front of the room.

Cador, King of Dumnonia, was, as befitted his rank, seated at one of the tables nearest to the king. As his son and heir, Constantine, ate hungrily beside him, Cador watched the king's table out of his deep-set dark eyes. He was considering once again the possibility of persuading the king to take another wife.

The boy Mordred was at least an heir, although Cador would have preferred a son of unquestioned legitimacy. But even if Mordred were to be given the preference over younger children, Cador felt it would be safer to have others behind him. Life was precarious.

It was not possible for Arthur to marry the boy's mother. She was still a handsome woman—and here Cador's eyes flicked approvingly over the vibrant figure of the Queen of Lothian—but too old for childbearing. Besides, there was always the question of incest.

A few murmurs had been heard when Arthur had announced the name of Mordred's mother, but by and large the tribal Celts had a forgiving view of such things. They were all accustomed to blood marrying blood within the clan. It was almost impossible to avoid, given the nature of Celtic society. But Morgause could never be his wife.

Cador's eyes circled the tables, stopping at the face of a particularly pretty young girl who was seated toward the bottom of the room. Nola, Madoc's daughter. Madoc, a prince from the extreme west of Wales, was of good blood. And the girl was very pretty. She would have to be, if the king were to be brought to consider putting aside Gwenhwyfar.

Cador's eyes moved back to the head table, to the face of the queen. It was sheer physical pleasure just to look at her, he admitted. He could quite understand Arthur's reluctance to put her aside. Any man who had got Gwenhwyfar into his bed would feel the same.

But she was barren. Five years they had been married, and never any sign of a child. Not even a miscarriage.

The boy, Mordred, was the final proof. Until his appearance it had always been possible to wonder if the fault was perhaps Arthur's. One had never heard of his leaving any bastards behind during all the long years of his campaigns against the Saxons. But then, even as a boy he had been fastidious.

Cador wondered if perhaps Arthur himself had feared to find out if he were the one responsible for his childless marriage. Perhaps that was why he had so adamantly refused to consider replacing Gwenhwyfar. He might feel differently now, with the proof of his own potency sitting at the table with him, looking so uncannily like Arthur himself had looked when first he came to Venta.

As Cador watched, the king's dark head bent closer to the red-gold one of his wife. Gwenhwyfar looked up at him, saying something. The green of her eyes was visible all the way across the room. Cador's senses leapt, and his mouth curled with wry self-knowledge. No, it was not going to be easy to persuade the king to set aside Gwenhwyfar.

The seat to the right of the queen was empty, and it was not until the main course was being removed that Bedwyr put in an appearance. Cador watched him stride across the floor, his fair head held with unconscious arrogance, his big body as powerful and graceful as the lion he was called after. There had been some problem with a horse, Cador knew. That was why the prince was late.

"I wish I could join the cavalry," Constantine said, and Cador looked at his heir.

"Would you like to? There is not likely to be much fighting now, you know."

"But to serve under the prince!" Constantine's dark eyes were shining.

The prince. In a room full of princes, there was only one who was the prince. In all of Britain, when you spoke of the prince, there was never any doubt as to whom you meant. Cador watched as Bedwyr took his usual seat next to the queen and leaned across her to speak briefly to the king.

They would be talking about the horse.

Gwenhwyfar listened quietly and said nothing. Then Arthur gave Bedwyr a quick smile and turned away to talk to the woman on his other side, Morgan, the Lady of Avalon. Gwenhwyfar poured wine into Bedwyr's cup while a servant filled his plate. Then the queen watched with amused affection as Bedwyr began to eat. He glanced up from his plate, saw her watching him, and they both laughed. A thought flitted across Cador's mind and he frowned and looked quickly at Arthur.

The king was talking to Cai. Morgan, seated between them, appeared to be listening. Cador had never before seen Merlin's youngest daughter, and he had been surprised by how small she was, how young. He had expected her to be a much more imposing figure, the famous Lady of Avalon. It was a title that somehow did not suit this small, fragile woman with the great brown eyes.

She looked up suddenly and those eyes met his. She had felt him watching her, he realized, as she held his gaze with her own. They looked at each other for a long moment, their faces grave, and then she smiled very faintly and nodded. Cador had the disconcerting feeling that his mind had been read.

There was obviously more to that small figure than appeared on the surface.

The after-dinner entertainment consisted of some excellent jugglers, then a troop of acrobats, and then a harper. As the program concluded, Arthur rose and said pleasantly that he had not yet met all of the wives and sons and daughters and would be happy to do so now. Prince Mordred, he added, would also be pleased to speak to any of the princes who had not yet had a chance to be introduced.

As Cador watched, the center of the dining room became filled with people, talking among themselves in small groups, waiting for their chance to speak to either the king or to Mordred. The boy, Cador was happy to see, appeared to be carrying out his role very well. Morgause was not far from him, but he never once looked her way for guidance.

He might do very well, this Mordred. He was not Arthur, of course. You couldn't picture this boy taking the kind of instant command Arthur had. But he did not have to. The king was only thirty-one. There would be many years for Mordred to grow in authority.

But it would be safer to have other sons behind him.

Arthur was talking to Madoc now, and as Cador watched intently, the Welsh prince presented his wife and his golden-haired daughter.

The king said something to the girl and she smiled, showing pretty white teeth. Then Arthur's head turned—like an animal scenting danger, Cador thought. With a murmured excuse, the king moved over to the group around Mordred, which now included the Lady of Avalon.

Before Cador could see what it was that had brought Arthur so quickly, his attention was claimed by Ban of Dyfed. The two of them backed into a corner and proceeded to talk about the problems of the succession.

Morgause had called Mordred and Morgan to her side, and in too public a fashion for either of them to demur. Morgan reluctantly left her small group of former patients and walked over to stand beside her sister.

It had quite obviously never occurred to the Queen of Lothian that the formerly happy relationship between Mordred and Morgan was necessarily going to be changed. Mordred was very pale as Morgan arrived at Morgause's side. He did not look at his mother. The occasion for the queen's summons was an old man who, she told them triumphantly, had actually fought under Merlin in Constantine's wars. Wasn't that amazing?

Morgan made some sort of remark which must have been acceptable, as the old man beamed at her. Mordred stood stiff and white and said nothing. Morgan wondered despairingly how she was going to extricate them from this awkward situation, when there was a quiet step at her side and Arthur was there.

He spoke to the old man. He was charming to Morgause. He called over a prince whose father had fought under Merlin too. Then he excused himself and Morgan, saying there were other people who wanted to meet her, and in a gesture that dated back to their childhood, he put his hand on the nape of her neck and steered her away.

It was silly to be distressed by such a small incident, Morgan told herself. But she was nonetheless grateful for the comforting pressure of Arthur's familiar hand on her neck. The hand tightened suddenly and she looked up to see Urien approaching her, a faintly apprehensive look in his light blue eyes. He looked at the king's face, faltered, and stopped.

Don't be an idiot. The thought ran in Arthur's mind as clearly as if she had spoken to him. He glanced down, saw the look in her eyes, and suddenly grinned.

"Urien," he said cheerfully. "Come and say hello to the Lady Morgan."

The handsome face brightened and the Prince of Rheged came to join them. Arthur dropped his hand and turned to speak to Urien's father, who had come up beside him.

The crush of people around Mordred seemed to have lessened and Arthur judged he could now properly make a formal departure from the dining room. He looked around for his wife. She was surrounded by a group of admiring men, not all of them young. His eyes passed on and found Bedwyr, talking to his brother on the far side of the room. Cai, Arthur knew, had already left.

Arthur caught Bedwyr's eye and the prince moved to join him. "The queen and I are going to retire," Arthur said. "Will you escort the Lady Morgan?"

"Of course," Bedwyr replied promptly, and turned to Morgan, offering her his arm. Urien reluctantly stepped back. Bedwyr was wearing a short-sleeved tunic and his bare muscular arm was covered with short golden hairs. Morgan put her small square hand on his forearm and smiled up at him. "I'm sorry I missed your program this afternoon," she said. "Cai tells me you got Arthur out on the field. How clever of you, Bedwyr."

He smiled back, very blond and blue in the light from the chandelier, and answered her humorously. They chatted with ease while they waited for Arthur to collect Gwenhwyfar and make a ceremonious exit.

The queen's admirers parted at the king's advance. He came to a halt beside her, said, "Time to let all these people go to bed," and with a polite formal gesture, he offered her his arm. They began to walk with dignity down the center of the room. Bedwyr and Morgan fell in behind them, followed by Morgause and Mordred.

Gwenhwyfar looked at her hand reposing so formally on her husband's arm. He had put his hand on Morgan's neck in a gesture that had looked to Gwenhwyfar to be purely instinctive. Arthur, who never touched anyone without making a conscious decision to do so.

Jealousy, so physical that it made her feel sick, rose within her. I will not feel like this, she told herself fiercely. I will not.

Behind her she could hear Morgan saying something to Bedwyr. His deep voice replied, sounding so natural, so familiar, so sane. Bedwyr, she thought, and clung to the image of him as a person caught in a swamp would cling to the one piece of solid ground that remained under his sinking feet.

* * *

The following morning Cador and Ban requested an audience with Arthur. Gwenhwyfar saw her father in the little hall, saw the angry look on his face, and thought she knew what the meeting was likely to be about. They wanted Arthur to take another queen.

Gwenhwyfar left the hall and went down the long corridor that led to the kitchens at the back of the house. Then she walked around the outhouses: the bakehouse, the storehouses, the meat house. She was watching a wagonload of vegetables being delivered when she saw Cai approaching. He squinted a little in the sun, then put up his hand to shade his eyes. "Are you all right?" he asked. "You look pale."

"I'm not suffering from morning sickness, if that is what you mean," she replied.

There was a pause. "Come for a walk in the garden with me. It's too dusty for you here."

She fell into step beside him and they walked in silence until they had reached the cool green oasis of the garden. "What is it?" he asked then quietly. "Can I help?"

Gwenhwyfar looked at him in surprise. He had sounded genuinely concerned. She and Cai had always got along well enough, but she had never been able to get over the feeling that Arthur's foster brother disapproved of her. Or disapproved of her and Bedwyr.

His hazel eyes looked very kind, however, and much to her own astonishment she said, "Cador and Ban are going to ask Arthur to take another wife."

"Probably." He sounded unconcerned. "It won't be the first time. You must know that."

She averted her face. "Yes, I know. But it is different now, Cai. Now that Arthur has Mordred. Now it is quite clear why Britain still has no heir from Arthur's marriage."

"It doesn't matter." He sounded genuinely puzzled. "That will make no difference to Arthur."

"Won't it?" Her voice was muffled. "He said to me once that our childlessness might be his fault, but now that he knows it isn't . . ."

"Gwenhwyfar." His voice was a curious mixture of impatience and compassion. "You are torturing yourself for no reason. Arthur will never put you aside. I am surprised I should have to tell you that."

Her eyes went back to his face. "How can you be so certain?"

"Because I know Arthur. He would no more replace you as queen than he would replace Bedwyr as cavalry leader or me as his second-in-command. Arthur is always loyal to his friends."

There was a long silence. A fish jumped in one of the decorative basins near them. "Sometimes, Cai," Gwenhwyfar said at last, "I don't know where loyalty lies."

It was a remark that took them precariously close to things they both knew were too dangerous to discuss. Yet she was asking for his help; he knew that too.

"Think of him as a friend," he said finally. "That is the feeling he has for you and for me and for Bedwyr. And one is not jealous of one's friend; one rejoices to see him happy, as he rejoices for you. You will not find a better friend in the world than Arthur. He will stand by you till death. Never doubt that for a minute."

The fish jumped again, making a little plopping sound as he reentered the water of the basin. "Where did you learn to be so wise?" Gwenhwyfar asked.

He smiled wryly. "In a hard school, believe me."

"Why does life hurt so much, Cai?" she asked suddenly, despairingly.

"It always hurts for those who feel deeply," he replied. "It is the price we must pay."

"It would be nice sometimes not to care."

"Easier, certainly. But would it really be worth it?"

She smiled at him, her beautiful face flawless in the morning light. "I suppose not. Come along. You and I have to get through yet another day of this festival!"

Cai grinned at her approvingly and they moved toward the palace together.

Chapter 36

*I*N the months that followed the festival, a number of things vital to Britain occurred.

Cai left for Rome to meet with the new Emperor of the West, Anthemius. It was the first official British embassy to Rome since the days of Constantine. Cai was the obvious choice for ambassador. Thanks to Merlin, his Latin was educated, grammatical, entirely Roman. He was also shrewd, intelligent, and a good judge of men. Cai would make the proper impression at the court of the emperor.

Gawain decided he would rather remain in Camelot than return to the north, even as a king. Arthur insisted that he hand his rights over to Gaheris formally and, in order to legitimize the transfer of power, went himself to Lothian to see Gaheris installed as king.

Morgause went with Arthur and Gawain, and once back in Lothian, she had decided to remain. In the north she was still the undisputed queen, and would be until Gaheris married. In Camelot she was ecliped by the younger, more beautiful Gwenhwyfar. Both Gwenhwyfar and Arthur were privately delighted by her decision.

Arthur began to build ships, to repair the roads, and to mint coins. He also levied a tax on all the regional rulers. They protested bitterly, but in the end they paid. The projects the high king was undertaking were too valuable for the Celtic leaders to risk seeing them halted for lack of funds. For the first time in living memory, Britain began to export grain to Ireland and to Gaul.

Cador asked the king if he might send his son Constantine to Camelot to train with the cavalry. What Cador wanted for his son, Arthur realized, was an education in the art of leadership. It was what Arthur wanted for his son too, a school of the kind Merlin had arranged for him and for Cai. In talking it over with Bedwyr, they decided that Constantine would make a good companion for Mordred.

As soon as the other kings and princes realized what was happening, Arthur found himself besieged by a horde of other applicants.

"Send some of them to Valerius," Bedwyr recommended as he and Arthur discussed the situation one autumn morning.

Arthur looked amused. "They don't want to go to the foot, Bedwyr. The cavalry is the fashionable choice. After all, Valerius does not prance around on fire-breathing black stallions and thrill the populace."

Bedwyr looked down his arrogant nose. "Very witty."

Arthur's amusement deepened. "You're saddled with them, my friend. I cannot say yes to Cador and no to Edun."

"What do you want me to do?" Bedwyr asked. "Make a special cavalry unit for them?"

"I think we had better give them their own quarters. They will need more than just the training we give to the ordinary cavalry officers. They are princes, after all, and will be the leaders of their tribes. You needn't do it all yourself. We have experts enough in Camelot. But I would like you to be in charge of this project, Bedwyr. It will take a strong hand to guide it properly."

"How many princes do you mean to take?"

"We had better set an age limit, let us say between the ages of fifteen and eighteen. That will give you a manageable group."

"What it will give me is a group of restless young colts who will have to be kept busy morning to night if they're to stay out of trouble. Unfortunately, there is no war to keep them occupied."

Arthur crowed with delighted laughter. "You should understand the problem better than anyone else," he retorted when he got back his breath.

Bedwyr had watched the king's mirth with resigned good humor. "Oh, all right," he said. "I'll take on your princes for you. But make the age limit nineteen. Agravaine is too good to exclude."

"Nineteen," the king agreed, and by the beginning of spring a collection of twenty noble princes, including the king's own son and cousin, were lodged in their own house in the cavalry enclave at Camelot.

Spring passed into summer. Cai returned from Rome with news of trouble in Gaul. Euric, King of the Visigoths, was seeking to throw off the empire and hold Gaul for himself. The Emperor Anthemius, hearing of Arthur's great victories, was requesting an alliance with Britain.

"It is almost unbelievable," Bedwyr said when he was told the outcome of Cai's embassy. "Rome cast us off, told us to fend for ourselves. And now we are being courted by an emperor!"

"Flattering, certainly," Arthur replied dryly. "I am not quite certain, however, that I want to be the last prop for Rome's tottering empire. It will take a more direct threat to Britain than that posed by Euric to get me to send my army beyond the Narrow Sea."

It did not seem possible, as Britons worked together in peace all during that golden summer and fall, that any outside threat could trouble them. The Saxons had signed a treaty and were subdued and docile within the borders of their shore kingdoms. The land was safe for those who worked it. Farms and villages and towns were beginning to flourish. Industry was beginning to revive. The king reigned in Camelot and all was well with the world.

Chapter 37

*T*HE princes of Britain sat around a large table in the dining room of their quarters in Camelot, eating, talking, trading jests and stories. They had practiced with lances all morning and now were having a midday meal before they went down to the riding ring. The center of the table's interest was, as always, Agravaine. He had been the undisputed leader of the boys since the School for Princes had started.

Mordred sat next to his brother, for he could never think of Agravaine as anything else, and listened with amusement to the light, mocking voice recounting a story. They were all roaring with laughter when the door opened and Bedwyr came in.

Agravaine smiled. "Our prince and leader," he said. His blue eyes were celestial. "Behold us, aching and callused, having heaved at least a hundred lances each this morning."

Bedwyr gave Agravaine a sardonic look. "Did you break a sweat?"

Agravaine's while teeth flashed. "It was very cool on the field."

"Gods, but you're a lazy lot." Bedwyr's eyes went around the table. "Come along. There are horses to be exercised."

"My digestion," Agravaine complained.

"Up," said Bedwyr inexorably, and they got to their feet and obediently began to move in the direction of the riding ring. Agravaine, as always, fell in beside Bedwyr.

They were riding without reins this afternoon, practicing guiding their horses with their legs and seats only. If the reins should ever be cut in a battle, it was important that they not lose control of their mounts.

It was one of the exercises in which Mordred excelled. He was even better than Agravaine, and he and Cloud did patterns up and down the ring, the two of them absorbed in happy partnership.

Suddenly there was a horse in front of him. Cloud stopped abruptly and Mordred's absorbed attention snapped as he looked up and into

Agravaine's face. His brother was blocking his way, sitting stock still in his saddle, arms folded across his chest. "Very pretty, little brother," Agravaine said. His hair framed his face in a fall of bright yellow silk, and his eyes were a much darker blue than the cobalt sky.

Mordred looked at him warily. He knew, from many years' experience, that Agravaine did not like to be bested. The only person Mordred had ever seen Agravaine defer to gracefully was Bedwyr. But then, none of them could expect to be better than Bedwyr the Lion. He was the undisputed best.

Except the king, of course, Mordred thought loyally. But Arthur left the day-to-day supervision of the princes to Bedwyr. It was Bedwyr they strove to emulate, Bedwyr they desired to impress. The king was a figure of awe, seen from a distance, admired, revered, but essentially unknown.

Mordred was the only one of the boys to spend any time with Arthur. He had dinner with the king and queen twice a week and spent at least one morning a week with Arthur in his office. This special treatment set him apart from the other boys, of course, but then, he was set apart anyway. They all knew that someday he would be their king.

"Cloud is a good horse," Mordred said now to the faintly antagonistic face of his older brother. "Very sensitive."

The other boys were riding around them, laughing and calling out as they narrowly avoided collisions. Then Constantine's horse broke into a canter.

"Pick up your reins!" Bedwyr called, knowing that the rest of the horses would follow suit if they were not restrained. Mordred picked up the reins that were knotted on Cloud's neck and watched as Constantine did the same and brought his mount back to a walk. Bedwyr summoned them and they all moved to stand in a semicircle around the prince and Sugyn.

"I think that's enough of work without reins for the day. Next we will do some exercises in lateral movement. Now, watch. I am going to walk Sugyn down the center of the ring, then, using my leg and a little rein, ask him to move sideways while he is still going forward."

Bedwyr demonstrated, then watched as each of the princes tried to emulate his example. Agravaine, as usual, got the most immediate results. He was a controlled and deliberate rider and he demanded, and usually got, obedience from his mount. Mordred and Cloud were not as successful. Cloud was not certain he wanted to do this, and Mordred, instead of forcing him, just kept on asking.

He rode like his father, Bedwyr thought with pleasure. Cloud would end up being a much better horse than Agravaine's Azur.

Half an hour later, just as Bedwyr was about to call a halt to the lesson, Gwenhwyfar rode up to the outside of the ring. Bedwyr trotted Sugyn over to stand in front of her.

"What are you doing out alone?" he asked over the fence that divided them.

"I was down to the bazaar," she answered. "And I had two men with me. I sent them up to the palace when I heard the sound of your voice. It's such a nice day, I wasn't ready to go home quite yet."

A horse came up behind Bedwyr and he heard Agravaine's light, distinctive voice. "Shall we put the horses away now, Prince?"

Bedwyr backed Sugyn a little so he could see both Gwenhwyfar and Agravaine. "Yes," he said. "They've done enough for today."

"Good afternoon, my lady," said Agravaine, and he bowed gracefully from the saddle.

"Good afternoon, Prince," Gwenhwyfar replied. She scarcely ever saw Bedwyr on the grounds of Camelot anymore without this golden-haired young man beside him. They made a striking pair, certainly, both of them so distinctively blond. Agravaine's coloring was more spectacular than Bedwyr's, but Bedwyr's size made the younger man look almost fragile.

Gwenhwyfar did not think that Agravaine was fragile. In fact, according to Bedwyr, he was the most talented student of weaponry among the group. He was handsome, charming, clever, popular with his peers. But there was something about him that repelled her.

She said nothing about her feeling to Bedwyr, simply because she found it hard to account for herself. But she was quite sure of one other thing. In spite of his extravagant courtesy, Agravaine liked her as little as she liked him.

Her eyes moved away from Agravaine's exaggeratedly respectful face and encountered a familiar pair of eyes regarding her with honest admiration. She smiled. "How are you, Mordred? Have you had a successful afternoon? I hope the prince has not worked you too hard."

The boy's darkly beautiful face lighted. "Oh, no, my lady. Not any harder than he usually does."

"Good," replied Gwenhwyfar with amusement. Then: "I did not mean to interrupt your training session, Prince."

"We were finishing anyway," Bedwyr replied. "Agravaine, make sure all these horses are properly cool before you turn them out."

"Yes, my lord," said Agravaine with faintly mocking deference.

"Do you want to go for a ride before returning to the palace?" Bedwyr asked the queen.

"That would be lovely," she replied promptly.

Agravaine sat his horse in silence as Bedwyr bent from Sugyn to unlatch the gate. Then, as the gilt and red-gold heads moved toward the road, he turned to the men and horses still in the ring. "All right. Let's take these horses back to the stable."

His face was white and his eyes were burning and the rest of them obeyed him in silence, knowing that any comment would only provoke a lash from that razor-sharp tongue.

"Why do you put Agravaine in charge?" Gwenhwyfar asked Bedwyr as their horses walked side by side through the cool March sun. "After all, he is less important than most of the other boys. Certainly he is less important than Mordred."

"Less important, perhaps, but Agravaine is a natural leader." He was looking straight ahead, directly between his horse's ears. Still without looking at her, he added, "Mordred is not."

She became instantly defensive. "He is still a boy. You must give him time to grow up."

"He is seventeen. At seventeen Arthur had been high king for a year."

"It isn't fair to compare him with Arthur."

"Perhaps not. There will never be another Arthur. But there's no hardness in this boy, Gwenhwyfar."

"And there is too much hardness in Agravaine! Given the choice, I would take Mordred's gentleness every time."

"So would I, if I were choosing just a son. But not a king. It is better for a king to be too hard than not to be hard enough."

"Then teach him."

At last he looked at her. "I am trying. Arthur is trying. As you said, he is young. Perhaps we will succeed."

"Is it that he cannot do what the other boys can? On the training field, I mean?"

"He accomplishes what he has to accomplish. His heart is not in it, Gwenhwyfar. He wants to please Arthur, so he tries, but he really isn't interested. He enjoys working with the horses. He likes music. He is a very fine harper." Bedwyr's voice was expressionless.

Gwenhwyfar ran her knuckles along the satiny neck of her bay horse. Then she said, very low, "Arthur loves him."

His answer was equally quiet. "I know, little bird. But Arthur isn't blind. He sees what I see."

She raised her face to the sky, as if searching for guidance. "How can Arthur's son not be a leader? He just needs time, Bedwyr. And I do not think it is wise to give Agravaine such preeminence. He has dominated Mordred since they were children. It is not a pattern that should be encouraged."

"No one dominates Mordred," he contradicted her. "He is not a leader, but neither is he a follower. He is a dreamer, Gwenhwyfar. That is where he differs most from Arthur, I think. Arthur is practical, intensely practical. That is his great gift, the combination of vision and practicality."

Their horses walked side by side in silence for almost a full minute. Then Bedwyr said, "Arthur needs to get him the right wife."

Gwenhwyfar stopped her horse. "I like him, Bedwyr," she said softly. "He is a very sweet boy."

Bedwyr's eyes were very blue. "I know," he answered. "That is the problem."

"I want you to come to the boys' training grounds," Bedwyr said to the king. He and Arthur and Gwenhwyfar were having dinner together in the small room off the little court they used for family meals. "In the old days," he continued, "there was not a man in the army who doubted where his personal allegiance lay. They all worshiped you, Arthur. The veterans still do. But these boys don't know you, scarcely see you. I'm not sure that is wise."

"The old days," repeated Arthur with amusement. "You speak with such nostalgia, Bedwyr. It's been only three years since Badon."

"These boys were not at Badon. And they will be the next Council of Princes. You ought to get to know them better."

"I have been busy with matters other than the army." Arthur's voice was undisturbed.

"Bedwyr is right," said Gwenhwyfar. "I think you ought to spend more time with the princes too."

Arthur looked from one face to the other. He raised his black brows. "Very well. I will come to see your charges, Bedwyr. Do you want me to hold their hands?"

"No," said Bedwyr with satisfaction. "I want you to show them how to use a sword."

Arthur rode down to the training field the following morning. The March wind was blowing white clouds briskly across the sky and the air was chill, but all the boys on the field wore short-sleeved tunics. They were practicing their swordplay, sparring with each other and with large sandbags marked with targets. Arthur dismounted and stood silently watching the activity. After a moment Bedwyr came toward him.

The two men leaned companionably against a wagon and watched the youngsters practice. Agravaine's brilliance was immediately apparent. He disarmed the Prince of Elmet with whom he was sparring, lowered his sword, and watched the king and Bedwyr as they stood together talking. Then Arthur moved away from the wagon and began to walk across the soft ground, with Bedwyr at his side. Bedwyr's head was bent toward the smaller, slimmer black-haired man next to him. Then the prince raised his voice and called the boys.

They came instantly, respectful and nervous. Bedwyr then had each boy perform a maneuver, using the sandbag as an opponent, and Arthur watched each one of them with flattering attention. He had a compliment for each prince and a suggestion for improvement. It was not until later, when they tried putting the suggestions into practice, that they realized how perceptive the king had been.

Agravaine struck the practice bag right through the marked heart and turned to Arthur, expecting only a compliment. "Your wrist is a little weak," Arthur said.

Agravaine's eyes widened. He waited until the last prince had finished his exercise before he made the suggestion. "Why don't you and the prince show us some real swordplay, my lord king?" His voice was silky, his blue eyes guileless.

Arthur turned to him, his face looking merely thoughtful. If he recognized the words as a challenge, he did not show it.

"No, thank you, Agravaine," said Bedwyr with humor. "I like to keep my reputation for invincibility."

It was the business of the cavalry demonstration all over again, Agravaine thought with anger. The prince had a compulsion to share all his honors with this king.

"I'll spar with *you*," said Arthur.

Agravaine flung back his hair and laughed, a clear musical sound of sheer joy. This was even better. His hand flexed unconsciously on his sword handle as he accepted the challenge.

The boys looked at each other in silence. Agravaine had beaten the best of the veteran cavalry officers just last week. There was no one at present in all the army who could beat him at swordplay, save Bedwyr the Lion.

"You had better roll up your sleeves," Bedwyr was saying practically to Arthur. "You can use Mordred's sword. It's your length and weight."

Mordred handed his father his sword, a very slight frown on his brow. Arthur lifted the sword, trying the feel of it. He smiled at Mordred and walked a little way onto the field. "Well?" he said mildly to Agravaine. "Are you ready, Cousin?"

Agravaine moved onto the field. He was twenty-one years old, in the full strength of his young manhood, of much the same height and weight as the king. Arthur would be thirty-three in a month, an age when reflexes start to slow and feet to move less quickly. The watching boys had little doubt that Agravaine would make full use of his advantages.

Arthur lifted his sword and Agravaine did the same. The king waited to let his opponent make the first move and Agravaine obliged, moving forward like a cat, his sword flashing and flashing and flashing again in the brilliant sun. There was the briefest flicker of expression on the king's face, and then he began to give ground.

Mordred felt his heart thudding inside his chest, as he was sure his father's heart must be. Arthur had been surprised by Agravaine's aggressiveness. And the king had not yet made a move that was not purely defensive.

There was a smile of unholy pleasure on Agravaine's face. He was breathing audibly as he pressed the attack on the still-retreating king. Mordred cast an anxious glance at Bedwyr, but the prince looked unconcerned.

"Very nice." It was the king's voice, cool and precise in the clear air. Arthur was not out of breath after all. He stood his ground and held off a fierce rain of blows. With all his pyrotechnics, Agravaine had not yet been able to get through the king's guard. "You must not go so consistently to the right, however. It makes the attack too predictable." Arthur's sword flashed to parry a blow aimed from the left. "Yes. That's better. But the biggest problem is still that wrist."

The king took a step forward, for the first time aimed a blow that was not defensive, and Agravaine's sword was on the ground. "You're so fast that you cover the weakness well," Arthur said pleasantly to the startled Agravaine. "Bedwyr will be able to give you a few exercises that will make a difference."

Arthur began to walk off the field and was immediately surrounded by a circle of awestruck boys. He smiled at them with perfect friendliness and began to answer questions.

It was Mordred who turned to go back to his brother. Agravaine was holding his wrist and watching the king. "Go away," he snarled when he saw Mordred approaching. Mordred looked at the pinched white face and blazing eyes, sighed, and turned back. There was no talking to Agravaine when he was like this.

As Mordred rejoined the group of princes around his father, they began to move off the field and toward the stables. Mordred pushed between Constantine and Lachlan to come up at Bedwyr's side. "Agravaine," he said in an urgent undertone to the prince.

Bedwyr paused, turned, and saw the solitary figure still standing on the field. He muttered something under his breath, called to Arthur, "Go on down to the stables. I'll meet you there," and turned to retrace his steps. Before making the turn that would put him out of sight of the field, Mordred looked back once to see what was happening.

Agravaine and Bedwyr were following them, walking slowly. Bedwyr had laid an arm across Agravaine's shoulders and was saying something to the younger man. Agravaine walked beside the prince, his golden head slightly bent, listening.

Chapter 38

"THE Saxons have sacked Angers." Arthur picked up a scroll from his desk and read its contents aloud to Cai and Bedwyr. It was from Syagrius, the king who ruled northern Gaul. Like Arthur, Syagrius espoused the idea of Romanitas without necessarily espousing allegiance to the person of the emperor. And like Arthur, he had a disparate group of tribes under his rule: the Franks, the Burgundians, and the Britons in Armorica being the chief among them.

" 'Odovacar now occupies the south bank of the Loire and most of its islands,' " Arthur read aloud. " 'His presence poses a direct threat to all British settlements along the Loire. The Saxon army numbers some fifteen thousand which is more than I can raise. Between myself and Childeric, King of the Franks, we can raise perhaps eight thousand men. If we are to deal with this Saxon threat, we must have assistance from Britain.' "

Arthur looked up.

"Odovacar," said Cai. "Another Saxon chief like Offa. Never content with what they have, always wanting more."

"If Odovacar gets more," said Bedwyr, "he may well look next across the Narrow Sea to Britain."

"That thought," said Arthur, "has crossed my mind."

The three men looked at each other. "Better to fight him in Gaul than in Britain." Cai spoke the words all were thinking.

Arthur's dark face was grave. "Cai, you are to leave for Gaul immediately. See Syagrius. Find out exactly the kind of campaign he is planning and the number of men he can actually count on."

Cai nodded. "What ship?"

"Take the *Gull*. It's at Portus Adurni now. And make certain you see Childeric as well. I do not want to land in Gaul and find the Franks at my throat. Take Lionel with you. His opinion would be useful."

Bedwyr grunted agreement and Arthur turned to him. "It seems as if the 'old days' may have returned after all, Bedwyr the Lion."

Bedwyr's blue eyes glinted. "But the 'old days' did not take us out of Britain. If you go to Gaul, who will act as your deputy in Camelot?"

"Mordred," said Arthur. "And Gwenhwyfar."

Cai and Bedwyr exchanged a look but said nothing.

"It will be as well to learn now if he can do it," Arthur said. "If he cannot, then we must look elsewhere for the next high king."

Bedwyr felt a relief so great that he was momentarily dizzy with it. *Arthur sees what I see*, he had once told Gwenhwyfar. But Bedwyr had not been as certain as he sounded of the clarity of Arthur's vision in the matter of his son.

He should have known that Arthur was always a king first.

"If Mordred cannot handle matters at home, Gwenhwyfar will," said Cai matter-of-factly. "She is fully as competent as Igraine ever was."

"I know." Arthur was slowly rerolling the scroll. "The army is to be put into full preparation, Bedwyr. I shall speak to Valerius. Supplies and transports will have to be readied as well."

Both Cai and Bedwyr recognized the note of dismissal and rose to their feet. Bedwyr grinned suddenly. "I feel as excited as an old warhorse when he hears the trumpet finally sounding."

Cai slapped him affectionately on the back and Arthur laughed.

Mordred lay on his back in the grass, his eyes half-shut against the August sun. He had escaped from Camelot early in the morning and ridden Cloud partway along the track he knew led to Avalon. He was not going to see Morgan, he simply wanted to get away by himself for a while.

In Lothian there had never been any problem finding solitude. No one had checked on his movements, no one had greatly cared whether he came or whether he went. In Lothian he had been free.

He was not free in Camelot. He was scarcely ever alone. It wore on his spirit, and occasionally he took a horse and just disappeared for a day. Bedwyr did not like it, but took no steps to prevent Mordred's periodic disappearances. It was the only way he exploited his position as the king's son.

He wondered if he got this desire for quiet and solitude from Morgan. His father did not seem to mind being a public person, but Morgan stayed quietly at Avalon, leading her life away from the busy forum of public life. He had met his mother only once since their first

302 • JOAN WOLF

emotional encounter. They had been polite to each other—very careful and very polite.

Morgan came rarely to Camelot. For the first time it occurred to Mordred that perhaps she was like him in her preference for a quiet life. He had thought before that she stayed away because of Gwenhwyfar. It was quite clear to Mordred that the queen did not like Morgan.

Gwenhwyfar. Camelot could never seem a prison to him as long as Gwenhwyfar was there. His heart sang whenever he thought of her. It never worried him that he should feel this way about his father's wife. It never occurred to him that he could ever be more than her adoring servant. Only his father was great enough to deserve Gwenhwyfar.

He pushed himself up on his elbow and rummaged in his saddlebag for his small harp. He ran his fingers across it once, then plucked a few separate notes. He was deeply concentrated on his music when a dog came panting up to him and tried to lick his fingers. Mordred laughed, put the harp down, and scratched the dog's ears. "Where did you come from, eh?" he asked, and the dog moved his head so Mordred could scratch another spot.

There came the sound of a horse moving through the trees behind him, and he turned his head. A pony and rider appeared from a narrow track that wound deep into the heart of the woods. With a small shock of surprise he recognized his mother. After an almost imperceptible pause she advanced toward him.

"An escape?" she inquired sympathetically.

He looked into her small, delicate face and quite suddenly remembered what he had refused to think about for a very long time: all the long summer days of his childhood that he had spent in her company. It was Morgan who had roamed the hills and burns of Lothian with him, Morgan who had lain beside him in the grass and watched birds, who had helped him return frightened babies to their nests. It was Morgan who had given him his harp. He smiled quite naturally and said, "Yes."

Another dog came cantering out of the woods and joined the first dog around Mordred. Morgan laughed and got off her pony. The dogs immediately came to her side.

"Any reason in particular?" she inquired. "Or just general suffocation?"

He gave her a charming, rueful look. "Bedwyr and my father rode down to Portus Adurni to look at ships. It seemed a good opportunity to get off by myself."

"I see." She left her pony to graze and came to sit beside him. It was the first time the two of them had been alone since that disastrous interview when he had first been told she was his mother. He found, a little to his surprise, that he was no longer angry with her. He was, instead, curious. He looked out the corner of his eye at her profile, at the long, shining, evenly cut brown hair. She didn't look old enough to have a seventeen-year-old son, he thought.

"How old were you when I was born?" he asked, a little shyly.

"Fifteen."

Fifteen. Two years younger than he was now. And his father had been sixteen. Hard to imagine them as being younger than himself.

He picked up a blade of grass and put it between his teeth. "Morgause has got married again," he said.

Her head turned and the big brown eyes looked at him. "I didn't know that."

"Gawain heard from her only yesterday."

There was a faint line between her brows. Seen up close like this, she did not look like a young girl any more. "Who?" she asked.

His mouth compressed itself into an austere line. "Lamorak."

"Lamorak?"

"Yes."

"I see."

There was a long pause before she asked, "What did Agravaine say?"

Lamorak was the son of a minor Lothian chief. He was twenty-five years old, twenty years younger than Morgause. Most of all, he and Agravaine had been inseparable for a whole year before Agravaine had left Lothian for Camelot.

"He seemed to find it funny." Mordred was clearly puzzled.

Morgan called to the pony, which had been moving closer to the woods as he grazed, and he raised his head and looked at her. She made a sound in her throat and the pony obediently began to graze back in her direction.

"Whatever can have possessed her, Morgan?" Mordred burst out. "Lamorak is so much younger than she is!"

"He probably makes Morgause feel young too."

"I should have thought two husbands were enough," he muttered.

He took the grass from between his teeth and stared darkly at his shoes.

"Evidently Morgause did not agree."

"But she looks so foolish!"

"I'm sure she doesn't think so. She is probably happy. I hope she is. She deserves to be."

His eyes jerked up from his feet to her face. Color stained his cheeks. "You're right," he said with swift contrition. "I've been thinking of myself, not of her."

"Tell me of yourself," she invited. "I hear you are to be regent while the king is in Gaul."

He heaved a great sigh. "Yes."

"Are you worried?"

He looked at her, Arthur's eyes without Arthur's power. "Yes. Everyone seems to expect me to be like my father. I suppose it's because I look so much like him. But I'm not like him, Morgan. He sees things so clearly, makes such quick decisions . . . I'm not like that."

"Because you are not like Arthur does not mean you cannot be a good king. You may be a fine king, but it will be in your way, not in Arthur's."

"I would rather be a doctor," he said, and shot her a quick look.

She was watching him steadily. "You have a duty to your country to try to be a king."

He sighed again. "Yes. And I have been trying."

"Good." She smiled at him, a warm, loving, approving smile, and got to her feet. The dogs, which had been sniffing around in the woods, came flying to her side. "I have been collecting herbs," she said, and for the first time he noticed the sack hanging from her pony's saddle. "I must be getting home."

"I have never seen Avalon," he remarked.

She paused, her hand holding her reins, and looked at him. "You are welcome anytime."

He smiled at her shyly. "Thank you."

A group of monks from Glastonbury rode to Camelot every Sunday to say Mass for the Christians in the capital. The abbot Gildas usually said Mass in the great hall of the palace for the king and queen and army officers, and the other monks held Mass in the common rooms of the main garrison buildings for the ordinary soldiers and civilians who were Christians.

After Mass it was Arthur's practice to mingle with the men in the great hall. It was everyone's chance to have a brief personal moment with the king. Agravaine, watching Arthur with a group of lowly foot officers, thought cynically that the king was well aware of his own personal powers. He was giving the men such flattering attention that they fairly vibrated with pride and pleasure. Fools. They had no idea that they were being manipulated, that Camelot was peopled with the victims of the king's cleverly wielded magnetism. Even the prince lit up like a candle when Arthur put a hand on his arm.

It infuriated Agravaine that no one saw through him. Agravaine did, though. Probably because he himself traded on his own charm quite as ruthlessly as did Arthur, he thought.

Gwenhwyfar had taken the abbot back to the little hall, where she always entertained him to breakfast. Agravaine looked around the crowded hall for the massive figure of Bedwyr. The prince never attended Mass, but he usually made an appearance at the reception afterward. Sunday was a day off for the army, and he and Bedwyr were going hunting together.

Time passed and the great hall began to empty. Arthur and Mordred disappeared in the direction of the little hall. Agravaine hesitated, wondering if he ought to go back to the princes' quarters to await Bedwyr there. Just as he had decided that was what he would do, Bedwyr and Gwenhwyfar appeared on the far side of the hall. Gwenhwyfar was dressed for riding.

Agravaine stood stock-still as they came up to him. "I thought we were going hunting," he said to Bedwyr.

The golden brows rose and the prince looked down at him. "I'm sorry, Agravaine. I forgot. You can find one of the other boys to go with. I have promised to take the queen for a ride."

Gwenhwyfar smiled. Her hair drifted like silk across the green wool of her riding tunic. Her eyelashes were long and dark. She really was extraordinarily beautiful, Agravaine thought, and he hated her.

He looked again at Bedwyr. "But I wanted to go with you." Even he could hear that he sounded petulant.

Bedwyr frowned. "Go with Constantine. Or Gawain. I am taking the queen for a ride."

Agravaine was certain he saw a flash of triumph in Gwenhwyfar's green eyes. Then they were past him and moving into the vestibule. Agravaine looked after them, an expression of hate and fury marring the usual beauty of his fair-skinned face.

Chapter 39

"WILL you be ready to sail before the storms come on the Narrow Sea?" Morgan asked. She and Arthur were walking hand in hand through the small copse of wood that stretched for a mile behind the villa of Avalon. The wood had been left when the villa was built in order to protect it from the noise and the smells of the livestock. There was a path that led halfway into the wood, then turned and doubled back to the house. This was Arthur's and Morgan's habitual walk, taken just before they went to bed. A fine mistlike rain such as was falling tonight was never enough to keep them indoors.

"I think so," Arthur answered. "Everything is in good order. We should embark in about two weeks."

"No further trouble from the north?"

"No. At this point everyone seems reconciled to the necessity of our going."

The council had been divided about taking the army to Gaul. Dumnonia and Wales had been in favor of the expedition, but the northern kingdoms had not been. Arthur had prevailed, as always, but there had been some rebellious mutterings about his "Roman" ambitions.

"Good," she said, and curled her hand inside his. His fingers tightened. He had ridden into Avalon late that afternoon, and would have to leave the following morning. The army preparations had given him less time than usual to spend with her.

Morgan wished he was not going to Gaul. She had had an uneasy feeling of late that it would not be wise for him to leave the country, but she had said nothing to him. Arthur the man would have been sympathetic, but the king would never let his judgment be swayed by her "feeling." It was better not to worry him at all, she thought.

The wood smelled sweet and damp and they heard the soft hooting of an owl, then the sound of its wings overhead. The dogs followed at their heels, making occasional forays off the path to chase some small

306

nocturnal creature. They walked side by side, so familiar with their surroundings that the dark was no handicap. Their steps matched together perfectly. Arthur's head was bent a little toward hers, and their voices were low and intimate.

"Mordred came to Avalon a few days ago," she said. "Did he tell you?"

"No." He didn't need to ask; he could feel the happiness that the visit had given her. "I told you he would come around."

"I showed him our old tree house."

"I hope you didn't climb into it. It can't possibly be safe after all these years."

"Don't worry. We just looked at it from the ground." He could hear the amusement in her voice.

They had reached the end of the path and the house loomed a hundred feet ahead of them. A lamp was lit in the small vestibule that was just inside the back door, and they entered into its pool of brightness, blinking as their eyes adjusted from the dark. The dogs crowded in behind them and began to shake the rain from their coats, sending a small shower of drops in all directions.

"Dure has a tail full of burrs," Arthur said, and bent to pull them out. Morgan watched his strong, slender hands dealing expertly with the burrs. He had not had a dog himself since Cabal died.

Arthur straightened. "There, that's better." He went to open the door of the small room off the vestibule where the dogs slept, and whistled to them. They both obediently trotted inside. He closed the door, tossed the wet hair off his forehead, and gave Morgan a faint smile.

She lit a candle, extinguished the lamp, and they both began to walk toward the passage that led to the bedroom wing of the house. In the villa's prime there had been slaves sleeping in every nook and cranny, but the house was empty now save for a few servants who slept in the rooms near the kitchen. There were still large numbers of people working for Avalon, but they lived these days in the village Morgan had built for them and their families. There were no more slaves; Merlin had freed the last of them in his will.

"It's always so peaceful here," Arthur murmured. He rested his hand on the nape of her neck as they walked toward her bedroom.

They had long ago given up any pretense that Arthur slept in his own room. On the rare occasions when there was someone other than themselves in the house, they observed the fiction, but otherwise they trusted the servants to keep silence. Everyone left working in the house had known the two of them since they were children.

The window in Morgan's bedroom was open, and the damp night air had filled the room. Arthur went to close it and Morgan lit the lamp with the candle she had been carrying. She blew out the candle, laid it on the table, and turned to him.

He was still standing at the window, pulling his tunic over his head. In the light from the lamp she could see the thin white scars that crisscrossed the smooth brown skin of his back. He turned around and tossed the tunic onto a wicker chair.

"I don't want to go to Gaul either," he said. "It will mean months and months without you."

So he knew she did not want him to go. So much for trying to keep something from Arthur. She smiled a little wryly. "I've grown used to having you."

He left the window and came to stand before her. He did not reply at once, but reached out to trace the curve of her cheek with his forefinger. Then: "We have been happy." Their eyes held together, and then he bent his dark head to hers. His lips were hard and soft, cool and burning. She ran her hands up and down his bare back. "Come to bed," he murmured against her mouth.

He undressed her and then she finished undressing him. They lay down together on her bed, surrounded by the vast peaceful quiet of the empty villa. They might have been the only two left living in the world.

He was fierce and he was gentle. She loved the touch of his hand, his mouth, the feel of his strong hard body against hers. It never lessened for them, the wild desire to be together, to be complete, as they could be only with each other and with no one else. He went to sleep with his arms wrapped around her, his head pillowed on her breast.

Morgan lay quietly so as not to disturb him, but she herself was wide awake. She had not blown out the lamp, and it glowed on the blackness of Arthur's hair. She touched the top of his head with her lips. He was deeply asleep, his breathing slow and even. He had been tired.

Why was she so uneasy? The night was quiet. There was no sound from the dogs. Finally Arthur's untroubled breathing began to soothe her, and she too drifted off into sleep.

She awoke to the sound of an urgent knock on her door. "My lady! My lady!" It was Marcus. Arthur was already swinging his legs out of bed and reaching for his clothes. "There are men here from Camelot for the king. He must go back. Something terrible has happened!"

Gawain joined Gwenhwyfar and Bedwyr for dinner that evening. Arthur was at Avalon and Bedwyr always took care not to dine alone with the queen. Usually Cai was present, but he was still in Gaul and so Bedwyr had invited Gawain. He had actually invited Mordred first, but Mordred had made an excuse.

Gwenhwyfar was not in the mood for making conversation with Gawain. Bedwyr would be leaving for Gaul very shortly, and she wanted him to herself while he was still in Britain. Arthur could go alone to Avalon, she thought irritably. She did not see why Bedwyr was so insistent about providing her with a chaperon.

She excused herself from the table early and left Bedwyr with Gawain. Let the two of them entertain each other, she thought with uncharacteristic petulance. She was weary of all the talk of army preparations and transport.

Like Morgan, Gwenhwyfar was apprehensive about Arthur leaving for Gaul. The queen was troubled by no premonitions of disaster, however; she was nervous about the responsibility Arthur was delegating to her.

"Why not leave Cai to help Mordred?" she had asked when he told her she was to be co-regent.

"I want Cai to go to Gaul for me. Besides, if I leave Cai to help Mordred, the boy will never make a move without Cai's consent. He will have more pride where you are concerned; he will want to appear to you as a capable and competent leader. And I want Mordred to have some actual experience of being king."

"Then why name me at all?"

"He is completely untried, Gwenhwyfar. He needs someone. And I need to know there is someone knowledgeable at hand with the power to step in if something should go wrong."

The glow of pride Arthur's words produced had lasted her for several weeks. It was only now, with his departure so close at hand, that she was beginning to worry about the responsibility. "Don't let him do anything foolish," Arthur had said.

She hoped to God that Britain stayed quiet while its king was gone.

She had dismissed her women and was sitting up in bed, propped against a pillow, when Bedwyr finally came in. "You took your time," she said crossly as she watched him coming toward her. "You could have spent the whole night with Gawain as far as I am concerned."

He reached the bed, stopped, and looked down at her. A flicker of amused comprehension showed in his eyes. "Gawain isn't as pretty as you," he answered, and began to unbuckle his belt.

The lamplight picked out the gold in the handle of the knife he wore in his belt, and the gold in his hair. He dropped the belt onto the floor. Her body wanted him but she was still angry about the dinner, and so she said what she had sworn she would not say: "I don't suppose *you're* planning to sleep alone once you get to Gaul."

He sat on the edge of the bed and began to untie the rawhide laces in his shoes. "What has that got to do with anything?" The shoes followed the belt to the floor and he stood up again. "You're annoyed because I invited Gawain to dine with us. You know why I invited Gawain. After all, it's your reputation I'm concerned about." He stripped his tunic off over his head.

She stared up at his massive chest and shoulders. She hated the thought of his touching another woman. He would not promise her to be faithful; she knew it. "If you're so concerned about my reputation," she said furiously, "you can just get out of my bedroom."

"You don't mean that." He was unperturbed by her hostility. He finished undressing and came back to the bed. His forearms and thighs were covered with the scars of the cavalryman. "You get more beautiful every day," he murmured, and then he was bent over her, sliding the pillow out from behind her, his powerful body following her down to the bed. His weight crushed her. For a moment she knew the impulse to resist, to stiffen against him, to fight. Then his mouth closed on hers, and the old fire of burning passion blazed up between them. She arched her neck to feel the fire of his kiss on her throat.

What did anything matter when they had this between them? His body vibrated, taut and powerful with the extremity of his desire. She thought for a moment that she would faint from the intensity of the sensation he was creating in her body. Her nails dug into the muscles of his back and she said his name.

Afterward they lay together, returning slowly to life and thought from the mindless, shuddering, sensation-seared caldron of physical desire they had just been plunged into. Now was the time to be quiet together. On the nights that Arthur was away, Bedwyr would stay with her until dawn.

He propped himself on his elbow and looked down into her face.

"What's the matter, little bird?" he asked finally. "What is troubling you?"

She smiled a little ruefully. "Nerves. I wish Arthur had left someone else as co-regent."

"There is no one better than you. Besides, we won't be gone for long. What can possibly happen in six months' time?"

Six months. She stared up into his face. His thick gilt hair was tousled from the touch of her hand. His eyes were absolutely blue. No one's eyes were bluer than Bedwyr's. "I'll miss you," she whispered.

"And I you." He smiled. "I've grown quite like an old married man these days. I find I've lost all my interest in women who are not you."

Her heart leapt. She was about to answer when there came the sound of noise in the corridor and then the door to her room was pushed open violently. There were shouts and a blaze of light and a single cry of triumph, and the room seemed suddenly filled with men.

She felt Bedwyr moving, reaching for his belt on the floor beside the bed. "No!" she cried, and hung on to his arm with both her hands and all her strength. She forgot for the moment that she was naked, that all these men were looking at her. She only knew she must keep Bedwyr from that knife or he would murder someone. "Bedwyr!" she shouted. "No!"

She felt his arm relax slightly and for the first time looked up to see who had broken in on them.

Agravaine was holding the lamp. She might have known. And behind him was Mordred, looking as if he were going to be sick. There were three others whom she recognized as princes from Bedwyr's school.

Bedwyr, thank God, had got himself under control and was taking charge. He pulled the blanket over her and got out of bed. "Mordred, go and get Gawain," he said.

Mordred stared at him, his gray eyes filled with disbelief and horror. "How could you?" he asked, his voice low and trembling. He looked at Gwenhwyfar and then back again at the prince. "How could you do this to my father?"

Bedwyr's face was impassive. "Go and get Gawain," he repeated, and this time Mordred left the room.

Bedwyr turned next to Agravaine and his followers. "Get out of here. Go and wait for Gawain in the little hall. I'll join you in a moment."

The habit of obeying Bedwyr was strong, and the three princes began to move to the door. Their looks of triumph had changed to uneasiness. Only Agravaine stood his ground, and the lamp he was holding gave Gwenhwyfar a clear view of his face. There was still triumph there, but as he stared as if spellbound at the splendid naked beauty of Bedwyr, another expression appeared. Gwenhwyfar, watching him, realized with deep shock that Agravaine was looking at Bedwyr the same way she did.

Bedwyr said something else, which she did not hear because of the roaring of the blood in her ears, and Agravaine finally turned and left the room. The door closed behind him and Bedwyr turned to her.

She did not think she had ever been so frightened in her life. For herself, yes, but mainly for him. "What are you going to do?" she whispered.

"Have Gawain send for Arthur." His mouth was a straight, ominous line. "It was Agravaine."

"Yes."

"But why?" He came to sit on the bed beside her. "Why, Gwenhwyfar, would he do such a thing? What purpose can it possibly serve?"

He did it because you love me instead of him, and he can't forgive you for that. But she didn't say it. Later, perhaps. Not now. "What will Arthur do?" she asked instead.

For a brief moment his big hand rested on her shoulder. "I don't know. I don't know what he can do." He stood up and began to dress. "He's the only one who can deal with this, though. There's no hope of keeping it secret."

"Keeping it secret was not what Agravaine had in mind."

"No." He pulled his tunic over his head. "Gods! And just when we were getting ready to sail for Gaul!" For the first time there was a note of despair in his voice.

"Arthur won't keep you from going to Gaul with the army, Bedwyr. I know he won't."

He passed his hand over his face. "I don't see how he can do otherwise, Gwenhwyfar. But we must wait for him." His blue eyes met hers and it was as though he were saying good-bye. "I'm sorry, little bird," he said. She did not answer and he bent to kiss her on the mouth, hard, and then he was gone.

Gawain followed Bedwyr's advice and confined Agravaine and his friends to one room, the obviously distraught Mordred to another, and Bedwyr himself to his own apartment. Then he sent for the king.

Dawn was beginning to lighten the sky when Arthur rode into Camelot. He found Gawain keeping guard over all parties from the little court.

"What has happened?" Arthur asked tersely. Gawain, being cautious, had told the men he sent to Avalon nothing except that the king must return immediately. He told Arthur the story now, and watched the king's face close, hard as a fist. "Where is Bedwyr?" he asked as soon as Gawain was done.

"In his rooms, my lord," Gawain stammered in reply.

Arthur turned without another word, strode to the door that led to Bedwyr's apartment, and went in. The door slammed shut behind him.

Gawain sat, solitary and miserable, as servants began to pass to and fro with fresh water for the bedrooms. The sky was completely light when Arthur finally emerged from Bedwyr's room. Gawain felt slightly sick as he watched the king crossing the hall toward him. He would not be Bedwyr now for all the glory of Caesar, Gawain thought. Arthur had trusted him, honored him, loved him. And he had repaid the king like this! Gawain wondered if Arthur would kill him. And Gwenhwyfar too. He had refused so steadfastly to put her aside, even though she was childless. He would put her aside now. Nothing would ever be the same again.

"Where is Agravaine?" Arthur asked. "And Mordred?"

Gawain told him.

"Very well. You may go to your own quarters now, Gawain. The prince will be leaving for Portus Adurni within the hour. I am sending him to Gaul to buy horses for the army."

Gawain could feel his eyes widening. "The prince is still going to Gaul?"

Arthur's face was absolutely remote. "The prince is my cavalry commander. I cannot imagine launching a campaign against the Saxons without him."

"No. Of course not, my lord." Gawain could not meet those winter-gray eyes.

"You are to say nothing to anyone of what happened here tonight, Gawain. Is that clear?"

Gawain's startled blue eyes flew to the king's face. "Yes, my lord."

"Thank you for your assistance," Arthur said then. "If we can manage to save anything at all out of this night's debacle, it will be largely due to your good sense."

Gawain bit his lip, nodded, and fled before he disgraced himself by bursting into tears.

Next, Arthur went to see his wife.

It was the longest night of Gwenhwyfar's life. Olwen had come in white-faced and petrified, and Gwenhwyfar had sent her back to bed. Then she had got dressed and done her hair by herself, taking immense pains to braid some gold thread into one long red-gold lock. That done, she sat and waited. And tried to think what she could do.

She was under no illusions as to the seriousness of what had happened. Adultery by the queen was a very serious matter indeed. A state matter. Agravaine had known that when he arranged his little visit this night. He had known he would force Arthur's hand.

It had been an attack against her, and in one way it had succeeded. Arthur would have to put her away. There was no way now that he could honorably keep her as his wife. She knew that, and accepted it. Her greatest fear was for Bedwyr.

Arthur would never physically harm Bedwyr, but if he dismissed the prince from his service, he would destroy him as surely as if he had run him through with a sword. It would break Bedwyr, to be parted from Arthur and from his beloved cavalry.

Perhaps if she offered to take all the blame, if she offered to go into a convent, Arthur would not have to punish Bedwyr.

God, what was Arthur going to do?

He had trusted them to be careful, and they had failed him.

Dawn streaked the sky, but none of her women came in to do the usual morning arrangements in her room. Olwen must be keeping everyone away. They were all waiting, as she was, for the king. Finally, in the quietness, she heard a familiar light step in the outer room, and then Arthur was standing in the doorway.

She had risen as soon as she heard his step, and they stared at each other now, the width of the room between them.

"God, Gwenhwyfar," he said. "I am so sorry. What an unspeakable thing for you to have gone through."

Her vision suddenly blurred and her throat closed. She found she couldn't breathe. Before she realized what was happening, he was across the room and was taking her into his arms.

She couldn't believe that she was actually here, being held comfortingly against him. She shuddered and he only held her closer. She buried her face in his shoulder and broke into deep, wrenching sobs.

"I am so sorry," he kept repeating. "Gwenhwyfar, I am so sorry."

She had braced herself for that remote, forbidding look, and to find instead this warmth and sympathy . . . It broke her, as sternness would not have. "We have to talk, Gwenhwyfar," he was saying. "Try to stop crying."

She made a heroic effort to get herself under control. "That's my girl," he said, and guided her over to sit beside him on the side of the bed. He handed her a cloth and she blew her nose.

The first thing she said, when she was able to speak, was, "Arthur, you must not put away Bedwyr."

His face was calm. "I have no intention of putting away Bedwyr," he answered.

His calm was infecting her. Perhaps it was not as terrible as she had feared. Perhaps she would not have to go to a convent. "I will go home to my father," she offered tentatively. Then, when he did not answer immediately: "Or if that will not do, I will go to a convent."

For the first time he looked angry. "I have no intention of discarding you, either. We will see this through together, all three of us, the way we have always done."

"But . . ." A strand of hair, wet from her tears, was clinging to her cheek and he reached out absently to unstick it and smooth it back. "But the scandal," she said.

"There will be no scandal. Not on the surface, at any rate. I am sending Bedwyr, Agravaine, and his friends to Gaul immediately. They will sail on the next tide. No one else knows exactly what happened here tonight except Gawain, and we can trust him to hold his tongue. Thank God he had the sense not to say anything specific to the men he sent to Avalon to fetch me. There will be talk, of course. The servants won't keep quiet. But we will ignore it."

She was staring at him with brilliant green eyes. "Are you certain this is what you want to do? You haven't had much time to think it through if you only just learned the truth."

"I've had a chance to talk to Bedwyr. And yes, I'm sure this is what I want to do."

"There is nothing you can do to keep this story from going beyond the palace walls, you must know that. And it's just the sort of thing any man who has no love for you will jump on."

"I know there will be talk, Gwenhwyfar. But there will be no one left in Britain for anyone to question, except us." He permitted himself a brief wintry smile. "And I do not think anyone is likely to broach the matter to you or to me. By the time the army returns from Gaul, the story will be an old one. It will be seen that Bedwyr is still my cavalry commander and that you are still my trusted and well-loved wife. I think the very fact that I am leaving you as co-regent will silence much of the talk immediately."

They were sitting very close, shoulder to shoulder, and now he picked up her hand and squeezed it gently. "It will all come right," he said. "I won't allow a destructive little weasel like Agravaine to destroy what we have built so carefully for all these years."

Quite suddenly words that Cai had once spoken to her sounded in her brain. "You will not find a better friend than Arthur," Cai had said. "He will stand by you to the death."

Cai had known his man.

She ran her tongue over dry lips. "Arthur," she said in a low voice, "there is still Mordred. I think that was the worst part of it all"—her voice quivered—"the look on his face as he said to us, 'How could you do this to my father?' " She bowed her head. "He won't consent to have me as co-regent. I know he won't. And," she added sadly, "I cannot really blame him."

He let out his breath audibly. There was the briefest silence before he said, "I am going to tell Mordred the truth about me and Morgan. This is a situation of our making, not of yours."

For the second time in ten minutes all her faculties for breathing seemed to shut down. Never had he acknowledged his relationship with Morgan to her. He knew, of course, that she knew, but never once had he admitted it. And to say, "This is a situation of our making, not of yours"! He had, quite literally, taken her breath away.

He was still holding her hand, unconsciously, as if he had forgotten it was there in his. Never before had he touched her like that. Never before had he let her inside the space he kept around himself. She was there now, and she went very carefully. "Morgan may not want you to tell him," she said at last.

He pushed his hair off his forehead. "Morgan is the one who said to tell him. He knows she is his mother; I told him the truth of that. He knows I go to Avalon. He, of all people, should have understood why."

"He is a curiously innocent boy."

"I know." Arthur smiled wryly. "Not at all like me."

Something had struck her and she turned to him, frowning. "Arthur, how can Morgan know what happened here? You said the men Gawain sent to Avalon told you nothing."

He dropped her hand and linked his own together on his knee. He was not looking at her. He seemed to be trying to decide whether or not to tell her something. She watched his profile. He looked tired, she thought. There were marks of fatigue under his eyes. Finally he looked up. He had made up his mind. "She knows because I told her," he said.

"But you haven't been back to Avalon."

"I know."

His long-sleeved white tunic was open at the throat, and the light from the hanging lamp played upon the bones of his face. From deep in her subconscious a picture floated to the surface of her mind: Arthur, dying, and Morgan standing beside his bed. She breathed hard through suddenly constricted lungs. "Are you saying that you can talk together with your *minds*?"

"Yes." He looked back at her, a little wary, not quite sure he should have told her this. She realized, abruptly, how astonishing this confidence was. Not only what he had told her, but the fact that he had told her at all. He was not even sure if she would believe him; she could see that in his face. Yet he had told her anyway.

"When you were so sick after Badon," she said. "*That* was how she brought you back, wasn't it?"

The wary look lifted. "Yes. The Saxons had been defeated, and I was so sick of being alone. I just decided it was time to go." She remembered vividly how it had been, the long, weary vigil, the despair at watching him slip farther and farther away. "Then Morgan came and I knew I wouldn't be alone anymore." The simple words struck her like a blow.

She looked away from him. "Have you always been able to talk to each other like that?"

"We had never tried before. There was no necessity, you see. When we were children we were always together. Then, when we were separated, we both thought we would have to live the rest of our lives apart, so it was better not even to try."

She saw. And, painful though the knowledge was, it was also a relief. She had not failed with Arthur, nor had Morgan stolen him from her. He had belonged to Morgan long before she came into his life.

How extraordinary, she thought. She had just been caught out in adultery with another man, and she and Arthur had never been closer than they were at this minute. For the first time in all their years together, he had let her in.

She was intensely curious about what he had just told her, but she sensed that he did not want to talk about it anymore. She changed the subject. "Mordred will take it hard. He idolizes you, Arthur. You must know that. He thinks you are a hero."

"It's time Mordred learned that there are no heroes outside the works of the epic poets," his father replied. "There are only men trying their best to do the job they have to do."

She sighed. "And women."

He smiled at her, the smile that had always been able to turn her heart. "And women," he agreed. "Now, have something to eat, wash your face, and put on your riding clothes. As soon as Bedwyr has left, you and I are going to visit every nook and cranny of Camelot. Together."

She smiled back. "Yes," she said, "my lord king."

Chapter 40

ARTHUR went next to talk to Agravaine. The Lothian prince and the three princes from Elmet and Manau Guotodin who had accompanied him on his visit to the queen's bedroom were waiting for him in one of the private reception rooms in the king's apartment.

His followers were nervous, but Agravaine felt only triumph. He had caught her, like a bitch in heat. No more would she be able to flaunt herself all over Camelot at the side of the prince. Now Arthur would know. Bedwyr's beloved friend would know. Really, Agravaine thought with pleasure, it could hardly have turned out better. And Mordred, poor besotted devil. He had found out the truth about her too.

The door opened suddenly, and the king was in the room. The four young men, who had been lounging in chairs, jumped instinctively to their feet. Even Agravaine came upright when Arthur walked in.

The king paused in front of the closed door and regarded them for a moment in silence. His face was utterly remote, his gray eyes cold. Mordred had his features, Agravaine found himself thinking reluctantly, but Mordred could never look as frightening as this.

"I have sent a servant to your quarters with instructions to pack your things," the king said when the silence was beginning to make the air too thick to breathe. "You will all be leaving for Gaul on the next tide."

"For Gaul?" It was a startled exclamation made by Baird of Elmet.

"Yes. I am sending the prince on ahead to purchase wagon horses for the army. You will accompany him."

Jesus Christ, thought Baird in horror. He was going to put them on a boat with the *prince*? After what they had just done to him? He exchanged a look of terror with his brother and with Innis of Manau Guotodin.

Only Agravaine did not appear alarmed by the king's words. He was staring at Arthur, and the pupils of his eyes were so dilated that the irises looked black, not blue.

He isn't going to do anything, Agravaine thought with incredulous fury. He is still sending the prince to Gaul. He doesn't care about Gwenhwyfar. He is going to cover it up.

"You will ride for Portus Adurni in half an hour," the king was saying in that flat, cold voice. His eyes moved from one face to the next, like the flick of a whip. "I will not prevent your communicating with your fellows once we are in Gaul. But I should advise you to take care. I am not a good enemy to make."

In the charged silence, Arthur looked at Agravaine. Alone of the princes, his face held no fear. Only fury; blind, sick fury. The two men stared at each other, and then the king said softly, "If you enter into a contest with me, Agravaine, I will smash you to pieces."

The faintest glimmer showed in those fixed black eyes, and then Agravaine looked away.

"Don't leave this room until you are sent for," Arthur said, and shut the door behind himself, leaving the four young men alone together once more.

He had left Mordred to the last. This was the interview he was most dreading. The boy must be made to understand the consequences of what he had done.

It was not going to be pleasant.

Even though Mordred lived down at the school with the other princes, he still had his own bedroom in the palace and it was there that Arthur went next. The bedroom was in Arthur's private suite, only a few doors down from the reception room that held Agravaine. Arthur put his hand on the door latch. How in Hades had the boy allowed himself to be so manipulated by Agravaine? he thought. And pressed down on the latch.

Mordred was standing by the window with his back to the room, a slender, almost fragile-looking figure. He appeared to be watching the sky. Morgan was right, Arthur thought: he had been better off in Lothian. He closed the door behind him and spoke Mordred's name.

The boy by the window turned slowly to face him. Mordred's face was pinched and sallow-looking, his eyes smudged with unhappiness and fatigue. "I'm sorry, Father," he said miserably. "I didn't believe him, you see. He was saying filthy things about the queen and Bedwyr, and I thought I would let him make a fool of himself and shut him up once and for all." The thin, beautiful face looked utterly stricken. "I never for a minute thought that he was right."

Arthur ruthlessly stifled the pity he felt for his son. Mordred had to be made to understand what he had done. "I know you didn't mean to cause such trouble, Mordred," he said in a quiet, level voice, "but you have put me in a damnable position. You must realize that."

"How *could* they?" Mordred cried passionately. "How could they do that to you? Betray you? Deceive you?"

The king walked slowly across the tiled floor. "*They* have not betrayed me," he said. "You have."

Mordred's head jerked as if he had been struck in the face. "Nor have they deceived me," Arthur went on remorselessly. "I have known about the queen and Bedwyr for years."

Mordred's face was chalk white. "I don't understand."

They were standing with but three feet between them. "How old are you?" his father asked.

"Seventeen."

"Seventeen. When I was seventeen I was high king and had lost the only person in the world I loved. I have never told this to anyone, but I thought quite seriously about taking my life." Mordred's gray eyes were clinging to his face with horrified attention. "I did not because I had responsibilities that went beyond my own personal needs. It is not a privilege to be king, Mordred. It is a responsibility. No matter what may happen, you must always remember that you are a king. That always must take precedence over your private feelings. Do you understand what I am telling you?"

"I . . . Yes."

"You let Agravaine use you for his own ends. You were thinking like a child, not like a king."

Mordred pushed the hair back off his forehead. Some color had come back into his face and he stared at his father with a glimmer of defiance. "Well, if to be king means that I can no longer allow myself to feel, then you must find a new candidate for the job. I can't do it."

Arthur's reply was measured. "I did not say you cannot allow yourself to feel. I said that you must not allow your feelings to influence your public acts."

"Don't you *care* about what they have done?" It was said wildly, passionately.

"I just told you that when I was your age I lost the only person I ever loved." Arthur was watching him with an odd, alert look in his eyes.

"After ten long years I got her back again. Why do you think I go to Avalon, Mordred?"

The blood was pounding in Mordred's ears. "To . . . to see Morgan."

"To see Morgan. Your mother. I have not touched Gwenhwyfar in years. I certainly never begrudged her the happiness she found with Bedwyr."

This is not happening, Mordred thought. My father is not saying these things to me.

"We were all managing quite well," Arthur said, "until tonight. Do you realize how you humiliated her, Mordred? Do you understand the danger you have placed her in?" The voice was remorseless, giving him no room for escape. "Under Celtic law, adultery by the queen is punishable by death."

"No!" It was a cry of shocked protest. "You wouldn't!"

"Of course I wouldn't. But if word of what happened here tonight gets out, there will be those who will call for punishment. I have enemies. No man can hold the power I do and not have enemies. There are those who would use her to get at me. And she has enemies too. She has no children, Mordred, so she is particularly vulnerable. There will be an outcry for me to put her aside and take another wife."

"Would you do that?" The words were barely a whisper.

"No. But you have not made things easy for any of us, have you?"

I won't cry, Mordred thought desperately. I won't let him see me cry.

"I am sending Bedwyr, Agravaine, and the others to Gaul immediately." Mordred was pinned down by that voice, the sound of sovereignty, empty of all emotion save authority. "When I leave with the army in two weeks, you will remain as co-regent with the queen. There will be talk; we cannot avoid that. You will not listen to it. You will behave toward Gwenhwyfar with the same devotion and respect that you have always shown her. Do you understand?"

"Yes," Mordred whispered.

"Look at me."

Reluctantly Mordred raised his eyes. For the first time since he had known his father, he recognized the signs of fatigue in Arthur's face. He supposed he did not look much better. He straightened his spine. Their eyes were now almost on a level. Mordred said, "I realize that such a statement cannot undo the damage, but for what it's worth, I'm sorry."

The face that was such a mirror image of his own suddenly warmed.

"I know," said his father, and the warmth reached to his voice as well. Mordred felt a wild desire to throw himself into Arthur's arms and beg for reassurance that all would be well. It would be, he thought desperately. His father would handle it; he always did.

"Mordred," Arthur asked, "why would Agravaine want to do such a thing?"

"I don't know," Mordred answered in obvious bewilderment. "He worships the prince. I can't understand why he would want to hurt him. But there was no talking to him, Father. And he has a vicious tongue. He just got me so angry that I didn't think."

"All right." Arthur not only looked tired, his son thought, he looked as if he were in pain. "We'll just carry on as if nothing has happened," Arthur said.

"What shall I do now?" Mordred asked uncertainly.

"Go back to the school. I shall be coming down with the queen very shortly. I will be putting each of the princes into a cavalry regiment. The School for Princes is now officially over."

He had to collect Gwenhwyfar and start on his rounds, but he needed to be alone first. He went to his bedroom, told Gereint to see he was undisturbed for fifteen minutes, and went to lie on his back on the bed.

His head was pounding and all his senses were raw. He felt as if the air were full of flying glass. God! The look on the boy's face.

He closed his eyes and out of the quiet and the dark came a feather-soft shower of love.

Morgan?

Yes. It's all right. I know. He will survive it, Arthur. We will all survive it.

Not words, actually, but feelings. She knew. She understood. He was not alone.

How had he lived for so many years without her?

Only part of him had lived through those years, he thought now, as the tension in his head slowly relaxed. The deepest part of him had been dead and dry, like a tidal pool that has been cut off from the sea.

He lay still, his eyes closed. The feeling of being stripped of his skin, of having all his nerve ends exposed to the searing air, had gone. He would be able to do what had to be done.

What devil had driven Agravaine to do this thing? There had been hatred in his cousin's eyes this morning. Surely all this could not have come about because Arthur had beaten him in a practice swordfight? Not even Lot's son could be as overweeningly proud as that.

The temptation to kill the four of them had been great. What had saved them was the fact that Agravaine was Morgause's son as well as Lot's. He owed too much to Morgause to allow himself to take that particular road, however tempting it had been.

They had none of them liked the idea of being cooped up on a boat with Bedwyr. They should know how close they had come to death when he had walked in the door and seen their faces. If there had been any hope of keeping the matter completely quiet, he would have killed them. But there was no way he could silence the servants' tongues. Agravaine had seen to that.

He forced his mind to practicalities.

He would have to see to the horses they were taking to Gaul now that Bedwyr was no longer here to do it. He hoped to God they had a calm crossing and he could get the horses safely across the Narrow Sea. In a battle against the Saxons, the horses were almost more important than the men.

With both Cai and Bedwyr gone, the whole of the job of moving the army was going to fall on him.

He sighed and swung his legs to the floor. No point in lying here thinking about all there was to do. Better get started.

He ran his hand through his hair. Damn Agravaine. If Bedwyr drowned all four of them on the way to Gaul, Arthur wouldn't say a word.

Chapter 41

*F*OR the following two weeks it seemed to Mordred as if his father never slept. Arthur was everywhere in Camelot, directing and encouraging, quiet, patient, quite formidably efficient. When he was not with the army he was in his office meeting with suppliers and coping with a mountain of paperwork.

Never again did Mordred see the marks of fatigue on his father's face. His energy seemed inexhaustible.

Toward the end of the second week, Arthur spent one night at Avalon. Then he moved five thousand men and three hundred horses to Portus Adurni, loaded them on ships, and embarked for Gaul. The messenger Arthur sent back to Camelot arrived two weeks later with the good news that the army had crossed the Narrow Sea safely and sailed into the mouth of the Loire, where Arthur had been formally greeted by Syagrius. The plan was for the two armies to combine and advance up the Loire to fight the Saxons.

Autumn came to Camelot. Arthur had left but a skeleton garrison in the capital, and the falling leaves blew around empty barracks and deserted training fields. Many of the shops closed for lack of customers, and the bazaar outside the gates slowly drifted away. The heart of Camelot had gone with the king.

Mordred found that his main business as regent was to dispel the rumors that had spread like wildfire about Bedwyr and Gwenhwyfar. His most trying test came with the arrival of Cador, King of Dumnonia, who rode to Camelot to find out the truth for himself.

"What is this story I hear about you and Agravaine catching the queen in bed with Bedwyr?" Cador asked Mordred bluntly as soon as he was alone with Arthur's son.

It was the first time Mordred had been directly confronted with such a question. He answered steadily, around the thumping of his heart, "Just that, my lord. A story."

Cador's eyebrows, gray and bushy, drew together. "It is not true, then?"

"It is not true."

"Then how in Hades did such a story get started?"

Mordred had had time to think about that question. "The queen has enemies," he replied. His gray eyes were as steady as his voice. "There are those who would like to see the king put her aside and take a new wife." To his amazement, Cador looked uncomfortable. "I suppose someone tried to take advantage of her friendship with the prince," Mordred concluded.

"Someone. Who is this someone, Prince Mordred?" Cador met his eyes once more.

"I don't know. But it is unfortunate that people are willing to believe such an ugly and improbable story. Bedwyr is devoted to my father. He would cut off his right arm before he would do anything to hurt the king."

This last statement was so true, and so universally known to be true, that Cador seemed convinced. At any rate, he left the following day, to be succeeded by Bedwyr's father come upon the same errand. Mordred dealt with him in much the way he had dealt with Cador.

"If such a story were true," he said to Ban, "the king would hardly have kept Bedwyr in his service. Nor would he have left the queen as co-regent with me." Mordred raised his black brows and for a moment he looked uncannily like Arthur. "Someone must hate your son very much, my lord, to have started such an ugly rumor."

"My son, or the queen." Ban's face was heavy with thought. "A childless queen is never popular."

Mordred had agreed, and after a visit of several days, Ban and his retinue had left again for Wales, apparently satisfied.

Gwenhwyfar wrote to her father and assured him that the rumors were not true and that she did not need him to come to Camelot. Maelgwyn apparently believed her, for he stayed home.

"Dumnonia and Wales are all right," Gwenhwyfar said to Mordred as they sat together at dinner the first night after Ban's departure. "But there has been nothing from the north."

"I wrote to Gaheris and told him that Agravaine had tried to cause trouble by starting an ugly rumor but that it was not true. Gaheris has no love for Agravaine. He should be satisfied."

"It is Elmet and Rheged I'm worried about. And Manau Guotodin, to a lesser extent. They are the kingdoms that opposed Arthur on this expedition to Gaul. And they will have the direct word of their own princes to oppose ours."

Mordred sighed and looked down at his plate. "I know. But there is little else we can do, save continue to act as if nothing has happened." He picked up a piece of meat, then put it down again, untouched. The servants were out of the room for the moment and the two were alone. "I have never told you how sorry I am for the trouble I have caused," he said in a low voice. "If I could undo it, I would."

They were seated at the small round table in the family dining room and Gwenhwyfar looked for a long, aching moment at Mordred's averted face. They were in their usual places and she had a good view of the hard line of his young cheek, shadowed by the down-looking black lashes. "Mordred," she finally said sadly, "I am the one to be sorry."

"No. My father explained it all to me. It was my fault, anyway, for listening to Agravaine."

She tried for a lighter note. "Well, there is little point in our arguing over who is sorrier. We must simply go forward as best we can."

He looked up at that and the glimmer of a smile lightened his set mouth. For a moment he looked so like Arthur—not just the bones, but the expression—that her breath caught. "Yes," he said. "We must."

She rinsed her fingers daintily in the water dish near her plate. "If . . . if you would like to invite Morgan to Camelot sometime, it is all right with me," she offered diffidently.

His face closed. "That won't be necessary," he said. Then the servants came in with the next course and he changed the subject.

Gwenhwyfar did not raise Morgan's name again, but she knew that since that fateful night of disclosure, Mordred had not spoken to his mother. Whatever Arthur had said to his son, it had been enough to exonerate Gwenhwyfar's sins in the boy's eyes and, evidently, shift the blame to Morgan. Gwenhwyfar was quite sure this had not been Arthur's intention, but it was not a subject she was fool enough to open with Mordred. He would have to separate the sinned-against from the sinning in his own mind. God knows, she was not the person to help him with that particular problem.

The storms of November closed in on the Narrow Sea and there was no word from Gaul. Mordred felt little worry. Arthur was invincible;

everyone in Britain knew that. Alone with Gwenhwyfar at Camelot, Mordred was happier than he knew he had any right to be.

Morgan knew what was happening in Gaul. It seemed that not even the Narrow Sea could separate them now, and she was able to see clearly in her mind what it was that Arthur wanted her to know. She knew the day that the combined British and Gaulish army smashed the Saxons near Angers. She knew that Arthur and Bedwyr and Cai were safe and that Arthur had sent a messenger to Camelot with news of the battle. She knew that Agravaine was apparently dead on the field. The army was moving north, toward Bourges, Arthur said. All was well.

Mordred had made no attempt to contact her since Arthur's departure and Morgan respected his silence. She had a very good idea of what he was feeling, a better idea than Arthur had, she thought. She had seen the expression in her son's eyes whenever he looked at the queen. "How could you do this to my father?" he had said to Gwenhwyfar. He had meant, Morgan thought: How could you do this to me?

If Mordred could find an excuse for Gwenhwyfar, he would. And Morgan had provided him with one. There had been no choice, unfortunately. Nor was Mordred wrong in what he was thinking. She and Arthur *had* driven Gwenhwyfar into Bedwyr's arms. It was what her son thought, and it was true. So it was best for her to leave him alone.

Consequently she did not try to communicate to him the news of Arthur's victory. Let him learn by the more orthodox means of official messenger. Without Arthur's weekly visits, and without the wagons rolling to Camelot with food for the army, Avalon was cut off from the world, a quiet little island of peace. Morgan spent the winter working on her book of herbal medicine.

Agravaine had been back in Britain for more than a month before she heard of it. And the news he had brought with him was quite the opposite of what she knew to be true.

Agravaine told a tale of total disaster, of the British army routed by a combination of Saxons and Visigoths, and of the death of the king and all his captains.

"*What!*" Morgan said in horror to the traveling harper who had stopped at Avalon for hospitality and who was the first to give her the news.

"Yes, my lady. Only Prince Agravaine and his own cavalry unit escaped the disaster. It was treachery, Lady Morgan. Arvandus, the imperial prefect in Gaul, betrayed the Roman emperor by bringing in Euric and the Visigoths. King Arthur was the victim of his treachery. Our men were overwhelmed by sheer numbers. Prince Agravaine himself saw the king go down. And Prince Bedwyr too."

Morgan was icy cold. This was what she had feared. Treachery. But the treachery had not been in Gaul. Her lips were white as she asked, "What is Prince Mordred planning to do?"

"There is to be a council, my lady. Prince Mordred will surely be named the next high king."

Morgan closed a channel in her mind. She must see Mordred first before she let any of this reach Arthur.

Agravaine. Arthur had thought him dead. He must have left the battlefield unobserved. He and his cavalry unit, the harper had said. This was something he had planned carefully.

She called Marcus and bade him see the harper was properly fed, but all the time her brain was occupied with what he had told her. What in God's name could Agravaine hope to achieve by this ploy? It would come out soon enough that he was lying. Did he think Arthur was just going to hand the kingdom over to him?

Time. Time was what Agravaine hoped to gain. The answer came almost as quickly as the question. It would give him time to organize the north against Arthur. He was, after all, Lot's son.

They must have intercepted Arthur's own messenger.

Dear God. Mordred had thought for the whole of this last month that his father was dead. And she, only twelve miles away, had known nothing! Why hadn't he sent to tell her? She couldn't believe he would be so cruel as not to tell her about Arthur's death. He was angry with her, but he would never do that. Not the Mordred she knew.

She sent a servant to saddle a pony. She had to see Mordred immediately. And Gwenhwyfar. Gwenhwyfar, of all people, should know what Agravaine was. How could the queen have believed him?

It had been the ravaged look on Agravaine's face when he spoke of Bedwyr that had convinced Gwenhwyfar. His eyes had been terrible. "There were just too many of them, even for the prince," he had said. "He went down." And his dark blue eyes had met hers in a strange, anguished intimacy. For a brief moment they were locked together in the shock of grief and lost love, and she had known then that Agravaine was speaking true.

No one had dreamed that Arthur might not be victorious. She felt sometimes as if she were walking at the bottom of the sea: nothing was clear, everything was such an effort. The world without Arthur. It did not seem possible.

They were all gone. Arthur. Bedwyr. Cai. And in their place now was Agravaine. Agravaine of the golden hair and midnight-blue eyes. Now that Bedwyr was dead, his hostility toward her seemed to have evaporated. There was even sometimes a kind of comprehension between them, dark and subterranean; frightening. She thought that when he looked at her, he saw Bedwyr.

The barracks were slowly filling with men from the north. A large contingent had ridden in from Lothian, headed by a blond-haired young man Agravaine had addressed mockingly as "Father." More and more, Mordred seemed to be slipping under Agravaine's bright shadow. He had been so quiet since the news of Arthur's death, so distant. As the grief and shock lifted slightly, Gwenhwyfar began to realize that she was afraid.

She waited until she was certain that Agravaine was not in the palace and then she sent Olwen to bring Mordred to her. They had scarcely had a moment alone and now she was going to force the issue. Arthur had counted on her to give his son guidance, and it seemed to Gwenhwyfar that he was in need of it. She waited for him in her pretty salon, rehearsing the things she would say. She had told Olwen to see that they were not disturbed.

He came in quietly and shut the door behind him. His thick black hair, grown longer than he usually wore it, had fallen forward over his forehead. There were hollows under his cheekbones that had not been there before. He looked older, she thought. "Mordred," she said, "I thought you and I should have a talk."

He nodded and advanced a little way into the room. His gray eyes were veiled by his lowered lashes and she could not read his mood. She tried to sound very calm. "It seems to me that Agravaine is taking rather too much upon himself."

The lashes lifted and then dropped again. "Agravaine is my brother. He is trying to help me."

"There have been other times when Agravaine's help was less than useful," she returned.

His eyes were on her mouth. "Agravaine is arranging for the council, with my coronation to follow. Once I am really king, I will have more power than I do at present."

A king does not wait for power to be given to him; he takes it. But she did not say the words. She had to be tactful with him. "What does Agravaine want for himself?" she asked instead.

"He wants to be my cavalry commander."

"Ah." She bent her head slightly, thinking. So Agravaine wanted to play Bedwyr to Mordred's Arthur. If he could not have Bedwyr, then he would be Bedwyr. She felt an unexpected flash of pity.

"Gwenhwyfar." Mordred crossed the small space that divided them and looked directly into her face. For the first time she could read his eyes, and her heart skipped a beat at what she saw there. "Gwenhwyfar," he said again, "I want you to marry me."

Her beautiful green eyes dilated in shock. She stepped back. "Don't be ridiculous, Mordred. Of course I cannot marry you."

"Why not? It is an old Celtic custom for the queen to marry the new king. And we are Celts, you and I. The day of the Romans is over. It was Rome that killed my father."

"That is Agravaine talking," she said sharply, "not you."

"I may have listened to Agravaine, but I have thought things through for myself. Arthur tried to extend Britain beyond her own shores, to bring her once again into the orbit of the larger world, and he failed. That attempt lost us the greatest king we have ever had, perhaps the greatest king we ever *will* have. I do not aspire to be Arthur's equal. I only want to keep Britain peaceful within her own borders."

"That is job enough," she said shakily.

"You could help me, Gwenhwyfar." His dark face was so grave, so intent. "Arthur appointed you co-regent because he knew I would need your help. I still do. Marry me."

"I can help you without marrying you, Mordred." She knew what the flame meant that was burning in those gray eyes, and her own blood began to race treacherously. "I cannot marry you," she said angrily. "I am your father's wife."

"My father is dead."

There was a silence as they both listened to the sound of those words. Gwenhwyfar twisted her hands together. The winter day was gray and she had lighted the hanging lamp to brighten the room. It cast its glow on her bright hair, on the beautiful, sweet curve of her cheek. When she spoke again her voice was hard. "You need a wife who can give you children. I am no wife for the High King of Britain."

He cupped her face in his hands and smoothed his thumbs along her cheekbones. Those thin, hard hands. She felt the calluses on the tips of the fingers and she shuddered. His dark head was close to hers. She could smell the youth of him, the fresh male youth. "I will give you children, Gwenhwyfar," he said. "I am sure of it."

She could feel his words within her womb. I should not do this, her mind was telling her over and over. But he was so strangely compelling. And Arthur and Bedwyr were gone. "Is this Agravaine's idea?" she asked.

The dark head moved from side to side. "No. It is my idea. Gwenhwyfar . . ." Desire and longing and love, looking at her out of Arthur's eyes. She made one more attempt to escape the net.

"You could have anyone, Mordred. There are princesses far younger than I who would be honored to marry the high king."

"Why should I want anyone else when there is you? After you, there can be no one else who matters."

She tried to think logically. "What will the council say?"

"The council will do as I tell it to." For that brief moment, he might have been Arthur incarnate. She must have swayed a little, for his hands moved to grasp her shoulders. "Will *you* do as I tell you?" he asked. "Will you marry me, Gwenhwyfar?"

"Yes," she heard herself saying in a voice she did not recognize. "I will."

Chapter 42

THE thin winter sun was still bright as Morgan passed through the gates of Camelot. She was surprised by the amount of activity she saw as she rode up the main road to the palace. There were far more men in the capital than she had expected to see. She detoured off the road to go by the large training field where the festival had been held. There were contingents of men marching on the dead February grass. Men dressed in the distinctive checkered cloth of the north. In the distance Morgan could see a yellow-haired man on horseback directing the action.

At least Agravaine wasn't at the palace.

She waited in the great hall while a servant went to inform Mordred that the Lady of Avalon was asking to see him. He came himself to greet her, his face carefully expressionless. He would never be as impenetrable as Arthur, however, and she read his eyes quite clearly. She glanced around the huge public room and said, "I do not wish to talk to you here, Mordred. Let us go into Arthur's office."

He hesitated, then nodded and led the way to a door that opened off the colonnaded gallery. She went in first and watched as he closed it slowly, reluctantly, behind them.

"A harper came to Avalon today," she said without preamble. "He told me that there has been a great battle in Gaul and that Arthur and most of the army are dead. Is this true?"

"Yes. Surely you knew?"

"I knew nothing. You did not think it was worth your while to inform me?"

He was looking appalled. "Morgan, I am so sorry. I thought you knew. I would never have let . . . have left you to find out like this. I thought you knew."

She stared levelly at his distressed face. "How could I know, Mordred, if you did not send someone to tell me?"

333

"Gwenhwyfar. Gwenhwyfar said it was not necessary to send news to you, that you would have known before we did."

"I see." The large brown eyes of his mother registered comprehension. "Did she say why?"

"No. Merely that you would know. She was very sure of it."

"I see," Morgan said again. Her small face looked quite composed. Mordred shifted from one foot to the other. "And your source for this story was Agravaine?"

"Agravaine and the men who escaped with him. It was treachery, Morgan. Arvandus, the Roman prefect, called in the Visigoths. Even Arthur could not prevail against the numbers they sent against him."

"And you believed this, solely on Agravaine's word?"

His eyes widened. "Of course I believed it! Agravaine may have a temper, but he is not a monster. Nor is he a fool. Of course he is telling the truth."

It was not Agravaine who was the fool. But she restrained her own temper and said calmly and rationally, "He is lying, Mordred. There *was* a battle. And the Saxons were routed. Your father and Bedwyr and the army are perfectly safe. Agravaine is lying."

He had gone pale. "How do you know this?"

"I just know it. It is true, believe me."

He stared at her out of wild and wary eyes. "What do you mean, you just know it? Have you received a message from my father?"

"In a way, yes."

"Stop talking in riddles, Morgan! If you have had a message, I want to see it."

"It was not written down."

"Let me talk to the messenger, then."

"There was no messenger."

There was the faintest trace of hysteria in his laugh. "And you expect me to believe you on *that* evidence? I know what an accomplished liar *you* are, remember."

She walked slowly across the space of floor between them. The top of her head was just level with his eyes. She looked up at him, and despite her size, there was authority in every note of her voice. "I want to see Gwenhwyfar. Gwenhwyfar will understand better than you."

He was shaking his head. "Oh, no. You have inflicted quite enough pain on Gwenhwyfar already. I am not going to give you the chance to hurt her again."

Her delicately arched brows drew together. "Nonsense, Mordred. I have no intention of hurting Gwenhwyfar. I just want to talk to her."

"You will keep away from Gwenhwyfar." His voice was curiously hard. "Whatever you have to say can be said to me."

The slight, tense frown between her brows deepened. There was something here . . . something she knew wasn't right . . . The door to the office opened and Agravaine walked in. His pale yellow hair framed a smiling face; his blue eyes were cloudless. "Aunt Morgan," he said. "I heard you had come to visit. Welcome to Camelot."

Morgan let her eyes travel slowly from the tips of Agravaine's shoes to the top of his polished head. "I used to think that it was Pellinore's fault," she said. "That he handled you wrong. I see now that I was mistaken."

Something flashed across that angelic face and then it was smiling again. "Pellinore," he answered, "was a fool."

"Agravaine." Mordred's voice was urgent. "Morgan says that there was a battle and that we were victorious. She says that you are lying, that my father is alive."

Agravaine hooked his thumbs in his belt and regarded his aunt. "May I inquire as to the source of your information?" he asked with exaggerated courtesy.

Morgan looked into the smiling violence of those blue eyes. Until this moment she had not realized how dark were the clefts in Agravaine's character. "I will reveal the source of my information to the queen." She would get nowhere with Mordred or Agravaine, she realized. But Arthur must have told Gwenhwyfar about the link between them. He must have, or she would not have said to Mordred that Morgan would know of Arthur's death first.

"Ah yes, the queen." Agravaine looked at Mordred. "Have you told her the good news, little brother?"

"What good news?" asked Morgan sharply.

"Mordred and Gwenhwyfar are to be married. On the day of his coronation. Is that not wonderful?"

"What?" Morgan looked at her son in horror. "Mordred, you cannot do this. Surely you must see that. Gwenhwyfar! I must talk to Gwenhwyfar!"

"No." Mordred's young face was grim and set. "If you have proof that Arthur is alive, then produce it for me. I will not have you distressing the queen. She has had quite enough to bear from you already, I think."

There was silence as the two young men looked at her. She could see behind Mordred's angry eyes to the fear and the dread that he was suppressing. Agravaine . . . Agravaine was looking alert. Alert and suspicious. It would not do to underrate Agravaine. They had all been guilty of that, and look where it had got them. "I would know if Arthur were dead," she said finally. "I would feel it."

Relief glimmered in two sets of eyes. "Woman's intuition," said Agravaine contemptuously. "Go back to Avalon, Morgan, and play with your garden. I tell you, Arthur is dead. I was there. I saw him fall. And there is an end to it."

"Agravaine!" It was Mordred. "She has only just found out. There is no need to be cruel."

Agravaine shrugged.

Arthur's office was cold and none of them had taken off their cloaks. Morgan walked past Agravaine to the door. "If you will have a servant bring around my pony, I will be returning home," she said quietly to Mordred.

Agravaine opened the door for her.

He did not leave her alone with Mordred again. The pony was brought to the door of the palace and both young men watched as she mounted and rode off down the road.

She waited until she was outside the gates. Then she pulled the pony up and closed her eyes. She sent the message out urgently in their own private signal: *Arthur. You must come home. Now. Immediately. Leave the army and come yourself. Danger. You must come home!*

The council convened in Camelot at the beginning of March in order to confirm Mordred as the next high king. The vote was unanimous and the kings and princes who composed the council proposed to stay for a few extra days in order to see him formally crowned. The day before the coronation, word came to Camelot that Arthur had landed in Cornwall with three hundred men and fifty horses. The news was brought to Cador by a few of his men who had been in contact with the king, who had actually seen him. Bedwyr and Cai and Gawain and Constantine, Cador's son, were with him. He had left Valerius in charge of the army in Gaul.

Mordred stood transfixed. He listened to the Cornishmen's words and then to Cador's and Ban's, and all the time he stared at Agravaine, his brain echoing in horror. *He lied. Arthur is not dead. Agravaine lied. Not dead. Not dead. Not dead.* The words reverberated through his skull as the angry words of Cador washed over him unheard. Then: *Gwenhwyfar. I must speak with Gwenhwyfar.*

"Are you coming with us, Prince Mordred?" It was Cador speaking to him.

Mordred looked at him blankly. "Coming?"

Cador had never looked more like an angry bull. "To join the king."

He couldn't see his father. Not yet. Not until he had spoken with Gwenhwyfar. "L-later," he said. "I'll come later."

After Cador and the Welsh kings had gone, he turned to Agravaine. "How could you do it?" He was not even angry, only numb. "How could you, Agravaine?"

They were standing on opposite sides of the council chamber's round table and his brother's eyes were hard and bright. "Arthur wants to bring back the empire," Agravaine replied. "We of the north think Britain ought to be a Celtic country. This king has taken too much upon himself, Mordred. It is time to turn him out and replace him with someone more sympathetic to Celtic ideas."

"But you always loved Arthur. When we were children, all you ever wanted was to be one of his captains. Don't you remember?" He was almost pleading with Agravaine, trying to make him see the horror of what he had unleashed. Now, sickeningly, Mordred understood the reason for the barracks full of north-country troops.

"I loved him when he was fighting the Saxons. Not when he was fighting for the emperor in Gaul." Agravaine's eyes were like blue glass.

Mordred was beginning to comprehend. "And so you used me for your own ends."

"I am making you a king, little brother. You ought not to complain about that."

Mordred continued as if he had not heard. "You lied to me and then you saw to it that I was as compromised as you." He was figuring it out as he spoke. "You were the one who suggested that I marry Gwenhwyfar."

"You ate her up with your eyes every time you looked at her," Agravaine answered brutally. "You didn't need much persuading."

"No. I didn't, did I? I made everything so easy for you. It must have seemed like child's play." He closed his eyes for a minute. "Morgan tried to warn me, and I wouldn't listen."

"For God's sake, stop whining. You chose to stay with me, and we'll settle the question of who is to be king on the battlefield. I had expected to have another month at least before he heard, but no matter. He left the army in Gaul. We shall still have the advantage."

"I didn't choose to stay with you!" Mordred cried. "I did not want to leave before I spoke to the queen, that is all. Of course I shall join my father."

There was a long pause and then Agravaine smiled with genuine amusement. "Wrong, little brother. Go and see the queen. After I have smashed Arthur, perhaps you can even marry her. But you are not leaving Camelot, Mordred. Not until we march to fight the king. Once Arthur is dead, then I will decide what to do with you."

The meeting with Gwenhwyfar was terrible. She was so pale, so strained-looking. He took her hand and she let him hold it for a moment before withdrawing it gently.

"Bedwyr is with him. Did you know?" he asked in a low, unsteady voice.

"Yes. My father told me before he left."

"I still cannot believe this of Agravaine." His gray eyes were shocked. "I grew up with him, Gwenhwyfar. I thought I knew him."

"*I* knew him," she answered bitterly. "I, of all people, should not have trusted him. But he seemed so . . . distraught. I did not think he could be acting."

"I should have let you see Morgan that day. But I did not want her to upset you." He rubbed his left temple as if it hurt. "I did not want her to persuade you out of our marriage—that was the real reason, of course."

"What is this about Morgan?" She was looking directly at him for the first time since he had come into the room.

"She came to see me not long ago. She had only just heard that day the story of Arthur's death. I was horrified at the thought that she had heard it like that, from a wandering harper and not from me. Then she told me it was a lie, that Arthur was not dead at all. I didn't believe her." The gray eyes were full of misery. "She had no proof, Gwenhwyfar. No message. No messenger. Then Agravaine came in. She asked to see you, said you were the only one who would understand." His head drooped. "We wouldn't let her."

Gwenhwyfar shaded her eyes. "You should have."

"Yes. I know that now." Silence fell between them. He looked around at the pretty, feminine room. "What must he think of us?" His voice was almost inaudible.

"He thinks what Morgan thinks. She is the one who told him, of course."

"What do you mean?"

"Morgan was the one who called him home. He couldn't have heard this news from anyone else; everyone in Britain thought he was dead. There are no ships crossing the Narrow Sea at this time of year to bring news to Gaul of what is happening in Britain. He knew as soon as Morgan knew. God, if I only had let you tell her when Agravaine first came home with his story, Arthur would have been here a month ago!"

"What are you saying, Gwenhwyfar? That Morgan can reach my father's *mind?*"

"Yes," said Gwenhwyfar. "That is what I am saying."

He looked all at once very young and very lost. "And Agravaine sneered at her woman's intuition."

"Agravaine," said Gwenhwyfar, and Mordred shuddered at the note in her voice.

"I made another mistake," he said, "to add to my already considerable collection. I should have ridden out with Cador and the Welsh. Agravaine couldn't have stopped me from doing that. Now I am trapped."

Her green eyes widened. "He isn't going to let you leave?"

"He isn't going to let me leave."

"Dear God, Mordred," she whispered. "What are we going to do?"

Agravaine came to the queen's salon next. Gwenhwyfar tried to keep Olwen in the room with her, but Agravaine dismissed the girl, and Gwenhwyfar, in an effort to maintain some semblance of dignity, allowed her to go.

"My lady the queen," he said gently as soon as they were alone, and laughed. He was dressed now in all the glittering splendor of the Celt. There was gold at his throat and on his arms. A gold brooch held his cloak, and gold flashed on his belt. His hair was as bright as his jewelry. "You were the one I was most afraid would not believe me," he said.

"I shouldn't have, of course. It was the way you spoke of Bedwyr's death that convinced me. You seemed so genuinely grief-stricken."

"Bedwyr *is* dead, to me at least. He wanted to murder me the whole way to Gaul. You are the one for Bedwyr, unfortunately. He would have come back to you, after Gaul. It seems I made a mistake. Arthur doesn't care."

She swallowed. There was something about him that was absolutely petrifying. Why had he come here? She made herself speak calmly. "And so, if you cannot have Bedwyr, you will see to it that no one else can. Is that it?"

"Something like that." He smiled maliciously. "I wonder how he felt when he heard you had agreed to marry Mordred?"

"It was *your* idea, that marriage. Wasn't it?"

"Of course. Mordred would never have had the nerve to think of marrying you. It didn't take much persuasion, though, Gwenhwyfar. Like Bedwyr, he was hungry."

He was coming toward her, all of his gold flashing in the shaft of sunlight from the window. Before she could stop herself, she took a backward step.

A slow, mocking smile dawned on Agravaine's face. "Frightened, little bird?"

Her heart jolted. Little bird. That was Bedwyr's name for her. He was staring at her out of suddenly dilated eyes and it was there between them again, that frightening, pitiless intimacy which was either hate or love, or both. "It would be interesting," he said, "to plow where he has plowed. Would you like that, Gwenhwyfar? Gwenhwyfar my enemy, the love of my love. Would you like to lie with me?"

"You . . . wouldn't."

"I think I might." He raised a hand. "Your hair is very beautiful."

She was like a creature mesmerized. He ran his fingers through her hair. His eyes were purely black.

She forced her mind to function. "Do this, Agravaine, and you will lose Mordred."

His hand continued to stroke her hair. "I don't need Mordred."

"Yes, you do. He will give at least a semblance of legitimacy to your fight against Arthur. And you may yet win him to your side. As you said yourself, he wants me."

"I have legitimacy. The legitimacy of the Celt trying to win his country back." His hand moved to her face. "And I may want you too."

Think. "It would hurt Arthur so much more, to think that Mordred had turned traitor."

His hand dropped and his lightless eyes searched her face and she knew she had said the right thing. Her own eyes narrowed. "It's Arthur you hate, isn't it?" she said slowly. "You hate him more than you do me. Why? What has he done to you?"

"Bedwyr loves him," came the devastating reply. "I might have been able to forgive Bedwyr you. You are just a woman. But not the king." He looked at her coldly, all the frightening intimacy gone from his face. "You are right. It would be best to have Mordred on my side, or at least appearing to be on my side." He smiled at her. "Too bad, Gwenhwyfar. It might have been . . . interesting."

As soon as the door closed behind him, Gwenhwyfar collapsed into a chair. She was still shaking five minutes later when Olwen came into the room.

Chapter 43

THE men of Dumnonia and Wales, many of whom had fought in Arthur's wars against the Saxons, began to stream into Cornwall to join the standard of the king. This, the ultimate battle for Britain, would be fought almost entirely by auxiliary troops. The standing army, that perfectly trained instrument of war, was still in Gaul.

Agravaine made no attempt to move south of Camelot. Clearly his strategy was to make Arthur come to him. And so, at the end of April, the king put his newly collected army on the Roman road at Isca Dumnoniorum and moved without impediment to within twenty-five miles of his occupied capital.

It was a wet, gray spring day when Morgan rode the ten or so miles down the Camm from Avalon to Arthur's camp. The woods were full of burgeoning green growth and white and yellow and purple blossoms. Fresh new life was coming to Britain. Morgan inhaled the damp, cool air, full of the smells of dirt and growing things. Two armies were facing each other on either side of Avalon, and her heart should be heavy, but today it was light. She was going to see Arthur. At the moment, that was all that mattered.

The king's camp was humming with the busy confidence all of Arthur's armies immediately acquired. Morgan rode her pony down the roped-off street and looked around curiously at the neat row of tents backed by the competent-looking earth wall that had been thrown up as a defense against surprise attack. Arthur knew she was coming, of course, and had sent Cai to look for her.

"Morgan!" She heard Cai's familiar voice and turned to see him striding toward her. He was wearing the scarlet cloak of the foot and his big-boned face wore a luminous smile. He lifted her out of the saddle and hugged her soundly before he set her on her feet.

"It's good to see you too, Cai," she said laughingly.

He called to a soldier to see to her pony and put his hand on her shoulder. "Come along to Arthur's tent. He'll be there shortly. He's reviewing the Dumnonian troops with Constantine. Cador broke his leg. Did you know that?"

They stopped in front of a tent that did not look very different from any of the others and Cai held the flap for her. She went in and he ducked his head and followed. "No," she said, "I didn't know that. What happened?"

"His horse slipped in the mud and fell on him. Young Constantine is going to lead the Dumnonian troops in his stead. Bedwyr says he's very competent. He was one of the princes in Bedwyr's school, so we can be certain that he has had good training."

The tent was very dim and Cai lit the lamp that was on the single table. The king's tent was very simply furnished. There was the table, one chair, and a bedplace. Cai saw her looking around and said ruefully, "We crossed the Narrow Sea in rather a hurry."

"It's a good thing you did," she replied, and unfastened the brooch that held her cloak to her shoulder. She removed the cloak and laid it, neatly folded, on the back of the single chair. She was dressed in the garments that were so familiar to Cai from their childhood: a pair of boy's breeches and a plain long-sleeved tunic. Morgan's riding clothes. She had never altered her taste. She walked to the bedplace and dropped to the blankets, sitting cross-legged with the ease and flexibility of a young child. Cai turned the chair to face her and sat down himself.

Outside it began to rain. The lamp illuminated the small tent quite efficiently and Cai looked in silence at the small figure sitting so comfortably on Arthur's bed.

Her long hair was still as brown and straight and evenly cut at the ends as he remembered. Her small, delicate face and large eyes were the same too. But it was the face of a woman now, not a girl; a face that had known suffering as well as joy; a face whose beauty went deeper than a mere arrangement of skin and bones. The difference between Morgan and Gwenhwyfar, he found himself thinking, was that while both knew how to give, it was Morgan who knew how to give up.

She bore his scrutiny in patient silence. Then she smiled. "I don't suppose Syagrius was happy to see you leave?"

He shook himself out of his reverie and answered her. They were discussing the situation in Gaul, and studiously refraining from mentioning the treachery at home, when the tent flap opened again and Arthur was there.

He looked at Cai and not at her, but the emotion she felt emanating from him was very strong. He said something to Cai and Cai answered. There was rain on Arthur's hair and lashes. He looked thinner than she remembered, and harder. His cloak was wet too. The rain was coming down hard now.

Finally Cai ducked out of the tent. Morgan could hear his voice outside telling someone that on no account was the king to be disturbed. Arthur unpinned his wet cloak and dropped it on the chair over hers. Then he came to join her on the blankets.

"Let me look at you." She put her hands on either side of his face. The gray, long-lashed eyes looked back at her hungrily. She moved her thumbs across his mouth and then let her hands slide behind his neck and encircle it. He held her close, his mouth against her hair.

"Not all the herbs in your garden are as good a medicine as you yourself," he murmured.

"You're too thin," she said.

She felt his shoulders quiver. "It isn't food I'm hungry for." She looked up. His face was lit with laughter that all at once made him look sixteen again.

"I missed you too," she said.

They were already sitting on the bed, so they hadn't far to go. Outside the sky was gray and it was raining and an army was preparing to fight for its life. Inside the lamplit tent Arthur and Morgan stepped out from under the ugly shadow of betrayal and treachery and into the brilliant sunshine of love.

A long time later Arthur looked down at the smooth, round head that was tucked so comfortably into his shoulder. "Morgan," he said, and there was bewilderment as well as anger in his voice, "why in the name of God did Gwenhwyfar agree to marry him?"

He felt the soft, warm breath of her sigh, but the shining hair that curtained his bare chest never moved. "She thought you were dead. And Bedwyr too."

"I know, but that still doesn't explain it. Gwenhwyfar enjoys being queen, but that doesn't explain it either."

She raised her head to look down into his face. Her hair streamed down around them, enclosing them in a tent within a tent. "You blame Gwenhwyfar?" she asked. "Not Mordred?"

"Gwenhwyfar is the older. She should have known better." His black brows were drawn together in a straight line. "Good God, Morgan, suppose Agravaine's story had been true? Suppose I were dead and Mordred king. The last thing Britain needs right now is another barren queen!" She began to laugh. "It isn't funny," he added a little irritably.

"It's you who are funny. You're so predictable."

He looked absolutely astounded. "I? Predictable?"

"Yes, you." She sobered. "You always think like a king." She touched his eyebrows with her finger, delicately smoothing away his frown. "I understand Gwenhwyfar," she said softly and sadly. The gray eyes waited. "Mordred adores her. And Mordred looks just like you."

She watched his face as he took that in. "Gwenhwyfar loves Bedwyr," he said at last.

"Yes."

His eyes searched her face. "How do you know what motivated Gwenhwyfar?"

"If I were Gwenhwyfar, I should probably have done the same thing."

But he was shaking his head, the faintest of smiles on his mouth. "Oh, no, not you. You are as predictable as I am, Merlin's daughter."

She gave him a rueful look. "I fear we are both Merlin's children." She sat up. "Speaking of children, Arthur, what are we going to do about Mordred?"

He lay still for a minute, looking at her. Then he sighed and sat up. "Do you think you can get into Camelot to see him?"

"Yes. I'm sure I can."

He looked around for his breeches. She unearthed them from the tangle of blankets and handed them to him. After a minute she began to dress as well. "Tell him he must get away from Agravaine," Arthur finally said as he tied the rawhide string at his waist. "Agravaine needs him now, but he won't let Mordred survive the battle."

It was what she had thought also. "But how is he to get away?" she asked breathlessly.

Arthur pulled his purple-bordered tunic over his head. "He must do it somewhere on the road between Camelot and the battlefield. I can't tell him exactly how, Morgan. He must sieze whatever opportunity arises. But tell him he must get away. If he doesn't, he is a dead man."

His hair was ruffled and she reached up to smooth it down. "Should he come to you?"

His face was somber. "No. Not yet. He is not precisely popular with my followers, love. Most of the men think exactly what Agravaine wants them to think. No, the safest place for Mordred just now is

Gaul. Tell him to join Valerius and the army in Bourges. He'll be safe there; they don't know what is happening here in Britain."

The fear that his presence had so magically lifted settled once more on her heart. "And after the battle?"

"Once I have things in order here, I'll send for him. But I want him in Gaul for now. It's the only safe place."

He seemed to be in no doubt as to the outcome of the battle. She felt a little better. "All right. I'll tell him. But what if he can't get away on the road?"

"Then the minute the battle begins, he is to ride like Hades off the field and head for the coast. Agravaine will not let him survive the battle, Morgan. Make that quite clear to him."

"I will." Her face was white but composed. "Don't worry about Mordred, Arthur. I will see that he gets himself to Gaul."

"You're certain you will be able to see him?"

"Oh, yes. Agravaine won't let Mordred out of Camelot, but he will let me in. He won't be able to resist the opportunity to gloat."

"If he holds you there, don't worry. I'll be back in Camelot within the week."

She searched his hard face, which did not look young any longer. "You think you will win this battle."

It was a statement, not a question, but he answered it anyway. "Yes. I got here in time. I think I will win."

She reached up to tie the laces at his throat and he caught her wrists in his hands. "Morgan," he said urgently, "when all of this is over . . ."

But she was shaking her head. "When all of this is over, then we'll talk."

"We can't go on—"

"I know. I know, Arthur. But not now." They looked at each other for a long minute, and then he smiled.

"All right. First let me get rid of that treacherous bastard Agravaine."

She smiled back a little sadly. "He was such a bright, charming little boy."

"Well, he's grown into a viper." Clearly Arthur was in no mood to be nostalgic over Agravaine's childhood. Under the circumstances, she could scarcely blame him.

"Yes," she said. "I'm afraid he has."

"Arthur!" It was Cai's voice from outside the flap of the tent. "Gaheris has just ridden into camp with three hundred men!"

"Gaheris!" Arthur's head snapped up and he began to move toward the tent door. Morgan followed more slowly. She knew how important this addition to Arthur's forces was. Gaheris joining the king meant that this upcoming battle would not be just the south and Wales against the north. Gaheris was far more vital to Arthur than a mere three hundred men.

Gaheris, Morgan remembered as she followed Arthur out into the rain, had never liked Agravaine.

Morgan had been right when she told Arthur she would have no trouble getting into Camelot. They let her through the gate with no questions and she rode up the road to the palace without once being stopped. She passed two wagonloads of food on the road and she looked sharply to see which farmers were supplying Agravaine's army. She had refused to send any food from Avalon.

She did not recognize the men driving the wagons. Agravaine must have had to import food from outside the immediate area.

A soldier took her pony in the palace courtyard and they kept her waiting for fifteen minutes in the vestibule after she said she had come to see Prince Mordred. They were checking with Agravaine, she assumed, and hoped she would get at least a few minutes alone with her son.

She did. They finally escorted her to one of the reception rooms that opened off the great hall, and in five minutes Mordred joined her. He was alone.

He looked young and solitary and lost and her heart ached for him. If only he had not looked so much like Arthur he could have spent his life safely and happily in Lothian, she thought. "Agravaine won't let me leave," he said to her as soon as he was in the room. "I know you probably won't believe me, but it's true. I wanted to go to the king, but Agravaine wouldn't let me."

"I know," she said softly.

"You know? But how?"

"Because I know you. I never for one moment supposed that you would wish to overthrow your father. Nor does Arthur think that." The unhappy gray eyes widened. "Now, listen to me, Mordred. I have brought you a message from your father. He says you are in great danger. Agravaine cannot afford to let you survive the battle. You must get away from him. Arthur says the best place will probably be on the road to the battlefield. Get away and go to Gaul. Do you understand?"

"I . . . Yes."

"If you cannot get away on the road, then you must ride off the battlefield as soon as battle is engaged." She was speaking quickly and in a low, urgent voice. Her eyes kept going to the doorway. "Join the army in Gaul. Your father will send for you once he has things under control here in Britain."

His mouth trembled. "I don't deserve that you should believe in me, either of you. I may have been fooled about Arthur's death, but . . . Gwenhwyfar . . ."

She said, "Of all of us, Mordred, you are the least to blame." And held out her arms.

He was even thinner than Arthur, and his shoulders were bony. He was quivering all over. "I'm so sorry," he was saying next to her ear. "Mother. I'm so sorry."

She patted his back. "I know, Mordred. We both know. Now, quickly, before Agravaine comes, will you go to Gaul?"

She could feel him trying to pull himself together. "Y-yes," he said.

She heard the step at the door, quiet though it was, and so had a second to prepare herself before a light voice said mockingly, "Such a touching sight."

She felt Mordred shudder and squeezed his shoulders bracingly before allowing him to step back from her. "Family affection is not something you would understand," she said to the chill blue eyes of her nephew.

"Aunt Morgan." His smile was full of meretricious charm. "And did you come just to hold my little brother's hand?"

Mordred was facing Agravaine now, and when he spoke, his voice was perfectly steady. "She didn't come to spy on you, Agravaine. She came for reasons you would never be able to honor or to understand."

Morgan looked at her son. He was standing straight as an arrow and the eyes he had turned on Agravaine were full of contempt. So was his voice.

Good for you, she thought. And he gave her a quick, startled look, as though he had heard her.

Agravaine's eyes went from Mordred's face to Morgan's. "You didn't think that it might not be as easy to get out of Camelot as it was to get in?" he asked gently.

She shrugged. "It doesn't matter to me one way or the other. Arthur will be in Camelot in a matter of days."

The fair face darkened with anger. "Don't be too sure of that."

Her eyebrows were two perfect delicate arches above her clear brown eyes. "I'm very sure of it, Agravaine."

"Get out!" he said with sudden violence, "while you still can! As you pointed out earlier, I don't have the same reverence for family ties that you have. Go back to Avalon. And when this battle is over, Morgan, I will expect your farms to send the same supplies to Camelot that they did in the days of Arthur."

She looked at him consideringly. He could not bear to be crossed at all these days, she thought. Would Mordred really be safe here? And what about Gwenhwyfar?

"Go," Mordred said commandingly. "And . . . thank you for coming."

Her son's eyes were clear, his face suddenly and oddly mature-looking. The young, lost look had quite gone. A little of the weight of fear she always carried for him lifted and she smiled. "God keep you, Mordred."

"And you," came the grave reply. She brushed past Agravaine and walked out through the beautiful colonnaded great hall, out the great double doors of Arthur's palace, and for the last time rode her pony down the main road of the famous capital city of Camelot.

Chapter 44

*I*T was a wet, misty April morning when Agravaine's army finally rode out of Camelot to fight the king. There had to be a battle; both sides understood that. Agravaine could not afford to hide in Camelot indefinitely and allow Arthur time to call his army home from Gaul.

Mordred rode beside his brother at the head of the neat rows of marching men. As Arthur had told Morgan, Agravaine needed the king's son. He needed his army to see that Mordred, Prince of Britain, was riding to battle with them. Two of Agravaine's men rode beside Mordred and two behind him, effectively cutting off any chance of escape. The morning air was cold and damp on Mordred's face. The woods on either side of the road were hung with wet white blossoms and purple twigs. Mordred watched the men beside him out of the corners of his eyes.

It was not his personal danger that was worrying him; it was the thought that his presence was helping Agravaine. He turned his head slightly and looked at his brother. Agravaine was helmetless, and even in the morning gloom his hair shone bright. He must have sensed Mordred's regard, for his own head turned. For a brief wordless moment their eyes held. Then Agravaine said regretfully, "I always liked you, Mordred."

There was an ache in Mordred's stomach. "I know," he said. But the Agravaine whom he had grown up with, the big brother he had admired and pitied, was not the man who rode now by his side. Or was he? Was he so clever a dissembler that he had been able to fool them all for so many years? Had this ruthless egotism always lain at the heart of Agravaine's character?

Abruptly Mordred remembered Gaheris asking: "And where were you when Pellinore fell down those stairs?"

There had been regret in the blue eyes looking at him just now, but no mercy. Agravaine would have him killed, all right. The possibility which he had never quite believed, now became a certainty. Mordred stood between Agravaine and the high kingship; therefore Mordred would have to die. In Agravaine's mind, it would be as simple as that.

Mordred felt suddenly nauseated. It was not the danger he was in that sickened him; he had a great deal of physical courage. It was Agravaine. God, what would happen to Britain should Agravaine become high king?

The setting sun was still streaking the sky with red when Agravaine's army entered the small village of Camlann some five miles west of Avalon. On one side of the village was the river Camm; on the other were the wide, neatly plowed fields of the villagers, already sown with spring seed. It was not life but death that would be sown on those fields tomorrow, however, for it was this flat, fertile valley that Arthur had chosen to be the scene of the ultimate battle for Britain.

It was a field that afforded little in the way of topographical advantage. Mordred was surprised that his father had chosen a site that would so clearly favor the army with the greater number. Agravaine had some eight thousand men under his command; his spies had reported that the king's army was two thousand less than that.

Mordred had not been able to effect an escape on the road, and so he was present when Agravaine made his battle dispositions for the morrow. The men of Elmet, under the command of their own prince, Baird, were given the right. Baird's father, Elmet's old king, was said to be very ill. Mordred doubted that he even knew of the enterprise his son was involved in. There would be two thousand men from Elmet and one thousand from Rheged under Baird's command tomorrow, mostly all troops who had fought at one time or another in Arthur's wars. The left wing, under the command of Innis of Manau Guotodin, was less experienced. The center, led by Agravaine himself, was a mix of seasoned veterans and youngsters from Lothian who had grown up under Pellinore's imposed state of isolation. These were the troops Agravaine had been training so intensively and he was confident they would not panic when faced with actual battle.

The sun was setting when the soldiers took up their positions and lay down in their cloaks to sleep. On the other side of the now-darkened field the king's army was presumably doing the same.

The night dragged on. The man sleeping beside Mordred, Agravaine's man, began to snore. Noiselessly Mordred rose to his feet and started to move toward the wooded banks of the Camm. He was challenged by a sentry, but when he said he was going into the woods to relieve himself, he was allowed to pass.

Once he was within the trees, Mordred wasted no time. His eyesight was very keen and he could move as silently as a woodland creature when he wanted to. By the time he was missed, and men were sent to look for him, he was far down the river, hidden by the dark and by the forest.

Go to Gaul, his mother had said. Your father understands. Go to Gaul, where you will be safe.

He could get away now with little trouble, head for the coast, where there would surely be some kind of boat to take him to Gaul. The branches of the trees rustled above him and he heard the soft sound of the water of the Camm as it lapped against the rocks of the shore. The decision was made and he was moving before he consciously realized that he had even made a decision. He could not go to Gaul until he had first seen his father.

He took a few more steps and the thought settled, solidified, and became a conviction. He must see his father. He did not know why, just knew that it was a necessity. He could not run away to Gaul until he had first seen Arthur.

He changed direction and began to return to the field from a different angle. His sense of direction was always accurate, and as the sun began to rise in the sky he found himself exactly where he had aimed to be, hidden in the thicket of woods that jutted out to the left of Innis' wing. He looked across the neatly plowed field to the army that was assembled on the other side, a quarter of a mile away.

The morning air was clear and the dragon banner of the king was easily visible in the early sun. Mordred's long-sighted eyes were able to make out Arthur's dispositions without difficulty. Bedwyr and the small cavalry unit were on the king's right. The prince would throw terror into the untried troops from Manau Guotodin, Mordred thought with approval. He squinted a little to see what foot Arthur had given to Bedwyr and was surprised to see a troop of men led by Gawain. Gawain should be with the cavalry, he thought. He looked harder and realized abruptly that the auburn head of the man he was watching did not belong to Gawain after all.

Gaheris. He almost said the name aloud. Gaheris, King of Lothian, had come to fight with Arthur. Mordred felt a moment of fierce pride in his brother. Then he moved his eyes to Arthur's left wing, expecting to see Cador and Cai.

Neither Cai nor the King of Dumnonia was commanding the left wing, however. Mordred looked at the slender, dark-haired man who was walking his horse up and down in front of his troops of foot, and felt jealousy sear his heart. Constantine. Constantine, where *he* ought to be, at Arthur's side. And instead, he was here, skulking on the edges of the field, a branded traitor. The conviction that he must see his father burned even deeper than before.

Finally, almost reluctantly, he allowed his eyes to come to rest on the figure under the great banner. He was riding Ruadh, Mordred saw at once. The center, which Arthur was commanding today, was placed on a small rise of land and the early-morning wind was blowing from its rear, causing the dragon banner to ripple almost directly over the king's head. As Mordred watched him, Arthur moved Ruadh forward to the edge of the small hill. Standing there in front of his men, alone, he raised his voice.

"Men of the north!" There was absolute silence in Agravaine's ranks as they listened to the clear, strong voice coming to them so effortlessly on the morning breeze. "You have fought with me before, many of you. Gaheris of Lothian fights with me today." Mordred could hear the murmurs of surprise that ran through Agravaine'a army as Gaheris came forward to the front of the right wing. The king raised his hand and silence descended once more. "Britons!" came Arthur's call. His black hair was blowing in the wind. "You have been deceived by a treacherous prince. Join with me today, and I will receive you like comrades."

"You lie!" It was Agravaine's voice, lighter than Arthur's but audible to his men. "It is you who are the deceiver, servant of Rome!" Agravaine moved his own horse forward so he was visible to all his army. Like Arthur, he was unhelmeted. "Do not listen to him," he cried to his men. "He is afraid because we outnumber him!"

The sound of a horn from Arthur's lines cut across his words. Agravaine gestured and his own trumpets blew. His men raised their weapons.

This was why Arthur had chosen this ground, Mordred thought as the two armies began to move toward each other. He had wanted to make that appeal to Agravaine's men.

Mordred had never seen a battle before, and at first he watched in horror as the two masses of men clashed and mingled and began to kill. It was perhaps ten minutes before he realized that there was a steady stream of Agravaine's men leaving the field. They were all moving toward the small rise of land from which Arthur had addressed the troops. Mordred looked and immediately recognized the figure who was so competently forming Agravaine's men into a unit of reserve for the king. Cai. Someone all these veterans would know and trust.

With a thrill of triumph, Mordred realized that Agravaine's army was slowly deserting to the king.

Suddenly Mordred could stand being an outsider no longer. He grasped his sword firmly in his hand and went onto the field to find his father.

"Mercy, Prince!" A terrified face stared up at Bedwyr. "I want to declare for the king!"

"Go and join Cai on the hill, then," Bedwyr said. He raised his voice. "Anyone who wishes to join the king is to go to the hill."

The crowd around him began to thin noticeably. Bedwyr grinned and turned to Gawain, who was beside him. "Gods! I'm afraid to kill anyone lest he be one of ours!"

Gawain laughed. "There were at least five hundred with Cai the last time I looked. The number must be double by now." His eyes narrowed. "Hold on. This is a group that isn't friendly."

"You deal with them," Bedwyr said. "I have another job to do." And he wheeled Sugyn away from the cavalry unit and drove him toward the center of the field. As so many years ago Cai had once searched a battlefield for Lot, so now Bedwyr searched for Lot's son.

Agravaine saw him coming, a great golden god of a man on a huge black horse. Agravaine raised his sword and watched as Bedwyr approached, cutting his way through the northern army as easily as a hot knife going through butter.

"Prince," he said when finally they were face-to-face. His blue eyes were fearless. "This is for you," Agravaine said. He gestured around the field. "All for you." And he laughed.

"You treacherous bastard!" There was no understanding in Bedwyr's eyes, only murderous rage. Bedwyr would never understand, Agravaine thought. It was supremely ironic, really, that the only one to understand had been Gwenhwyfar.

Bedwyr's sword was descending and he parried it. The prince was immensely strong and Agravaine's wrist ached from the blow. Then, as he was launching his own sword, he saw another blow on its way. He just managed to get his shield up in time. Bedwyr was so fast! Then

Sugyn was moving sideways, taking Bedwyr under his guard. "You always did stress the importance of lateral movement," Agravaine managed to gasp before the last blow came down on his unprotected golden head.

Mordred was aiming for the dragon banner. He cut his way through the shifting groups of men on the field, reacting automatically, in the way he had been trained, whenever a sword was raised against him. The dragon banner, however, instead of getting closer, seemed to be getting farther away. Arthur was leaving the field, Mordred saw. In a panic, he pushed forward even harder, his mind concentrated on this one thing only, that he must speak to his father.

The battle was breaking up around him. The death of Agravaine had taken whatever heart his troops had left. There were still patches of combat here and there, but clearly most of the fighting was over.

Arthur had pulled Ruadh up at the edge of the field and was watching the action, surrounded by a group of horsemen. Mordred saw Cai coming on foot to speak to Arthur, and the king turned toward him. Then Arthur dismounted and gave Ruadh to someone to hold. As he and Cai talked, Mordred began to run. Sweat stung his eyes and it was only instinct that made him turn to parry the blow that had been aimed at his back. He struck the man away and ran forward again, panting with exertion and emotion. He did not even realize his sword was still raised.

"Father!" he cried as he pushed through the circle of cavalrymen who had been watching the king and Cai and so had not seen him coming.

Arthur spun around. "I have come to beg—" Mordred was beginning when there came a bellow of rage from one of the horsemen. Mordred looked up in a daze to see the point of a lance hurtling straight at him. Then something was in its way.

"*Arthur!*" It was Cai's anguished cry. Mordred stared with horror as his father slowly slipped to the ground at his feet.

Someone was sobbing. Cai dropped to his knees beside the king. Mordred's sword slid out of his numbed hand. The lance that had felled Arthur had come out of the wound when the king had fallen and there was blood all over the front of his white tunic.

"Get a doctor," Cai said, and a horse galloped off. Cai tore off his cloak and tried to stanch the blood. Arthur's lashes lifted slightly.

"Get the boy away," he said. His voice was weak but clear. "To Gaul."

"I will," said Cai. "Just rest. We'll have you bandaged up in no time."

"Avalon," said Arthur. "Cai. Take me to Avalon."

The doctor came running up, followed by the thunder of hooves. "Arthur?" Even through the anguish and the fear, Mordred recognized Bedwyr's voice.

"He's hurt," said Cai.

"Hurt? But how? The battle is over."

"It was an accident," said Cai curtly. The doctor was bending over the king's now unconscious figure. He looked up at Cai, and Mordred read what was in his face.

"No." It was scarcely more than a whisper. Mordred stared in panic at Arthur's quiet face. "He's not . . ."

"Not yet," said the doctor. "But it won't be long, I think."

"Avalon is but a few miles away," said Cai. "We'll take him there."

Trotting hoofbeats this time, and Mordred turned to see Gawain. His brother checked in surprise as he recognized him, and then he saw the figure on the ground. Someone had led away the sobbing horseman and it was very quiet. Cai looked at Gawain and said, "You must get your brother away from here, Gawain. Take him to Gaul. It was the last thing the king said before he lost consciousness."

The freckles were stark on Gawain's pale face. "Did Mordred . . . ?" he began.

"No. It was an accident. Get Mordred to Gaul, Gawain. Will you do that for the king?"

"Yes." Gawain rallied visibly. "If that is what he wants."

Mordred felt himself being lifted into a saddle. It was not until much later that he realized he was riding Ruadh. He did not want to go, but he knew that he must. "We'll make a stretcher," he heard Bedwyr saying as he and Gawain rode slowly away through the beautiful April morning.

Morgan was waiting for them. She had known the moment that Arthur was hurt, but she did not know until she saw him how serious it was.

They put him on the bed in his own room, the room he had been given when, as a boy of nine, he had first come to Avalon. Morgan took one look at the wound and realized there was nothing she could do. It was a miracle he had survived the journey to Avalon.

Arthur had been in this place before, but then it had been by choice. He did not want to be here now, and he fought it. He was hurt and so terribly weary, but he fought. There was a long dark path before him, and at the end of it there was a light. The light was so warm, so welcoming . . . No, he said. *Morgan. I cannot leave Morgan.*

The light came closer and then it was as if someone were speaking to him. He heard it the same way he heard Morgan, but it was not Morgan this time. The voice seemed to be coming from the light. There was great peace in what it said to him, and Arthur felt the peace seeping into his spirit. The pain in his chest lifted and he opened his eyes.

She was there, as he had known she would be. But there were other obligations first. *Mordred?* he asked.

Gawain took him to Gaul.

That was a relief. *Cai?* he asked next. *Bedwyr?*

They are waiting outside. Do you want to see them?

Yes.

They came in, the two big men, and he would have grieved for their sorrow if he had not been too filled with peace. "Constantine," he said. For them, he had to talk. It was an effort. "I name Constantine as my heir."

There were tears running down Bedwyr's face. Arthur wanted to tell him not to grieve, but it was too hard to talk. He must conserve his energy for the essentials. "My dragon brooch," he said to Bedwyr. "Give it to Gwenhwyfar." Bedwyr knelt and pressed his wet face into Arthur's hand. Slowly Arthur's eyes went to Cai.

Always there, he thought. Whenever I have needed him. For all these years. "One of the finest things in all my life," he said to those familiar hazel eyes, "has been having you for a friend."

Cai was not crying, but with the peculiar clarity that characterized his vision just now, Arthur could see his whole face clench. Arthur closed his eyes. *Enough,* he said to Morgan, and he heard her taking them to the door.

She put them in her room, so they would be close. Later she would tell them not to reveal to anyone that Arthur's wound had been mortal. They would bury him secretly, and his sword with him. Let Britain believe that she had hidden the king away until he was healed. Let them believe that someday he would come again. It was the last thing they could do for Arthur, the king.

She would tell them that later. Just now the person they had lived for all their lives was dying, and they were lost in a wilderness of despair.

And she?

She had felt despair when first they carried him in, but it was gone now. He was still and white and blood had stained through the bandages and she knew he was dying. She could not call him back this time. But he was at peace. She could feel that in him, and she was glad. He had been going away and he had made one last great effort to come back, but not because he was fighting it. He had come back to share some of that peace with them, and to say good-bye.

She crossed to the bed and his heavy lids lifted. *Lie with me*, he said.

He was beyond pain, and so she did as he asked, resting her head against his arm. *We will be together*, he told her. *Believe that. This is only for a little while. We were always meant to be together, you and I.*

She did believe him, and some of his peace crept into her own heart. *Arthur*, she said. *Arthur, my love.*

She felt his head move, and his thought came through, faint but clear, *Your hair always smells like lavender.*